The P
"someo
Affaire d
write

T

"[*That Chesapeake Summer*] deftly uses the tools of the genre to explore issues of identity, truth, and small-town kinship. . . . Stewart offers a strong statement on the power of love and trust, a fitting theme for this bighearted small-town romance."

—*Publishers Weekly*

"A touching story of self-discovery and homecoming that is sure to warm readers' hearts . . . fans are sure to feel right at home in Stewart's idyllic seaside setting and follow this emotional journey with avid interest."

—*RT Book Reviews*

"Romance fans will enjoy their time on the Chesapeake Bay when they read this entertaining and heartfelt novel."

—*Harlequin Junkie*

"A well-told story with excellent pacing and smooth development on the romantic front . . . one of my favorites in the series."

—*The Good, The Bad and the Unread*

THE CHESAPEAKE DIARIES

"The town and townspeople of St. Dennis, Maryland, come vividly to life under Stewart's skillful hands. The pace is gentle, but the emotions are complex."

—*RT Book Reviews*

"If a book is by Mariah Stewart, it has a subliminal message of 'wonderful' stamped on every page."

—*Reader to Reader Reviews*

"The characters seem like they could be a neighbor or friend or even co-worker, and it is because of that and Mariah Stewart's writing that I keep returning again and again to this series."

—*Heroes and Heartbreakers*

"Every book in this series is a gem."

—*The Best Reviews*

"Captivating and heartwarming."

—*Fresh Fiction*

A DIFFERENT LIGHT

"Warm, compassionate, and fulfilling. Great reading."

—*RT Book Reviews*

"This is an absolutely delicious book to curl up with . . . scrumptious . . . delightful."

—*Philadelphia Inquirer*

MOON DANCE

"Enchanting . . . a story filled with surprises!"
—*Philadelphia Inquirer*

"An enjoyable tale . . . packed with emotion."
—*Literary Times*

"Stewart hits a home run out of the ball park . . . a delightful contemporary romance."
—*The Romance Reader*

WONDERFUL YOU

"*Wonderful You* is delightful—romance, laughter, suspense! Totally charming and enchanting."
—*Philadelphia Inquirer*

"Vastly entertaining . . . you can't help but be caught up in all the sorrows, joys, and passion of this unforgettable family."
—*RT Book Reviews*

DEVLIN'S LIGHT

"A magnificent story of mystery, love, and an enchanting town. Splendid!"
—*Bell, Book and Candle*

"With her special brand of rich emotional content and compelling drama, Mariah Stewart is certain to delight readers everywhere."
—*RT Book Reviews*

MARIAH STEWART

Driftwood Point

POCKET BOOKS

New York   London   Toronto   Sydney   New Delhi

Pocket Books
An Imprint of Simon & Schuster, Inc.
1230 Avenue of the Americas
New York, NY 10020

This book is a work of fiction. Any references to historical events, real people, or real places are used fictitiously. Other names, characters, places, and events are products of the author's imagination, and any resemblance to actual events or places or persons, living or dead, is entirely coincidental.

Copyright © 2016 by Marti Robb

First Pocket Books paperback edition July 2016

POCKET and colophon are registered trademarks of Simon & Schuster, Inc.

For information about special discounts for bulk purchases, please contact Simon & Schuster Special Sales at 1-866-506-1949 or business@simonandschuster.com.

The Simon & Schuster Speakers Bureau can bring authors to your live event. For more information or to book an event, contact the Simon & Schuster Speakers Bureau at 1-866-248-3049 or visit our website at www.simonspeakers.com.

Manufactured in the United States of America

10 9 8 7 6 5 4 3 2 1

ISBN 978-1-4767-9259-0
ISBN 978-1-4767-9260-6 (ebook)

For Kathryn C. Robb, MS, PsyD

Acknowledgments

Ask any writer and they'll tell you that writing is a solitary pursuit. Most of the time, it's you and your characters, your keyboard, or your pad of paper and a pen (or in my case, more often than not, a mechanical pencil). But the writing of it is only step one in getting a book into the hands of a reader. Along the way there's an editor (and often a very capable assistant), marketing people, publicity people, salespeople, an art department, and probably some other people that I still don't know about, even after my twenty years of sitting at the keyboard (or elsewhere with pen or the aforementioned mechanical pencil in hand and a lovely fresh Claire Fontaine writing tablet). So when a writer thanks their publishing family, it's with good reason.

This is where I thank my fabulous editor, Lauren McKenna (who truly is fabulous, by the way), for beating up on me to get the best of my best out of my head and onto the page. I must thank Elana Cohen as well—she's always there to answer questions and to help out, with humor and grace. Many thanks to Melissa Gramstad, publicity manager, for all she does to get my books out there and noticed. The art department has given my books quite possibly the best covers I've ever had on any of my books—you all have my gratitude. There are so many other people behind the scenes, in sales and copy and marketing . . . I sincerely appreciate everyone who has a hand in getting my stories out of my head and onto the shelves.

I owe a huge thanks to Louise Burke (and rock star editor Lauren) for bringing me back home to Pocket Books.

I also want to thank my late agent, Loretta Barrett, for twenty years of mentorship, love, and friendship. Loretta loved books—loved the making of books more than anyone I've ever known. She was totally devoted to the publishing business, and when she said that someone was a "real" editor, I knew exactly what she meant. It was her highest praise. She is sadly missed every day.

Thanks have to go to my friends who have been cheering me on since the beginning (Helen, and my homegirls Jo Ellen, Cathy, and Eileen), and the writer ladies who lunch (Kate Welsh, Martha Schroder O'Conner, Gail Link, Terri Brisbin, Gwen Schuler, and Cara Marsi).

And of course, to my family—Bill, Becca, Katie, Mike, Cole, and Jack. You are my world.

Driftwood Point

Diary~

It occurred to me this morning how much I love early summer, that sweet time between the cool mornings of spring and the humid days of deep summer. Most of the flowers I love best are in bloom or about to be—like the peonies that have bloomed here at the inn for more years than I can calculate. My Daniel's mother planted them, oh, I'm guessing around 1940 or so. Same with the roses. She had a green thumb for sure, that mother-in-law of mine did. In season, we have bowls of peonies and tall vases of roses all throughout the inn. No little plastic vials of air freshener required!

I'm thinking about Dan's mother and her black-eyed Susans and the hollyhocks that she planted so long ago—they've reseeded themselves over and over through the years—because I found out this morning that the seeds for those very flowers—the Susans and the hollyhocks—were given to Mother Sinclair by my dear friend Ruby Carter. Let me explain.

Ruby was here for our weekly get-together, and I had a

vaseful of those pretties cut just this morning for the table where Ruby and I would have our lunch. She smiled when she saw them and touched the petals, then said in that wonderful dialect peculiar to our Cannonball Island, "These be mine, once upon a time. Gave an envelopeful to Marion"—that was my mother-in-law—"one August when I had so many I was giving them away by the fistful."

Well, imagine my surprise. Yes, of course I'd noticed the proliferation of flowers around Ruby's place—that would be the general store over on Cannonball Island—and I had noticed that they were the same old-fashioned variety as those we had here at the inn. But I assumed that since both the inn and Ruby's store are historic buildings in the truest sense, the flowers had been planted around the same time.

It made my heart happy to know that something of Ruby's grows here, because she is the dearest of friends—may I even say my mentor in some things—and since she's one hundred years old, well . . . nothing lasts forever, if you get my drift. She and I had lots to talk about this morning—she sees changes coming into her life from all directions, and she's wisely sorting them out. Now, it's always been said that

Ruby Carter has the eye, but I'm here to tell you, it's much more than that. I have the eye, if you will, and friends on the other side—we prefer spirits to that silly term "ghosts"—who from time to time help me shed some light on things (though I confess that just as often they go silent when I need them the most). But like Ruby says, "Temperamental on this side, temperamental once you cross over." I've found that to be true.

Anyway, Ruby sees what she sees, and when she says change is on the way, you better believe it. And I do. It be time, she says, and so it must be. What form those changes will take, if she knows, she isn't sharing quite yet. But she will. She did share that her great-granddaughter, Lisbeth, is on her way home for a while. "She'll stay longer than she thinks she will," Ruby tells me, and I know that's more than wishful thinking on Ruby's part. "And once she's here, she'll find what she doesn't even know she's missing. It's been a long time coming, Gracie."

Yes, I know. And yes, it's about time.

She also mentioned that Owen, Lis's brother, will be back by and by, too. We both know that he's in for the ride of his life. But that's down the road a bit.

So. Exciting times ahead for my friend. If I hadn't taken her to Baltimore last year myself to have her heart checked, I'd worry that all the excitement might do her harm. But our Ruby is one tough lady—tougher than most—and I would not be surprised if she outlived the rest of us.

Grace

Chapter One

Mist rose off the Chesapeake and floated silently over the beach. The woman standing on the shore tilted her head slightly to one side to follow the distant whine of an outboard as an unseen craft headed south through the darkness. She took a deep breath and let the damp June air fill her lungs before turning back and crossing the dune. The soft glow of the full moon barely lit the way, but she knew by heart every step from the beach to the old general store. From the top of the dune, she could see the blue haze from the TV in the building's back room, and a faint light from a second-floor bedroom.

The back porch had been sagging on her last visit, so she dug into her pocket for the key to the front door while she walked around the building and climbed the steps. The old bait cooler still stood to the right of the door, its once-white exterior now faded and chipped, and pots of some undeterminable flowers yet to bloom were lined up along the railing. Surprised to find the door unlocked, she stepped inside. Standing in the middle of the room, she called uncertainly into the darkness beyond.

"Gigi?"

She heard low voices from the TV, the scrape of a chair leg on the random oak floor, slow, soft, shuffling footfalls. A floorboard creaked, and she smiled.

"That you, Lisbeth?" a voice called out from behind the closed door.

"It's me." Lisbeth Parker dropped her bag by the door. She'd barely crossed the floor when a figure emerged from the back room, backlit by that blue light.

"Gigi, I'm sorry I'm so late. You shouldn't have waited up for me."

Ruby Carter—Lisbeth's great-grandmother—greeted her with a shush. "I don't be needing the likes of you to be telling me when to go to bed. But I do be needing a hug from my favorite girl."

Lisbeth's embrace totally enveloped the old woman's slight form, and she held her for a very long time.

"You can let go now," Ruby—Gigi to her great-grandchildren—chuckled. "I'm still all in one piece."

"Just making sure." One last gentle squeeze and Lisbeth released the old woman and reached for the wall switch to turn on an overhead light. She was tempted to chastise her elderly relative about walking around in the dark, but knew better. Ruby Carter had tread these boards for most of her one hundred years, and she knew every nail and every loose board between the store's long wooden counter and the front door.

"I saw on the TV there was that accident on the big bridge." Ruby walked behind Lis and locked the front door. "I figured you'd be coming along a little late. I heard your car. Wondered what you been up to for the past time."

"I walked down to the bay. It's been awhile since I was home, and I just wanted to . . ." Lis paused. She hadn't questioned her walk through the dark to the water's edge. She'd simply gotten out of her car and followed the path over the dune to soak in the smell, the feel of the Chesapeake. The feel of home.

"Always did the same myself whenever I'd left the island for a time and come back."

"When was the last time you left Cannonball Island, Gigi?" Lis put her arm around Ruby's slight shoulders. "I don't remember you crossing that little drawbridge too often."

"Hmmph." Ruby sniffed indignantly. "Went over to St. Dennis just last week. How much you know."

"You did? What for?" Lis's brows rose almost to her hairline.

"Not that it's any of your nevermind, but I went to see a friend."

"In St. Dennis?"

"Yes, in St. Dennis. Any other place be right on the other side of the bridge?"

"I didn't know you had friends over there."

"There be a lot of things you don't know, missy." Ruby straightened her back and drew herself up to her full height of five feet, one inch—four inches shorter than her great-granddaughter. "Who my friends might be is just one of them."

"Well, then. I guess you told me." Lis turned her head so that Ruby wouldn't see her smile.

"Well, then. I guess I did." Ruby nodded once in satisfaction. "Come on in back and have some tea. Warm you up proper."

Lis followed her great-grandmother through the store toward the door that stood open along the back wall, noting that the old-fashioned wooden shelves were only partially stocked and that unpacked delivery boxes had been stacked near the counter. She'd tend to those herself in the morning while Ruby chatted with the early crew who would arrive for coffee and their newspapers. It was a marvel to Lis that the local papers were still delivered to the island. The last time she was there, it seemed there'd been fewer residents than there'd been the time before, and several homes appeared to be vacant.

Lis stepped through the doorway and stopped short. Gazing around at the jumble of moving boxes and furniture shoved into the four corners of the room, she exclaimed, "What the hell happened in here?"

"Mind your tongue, girl," Ruby chided. "Don't be taking hell lightly. You have other words. Use them."

"Sorry, Gigi. What's going on in here? Why is there such a mess?"

"I been having some work done."

"What kind of work?"

"Having a bedroom and sitting room down here." Ruby looked pleased. "New bathroom, too." She paused, then pointed to a closed door in the middle of the wall and added, "The kitchen be new, too. Well, almost. Just needs some paint, I think. Go on, now. Take a look."

Lis opened the designated door. Ruby came up behind her and switched on the overhead light.

"See here? New all." Now Ruby was beaming, her pale blue eyes sparkling. "Stove, refrigerator. Even a dishwasher. I told him I don't need such a thing, but he said it didn't make sense to do all this and not put in a dishwasher."

Lis gazed in silent shock at the renovations, which were near completion. She ran her hand over the smooth wooden counter.

"Counters be made of the wood from the old floor," Ruby told her. "Some of it was not so good now, so he suggested that we put down new and put the old to good use right here." Ruby slapped her hand on the counter. "I like it."

"I love it." The old red oak from the floor had been sanded and polished to a sheen. If Ruby hadn't told her, Lis would have thought the counter had come from a high-end home renovation shop. "It's beautiful. But who is he? And when did all this take place? And why didn't I know about it?"

Ruby got that look again. "You think you need to know all, missy?"

"It's just such a surprise. This used to be the storeroom and just, well, mostly shed space." She was still taking in the transformation.

"Time for some changes," Ruby replied. "Time for me to be living smaller right here, 'stead of upstairs."

Lis was beginning to understand. Ruby might be reluctant to admit that climbing the steps to her living quarters was too much for her, but perhaps she was finally beginning to feel the weight of her one hundred years. Lis had met people years younger than her great-grandmother who had far less energy, physical strength, and mental acuity and who could never have withstood the rigors of running a business and keeping up with the world. The woman was a miracle, for sure, but there was no question that she was better off not taking a full flight of steps several times every day.

Treading carefully, mindful that Ruby had her pride, Lis said, "This is a beautiful room, Gigi. Let me see what else you're having done."

"Bedroom be next over." Ruby pointed to a closed door. "Bathroom beyond there. Go on."

Lis opened the door onto a finished room. She recognized the walnut bed and dresser as those that had been in the front corner room on the second floor for as long as she could remember. A small lamp on the table next to the bed shed light on walls the color of spring violets.

"Wow, Gigi." Lis could hardly believe her eyes. The bedroom upstairs had been beige for, well, forever. "Who picked the color?"

"Who do you think?" Ruby sniffed indignantly. "As if someone else should be picking for me."

"No, I just meant . . ." Lis continued to look around the room. She reached out to touch a chair that stood in a corner. "Is that Pop's old chair? You had it re-covered?"

"Wasn't going to leave it up there by itself. My Harold would have had a fit for sure. Wouldn't have given me a minute's peace." Ruby smiled as she always did when she spoke of her husband of sixty years, long gone now. "My Harold loved that old thing. I tried to toss it but he wouldn't hear none of it."

"It looks so nice." Lis ran her hand over the new fabric that covered the back of the chair. "I like this plaid."

"It's right pretty. I wasn't sure anyone should be messing with it, but he told me it could be done good as new. Wouldn't do to have that dusty faded thing in this new room, he said. I couldn't say he was wrong."

"Who is *he*?"

"Boy from over town. He did all this." Ruby waved her hand around the room. "Alec Jansen."

"Alec Jansen?" Had Lis heard correctly? "*Alec Jansen?*"

Ruby folded her arms across her chest and stared at Lis. "You remember him. From school."

"Not really." Lis turned her head so she wouldn't have to meet Ruby's eyes.

She could feel those eyes boring a hole right through her.

"Okay, so maybe the name rings a bell." Lis picked up a toss pillow and appeared to inspect it.

"Hmmmph." Ruby leaned against the doorjamb. "Seems there were few enough in that class that you'd recall them all, each and every."

She never could bluff Ruby. Lis tossed the pillow back onto the bed and sighed. Alec Jansen was a name she hadn't heard in years. Just the mention brought up a flood of memories she had no intention of dwelling on—or sharing with her great-grandmother. "So is Alec into interior design these days?"

"He be handy with a hammer," Ruby said simply.

"Did he do the kitchen, too?"

"He did all. The kitchen, here, the bathroom." Ruby nodded in the direction of a half-opened door. "When I get the front room clear of the boxes, get unpacked and all tucked away, he be painting that room, too." Ruby looked toward the front room, her expression thoughtful. "Maybe have him make me some shelves for all my books, 'ventually."

Lis peeked into the bathroom. Besides the toilet and a vanity with a shiny new porcelain sink, there was a walk-in shower with a wide built-in seat. Alcoves for shampoo and soap were set into tile walls the color of sea glass within easy reach of the seat.

"This is lovely," Lis said. "No tub, though?"

"What I be needing a tub for? Kill myself getting in or getting out. Nearly did," she conceded.

"What do you mean, you nearly did? Did you fall . . . ?"

Ruby nodded. "I did, yes. Wasn't till Hedy Perkins came in to the store that I had help getting up. She be coming here for all her life, always I be at the counter or that old table by the window. I heard her calling my name and I called her right back. She 'bout set a new record for speed running up those steps. Moves good for a big girl. *'In here,'* I called to her. She opened the bathroom door and said, *'Good Lord almighty, Miss Ruby. What are you doing on that floor?'* And I said, *'Give me a hand up, Hedy,'* but she said no, she had to call someone because what if I be hurt, broke my hip or something? *'My pride be hurt but my hip be fine,'* I told her. *'Fetch me one of those towels.'* So she gave me a towel and took my hand and helped me right myself."

"I hope she got you to go to the emergency room at the hospital. What if you'd broken something?"

Ruby scoffed. "Nothing but maybe a little black and blue."

"You could have been badly hurt, Gigi." Lis studied the woman's face. Every line, every crease, was beloved. The thought of her falling and having no one there to help turned Lis's blood cold.

"Well, I don't know all, but I know that." Ruby nodded. "That's why he—Alec—said I should start thinking about maybe using the space back of the store for my living."

"Wait. Someone else suggested all this and you actually agreed?"

"Don't be looking so surprised."

"This"—Lis pointed to her own face with both index fingers—"is not the look of surprise. This is the look of shock, as in, I'm *shocked* that someone—*anyone* other than you—would have said you should move down to the first floor, and you just said okay."

"Time be right." Ruby straightened her back as much as she could and leaned past Lis to snap off the light, then turned and walked back through her new bedroom, leaving Lis momentarily in the darkened room.

"No, seriously, Gigi." Lis trailed behind into the front room, where the eleven o'clock news was just coming on. "How did he convince you? What did he say?"

"It be time." Ruby lowered herself into her recliner. "And in case you're wondering, when he paints out this room, this chair going to be gone. Ordered me a new one. Red leather."

Lis leaned against the doorjamb and felt somewhat like Alice must have felt when she fell down the rabbit hole.

"Owen and I have been telling you for years that you shouldn't be living upstairs by yourself. Why all of a sudden was it time?"

Ruby looked smug. "You and your brother had no plan. Alec, he drew it all out. Here the kitchen, there the bathroom. It looked right."

"How did Alec even know that you fell?"

"I 'spect just about everyone hereabouts knew. Like I said, Hedy Perkins be the one who found me. Woman couldn't keep a secret if the good Lord himself put her to it." Ruby glanced up at Lis. "You wanting the news?"

Lis shook her head. It was clear her great-grandmother had said all she was going to say on the subject of her newly constructed living quarters.

"I suspect you be ready for that tea now."

Lis, still in a bit of shock, nodded. "I'll make it."

"Let me know if you need help finding things."

"I'll figure it out." Lis went back into the kitchen, where she found everything exactly where she'd expected. Ruby was a creature of habit, one who was meticulously ordered. Lis filled the kettle and while the water boiled, she took two cups and saucers from the cupboard. Since both she and Ruby preferred their tea without cream or lemon, it was an easy fix. As Ruby had taught her long ago, Lis measured one scant teaspoon of sugar into the bottom of each cup and waited for the kettle to whistle.

She looked through the tall bottom cupboards to find the old wooden tray that Ruby preferred and placed the cups and saucers on it, then dropped in tea bags and filled the cups when the water was ready. She carried the tray into Ruby's crowded sitting room and looked for a place to set it down.

"Right here be fine." Ruby pointed to the table next to her from which she removed a stack of books. "Thank you."

"You're welcome." Lis took a seat on a nearby chair. "Aren't you going to ask me if I remembered how much sugar to put in?"

Ruby shook her head, a smile playing on her lips. "Not much chance you be forgetting."

Lis returned the smile and lifted the cup to her lips. She was just about to take the first sip when Ruby asked, "You be hearing anything from Owen?"

Lis returned the cup to the saucer and placed both on the floor in front of her. "Last I heard, my big brother was in Alaska flying a mail plane. Of course, that was two months ago. He could have moved on since then."

"I thought he said something about a shrimp boat in New Orleans."

"You spoke with him?"

Ruby nodded. "Not too long ago. He said he be having a fine time."

"When does he not have a good time?" Lis laughed. "He's a player, that's for sure."

"Playing at what?"

"Playing at being twenty again instead of thirty-eight."

Ruby took a sip of tea. "I'm looking to see that one grow up before my time is over."

"Good luck with that." To Lis, her older brother had always seemed bigger than life. Sinfully handsome and wickedly clever, Owen had been a magnet for mischief as well as for the girls in town. Growing up, she'd idolized him and wished she could have been more like him, carefree and daring and confident.

"He be getting his comeuppance, by and by."

Before Lis could ask her what she meant by that, Ruby added, "He be here for your art show, no matter where he be now."

"Did he tell you that?"

"He doesn't have to. He be here."

"I'd like that." It had been almost a year since Lis had seen her brother. She thought maybe she'd extend her stay to spend some time with him.

As if reading her mind, Ruby asked, "How long you be staying around, Lisbeth?"

Lis shrugged. "I'm not sure. The show is next week, but I don't have any real plans." She paused, then said, "To tell you the truth, my work hasn't been going all that well."

"Oh?" Ruby rested the saucer on her knee and waited for Lis to gather her thoughts.

"I'm just stuck," Lis blurted out. "I sit and stare at the easel and I can't seem to make anything happen. I want to paint—I love to paint—but I just . . . can't.

It's like whatever I had inside me, whatever it was that I saw when I looked at the paper, is gone."

"Go on."

"I've tried everything: different papers—cold press, hot press. Handmade. Paper on a roll, paper on a board. I've even tried painting on canvas, you know, like you usually use for oils?" Lis sighed heavily. "It's like it's just . . . gone."

"What you be trying to paint, Lisbeth?"

"What I've been painting. What I'm known for. Skylines and city scenes."

"Maybe what you be painting needs to change."

Lis stared at her.

Before she could ask, Ruby closed her eyes. "It be back, Lisbeth. Soon enough. You be fine, by and by. Let it be. In its time, it be back."

Lis knew better than to argue or question when Ruby made one of her pronouncements, so she bit back the protests that had been settling on the tip of her tongue and said nothing.

"Think I'll watch the end of the news." Ruby turned on the TV with the remote, and just like that, the conversation was over.

Lis gathered the cups and saucers and returned them to the kitchen, where she rinsed them and started to place them in the dishwasher, then remembered Ruby's comments. She washed the dishes in the sink, dried them, and put them away.

Still—a dishwasher. In Ruby Carter's kitchen. Lis shook her head. Would she believe it if she hadn't seen it with her own eyes?

She rejoined Ruby in the sitting room.

"You want to sit a spell?" Ruby asked.

"Actually, I'm pretty tired."

"You can find your way upstairs all right? Your old room be ready."

"I remember the way. I haven't been gone that long."

Lis leaned over to kiss her great-grandmother's cheek and felt the old woman's hand gently stroke the side of her head. The small gesture, so filled with love, caused Lis's throat to tighten, so that her words came out in a whisper. "Thanks for letting me stay with you, Gigi."

"Now, where else would you go, girl?" Ruby's voice softened. "You come home to the island, you come home to me, sure enough."

"Always, Gigi." Lis gave her a quick hug. "I will always come home to you."

Ruby grunted with satisfaction and patted Lis on the back. "Get on with you, now, get to bed."

"What are you going to do?"

"I'm going to sit right here and read me another chapter of this book, then turn in."

"What are you reading?" Lis reached for the book just as Ruby held it up. The cover was black with blood-red drops dripping down one side, the author a thriller writer known for his creepy and lurid tales. "Gigi! I can't believe you read this stuff."

"Why not?"

"It's so . . . scary. Doesn't it give you nightmares?"

"Honey, at my age the only thing that ever really scared me was the thought of the hereafter, and even that fear be gone these days." Ruby smiled and opened the book. "You be needing anything else?"

Lis, still in shock, shook her head.

"Then go on up and settle yourself. I'll see you in the morning."

"Right. See you in the morning." Lis kissed the top of Ruby's head.

She walked through the unlit store to pick up her bag where she'd left it, then turned on the switch for the light at the top of the stairs to the second floor. As Lis climbed she tested herself to see if she could remember which steps squeaked and which had been safe to tread on when coming in late back in the day. She was pleased when she'd made her way to the top without one squeal or groan from the floorboards, as if her feet remembered where the squeaky boards were placed.

The room at the end of the hall had been hers for as long as she could recall. The door was open and a small lamp cast shadows on the pale green walls. The furniture stood where it had always been, the poster bed in the center of the left wall, the painted dresser next to the door. The same old chair, its slipcover unchanged from the blue and white stripe of Lis's youth, still curled into the corner next to the window, the same old faded carpet covered the floorboards. The familiarity of it was comforting. There was nowhere on earth she felt as at home as she did beneath this roof, in this room. She'd moved in when she was seventeen, when her newly widowed mother decided that life on the island held no promise for her and decided to move to Arizona.

Having one year of high school left, Lis had refused to go. Gigi had sided with Lis and had convinced her granddaughter to allow Lis to remain there at least until she graduated. Lis had joined her mother for the following summer in Arizona, but that had been enough to convince Lis that the Southwest was not for her. She'd returned to the Eastern Shore briefly before leaving for art college in Philadelphia, and from there, she'd moved to New York, to an apartment where she had three roommates, which had proven to be three too many. Realizing she couldn't work with an audience and that peace and quiet were much more conducive to creativity than constant conversation at night and talk radio from dawn to midnight, Lis moved to a New Jersey suburb where rents were more reasonable and she wasn't subjected to the habits and lifestyles of others. Her work flourished, and deep inside, she knew it was only a matter of time before her work would hang inside the galleries whose showings she had attended so many times.

It was ironic, she'd once told her ex-fiancé, that it was only after she left the city that her paintings of cityscapes began to come to life.

Lis had gotten lucky when she met the owner of a trendy Manhattan gallery who offered to exhibit several of her paintings. Her reputation was made when the star of a popular TV talk show stopped by one afternoon and loved Lis's work so much that she not only bought all the paintings in the gallery but asked to see more. In the end, she purchased six paintings and showed them off on her show one morning before having them hung in her home. Lis enjoyed a quick uptick in visibility as an artist and a huge bump in her sales, appearing on that same talk show several times and having several newspaper and magazine articles cover her work. The eventual result of all the publicity was an invitation to exhibit some of her paintings in a showing of local artists' works in the new St. Dennis art center. The temptation to come back a rousing success on every level was more than she could resist. Besides, it had been six months since she'd been home—since the day after Christmas, and then she'd only stayed for an overnight—and it was well past time that she checked in on Ruby.

Lis took a quick shower in the bathroom across the hall, swinging her legs over the high side of the old tub, thinking it was no wonder that Gigi had fallen while trying to get out. Thank God she had a nice, new walk-in shower downstairs.

Thinking about the new bath made Lis think of Alec Jansen. What magic had he employed to talk her great-grandmother into a total renovation of the first floor?

He always was a sweet talker.

But Lis knew that Gigi never let anyone talk her into anything she didn't want to do, so she must have been thinking about it before Alec showed up. But how had that come about? Alec was a townie, a St. Dennis boy. How likely was it that he had just shown up one day with a sketch for Gigi's new first floor? Would a one-hundred-year-old woman know what such a renovation should cost? With no one there to look after her interests, how would she know if she was being ripped off?

Lis sat on the edge of the bed, towel-drying her dark brown hair, biting a nail, pondering the possibility that her great-grandmother was being taken advantage of. Alec Jansen had always been a smart guy with a smart mouth, but she'd never known him to be dishonest. Still, people had been known to change, and this was Gigi, and any responsible great-grandchild would look into the situation. She couldn't be too overt, however. Ruby wouldn't take kindly to anyone questioning her judgment, whether of the work itself or of her choice of contractor.

Lis finished drying her hair, then changed into a nightshirt and climbed into the big soft bed that always seemed to welcome her with a comforting hug. She turned off the light and lay in the darkness, savoring the feeling of being in this place where love and warmth had always been hers for the taking, where the sheets and blankets smelled of Ruby's laundry soap and the bit of lavender she always tucked under the pillow. From below, she heard the sound of a door closing as Gigi, too, prepared to sleep, and from the open window, she could hear the faint lap of the waves against the beach. A late spring breeze brought the once-familiar scent of the salt marsh on the western side of the island. There was no other place on earth like Cannonball Island, with its history and its traditions, its storied way of life, even its own odd speech patterns, which still prevailed through the centuries among the older residents like Ruby. It was music to Lis's ears.

Of course, every year there remained fewer and fewer who spoke in that distinct fashion. The thought gave Lis pause. She tried to recall how many islanders remained who were in their eighties and nineties, whose speech reflected Ruby's. Surely there was no one older than a hundred left on the island. Lis's heart saddened at the thought that islandspeak would be gone from memory within the next twenty years or so. With the older residents would go not only their speech but their stories. As far as Lis knew, there was no written record of the island's unique history of having been settled by residents of St. Dennis who'd been driven from the town for supporting the British during the War of 1812. She'd heard the tales of near famine and the iron-willed islanders who refused to be defeated by the poor soil that supported little more than scrub pines and hackberry trees.

The stories needed to be written down while there was still time, she realized, preserved for future generations. For her own children, should she have any.

It occurred to her then that there was a good chance that her children could be born into a world from which Ruby had already passed. The thought brought tears to her eyes.

Lis always did have trouble falling asleep after driving for more than a few hours, but now she willed her racing mind to turn it all off. Her worries about Gigi, the island and the stories she'd been raised on, the changes to the old general store, which had her mind settling on Gigi's contractor—all swirled around in her head.

Lis hadn't meant to share her frustration and

anxiety over her sudden inability to paint, but somehow Ruby always knew when something wasn't right, and she knew how to draw it out with barely a word. She made you want to bring things into the open, to talk things over whether you felt ready to or not.

Lis had decided to save the story of her breakup with Ted, her fiancé, for another day. There was only so much angst she could take in one night.

She turned over and punched the pillow.

Tomorrow she would think about how best to deal with Alec Jansen and the separate world that was Cannonball Island, and maybe tell Ruby that her engagement was off and try to explain why. Maybe she'd even try to paint. Tonight she would simply be happy to sleep beneath this roof again, where one floor below, Gigi, too, settled in for the night.

Chapter Two

Always an early riser, regardless of where she was or how late she'd been out the night before, Lis was awake before the sun her first morning on Cannonball Island. She was dressed and downstairs before the last wave of watermen stopped in to fill up their thermoses with coffee.

"That Kathleen and Jack's girl I see coming down those steps?" Joe Compton had called from the ancient counter where Ruby set out the coffeepot.

"It sure is." Lis smiled. Joe had been a friend of her dad's. "How's your family, Mr. Compton?"

"Right as rain." He nodded as he poured sugar into the thermos.

"How's Judy?"

"She and Justin have three little ones now," he told her. Half-and-half followed the sugar. "Living over outside of Baltimore. Justin owns his own shop, fixes computers and builds some custom. Got a nice little business going for himself."

"Good for Justin. Please tell Judy I was asking about her."

"Will do. How's that pretty mama of yours? Did I hear she snagged herself another husband?"

"You heard right."

"Number three or number four?"

Lis laughed. "Husband number three. It's been about three years now."

"She always was something else, that Kathleen." He hastened to add, "No disrespect meant. You tell her Joe was asking for her, hear?"

"I sure will." Lis knew exactly what Joe meant. From all she'd heard over the years, her mother had earned her reputation as a bit of a free spirit.

Lis got in line behind a man she didn't recognize. He gestured for her to go first but she shook her head. "No, no. I'm not in a hurry to get anywhere, but I suspect you'd like to be out on the water right now, checking your traps."

"True enough. Thanks." The man served himself, nodded to Lis, then left the store with Joe, who'd apparently paid for both of them.

Lis filled a paper cup with coffee and went to the counter, where Ruby was ringing up a customer.

"Good luck out there this morning, Paul. Hope that storm they warned about stays down around the other end of the bay till you all get your business done and get on home safe and sound."

"Thanks, Miz Ruby. I hope so, too." The customer nodded to Lis as he was leaving.

"You still pack 'em in in the morning, Gigi." Lis leaned on the counter.

"No place else for them to go this hour, less they want to drive to the mainland. I hear there's a new place over to River Road that's open at six or so. She gets the fishermen, they say. I get the crabbers and the oystermen. All works out."

"I can't believe you still get up this early," Lis made the mistake of saying. As soon as the words were out of her mouth, she could have kicked herself.

"And where else should I be, missy?" Ruby turned those blue eyes on her.

"I just meant . . ."

"I know what you meant. You meant I'm old and I should stay in bed and sleep away the rest of what I got coming to me." Ruby shook her head. "Plenty of time to sleep when I'm done breathing."

The last of her customers having left, Ruby went past Lis to the pile of boxes that stood inside the front door. To the left of the door stood a soda cooler. Several crates of both Pepsi and Coke products were stacked side by side in front of the cooler.

"I'm sorry, Gigi." Lis joined her and started to empty the crates to restock the cooler. "I just meant that you've worked hard for a long enough time that you earned some rest."

"I will take it when I'm good and ready." Ruby slit the top of the first box with the Swiss Army knife she pulled out of the pocket of her blue and white apron. "Not before."

Lis knew better than to respond, so she watched in silence for a moment, wondering how to offer to shelve the contents of the box without offending Ruby.

"Well, maybe you could stack these cereal boxes there on that top shelf when you're done there," Ruby said, as if she'd read Lis's mind. "It's a bit troublesome, reaching up."

Lis suspected Ruby was having problems with her left shoulder again, but since she seemed a bit touchy, Lis tucked the thought away to ask later. She emptied the last crate, then restacked them by the door for the distributors to pick up and refill. Next she dragged the box Ruby had opened to the shelves where dry cereals were kept.

Ruby acknowledged the gesture with a "Hmmph."

"It's nice that you still get deliveries here on the island," Lis said cautiously. When Ruby was feeling touchy, just about anything could set her off.

"Tom Parsons been delivering to me over forty-five years, his daddy before him." Ruby slashed the top of the next carton and left it for Lis to empty and find space on the shelves for its contents. "I been a steady customer all those years, expect this place be around another forty-five." She glanced at Lis and added, "At least that many."

Lis wasn't about to step into that trap.

"So you still stock mostly dry stuff, I see. Cereals, canned and paper goods, baking stuff," Lis said.

"Doesn't pay to carry perishables. The market over to St. Dennis is bigger, got the room for the big coolers and what all," Ruby told her. "Got the basics here, newspapers every morning 'cept Sunday. Most folks want a Sunday paper, they pick one up over to the mainland when they go to church."

"Who goes to St. Dennis for church?" Back when

she was growing up on the island, that would have been unheard of.

"Everyone who has a mind to church, that's who." Ruby looked up from her task of opening another box. "Been no preacher here for . . . four, five years or so."

"What happened to Reverend Foster?"

"Retired to someplace warm. I hear he passed not long after."

Lis knew what was coming next, so she turned back to the shelf lest Ruby see her smile.

"Folks need to know where they belong." Ruby delivered the anticipated pronouncement. "Some don't know when they're well off. Some move on when they should stay put."

Lis knew that her great-grandmother was talking about Lis and her mother, her brother, Owen, and everyone else who ever moved off the island.

"I think for some, the prospects are just better somewhere else," Lis said. "There are some things that you have to leave home to do."

"And what might that be?"

"Art school for me, to start."

"Art school be done. Seems to me you can paint anywhere."

"Can't find a husband here." Lis tried to add some levity to the conversation.

"You'd be surprised what you might find hereabouts these days."

"Gigi, there hasn't been a man under fifty living on this island for at least fifteen years." Lis paused. "Except maybe a few of the guys I went to school with when they came back to see their parents. And most of the parents have left as well. Last time I was here, I noticed more than a few of the old cottages were boarded up."

"Some boards go up, some might have come down since then." Ruby stood up and stretched. "Times be changing. Might be you should be taking a walk around sometime soon, see what is, not what was."

"I just might do that."

"Do you good." Ruby nodded and walked over to the counter, where she helped herself to a cup of hot water from the carafe she set out every morning for those few early birds who preferred tea. She made her selection from the tea bags she'd put out in a little basket.

"What sort of day do we have today, Gigi?" Lis asked once she'd emptied the boxes.

"Why don't you go on out and see for yourself?" Ruby took her tea to the old round table under the window on the right side of the room and sat in one of the four ancient wooden chairs. She opened a newspaper and, settling herself, told Lis, "Be a lull here till around nine or so. You go on, now. I have some news that needs reading."

"I won't be long." Lis headed for the side door and stepped outside.

The sun had risen just enough to warm the sand and sparkle off the scrubby tufts of grass. Lis walked around to the back of the building, heading for the path that led over the dune, but she was stopped in her tracks when she approached the back porch. Where previously the floorboards had sagged and the supports had leaned precariously and the roof had threatened to collapse, there was an entirely new structure, top to bottom.

"How . . . ?" she wondered aloud.

She stepped tentatively onto the first step, found it solid as rock, and climbed the next two to the porch, which was similarly solid. The wood had yet to be painted, but there wasn't a rotted board to be seen and the supports actually seemed to be holding up the roof. Funny Gigi hadn't mentioned it.

Lis stood on the new floorboards and leaned against the new railing and surveyed the island from the slightly elevated vantage. She paused, her gaze darting across the property from left to right and back again.

Something wasn't right. Something was missing. It took her but a moment to realize what that something was.

She all but flew back into the store.

"Gigi, where is Uncle Eb's boat?" Lis asked.

"Hmmm?" Ruby looked up from the newspaper. "Oh. The boat. Alec has it down to the marina."

"Why?" Lis took a seat at the table across from Ruby. "Why does Alec have our boat?"

"I guess because it be his now," Ruby said calmly.

"He bought it?"

"Sort of."

"What does that mean? Either he bought it or he didn't."

"Well, no money changed hands"—Ruby folded the section of the paper she'd been reading—"but he paid all the same."

"How much?"

Ruby's eyes narrowed. "Now, how do you suppose that might be yours to know? Last I heard, that boat be mine. Came to me through my Harold, left to him by his brother Eben. Don't remember Harold's will saying nothing 'bout Ruby *and Lisbeth*."

"Gigi, that was a *skipjack*. One of the old ones from back in Grandpap's day. It was worth a lot of money."

"You thinking I be too much a fool to know what that old hull was and how much it be worth?"

"No, I don't think you're foolish, but . . ."

"No buts. You think I can do for me or you don't."

"Of course I think you can take care of yourself," Lis said softly, "but sometimes when we trust someone too much, they can take advantage of us."

Ruby glared.

"Girl, I am one hundred years and three months on this earth. If I can't tell the true from the false, you might as well set me to my rest right now."

"The new porch . . ."

Ruby opened her paper and focused her attention on the page in front of her, signaling that the conversation was over.

Lis watched in silence for a few moments, but Ruby had nothing more to say. Lis suspected that Alec was responsible for the porch as well, but there was no point in asking. Not right now, anyway. Lis broke down the cardboard boxes the groceries had been delivered in, folding them flat and stacking them in a pile.

"You still leave these next to the door out front?" she asked.

Ruby nodded. "Tom'll pick 'em up when he comes back through."

"What if it rains?"

"Well, then, I expect they'll get wet." Ruby still hadn't looked up. "Less a tarp be spread over the lot."

"Where would I find a tarp if I needed one?"

"In the shed out by the garage."

Lis dragged the cardboard outside and set the pile to the left of the door where it would be out of the way. She went back into the store, poured herself a second cup of coffee, and told Ruby, "I think I'll take that walk now."

"Take your time."

The walk to the bay was a short one. Lis took off her sandals and picked her way carefully over the rocky jetty until she found a dry flat spot. She sat and sipped her coffee and watched the boats out on the bay. The local watermen had their own boats, their own crews, their own favorite spots for whatever they were after on that particular day. Generally they were courteous to each other, respecting their neighbors' territory. She'd heard all the old stories about how out-of-towners occasionally slipped into their waters and tried to lift crab pots that weren't theirs, how the locals would surround the interlopers until they turned over their ill-gotten catch to whomever they'd poached from. Few made a return trip, her uncle Eben used to say, once they'd been found out by the islanders.

For years the bay had felt the effects of both

overfishing and pollution, and watermen all around the bay had suffered terribly. Cannonball Island's crabbers and oystermen were no exception. Many a family had moved from the island, not to return, and many a father had sold his traps and gone onto the mainland seeking employment. Lis had heard that the bay was making a comeback, and judging by the number of boats out on the water that morning, she believed it was true. The Chesapeake had sustained her family since the early 1800s. She had only kind thoughts for it now.

Her thoughts turned to Alec Jansen, and they weren't as kind.

She couldn't help but be curious about how he managed to talk Ruby into making so many changes. The woman had stubbornly refused to listen to Lis or Owen or anyone else whenever they'd suggested making any sort of change in the old general store, so how had Alec succeeded where so many of Lis's relatives had failed?

"Time was right," Ruby had told her the night before.

"Yeah, well, time's *been* right for a long time," Lis muttered.

She finished the coffee and dangled her feet over the edge of the rock. In the water below, a large blue claw crab picked at the remains of a fish, probably bait that had been tossed overboard by one of the boats that by now was miles away. Lis peered closer, saw the red tips of its claws, and for a moment she was five years old and watching her older brother empty the bucket in which he'd kept the crabs he'd caught that morning.

"See that red on the claws?" Owen had held up a squirming crab. "That tells you this is a grown-up girl-crab. We call them sooks. The guys don't have red there on their claws."

Owen used to catch crabs by hand, but Lis had never learned the degree of stealth required to grab one quickly enough to avoid those claws. She'd been pinched enough by the time she was twelve to no longer make the effort.

She watched the crab feed until it disappeared among the rocks and she lost her excuse to avoid thinking about Alec and what he was up to.

He'd always been a handsome thing, and she couldn't help but wonder what he looked like these days. Was his hair still as blond, his eyes still as blue? In the seventeen years since they graduated, she hadn't run into him even one time. Not so unusual, maybe, since she spent little time in St. Dennis even when she was home. She didn't know if he'd stayed in the town, or moved away as so many others had, including Lis and her brother. She'd had no ties with anyone in town, and so there'd been no one to ask about Alec's whereabouts. For all she knew, he was married and had five kids.

Lis's father's prejudice and suspicions about all things St. Dennis had been drummed into her from the time she could crawl, and as a result, consciously or unconsciously, she'd never been comfortable in the town or among its residents, which had made things awkward when she was in school. Cannonball Island had a one-room schoolhouse that served the islanders through the fourth grade, after which they all went into St. Dennis to continue their education. Lis and Owen had been forbidden to make friends with anyone who hadn't been born and raised on the island, which drastically cut the list of potential friends—not to mention dates. Owen had mostly ignored his father, but Lis hadn't been as assertive.

But comfortable or not, Lis was going to have to make a trip across the drawbridge and hunt down Alec and interrogate him. It was the least she could do for Ruby. Someone had to protect her interests.

She didn't know where she'd find him, but St. Dennis wasn't all that big, and if he was into contracting, someone would know where to look. She sure as heck wasn't going to ask Ruby for directions.

Lis followed the rocks back to the beach. She considered returning to the store to get her car, but then she'd have to face Ruby, and chances were her great-grandmother would know exactly where she was going and why. Better to walk to town—it was only a few miles. Lis had walked that and more every day when she was living in Manhattan. Even after her move to a small New Jersey suburb, her daily routine had included a long morning walk.

It was still early, not quite nine, and the sun had yet to burn off the dew. Lis walked across the dune, sticking to the well-worn path, the grasses brushing against her legs as she passed. While she put her sandals on, a car pulled into the store's lot, and Estelle Detweiler got out. Lis knew that Estelle, the older sister of Hedy, the island gossip, was good for keeping Ruby occupied until noon. She set out for Bay Road and the one-lane bridge that separated the island from St. Dennis.

She paused at the bridge to permit a car to pass. The driver waved and Lis waved back, an acknowledgment more than a greeting, then walked across to the other side. She smiled as she stepped over the gridwork where the two points of the drawbridge met, just as she had as a child. Every kid who grew up on the island knew that if you stepped on that exact spot where the bridge opened, a troll would arise from the depths of the river in the blink of an eye, and just that fast, it would grab you and take you down into his lair and you'd never be seen again.

The morning was cool for late June, the large trees along Charles Street filtering the sun. She walked along the shoulder of the road—marveling that there were still no sidewalks on this end of the town's main street—past a pond where a heron fed, and then, further down the road, the Inn at Sinclair's Point, one of the town's landmarks. Back in the day, Lis had gone to school with Ford Sinclair, the youngest of the three kids whose family had owned and operated the inn forever. She wondered if they still owned the place, then realized if they'd sold it, it would have been considered the kind of news that someone—Ruby, Owen, or her mother, who still had friends on the island— would have told her.

She passed a park—she couldn't recall the name but remembered it had ball fields, though she'd never played there—and on to the center of town. St. Dennis still had only one traffic light. It was at the corner of Kelly's Point Road and Charles Street, and it marked the beginning of the shopping district. Lis slowed and noted the new arrivals since she'd last been back. The flower shop, Petals and Posies, had been there for years; likewise, Lola's Café, an upscale eatery. Cuppachino had opened right before her last long visit, and she fondly remembered the excellent coffee she'd had there. Across the road was Sips—beverages only—which had been around when Lis was in high school. Next to it, however, was a fancy-looking shop that had all manner of gorgeous things in the window, things like shoes and bags and swimsuits, sundresses and one knock-out dress-up dress, a black sleeveless V-neck number with tiny sparkly things scattered on it like stars against a dark night sky. The name of the shop—Bling—was painted on the window as well as on the door. She'd passed it numerous times on her previous visits home, but since she rarely stayed beyond two or three days, she'd never had the occasion to stop in. This time around she might check it out when she had a moment. But that moment wasn't now. She was on a mission.

The light was red and the DON'T WALK sign was flashing, so Lis waited at the corner for the go signal. There was a sign with an arrow pointing down Kelly's Point Road for the municipal building, the marina, Captain Walt's Seafood Restaurant, and One Scoop or Two, the local ice cream shop. Hadn't Ruby said that Alec had the skipjack at the marina? That was as good a place as any to start.

Lis headed left down the road, which had been sand and gravel the last time she'd been there. The macadam was a nice improvement: Stones had gotten into her sandals the last time she'd walked that road, a few years back when she was home for Owen's wedding. His bride had wanted the photos taken along the dock overlooking the bay. The photos had lasted longer than the marriage.

Must have been something he'd said, Lis mused. No one had liked his wife, Cindy, and no one had so much as blinked when she left him and filed for divorce less than a year later. Some guys weren't meant to settle down. Lis suspected Owen might be one of them.

At the end of the road a wooden boardwalk went left and right. To the left was One Scoop or Two, and the marina lay to the right behind Captain Walt's.

The sign out front of the marina read ELLISON'S—BOATS FOR THE BAY SINCE 1896. The building was as wide as it was long, of weathered white clapboard that was showing its age. The roof was slate and large double doors opened along the bay side. Windows ran across the front on both sides of a glass door with the name painted on it in black. Lis tried the door and found it locked, so she walked around to the side and followed the sound of machinery through the open double doors.

Ten feet in, the skipjack Eben Carter bought in 1932 was perched atop a series of cinder blocks. Pieces were missing from the hull and the rudder lay on the floor next to it. The boom, as long as the boat itself, lay alongside the empty hull. The mast, a full sixty feet long, stood at a wide angle to the wall. The whining noise from the other side of the boat was deafening. Lis covered her ears and ventured close enough to peer around the bow.

His back was to her, but she knew instinctively that she'd found the man she was looking for. He wore a pair of ripped khaki shorts and a gray T-shirt that had holes near the shoulder and the sleeves ripped off to show deeply tanned arms. His blond hair, mostly hidden by a baseball cap worn backward, was just long enough to inch over the back neckline of the shirt. He held a sander, which he ran back and forth over a length of wood.

Lis waited till the whining of the sander paused before saying, "That's my great-uncle Eb's boat."

Alec glanced over his shoulder and gave her a once-over, top to bottom. "Good to see you again, too, Lis."

He wore goggles upon which a layer of fine dust had accumulated. He wiped the lens with the bottom of his shirt and turned the sander back on. Lis waited for him to finish. When the machine finally went silent, Alec set it on the concrete floor.

"So what brings you to town?" he asked without turning around.

"I want to know what's going on," she said, annoyed that he'd taken his time in turning off the sander.

"In St. Dennis?" He lifted the smooth board and turned to face her, his eyes still the cornflower blue she remembered. "Well, let's see. The parade is on for Fourth of July, just like always. The annual garden tour starts in another week or so, I forget just when. I never did make it to that. But you know, you can pick up the latest *St. Dennis Gazette* and get the whole calendar of events from now right on through December. Grace Sinclair does a fine job tracking down everything that happens in town."

"You know that isn't what I meant." She glared at him. "What's going on with you and my great-grandma?"

"What's going on is that I'm helping her to stay in her home, keep her business going, without her ending up in the hospital with a broken hip or worse or inviting a lawsuit from someone who trips over those loose floorboards in the store."

"I didn't notice any loose floorboards."

"That's because I nailed them down."

"How did you talk her into letting you do everything you're doing?"

"Maybe you should be asking her that."

"I already did."

"And . . . ?"

"And her answer wasn't really an answer. I want to know how it came about and how much it's costing her."

"Don't you think that's her business? Hers and mine?"

"Not if she can't afford it."

"She can afford it. That all?"

"No. I don't get it. Owen and I both have tried for years to get her to make some changes in the place but she wouldn't hear of it. Now I come home and there's a whole new living space . . ."

"No way a hundred-year-old lady should be climbing stairs a couple of times a day."

". . . a new kitchen . . ."

"Old stove was about to set the place on fire."

". . . new bathroom . . ."

"She couldn't get in and out of that old tub without falling. One of these days she was bound to break something and that would'a been the end of her and the Cannonball Island General Store would have been closed for good. No way was that going to happen."

". . . a new back porch . . ."

"Oh, now, that was a necessity. That thing was headed south in the next big storm. Scared the life out of me to just walk past whenever a big wind kicked up." He nodded, his hands on his hips. "Yeah, replacing that was the first thing that had to happen."

"How did you talk her into it?" Lis was all out of patience.

"Well, since you're all hell-bent to know and you somehow feel you're entitled—I didn't ask her. I just started to work on it. She stuck her head out the back door, and I said, 'Miz Ruby, I'm fixing this old ramshackle porch of yours before it falls down on someone. So if you hear some noise out back, it's just me and my hammer. With your permission, of course.'"

"And just like that she said okay?"

"No, she said, 'Go on, then, boy.' Took me a couple of weeks, but once it was done, she liked it."

"Is that when she said, 'Gee, thanks, Alec. Take my boat'?"

"Our payment arrangement is between the two of us." He walked over to a cooler that sat on the floor and opened it and took out a bottle of water. He twisted off the cap and took a long, deep drink.

"Bottle of water?" he asked.

"No, thank you," she said, though she was thirsty as hell.

She tried not to watch as he lifted the front of his shirt and wiped the sweat off his face, but it was too much to ask that she look away from the sight of that tanned, toned torso.

"If you're worried that I'm taking advantage of her, that I'm going to bankrupt her or, God forbid, end up owning the general store, I can assure you that no one is taking advantage of anyone. She's being charged a reasonable amount. Let's call it the friends-and-family discount. Anyone else would have charged her a hell of a lot more. Believe me, the value of this old heap was a drop in the bucket for my time, but we called it an even exchange."

"If the work is worth more, why not charge her what you'd charge anyone else? Why take just the boat as repayment?"

"Because the boat is a bit of history. It was the first skipjack that Clifford Ellison built here in St. Dennis."

"So?" The name meant nothing to her.

"As to why didn't I charge her what I'd have charged anyone else? Because she isn't anyone else." He ignored the first question and finished the water before tossing the bottle end over end into a trash can near the door. "She's Ruby Carter. The last of her kind and one of the wisest people I've ever met. She's a legend around here—a treasure—which you'd know if you'd spent a little more time with her."

"Excuse me, but I've spent plenty of time with her over the years. I lived with her, remember?"

"Right. Seventeen years ago. How long has it been since you've spent more than a weekend home?"

"I've spent plenty of long weekends here—three and four-day weekends, actually—but I don't have to have that conversation with you."

"Hey, you brought it up. You want to know why I spent so much of my time over there?" He leaned against the hull of the skipjack, which Lis had to admit was rotted through in several places. "You being family, you'd have to know that Ruby's store is one of the original structures still standing on Cannonball Island. It's like something out of a movie set, with those old wooden floors and shelves and that oak counter—God, you can see how it's been worked smooth over the years from the wear it's taken. That's original glass in most of the windows on the first floor. The front door is four inches thick. And that Coca-Cola sign over the front door? It still works, still lights up, did you notice? I keep telling her she should have that thing insured. The store should be on the National Register of Historic Places. As soon as I have time, I'm going to work to see that gets done."

"Why does that matter to you? You're not an islander."

"Cannonball Island is a place unto itself, with its own strange history, its own mythology, and its own stories. It has its own heroes and its own villains. But it's going to undergo some changes in the not-too-distant future. The time to preserve what's there is now."

"What's that supposed to mean? What kind of changes?"

"Ask Ruby, she knows. Now, if your interrogation is over, I'd like to get back to work."

He put the goggles back on and picked up the sander.

"Oh, hey. I almost forgot to congratulate you. I hear you're a big-time artist now. Galleries in New York City displaying your paintings, celebrities lining up to buy them, appearances on TV, people writing about you. I heard there's going to be a special showing at the new art center." He set the sander on a nearby cinder block. "What kind of paintings do you do, anyway?"

"Landscapes, mostly. Cityscapes."

"Cityscapes, eh? Tall buildings, bustling traffic, that sort of thing?"

"Some. There's nature in the city, parks, too." He was making Lis feel defensive, but she wasn't sure why. "Lots of trees, some ponds."

"Trees and ponds." He rubbed his chin thoughtfully. "So you left the island and went all the way to New York looking for natural subjects to paint, and you found *trees and ponds*. There's a certain irony in that, don't you think?"

Before she could respond, he turned his back, flipped the switch on the sander, and went back to work.

Chapter Three

Alec finished sanding the board that he would eventually replace on the hull of the skipjack. He'd been working on the boat since early spring, since the morning Ruby Carter had agreed to hand it over in return for the time he would spend renovating the old general store and building new living quarters for her on the first floor. The only money that had changed hands since then went to materials. He had paid the plumber, the electrician, and the occasional helper he'd had to hire from his own pocket. When it was all added up, Alec figured Ruby was still ahead of the game in dollars, but he'd come to own the boat he'd been dreaming about since he was a kid, so in terms of overall satisfaction—as happy as she was with her new living space—he figured he was the clear winner.

Alec stood back to admire the *Annie G.* Even now, with her partially rotten hull and holes in the bow, to Alec, she was beautiful. He knew that part of her allure was due to the legend that surrounded her, that of the mysterious disappearance of her namesake, Anne Gregory. He'd heard the story over and over as a child, every time old Eben Carter had come into Ellison's to shoot the breeze with Alec's uncle Cliff and the two bachelors—the old one and his younger counterpart—would share a brandy or two. Alec would sit quietly at Cliff's desk doing homework or reading comic books, all the while listening to the tales the older men would tell. By the time he was twelve, Alec knew all the stories by heart, but that never stopped him from hanging on every word.

"Clifford, she was the prettiest girl on Cannonball Island." Eb would sit on one of the old metal folding chairs Cliff kept in the shop, and he'd prop his feet up on whatever was handy—a toolbox, some concrete blocks, a tall stack of newspapers Cliff kept in the shop to wipe off paintbrushes. "Loved that girl the first time I laid eyes on her, back when we were just kids. Even then, I knew she was the only girl for me. Yessir, it was love at first sight. Couldn't believe my good luck, that she loved me, too."

"No explaining love, Eb. No rhyme or reason to it, best I can see." Cliff would lean against whatever boat he was working on that day and light one of the cigarettes that would, in time, take his life.

"Yep. She was a beauty." Eb's eyes would glaze over. "Worst day of my life, the day she disappeared. Searched for her every which way, but it was like she just went *poof*! And she was gone like she was never even here."

Once Alec asked his uncle what Eb was talking about, what had happened to Annie.

"Nobody knows, Alec. That's the tragedy of it." Cliff's eyes had shifted to the photograph of Eb and his boat that hung on the wall. He'd taken it just before the skipjack races the previous spring. "Young woman vanishes into thin air like that, it's just not right. No one who knew her will ever know peace. For sure, old Eb won't."

"Who was she?" Alec persisted.

"Girl from Cannonball Island. Eb's sweetheart. They were going to be married that year at Christmas."

"Maybe she ran away," Alec had suggested. "Maybe she didn't want to marry Eb and have her name on the back of his boat."

Cliff had nodded. "More than one said the same thing back then, but according to everyone who knew her—including her sisters and her best friends—she was crazy about Eb and wanted to marry him."

"So she just was gone?" The eight-year-old Alec had a problem grasping the concept. "Like, one minute she was standing there and the next minute she wasn't? Like magic?"

"More like one night she was sleeping in her bed, the next morning she was nowhere to be seen. The police investigated and thought that someone had gotten into the house overnight and took her." Cliff had taken a long drag on his cigarette, blew out a mile-long stream of smoke. "It's a mystery, all right."

"A stranger came in and just carried her away," Alec had said softly.

"Looked that way. I heard it said they found a cut screen in the back door in the morning, so it seems

logical." Alec's uncle Cliff was always looking for the
logic in any situation. "Course, back then, just about
no one locked their doors at night. Not here in town,
not over there to the island. Folks trusted more back
then."

"If the door wasn't locked, why'd someone cut
a hole in the screen? Why didn't they just open the
door?"

"Well, now, that's a good question, Alec. My guess
is that whoever took her away didn't know the door
would be unlocked. Or maybe that night, the locks
were on, who knows? Only thing we know for certain
is that the next day, Annie was missing and there was
no trace of her left behind."

"I didn't know that could happen."

The idea worried Alec that some unknown person
could work his way into your house and steal you
away and no one would ever find you and no one
would ever know what happened to you because you
would never be found.

"Well, I don't think you need worry about that
happening around here." Cliff reassured Alec. "We've
got something the Gregorys didn't have."

"What?"

"Sadie." The German shepherd Cliff had gotten
for Alec for his birthday the year before had turned
out to be not only the boy's best companion but a
great watchdog.

"Sadie." Alec had nodded. "Sadie wouldn't let anyone come into our house."

"You bet she wouldn't." Cliff had patted Alec on
the head and gone back to work, and from that day

on, Alec slept soundly, secure in the knowledge that anyone who reached for him in the dark would find themselves in the vise of Sadie's strong jaws.

But he'd never forgotten the story, and the way his heart had skipped a beat the first time he'd heard it. As an adult, the boat made him think of romance and love that never died. Not that he'd ever known such a thing. He'd thought he'd been in love a time or two, but knew he'd never known the kind of passion that old Eben Carter had felt for his Annie, the kind that could last a lifetime.

Funny, he thought as he washed up before locking the shop for the day, that the object of his very first crush should pop up when he'd finally gotten his hands on the boat he'd coveted for so long, not that Lis Parker had been aware of his infatuation. He'd secretly had a thing about her from the time Mrs. Warner, their fifth-grade teacher, had moved his desk so that his seat was right behind the mysterious dark-haired beauty from the island. Mysterious, because she rarely spoke with anyone except other islanders. He'd even become friends with geeky Jerry Willets because he heard that Jerry lived across the road from Lis. The friendship had been short-lived, he recalled, because the hoped-for invitation to Jerry's house had never come, and because Alec discovered that he really didn't like Jerry after all.

Since Lis was always so aloof, he'd never gotten to spend much time in her company outside of school, so he made sure he signed up for every class she took, going so far as to enroll in a poetry class in which he had no interest. But she never gave him a second look. They'd been juniors the year he decided he would in fact be the master of his fate: He was going to go for broke and ask Lis Parker to the junior-senior prom.

He'd chosen a time when there were other kids standing around the student lounge, hoping their presence might bring him luck. After all, she wouldn't turn him down in front of all those other kids, right?

"So, Lis," he'd said as he walked up to her, his stomach doing flips and his heart pounding even as outwardly he exuded nonchalant confidence. "Want to go to the prom with me?"

"No." That was all she'd said. One word. No. No explanation, no excuse, no *thanks anyway*. Just . . . no.

He'd stared into her eyes as if he hadn't heard her. When he realized she wasn't going to smile and say, "Just kidding," he prayed for the floor to open, swallow him whole, then close over his head.

Humiliated, Alec had muttered something like, "Oh, okay, then," and walked away, his cheeks burning like they'd been set on fire, his confidence soundly shot in the butt.

The moment had remained in his memory as the single most embarrassing moment of his life. No one had ever made him feel quite as awkward as Lis had in the fifteen seconds it had taken her to respond, and it annoyed the hell out of him to discover that she still could make him feel just a little like that insecure adolescent he'd once been.

His phone rang in the back pocket of his shorts, and he wiped his hands on his shirt before answering.

"Jansen."

"Alec, you wanted me to call at eleven and remind you about your meeting with Brian Deiter at one." His assistant, Lorraine, was one of the very few people in his world that Alec couldn't live without. She had never failed to keep him on track.

He glanced at his watch. It was exactly eleven. Her call was, as always, on time to the minute.

"Thanks, Lorraine. I'll finish up here and stop home to clean up and then I'll be in. Can you have those latest wetland studies copied for me?"

"Already done and in a folder on your desk. And yes, I made a copy for Mr. Deiter."

"You are worth your weight in gold, lady."

"Platinum," she corrected him.

"Whatever makes you happy. See you soon."

Alec cleaned up his equipment and his workspace, then left through the side door. He padlocked the shop and headed for his car, which he'd left parked in front of the old showroom. Someday he'd get the boat sales business up and running again, but he knew that was a few years down the road. Right now, he was lucky he could steal a few hours away from his office to work in the shop on the skipjack.

And someday I'm going to build them, the classic Chesapeake Bay crafts. Deadrises. Skipjacks. Maybe even a bugeye. As far as Alec knew, there was only one of the latter left in operation. Might be fun to build one if he could find a buyer.

He made a quick stop at his house, where he showered and changed into what passed as summer business attire—khaki shorts and a polo shirt—and drove to his office on Elgin Road. He parked in front of the building he'd purchased the year before and got out. The sign over the door—ALEC M. JANSEN, PhD, ENVIRONMENTAL CONSULTANT—always gave him a thrill. Who'd have ever guessed that the boy who'd skipped school every chance he got would eventually achieve such status?

Lorraine greeted him with a nod and went straight to the important stuff. "Jesse Enright called to let you know the contracts for the Borden project are ready for you to sign. Said to stop in and take a look when you get a minute; he's in all afternoon and tomorrow morning."

"Thanks. Can you let him know I'll stop by around three?" Alec mentally added a visit to his attorney's office to his list of things to do after his one o'clock.

He skimmed through the stack of phone messages, all written down on pink *While You Were Out* slips in Lorraine's precise cursive. Even if voice messages had been left for Alec, Lorraine, who mistrusted most electronic devices, insisted on writing it all out herself.

"What if there's a power outage and you can't get your voicemail?" she'd asked archly when Alec told her she could just send to voicemail every call he was unable to take. Before he could respond, she added, "Besides, no one wants to talk to a machine. Everyone hates that."

By "everyone," Lorraine meant Lorraine. Alec never brought it up again.

While only in her forties, Lorraine had the mindset—not to mention the wardrobe—of a much older woman. She wore her long dark blond hair—streaked with gray since she was in her early twenties—in a long ponytail that lay flat and straight against her back. Her suits were gray or black, and if she wore a dress, it was a shirtwaist or a sheath that was at least a size too large. Flat-heeled shoes, always, and no jewelry. But Alec couldn't have cared less what she wore, or how she looked, though there were days when he did have to bite his tongue. Lorraine was efficient, doted on Alec, and nothing—but nothing—ever got past her. Alec wouldn't think of crossing her. To his mind, she was the perfect employee, and he was grateful every day to have her.

"I'm off to meet with Deiter," he told Lorraine after he'd taken a glance at his mail, which she'd opened and stacked on the middle of his desk in order of what she perceived as importance. She was rarely wrong. "I'll stop at Jesse's when I'm finished. If I'm not back by four, you can leave if you like."

"My hours are till five." She returned to her computer and the report she was typing from his hand notes. "I'll be here until then."

"All righty, then." Alec smiled to himself and left the office.

A quick trip down Charles Street brought him to Cannonball Island. Once he'd crossed the bridge, he was minutes from his destination, the island being only eighteen miles from the bay to the bridge. He passed few houses, most of the residents having built their homes closer to the interior, on the far side of the dunes. The few small cottages he did see had been abandoned and boarded up a long time ago, their once-white picket fences staggering to stay upright. Alec knew that within the fenced front yards he'd find the grave markers of those who'd lived and died there. It was a long-running tradition that islanders buried their dead on the property where the deceased had lived. Alec drove by slowly, careful to note where each of the family graveyards were located.

There were salt marshes on the right and a small cove where a dock of undeterminable age reached out into the bay. It still being morning and prime time on the bay, no boats were tied up, but Alec knew that by three o'clock there'd be several pulling in for the night. Many of the islanders still made their living as watermen, as their ancestors had done. When he'd told Lis that the island was a place unto itself, a special place, he meant every word.

It was going to take everything he'd learned over the years to keep it that way.

Alec winced at the sight of the white Cadillac Escalade parked off the road and partially on the dune. He pulled his Jeep onto the solid sand on the opposite side and cut the engine. The file Lorraine had put together for him was on the seat. He was debating whether to take it with him when he glanced up to see his one o'clock appointment walking toward him from the shore.

Brian Deiter wore neatly pressed shorts, a knit shirt that tried too hard to appear casual and that was stretched to its limit over his ponderous abdomen, and leather sandals that appeared out of place on his very large feet. Everything about the man screamed money, and he was there to spend as much

of it as he could. How much that might be would
depend largely on what Alec had to tell him.

Alec took a deep breath and got out of the Jeep.

"Brian, good to see you." Alec extended his hand.
"Am I late?"

"No, no, I'm early." The large man took the hand
he was offered, shook it, then turned to look out at
the bay. "Tell me that isn't the most beautiful view on
the Chesapeake."

"It's one of them, that's for sure." Alec nodded.

"Can't you just see a beautiful house right there?"
He pointed across the road to the dune. "Not one
of those modern, all-glass things. I'm talking about
classic architecture here. I've got the plans in my car.
Can't wait to show 'em to you."

"Well, I'm interested in seeing what you've got
in mind, but I have to remind you, you can't assume
that you're going to be able to build out here. The
wetlands—"

The developer made a sweeping motion with his
hand. "Hey, there are already houses out here, right? I
passed a bunch of 'em back that way. You must have
passed them, too. People live here already, right? Been
here since the 1800s, I read. So what's the difference,
a few more houses?"

Alec's head began to pound. Nothing about this
conversation was going to be easy.

"It's true, the island has been populated for a
long time, but the majority of those homes are built
toward the center of the island, and they're cottages.
The places that were built on this side closer to the
bay are all abandoned now."

"Perfect. So we'll find out who owns them, we'll buy them, and put up new ones in their place." Brian looked pleased at the thought. "We'll build along the road there, and then out here on the point."

He gestured in the direction of the acres of grass and pines on the opposite side of the road.

"Brian, the houses were abandoned because they got the crap knocked out of them every time it stormed. This side of the island is right in the track of every major storm that hits the Chesapeake."

"Oh. Isn't there some way . . . ?"

Alec shook his head.

"I'll bet my architect could find a way to make it work."

"It's a loser, Brian. There's a reason why no one rebuilt those places. Besides, every one of those houses has a private graveyard."

"A what?"

"Traditionally, families on the island buried their dead right in their yards. If you look closely, you'll see the small headstones marking the graves."

"So we'll move 'em all into one big cemetery. How's that for quick thinking, eh?" He poked at Alec with a forefinger.

"It's part of their traditions, Brian. If they think for one minute that you don't respect them, or their heritage, or their way of life, there isn't one person who'd sell as much as one square inch of land to you." Alec fought to keep the impatience out of his voice. He knew that Deiter was used to getting his way, and if this project was going to go through with Alec's involvement, he was going to have to let the client know where the lines were drawn. In a gentle way, of course. "Let it go."

"All right, then. Back to my original plan. How many houses do you think I can put up over there?" He pointed across the road.

"Not as many as you'd like, and not nearly as big as what you want, I'm afraid."

"How 'bout out on the point?"

"Same thing, Brian."

"But I thought I explained to you that I wanted—"

"Walk with me, and I'll show you." Alec crossed the road, and an increasingly impatient Brian followed.

Alec led the way across the dune, being careful to avoid stepping on the grasses.

"This is all wetland." Alec pointed to the salt marsh behind the dune. "It would be like building on a floodplain. There's no real solid underpinning . . ."

"Bah." Another wave of Brian's impatient hand. "We'll bring in fill, shore it up."

"I'm afraid the state of Maryland isn't going to let you do that, at least not here, and not to the extent you want."

"Didn't I hire you to figure this all out?"

"I have figured it out. You can build on three, maybe six to eight locations on the island at the most, but you aren't going to be able to put up a bunch of McShore mansions on the beach or on the dunes. These are protected areas. Now, do keep in mind that the fewer you build, the more exclusive the area will remain."

Brian mulled that over for a moment. "The

more I can charge. Yeah, I can see that. Fewer, more expensive homes. I can go along with that."

"And size is going to be an issue."

"Why? If I only build a few . . . maybe six, seven . . ."

Alec shook his head. "You might not get permits for that many in this location. The watershed is protected. Everything you do here is going to change the environment, from the concrete you use to build the footers to the amount of waste that goes into the bay. Everything has an impact, Brian. The state has gotten serious about the requirements that you, as a developer, will have to meet." Alec knew damned well that Brian was well aware of that. The man had been doing business on the Chesapeake for years. "If you go in with an acceptable plan, it should be easy to get your permits. If you go in with a plan that you know from the outset isn't going to fly, the appeals are going to cost you a bundle, go on forever, and you will not win. The only ones who come out on top will be the lawyers you hire to fight the decision. It isn't worth it. Trust me when I tell you, you're going to have to have a plan that works within the ecological and environmental parameters that have already been established. You're going to have to respect that. You may not make the killing you were hoping for, but you won't lose your butt in the process."

Clearly annoyed, Brian went to the top of the dune and made a three-sixty turn around. Alec figured he was debating his options. His plan, as originally laid out to Alec, was to develop the entire

eastern shore of the island, building large luxury
homes right on the bay all the way to the point. Alec
knew it would never be approved by any of the agencies that would be involved, but he also knew that
Deiter Homes had huge resources behind it, and a
track record of bulldozing ahead with a project and
letting the chips fall where they may. Given the wrong
advice—and encouragement of the wrong sort—Brian
would defy the regulations and he'd go ahead and
take his chances with the courts. Alec knew his client was debating those options at that very minute.
He knew, too, that if Brian looked long enough, he
could find a consultant who was crafty about bypass-
ing the laws and who wasn't above recommending a
little quid pro quo in the form of a payoff to the right
people to get what he wanted.

"Everybody told me you were the guy around
here. That you knew this area like the back of your
hand."

"That's true." Alex nodded. "Born and raised in
these parts." He couldn't truthfully say on the island.
"I know the people here. I know the laws. I know
how to go about getting the most of what you want
without tying up your project for the next ten years
while you deal with the EPA."

"So let's say you're me. What would you do?"

"I'd find out what properties might be available
for sale and I'd talk to the owners, see what
they might take. Then I'd see where the available
properties are located. You don't want to build a
big brand-new place next to a cabin that hasn't seen
a new coat of paint in two centuries and won't for

another two." He crossed his arms over his chest. "You need to know what's available, then sit down with your architect and see what he can do."

"I already told you my architect—"

"From what you've already told me about the plans your architect has drawn up, they're for houses that will never be built on Cannonball Island. Bring your guy out, let him see what the terrain is like, what the area is like. If he's good—and if you've hired him, I'm sure he is—he'll want to design places that fit into the environs here. Places that are plain but beautiful in their simplicity. Places that respect the unique historic nature of the island."

"Places that look like they coulda' been here all along." Brian nodded as if seeing the light. "Yeah. That could be very classy. My ad guys would go crazy with the concept."

"Keep in mind that the cabins that are already here are very small. Anything too large is going to look out of place."

Brian was still nodding. "Small houses are all the rage now, right?"

"I hear they're on trend."

"You think we can get the go-ahead on something like what you talked about? Think we'll find enough folks around here who'll sell?"

"I think there are enough that will make it profitable for you."

"I'd been thinking more like eight or nine on the point."

Alec shook his head. "That will never happen. As far as I know, the point is not for sale."

"You're killing me, Alec."

"Sorry. You need to know up front what's feasible and what isn't. I'm just trying to be frank with you. I wouldn't want to see you get into a situation where you sink a lot of money into the project and end up getting burned in the end."

"All right. I appreciate that," the builder told him, "and I respect your honesty. I'll talk to my architect. You get me a list of people to talk to out here, and I'll send someone out to—"

"No. If you want to buy, you have to do the talking yourself," Alec told him. "I've said before that the islanders are a different sort. They're not going to deal with a middleman. If you want their property, you're going to have to sit down with them, look them in the eye, tell them why you want it and how much you'll pay."

"How would you go about getting that conversation started?"

"I'd invite everyone to a meeting, here on the island. I'd have the plans for the houses I'd like to build, and I'd tell them what I want to do. I'd let them know I wasn't going to try to steamroll over anyone, but I'd like an opportunity to buy some land on the island, if anyone was interested in selling."

"And if no one bites?"

"Then you're looking for another place to build. You can't buy what no one wants to sell."

Brian scratched the back of his neck. "I'll think about it."

"Hey, if you find it's more trouble than it's worth, that's okay, too." Alec shrugged. He almost hoped

that in the end, Brian Deiter would walk away, but
something told him that wasn't going to happen. The
best he could do was to help protect the interests
of the islanders while still giving solid advice to his
client, the guy with the fat wallet and dreams of
building luxury homes on this historic bit of ground.

"I'll get back to you." Brian started to his car, then
turned back. "I heard you were a straight shooter. I
appreciate that."

"No point in encouraging you to waste your
money."

"Right. Thanks." Brian got into his car, started the
engine, and drove off, his left hand waving out the
window.

Alec let out a long breath, one he felt he'd been
holding since he got into his car back at the office. He
was used to dealing with developers like Brian Deiter,
but he'd never been comfortable with the situation.
He'd been referred to Deiter by his college roommate,
who was married to the developer's sister, and while
he appreciated the work, he had mixed feelings.

Cannonball Island had always held a deep fascination for Alec, one that went way beyond his crush on
one of the residents. There were the stories of how
the island had come to be inhabited, of the men and
women who'd been driven across the slow-moving
branch of the New River to a place where there was
no shelter and few trees—simply because they'd supported the British in 1812. That the small community
had not only survived, but thrived, had been nothing short of a miracle. Tradition had said that only
scrub pine and dune grass and beach plum grew on

the island back then, but that first year, the newly displaced band of exiles managed to raise crops and build shelters. Having brought with them what they could carry from their homes in St. Dennis, many had cash to spend, and more than one had relatives in other towns who were more than happy to supply the lumber they'd use to build their homes. Over time, the islanders settled in and made their own way, mostly on the water, but for many, the bitterness toward the residents of St. Dennis for what their families had been made to endure and what they'd had to leave behind never died but was passed from one generation to the next.

Like Lis's father, Alec recalled. It had been no secret that Jack Parker had never gotten over the fact that his family had once owned a handsome house on Hudson Street right around the corner from the storied Enright mansion, the largest home in town. Jack wasn't the only one who'd harbored resentment against St. Dennis and its residents, many of whose ancestors had been the very ones who'd driven their families off land they'd settled. It was a black mark against the town's history, but these days almost no one in St. Dennis gave it a thought except maybe on one of the days of the year the town celebrated its past. The injustice, however, still lived on in the minds of some of the descendants of those who'd lost so much.

Alec would do the best he could to protect the island environmentally and culturally, while at the same time offering economic opportunities to the residents. If the development was approved, there would be jobs to be filled. Alec knew of at least four guys from high school who'd left the island to find work only to discover that jobs were scarce in places other than Cannonball Island. And for those who had land to sell in the areas that were appropriate for building, there'd be fair market value offered from the buyer. Alec would see to that.

It was inevitable that someone, someday, would build there. In the right hands, a certain amount of development could be very good for Cannonball Island. In the wrong hands, it would be a disaster. Which meant that Alec had to ensure that the reins for this project remained where he could see them— preferably in his hands. He just hadn't figured out quite yet how to make that happen.

Chapter Four

L is sat on the new back steps of the Cannonball Island General Store and watched Ruby water her flower garden, which along with the family graves was enclosed by the newly painted white picket fence.

After a few moments of silence, Lis asked, "So what do you have growing this year, Gigi?"

"Much as every year," Ruby replied. She turned off the hose. "I started this garden when your mama was younger than you. Added on over the years. I like to think of it as my memory garden. When I see my flowers come back every year, makes me think of where they came from. There's a little bit of this from one, a little bit of another from someone else. Some folks gone now, but a piece of their garden still be blooming right here on the island." She turned the hose back on and continued with her task.

"Nice that your friends shared their plants with you."

"I did in kind."

"What did you share?"

Ruby turned off the hose again. "Some of that red hollyhock be growing over at Hedy's these days. She passed on seeds to her daughter and her grand-daughter who lives over to Annapolis. Gave some to Jenny Painter four years back. You go past the Painter place, you'll see 'em growing like weeds out front of their fence. Those black-eyed Susans, them come from Libby Allen. Grow so fast and spread so far I have to pull some out every summer. Take over the whole yard, if I had a mind to let them." She leaned over to check the buds on an airy-looking plant with lavender blue flowers. "This here is geranium," she told Lis. "Got a shoot of this from Mother Bristow when I first moved here from the old house on the point. She was the widow of Reverend Bristow, who used to preach at the chapel over to the village."

Ruby picked a flower and handed it to Lis as she straightened up. "She passed not long after giving her plants away. Some to me, some to Abby Turner, a bit to Virginia Larson. You walk around the island with your eyes open, you'll see this blue geranium growing here, there, and everywhere."

"It doesn't look like any geranium I ever saw." Lis held up the flower. "And I'm sure I never saw a blue one before."

"Well, that's what it be."

Ruby went back to her watering.

"Which one's your favorite, Gigi?"

Off went the hose. "All of them. Can't pick a fa-vorite amongst your children." She started to turn on the water, then looked over her shoulder at Lis and asked, "You 'bout done with your questions now?

You got anything else you need to know right at this time? 'Cause I would like to finish up here before the store gets busy. Right about two or three, folks start to stop by for this or that."

"I'm done." Lis nodded. "For now."

Ruby watered the flower bed on the far side of the porch, then turned off the water for good. She wound the hose around her arm and carried it to the hose bib, where she left it coiled on the ground.

"That's a neat-looking hose," Lis observed. "What's it made of?"

"Some sort of soft thing," Ruby told her. "Not near as heavy as the old rubber kind. Easier to carry, easier to put away."

"You buy that at the hardware store in St. Dennis?"

"Carl down to the store don't carry these, best of my knowledge."

"You send for it?"

"I thought you were all over your questions for today." Ruby planted her hands on her hips.

Lis made a zipping motion across her mouth.

"Guess then it's my turn." Ruby dried her wet hands on her apron. "You find what you be looking for over to St. Dennis this morning?"

Lis's jaw dropped. How could Ruby have known . . . ?

"Less my eyes be failing me, that be ice cream on your shirt."

Lis looked down at the front of her T-shirt. Sure enough, there, right in the middle of her abdomen, was a small blob of something faintly pink.

"Stopped at Steffie's, be my guess." Ruby folded her arms across her chest, a glint of *aha* in her smile.

"There's sure nothing wrong with your eyes," Lis muttered.

"Should there be?"

Lis shook her head. "You just . . . you never fail to amaze me, Gigi."

Still smiling, Ruby climbed the steps and folded herself into one of the rocking chairs. Lis shifted her body around to face her. In this morning light, the lines on the old woman's face were more noticeable than usual. Not for the first time, Lis was struck by the beauty that radiated from within her great-grandmother. The woman had an aura, a presence. What would it take, Lis wondered, to capture that radiance, that *knowing* Ruby seemed to possess? What color could re-create the clear blue of those eyes, the pure white of her hair, and the softly tanned skin of that remarkable face? Was Lis artist enough to even attempt such a thing? She'd never liked painting portraits, but maybe . . .

"Folks on my side live long," Ruby was saying. "Not that I'm fearing the hereafter, mind. Nothing fearful about seeing them who gone before. See my Harold, my sisters. My mother and father. The baby son we buried, me and Harold. The daughter we lost to influenza. Eight years old and pretty as them roses growing around the front porch. Resting all peaceful, just waiting for me. Now, Harold and my mother and father, they be laid right down there on this side of the fence. The babies, well, they were laid to rest down by the old house on the point. I been thinking about moving them up here so they can be with me and their daddy. Never did hear of anyone moving a grave, though." Ruby stopped rocking for a moment and asked, "You think that would be bad luck for them? Being moved after being in one place all that time?"

"I . . . I don't know." Lis was somewhat taken aback. "I never thought about . . . well, about doing something like that."

"I swear, I don't know what's right. Me and my Harold talked about it, but he died before he ever said." Ruby resumed rocking. "Decision might come to you and Owen, by and by, if I don't figure out before I go."

"I don't like to think about that, Gigi." The words stuck in Lis's throat.

"Why not?"

"Because I'd miss you too much."

"Much as you miss me when you're off doing whatever, and I be here?"

"I know. I should spend more time here. And I will." Lis nodded. "I will. Just don't leave me yet, Gigi."

"Got no plans for soon. We'll see. It's all in his hands, and he keeps his plans to himself, no reason to let me know ahead 'a time."

Ruby stood and turned toward the back door, then paused to glance over her shoulder and look Lis in the eye. "You don't be worrying about what you can't change, what's past or what's to come. Dying is like living, all part of the same. You be born when he say it's time, you go on back when he calls you.

Be up to you and Owen to bury me right. Don't be
forgetting where I need to be. And don't be letting
your cousin Chrissie Jenkins have a hand in it. That
girl be too fancy by a mile. Sent her grandmother to
her grave in a pink satin-lined coffin. I never saw such
a thing. A box is a box and you need to keep in mind
where it's going."

She patted Lis's head before heading inside. Lis
heard voices from the radio that Ruby had turned on
in the store, heard a window being opened to bring
in fresh air from the bay. When Alec had talked Ruby
into renovating the building, Lis wished he'd talked
her into central air-conditioning. It hadn't been too
hot the night before, but Lis was betting tonight
would be uncomfortable. The humidity already was
rising along with the temperature.

She picked at the little sludge of ice cream that
Ruby had noticed, and she smiled. Damn, but that
woman really didn't miss a thing. If Lis had to put
money on it, she'd bet that Ruby knew where she'd
been and whom she'd been talking to.

Alec Jansen. She hated to admit it, but as her
mother would say, he'd grown up real nice, but that
wasn't much of a surprise. He'd been all too hot for
his own good back in high school. Nice to see that
some things never change. She'd never let on to anyone, not even to her best friends, that she thought he
was the best-looking guy in their class. She'd been
grateful that he'd always sat behind her; otherwise,
it would have been all too apparent to everyone else
that she had a crush on him. She'd be staring at him
all day long, and her secret would be out.

Her mind wandered back to those days, when she and Judy Compton and Margaret Townsend were inseparable, mostly because they'd started kindergarten together and because the only other two girls in their class from Cannonball Island were the Doran twins and they only spoke to each other. The school on the island went up through fourth grade, and more often than not, grades intermingled because there might only be one or two students. Lis's year there were eleven—five girls and six boys—who eventually were sent across the bridge every day to the elementary school in St. Dennis.

Lis would have loved to have been friends with some of the girls she met there, girls who didn't live on the island but who were smart and seemed like they'd be fun to know, but her father wouldn't hear of it. Lis often wondered what those friendships might have been like. Jack Parker's dislike of all things St. Dennis had been the source of most of Lis's teenaged angst. She wouldn't dare defy him—he had a well-earned reputation as a hothead—but there were times when she came *this close* to going behind his back.

Lis would have given anything—*anything*—to have accepted Alec's invitation to the junior-senior prom, would have been the happiest girl on the planet if she could have said yes when he'd asked her. But the situation was more complicated than she'd been able to express that day. Maybe if he'd approached her in private, she'd have been able to explain. But he'd done it very publicly, and she couldn't find the words to talk about her father's deep-rooted prejudice in front of everyone in the lounge. So she'd just said no, and left it at that. She spent prom night in her room, staring out the window, pretending to be in the garishly decorated but dimly lit gym, dancing in a beautiful dress with the best-looking guy in the junior class. Of course, she was wearing a blue satin gown, à la Cinderella at the ball.

She was certain that Alec had forgotten the incident, especially since everyone knew he'd taken Courtney Davison, and from all reports, had himself one heck of a good time in the backseat of Ben McLemore's car. But Lis remembered the way her heart had first leapt with joy, then crumbled with pain and disappointment, and the look on Alec's face when she turned him down. Whenever she looked back on that day, she felt her heart fill with anger all over again. Anger toward her father, anger toward her mother, who wouldn't—or couldn't—stand up to him, anger toward the people in St. Dennis who drove her ancestors onto the island and gave her father an excuse to be a mean SOB.

"You don't be worrying about what you can't change, what's past or what's to come," Ruby had said, and she was right, of course. Lis couldn't go back in time, but if she could . . . well, what might *she* have done in the backseat of that car on prom night?

Lis grinned. She'd been such a Goody Two-shoes back then, chances were pretty darn good Alec would have wished he'd gone with Courtney after all.

She wondered what he'd been doing for the past seventeen years. She'd lost track of him after graduation, but she did remember he'd gotten a scholarship to . . . she tried to remember what she'd heard. University of Maryland, maybe? She wondered if he'd stayed for all four years. Obviously he was a carpenter now, and a skilled one at that, judging by what she'd seen of his work.

Shaking her head as if that would get him out of it, Lis stood and brushed off the back of her shorts, then looked down again at the ice cream stain on her shirt. She'd stopped at One Scoop or Two after she spoke with Alec, and was mesmerized by the many tempting flavors on the handwritten chalkboard that served as the shop's menu. Blueberry Butter Brickle. Strawberry Mousse. Mint Chocolate Divinity. The choices had made her head spin. She'd finally decided on one scoop of the Strawberry Mousse in a cone, and she'd sat on one of the benches overlooking the marina while she ate it. It had been incredibly delicious, and she was just debating whether she should go for seconds, maybe try that wonderful-sounding Chocolate Concoction, when a woman appeared in front of her. The sun was at her back, and Lis had to raise a hand to shelter her eyes in order to see.

"Excuse me, but aren't you Ruby Carter's Lisbeth?" the woman asked.

Lis had been startled, but she'd nodded. "I am. I'm sorry, do I know you?"

"Oh, once upon a time, I believe you did." The woman smiled good-naturedly, not at all offended at having been forgotten. "I'm—"

Lis snapped her fingers, remembering. "You're Ford's mother. Ford Sinclair. Mrs. Sinclair, it's nice to see you again."

"Lovely to see you, Lis. But you're all grown up now, so call me Grace. Everyone does." The woman's smile grew broader. "I really wouldn't have expected you to remember me, but how nice that you have. And you're back to exhibit some of your paintings, all of which are wonderful."

"Oh?" Lis was momentarily confused. "I didn't know they'd arrived in St. Dennis already."

"They were delivered yesterday afternoon. I just happened to be in the gallery when they arrived, and I begged a sneak peek. I hope you don't mind."

"No, of course not."

"I particularly liked the foggy day in the park."

"Actually, that's the name of the painting. *A Foggy Day in Central Park*." Lis smiled. It was one of her favorites, too.

"Well, it's a beauty. I told Ford—he was there helping Carly uncrate everything—"

"Carly? Oh, right. Carly Summit." Though they had never met, Lis knew that the woman who ran the gallery in St. Dennis owned several galleries of her own in different cities, and knew her by her New York reputation. Their only contact had been Carly's invitation to Lis to exhibit in St. Dennis, and Lis's acceptance.

"Carly's my daughter-in-law. She and Ford were married last year."

"I didn't know. Please give Ford my congratulations on his wedding."

"I certainly shall. And you tell my friend Ruby that I'll see her again next week, Tuesday or Wednesday, whichever she prefers. As always, I'm looking forward to it. We're happy to come pick her up. Now, if you're going back into Scoop for a second helping, I think I'll go along with you and treat myself. It's the first time I've been able to walk around on my own in a long time and I'm making up for lost time."

Lis had noticed the woman walked with a cane. "An accident?"

"I fell down the main steps in the inn's lobby." She rolled her eyes. "Cannot even imagine what I must have looked like tumbling down. I heard it wasn't pretty."

"You fell down a flight of steps?" When the woman nodded, Lis said, "You're probably lucky . . ." Lis paused.

"To be alive? Yes, so they tell me. I did have a few broken bones, though."

"But you're better now . . ."

"Oh, much better, dear, and so grateful to be out and about without someone looking over my shoulder. Now, let's go inside and see what Steffie has that neither of us can resist . . ."

Later, while walking back to the island, it occurred to Lis that she didn't recall mentioning to Mrs. Sinclair—Grace—that she was thinking about going back into Scoop for seconds. How, she wondered, had she known? And she'd referred to Ruby as her friend, and said she'd see her again next week, which implied that she'd seen her this week or possibly last week, but definitely recently. What was that all about? Lis couldn't remember her great-grandmother being that friendly with anyone off-island.

Though Ruby had made that remark about going to St. Dennis to visit a friend. That must have been Grace Sinclair. Lis continued to ponder the situation all the way back to the island. Since she'd stopped driving years ago, Ruby hated to go anywhere in a car, always said she didn't trust anyone behind the wheel except herself, so who was picking her up? First the redo of the store, now she's going off-island and being friends with one of the more prominent members of the St. Dennis community. What the heck was going on with her great-grandmother? So many changes from the woman Lis had known all her life.

Well, Alec had said changes were coming. Was this what he meant? He'd certainly seemed to have spent plenty of time with Ruby over the past however long it had taken him to renovate the old place.

Lis was still thinking about what changes he might be foreseeing when the door behind her opened just a crack and Ruby stuck her head out.

"There's tuna fish sandwiches in here for lunch, if you're getting hungry," she told Lis, "and iff'n you're not too filled up with ice cream. I'm pretty sure there be more than one color on the front of that shirt."

"Actually, I was just thinking about lunch. And trust those hawk eyes of yours. I did have two different flavors."

"Nothing to be ashamed of. Done that myself a time or two since Steffie opened up that pretty little shop of hers." Ruby opened the door a little wider. "Come on, then. Get a cool drink of something from the cooler and come sit with me over to my little table and we'll watch the rest of the island go by."

And it seemed the rest of the island did go by the store's windows over the hour that Lis and Ruby shared lunch on the round table that had served Ruby for all the years since her wedding when she was just fifteen. Lis was surprised at the number of vehicles that went by: a white Cadillac, a Jeep, and two pickups passed within a fifteen-minute period. By island standards, that constituted a traffic jam. Ruby hardly seemed to notice. She'd picked up that morning's paper, and from what Lis could see, was reading the movie reviews.

Before they ate, Lis had run up the steps and grabbed a small notebook from her nightstand and slipped it into her bag along with a soft pencil. She kept it next to her plate while they ate so she could begin a sketch of Ruby. Today she would concentrate on getting the shape, the contours, of Ruby's face right. Later she would work on the features. It had been years since art school—the last time she'd attempted to translate someone's face to paper—and she wasn't sure she could do justice to the subject.

"What you be drawing there on that pad?" Ruby finally asked.

"Nothing."

"That pencil be busy with a lot of nothing. Show me that nothing."

Lis held up the sketch. Ruby stared at it for a long while.

"Lisbeth, you be drawing a picture of me, you best be forgetting about that mole over my left eye." Ruby raised her fingers to her left eyebrow. "Shoulda' had that thing taken off a long time ago. Vexes me every time I look in the mirror . . ."

Lis made a mental note to nix the offending mole, and a satisfied Ruby went back to her newspaper.

After lunch, Lis called Carly Summit and left a message that she was on the island and would be happy to meet with her if she had any questions about the works that had already been delivered.

"Gonna be a big crowd at that gallery for you," Ruby had told Lis. "I suspect lots of folks be wanting to see how my Kathleen's girl grew up, see what she's done."

"Did Mom have any artistic talent?" Lis asked.

"Not she, not any of my other grandkids had more than a lick of sense about much of anything. No talents there far as I know. Nope." Ruby shook her head. "Though I did hear tell that a sister of my mama's—that be my aunt Josie, I have no recollection of her, she left the island before I was born—some say she was an artist of some sort. Lived over to Virginia somewhere. I heard my mama talking about it once or twice."

"Did she paint?" Lis asked.

Ruby shrugged. "If I knew, I've forgotten. Like I said, I never met her."

Ruby stood and worked out the kinks in her legs where arthritis had slowed her gait. When she picked up the two empty water bottles from the table, Lis saw that her fingers were twisted in a way she hadn't noticed before.

"I'll clean up here, Gigi," Lis told her. "You go back to that creepy book you were reading last night."

She cleared the table and went into the kitchen to put their plates into the dishwasher; then, as she'd done the night before, she washed, dried, and put away the dishes they'd used.

On her way back into the store, Lis picked up Ruby's book and her reading glasses from the table in the sitting room. She took them into the store and handed them to Ruby.

"I think I'll take that walk around the island now," Lis told her.

"Be a long walk if you're thinking of going all the way around," Ruby reminded her.

"I'll just go as far as the point." Lis helped herself to another bottle of water from the cooler that stood near the cash register. She started toward the door, then stopped. "Gigi, do you still own that land out at the point?"

Ruby stared at her for a moment, then asked, "What made you think about that old place?"

"I don't know." Lis shrugged. "I guess because I'm headed out that way, and don't want to be trespassing on someone else's property, maybe get run off with a shotgun."

"Don't need to be worrying 'bout that none." Ruby turned her attention to her book. "You have a nice walk, now."

It *was* a nice walk. The south side of the island was slightly more populated than the north, but even at that, Lis passed few people on her trek to what islanders referred to as "the point." Driftwood Point was the proper name given to the twenty-two-acre spit of land that stuck into the bay like a defiant child's tongue. Lis's family had owned it since the days when the island was first inhabited. As a child, she and Owen and their cousin Chrissie had spent many an afternoon exploring and playing hide-and-seek. Owen had learned to fish off the pier their great-grandfather—Ruby's Harold—had built and they'd spent hours catching crabs that hid in the seagrass that grew under the dock. They dared each other to go inside the crumbling ruins of the old one-room cabin that stood against a wall of pine trees and they made up stories about who had lived there and why it had been deserted. The old house that Ruby and Harold had lived in for the first years of their marriage was located closer to the bay, and by modern standards, had been pretty primitive. The kids had all loved playing there on rainy days. Most of the furniture had been moved to the living quarters above the store by the time Lis and her generation had been born, but there was still a fascination about the place.

Which brought to mind the real stories about the real people who'd lived on the island. Those were the ones that should be preserved. Lis reflected on her earlier conversation with Ruby, the one about Ruby dying and going on to the next place. Lis knew that much of the island's history would be lost once Ruby was gone, and once again, she found herself thinking that someone needed to write it all down, preserve the truth and the myths, separate fact from fiction. The stories were not only part of the island's history, but they reflected the fabric of life on the island.

That someone, Lis knew, was going to have to be her.

She should sit down with Ruby with a recorder every night for an hour or so, and ask about the family members she'd never known. She knew names, and had heard bits of stories about this one or that, but to the best of her knowledge, no one had ever written any of them down. Recording Ruby's voice telling of the tales would be much more effective in years to come, especially in those years after Ruby had passed on.

Lis couldn't bear to think about that. It made her heart ache too much. Ruby Carter was the most fascinating woman Lis had ever met. It humbled her to know that Ruby's blood flowed in her veins, and even at that, Lis felt unworthy.

She rounded a bend in the road and knew that she was almost there. Unless things had changed drastically, there'd be a wide stand of pines right on the other side of the bend, and from there the land stretched to where it would jut out into the bay. Her feet moved a little faster as if they knew they were close to their goal.

The pines were still there, as were the remnants of the tiny cabin, though the walls had completely crumbled since her childhood days, leaving just the outline to prove what had once stood there. Lis was trying to remember if they ever had discovered who had lived in that place, who had been born there and who had died, when she saw the black Jeep parked up ahead. She paused, scanning the property for movement. There, out on the end of the pier, was a figure, male if she wasn't mistaken, but he was too far away for her to recognize him. She stood still for a few long moments in the shade of the trees when the figure began to move toward her. It took a moment for her to realize it was Alec, though what he'd be doing out here was anyone's guess.

"Hi." Her greeting held a touch of a question.

"Oh, hey. Lis?" he called back.

"Yes." She began to walk toward him, to meet him halfway between the pier and Ruby's old house.

"Boy, twice in one day. I guess I hit the jackpot."

She couldn't tell if he was being sarcastic or not, so she replied in kind. "I guess you did."

"Beautiful day, right?" He was closer now, and as he moved into the shadows, he removed his sunglasses and tucked them into the open neckline of his shirt.

A shirt that was not a ripped tee, like the one he'd been wearing back at the shop. His shorts were different, too—not a hole to be found.

"Sure is." She watched him approach, wondering if he was going to offer an explanation as to why he was on her family's property.

"Out for a walk, I see."

She nodded. "You?"

"Just felt like getting out for a bit."

"The sanding dust getting to you?" She raised an eyebrow. St. Dennis wasn't exactly Manhattan, and Cannonball Island wasn't even St. Dennis. Why bother to change just to walk around?

"What? Oh. Right. Yeah, it does after a while."

"So what brings you out here today? Looking for another boat to buy?"

He shook his head and artfully deflected the

question. "One boat at a time. The *Annie G* is enough for me. She has all my attention."

"Isn't it hard to make a living that way?"

"I'm not going to be selling her," he said. "She's all mine."

"Oh. I thought you worked for the boatbuilder. Ellison's."

"Cliff Ellison was my uncle. He raised me after my folks died. He was the boatbuilder, he and his dad. He passed away when I was still in college."

"Is that when you decided to be a carpenter?" she asked.

"I learned all my carpentry skills from Uncle Cliff. If he couldn't build it, it couldn't be built. He taught me everything I know. Boats, houses, whatever."

"So you, what, build boats, then in your spare time you build back porches and kitchens and bathrooms? Or is it the other way around?"

Alec smiled. "I spend my spare time with *Annie*. She keeps me busy when I'm not otherwise engaged. Eventually, I'd like to build boats full time, like my uncle did. I have a real fondness for the classic Chesapeake working boats."

"That skipjack of Uncle Eb's—"

"Was built by my great-uncle. I found the plans for her and some photos taken of her when she was just a work in progress. They're not great—the lighting in the shop wasn't so good back then, and since they built her over a winter, the place was closed up most of the time, so the pictures are pretty dark. But you can see her lines, her bones . . ." He laughed self-consciously. "Yeah, I know, she's just a boat."

"But she's special, I get that. I never really knew Eben—he always seemed to keep to himself. Actually, I never really knew anyone from that generation on either side of my family. My grandmothers both died when I was a baby, so I guess that's why I always felt an attachment to the boat. It was a tangible link to . . ." She paused. "I don't know why I just said all that."

"I get it. The boat is part of your family."

"She was part of the landscape around the store. I can't remember a time when she wasn't there. I could look out my window at night and she would always be there." *Like a sentinel*, she could have added, watching over her and Ruby after her father died and her mother moved to Arizona and Owen was away at college. "Anyway, it's interesting that Gigi was willing to part with her after holding on to her for so long."

"I think she was happy to know the boat was going to a good home. Ruby knows how much I wanted her, that I'll do right by her. She was weathered pretty badly, but she's coming along. She will be as good as new—better than new—once I'm done."

"What will you do with her once you're finished? You going to give up your carpentry business to dredge for oysters?"

"I do a little oyster farming with a couple of other guys, but no. I don't plan to work her that way. They have skipjack races here and there during the summer months. I'll be signing up for a few of those once she's seaworthy."

"I didn't know there were enough skipjacks left to race."

"There are a number of them still around. There's a big race down at Deal Island in September."

"I hope you get her back out there, then. And I hope you win."

"Thanks. We'll give it our best." Alec took a step away from the car. "So can I give you a ride back to the store?"

"Thanks, but I think I'd like to hang around here for a while. I thought I'd check up on Ruby's old house."

"It's still standing." He pointed to the brick house—little more than a cottage—that was fifty feet or so from where they stood. "Needs some work, hard to tell how much. But considering the age and the fact that it's been uninhabited for . . . how many years, do you think?"

Lis shook her head. "No idea. I'll have to ask Gigi when she moved from here to the store."

He checked his watch, then said, "Well, be careful if you walk out on the pier. There's a lot of rotted wood. There are a couple of whole sections that need to be replaced."

"I'll tell Gigi. She should think about posting 'No Trespassing' signs, and she should probably get the pier fixed. It's an attraction for the kids on the island, I would guess. Assuming there are still little kids on the island."

He started to walk toward his car, and without thinking, Lis fell in step with him.

"Not too many little ones around here these days," he told her. "Not that I've seen, anyway."

"Oh? You spend a lot of time out here?" They'd

almost reached the Jeep, and she held back a few steps as he walked to it.

"I spent a lot of time at Ruby's." He opened the car door, slid behind the wheel, then slammed the door. "And in case you hadn't noticed, there are a lot of places on the island in need of repair."

"Lucky for you, then, right? Lots of work to keep you busy when you're not—" She stopped. She wasn't sure what he did in his spare time.

"When I'm not what? Conning old ladies out of their valuable property?"

"No, no," she protested. "I wasn't going to say that. Really."

"I'll bet you were thinking it. Same thing." He put the Jeep in reverse. "See you at the reception, if not sooner."

"Wait, Alec, I . . ." She paused. "What reception?"

"The reception at the gallery before your showing. I hear it's going to be a Big Event." He turned the car around and passed her, not bothering to wave.

Well, damn. Lis watched the Jeep disappear around the bend in the road and stood for a minute wondering what had just happened. She hadn't been about to insult him. She hadn't even been thinking it, but their earlier encounter that morning must have weighed heavily on his mind for him to have been so defensive.

It occurred to her that she never did find out why he'd been there.

She walked past the old house and out onto the pier, stepping over those spots where the wood had rotted, as Alec had warned. It really did need repair.

She went all the way to the end, then sat cautiously, her feet not quite reaching the water. She scooched a little closer to the edge so that her toes were visible beneath the surface. There had been a thousand summer days like this one when she'd sat right here, looking out at the bay and wondering what was on the other side. She'd watch the boats come back in late in the afternoon, hoping that her father had had a good day with his traps. The later he pulled into the cove, the more doubtful it was that he'd found his traps filled. Some days she'd bring a sketch pad and draw what she saw on the bay—the boats with their sails filled with breeze, the gulls that followed the fishing boats, picking at the chum. Ospreys that dove headfirst into the water to do a little fishing of their own. That time in her life had its own flavor, colored by sunlight on the water and the shadows of the scrub pines.

On her ninth birthday, Ruby had given her the first real art supplies she'd ever owned. There'd been a lidded basket filled with pads to sketch on and pads upon which to paint. There'd been charcoals and watercolors and tubes of oil paints, a variety of brushes and several small canvases. Years later, Lis realized it had been Ruby's way of encouraging her to find her medium. It had been the single greatest gift she'd ever received, and she'd guarded her treasures as if they'd been gold. She kept her sketches and her early attempts at painting to herself. She knew she had a lot to learn, but she also knew she'd never want to do anything but paint.

Now, as an adult looking back on that time, Lis

could see that Ruby's choice of gift was her way of saying that she recognized who Lis was. No one, Lis realized, saw her as clearly as her great-grandmother, and yet she'd never done one thing to adequately thank her.

Well, that was going to change. Lis resolved to stick around for as long as it took to make sure Ruby's stories were preserved. She'd drive back to her apartment in New Jersey and gather her work supplies and bring them back. There was no reason why she couldn't work here as well as there. Ruby wasn't getting any younger, and it would be a crime if she passed on and took everything she knew with her.

Resolved, Lis stood. Her feet were too wet to put into her sandals, so she walked barefoot back along the pier, careful to avoid the loose or missing boards.

As she stepped off the pier, she heard a bang. One of the shutters on Ruby's old place had come loose and was flapping against the wall every time even a light breeze blew. She went over to investigate and found that the hook that once held it in place was missing. She tried the front door but found it locked. She walked around to the back of the building and checked under every rock but there was no hidden key. She peered through the glass on the top half of the back door, using first her hand, then the front of her ice cream–splotched shirt to wipe away decades of dross. She could barely see inside, but she knew that there was a large room that had served as a living room and a dining room, with a square kitchen off to the left side in the back. There were two bedrooms and a small bath off a short hall to the left. The second floor had a loft where Ruby and Harold's four daughters—including her own grandmother, Sarah—had slept, their metal beds lined up in a tight row. The two boys had slept in the second bedroom on the first floor. Lis had heard stories over the years, but they'd never seemed important, until now. Now she wanted to know every one of them—the boys who'd gone off to war and the girls who'd stayed home and married and populated the island, until life on the island was no longer enough to hold them. She'd never thought about the ones who, like Lis herself, had left. She knew nothing about them other than the fact that they'd started their lives in this little cottage by the bay.

Lis hurried back to the store, wanting to jot down all her thoughts before they left her. She'd make a list of all the questions she wanted to ask about all the people who'd come before her, and she'd record Ruby's responses in her own voice. Maybe she'd take notes, write down as much as she could. In her mind's eye she saw a book, the cover of which bore the likeness of the cottage she'd just left. A likeness she'd paint herself, maybe right there in the cottage.

The thought came on in a flash of clarity: the cottage would make the ideal studio. The lighting was perfect and the views were inspiring. Already her hands were itching to hold her brushes, the colors in her mind eager to capture the exact hues of the water and the sky. Images began to take shape, and she knew that her days of painting cityscapes had come to an end.

She couldn't wait to get back to the store and ask Ruby for the key. She'd beg if necessary, but having rediscovered the cottage, she knew in her heart it had been biding its time, waiting for her.

Chapter Five

B e a lot of work to fix that place up." Ruby's expression was thoughtful after listening to Lis's idea about using the old cottage as an art studio. "I don't know you want to put all that into it."

"I think it would make the perfect studio, Ruby, and I can't think of anything better to do with the money I made from my paintings. I did pretty well this past year, you know, so I have a nice nest egg tucked away. If you don't have other plans for the cottage, I'd like to use it, if I could."

"Tell me what you be thinking."

"I thought maybe I'd close up the apartment in New Jersey for a while, see how things go here, if it's okay with you. I think I could use a change of scenery. I'd love to paint out on the pier, maybe some places around the island." Lis smiled. "And I'd like to spend more time talking to you, maybe even get you to tell some of your stories about the island, about our family. Being out at your old house today, I realized I know so little about Gramma Sarah and your other children. It's as if that entire generation is a big blank to me. I'd like to know about them."

Ruby looked as if someone had just walked in and told her that a dozen clowns were parachuting onto the roof of the store.

"I must be light-headed," Ruby said. "Think maybe I should sit a spell. Sure enough sounded like you said you'd be staying here a time, doing some painting out on the point, take some time to know your kinfolks. Time to set out to see Dr. Booth. Get my ears checked out. Maybe I got the vertigo."

Lis laughed. "There's nothing wrong with your hearing, Gigi. You heard perfectly well. Is it that hard to believe?"

"You been gone mostly since you were eighteen."

"I've been back," Lis protested, even as she knew Ruby was right. Her visits were few, far between, brief, and always at Lis's convenience.

"Not casting blame, just saying what is." She appeared thoughtful for a moment. "What you suppose *he* will say to that?"

"He?" Lis frowned.

"That man that lives in your apartment. The one who only showed up here one time and acted like he couldn't wait to leave."

"You mean Ted."

"Any other man be living in your apartment?"

"Actually, there are no men living in my apartment." Lis held up her left hand and wiggled her ring finger, knowing full well that Ruby would have noticed the absence of the diamond that had decorated that finger for the past year. "I gave the ring back."

Ruby nodded as if she'd been expecting the news.

But the last person Lis wanted to think about was Ted, so before Ruby could pump her for details, Lis asked, "Is it okay if I stay? Would it be all right if I fixed up the old place?"

"This island be your birthright, course you can stay. That old house been sitting there for more years than I can count back. Didn't think it would ever see life again." Ruby walked slowly to the counter, where she made herself a cup of tea.

When she returned to the table, she told Lis, "My Harold and me, we loved that old place. Wasn't no place on the island we loved as much. When my daddy passed, I helped my mama to keep the store going. When she passed, it fell to me. Harold and I moved here, wasn't no one else to do. People need their store on the island. We were happy there and happy here as well, but I always felt like I left something behind back there on the point. That old place be filled with memories. Maybe time for it to have a few more. New." She sipped her tea.

"Do you still have the key? Maybe I could walk through and see what's what." Lis studied Ruby's expression, one of sorrow at the passing of her days with the man she'd loved and made a family with, ran a business with, and one day buried in the yard behind the store. Lis wondered if it ever would be possible to do justice to that face.

"Key's on a chain near the back door here. Now, you tell Alec to take a look at the place, see if it can be saved. Been left alone so long, maybe has to come down. Alec will know."

"I think I'd like to check it out myself."

"Suit yourself," Ruby said. "But I don't see you poking in the walls. Never know what you'll be finding, once you do. And someone's going to have to be climbing up on that roof. That going to be you or Alec?"

"Alec climbed on your roof?"

Ruby nodded. "More'n once. Somebody had to. Weren't going to be me."

"Isn't there anyone else who does home repairs and carpentry around here?"

"Cameron O'Connor be a good man, good worker, right smart boy he is. But I hear he's turning people away, he's so busy." Ruby eyed her suspiciously. "You having a problem with Alec?"

"Not really. Of course, I'll call him if that's who you like."

"Did right by me," Ruby said simply.

"Gigi, did he really just show up and start taking down that old back porch without asking you about it?"

"He did that." Ruby grinned, the lines on her face folding into deep creases. "Shows what a good boy he be, what good upbringing he had. Saw a problem and just took it on himself to fix it."

"And it didn't bother you that he didn't ask?"

"What fool would want his house to fall down? That porch roof was gonna go in the next big wind, sure enough. I kept meaning to ask someone to look at it, but it kept slipping my mind."

Lis doubted that anything ever slipped Ruby's mind, but she let that pass.

"Well, what if you couldn't have paid for the work?"

"I guess we would have worked something out, by and by."

"You really think a stranger would have—"

"Who said something about a stranger?" Ruby interrupted. "How'd that thought get inside your head?"

"Isn't he?" It hadn't occurred to Lis that Ruby might have known him. When would she have met Alec? "How would you have known him?"

"Known Alec since he be a wee one. Known his kin all my life."

"You have?"

Ruby's white head nodded. "He left town for a time, been gone off and on since old Cliff passed, but that been some time ago. He been back here, oh, maybe a year, maybe a time more. Had some business of his own up in Havre de Grace, brought it here."

"Still, if you knew that the porch needed work, and you knew that you needed to move to the first floor, why didn't you ask Owen or me to take care of it for you?"

"You and your brother be off doing your own things, having your own lives. Alec be here and he didn't wait to be asked. He said, '*Miz Ruby, you need to be mindful of those steps, going up and down every day.*' He'd heard about my fall in the bathroom. I suspect everyone both sides of the bridge heard tell of that, Hedy being Essie's sister and they both being such gossips."

"So you just said, okay, build away?"

"No. He asked if he could see the back space, all the old storage behind the store. So I let him go on in back there and he poked around a time and came out when he was done poking. Went out to his car and came back in with paper and asked me for a pencil. Stood right there at the counter and drew some pictures. When he be done, he said, '*Miz Ruby, I think this would work.*' Showed me what he drew. All what you saw back there now." Ruby pointed to the back wall of the store. "Said if I liked it, he'd do it for me."

"Did you get another estimate to see if his price was fair?"

"Didn't feel inclined to do that. Price felt right. Charged me only what it cost him. Paid for the plumber and the electrician from his pocket."

"He did?" Lis couldn't hide her surprise. What contactor did things like that? Even she had to admit if Alec had been out to take advantage of Ruby, he hadn't done a very good job of it.

"Sure enough he did, bless his heart."

"I'm still surprised you let him take the boat. I'm pretty sure he could have found another skipjack to restore. It isn't as if that was the only one around up on blocks."

"That be what he wanted for his time. Wasn't just any skipjack he wanted. His folk built that boat back in the day. Guess he felt a kinship with it. Seems to me the barter be fair. We both be pleased with our part."

"He did tell me that. That his uncle . . ." Lis tried to remember the name.

"Clifford. Cliff Ellison. Ellisons be in St. Dennis since right before the Civil War. Owned the only newspaper in town. Still do. Cliff should have been the one to take it over from his daddy, but he had no mind for it. Fell to his sister, Grace. She still owns it, still runs it. Does a fine job, too."

"Grace . . . do you mean Grace Sinclair?"

Ruby nodded. "Alec be Gracie's nephew. His mother—Gracie and Cliff's sister Carole—and his father died in a car wreck. Hit by one of those big trucks that haul for one of them big companies, I forget which one. Carole and Allen be fine people. Doted on that boy. Them dying so sudden left the boy alone, but Clifford, he went to the courts and said he'd raise the boy. Courts said fine, Cliff brought Alec to St. Dennis. The company that owned the truck paid a lot of money, 'cause of the accident taking his parents, but Cliff put it all in some accounts for when Alec turned twenty-five. Cliff had the money for his college all set up separate, which was good, since Cliff passed before Alec was even twenty, best I recall. Grace would know the details, Cliff being her brother and all."

"I think maybe I did hear something about that when we were in school. I don't know that I knew all the details, but I'm pretty sure I'd heard about the accident. It must have happened before I started going to school in St. Dennis, because Alec was already there before me." *Poor Alec*, she thought. *What a horrible thing for a young child to endure.* She couldn't imagine what it would be like to lose both parents at the same time. She'd been in her teens when her father died, and while that had been a sad time, she still had her mother.

"Everyone in town knew. It was a terrible tragedy. Gracie was torn up about losing her sister, but Cliff, he never was the same after."

"I forgot to tell you I saw Grace earlier when I was out. She said to let you know she'd have someone come for you Tuesday or Wednesday."

"I suspect you could drive me," Ruby said.

"Drive you where?"

"Over to the inn. Grace and I be friends for a time. Known her since she be a girl. She used to come, spend a few hours with me. Share lunch. There be things we talk about. Every week for years till she be hurt last year and stayed pretty much at the inn. Saw to it that every week, someone would come for me, we'd have lunch and visit, someone would bring me back."

Lis would love to know what things Ruby and Grace Sinclair talked about, but she let it go, asking instead, "Who watched the store for you?"

"Put a sign up. Gone fishing. Be back at two." Ruby's eyes danced with mirth.

Lis laughed. "So you've been going into St. Dennis every week to have lunch with Grace at the inn?"

"Like clockwork. The cook over there knows what to do with rockfish. Does nice with blue claws, too."

"Oh boy, my dad would have loved that," Lis muttered. "You getting chummy with the townies."

"Lisbeth, your daddy was wrongheaded about a lot of things. St. Dennis just be one of them. Your mama be another." She shook her head. "Everyone says I should never have let my girl marry that man, but then I say, can't change what is. If Kathleen had married someone else, there'd be no Lisbeth. No Owen. Change one thing, change all. Kathleen made her choices all her life. Not all of them be good. But you and your brother . . . well, sometimes right comes from wrong. You and Owen are right. Best thing your mother ever did, had you two." She looked Lis in the eye and said, "The best thing your daddy ever did was die young."

Not for the first time that day, Lis's mouth dropped open.

"Shocked you, I see. But truth is truth. Jack Parker gave nothing good to this world but his children. He can rest in peace knowing he did that much. Now, you can get that look off your face. I never wished the man harm, but I never shed a tear for him, either."

"I did. I cried for him when he died," Lis said softly.

"I know you did. And that be right. He was your daddy and no matter what, you should have cared when he passed."

"I didn't cry 'cause he died, Gigi. I cried because of the way he lived. He could have been so much more than he was."

"True words, those. He wasted time he should have spent well. But he was content with the way he was and the way he lived. Could have been different, could have been better, but he lived his life looking over his shoulder, looking back at things that had nothing to do with him."

"It was hard trying to convince him that the War of 1812 had been over a long time."

"Always he be talking about the big house over on Hudson Street that should have been his. Always saying how life would be different, better, if that place had passed to him. Blaming others for what he was 'stead of looking inside himself." Ruby shook her head. "He couldn't see that it was him causing his own grief."

"It makes me sad to think about him."

"Don't be wanting you sad, Lisbeth." Ruby reached across the table and took Lis's hands.

"I'm mostly sad that he could have been happy and he chose not to be."

"Not the fault of you or Owen or your mama for that matter. Jack made his own path, that's a fact. Had nothing to do with you, hear?" Ruby squeezed Lis's hands, then let go. "Now it be your time to make your path. You choose to be here for a time, see what comes of that."

"The only thing I expect to come of it is— hopefully—some good art. Some *great* art," she corrected herself. "I have a feeling about that place, Gigi. I have a feeling that I'll find something new there."

"Like what new?"

"A new form of expression. A new look at life and the world and a new approach to my work. I think I was getting stale."

"Might have something to do with staying in that place after *he* moved out," Ruby said dryly.

Lis had been wondering how long it would take Ruby to toss in her two cents about Lis's broken engagement.

"It wasn't Ted's fault, Gigi. It was mine." Lis recalled The Talk, the look on Ted's face when she'd said, *"It isn't you, it's me,"* and realized she'd just uttered the biggest cliché, the world's worst breakup line. "Something just didn't feel right. I can't explain it."

"Don't need to. You find what you need when you need it. You weren't in the right place. Told you a hundred times or more, you got to know where you belong. Right always feels right."

"Oh, and I suppose you think this is the right place?" Lis tried to make light of a touchy subject. "That you know where I belong?"

"Be surprised what I know, missy." Ruby smiled that enigmatic smile that had driven Lis crazy all her life, finished her tea, and went to the counter a full thirty seconds before a customer came through the door.

LIS SPENT THE rest of the afternoon unpacking and shelving a soda delivery.

"Soda's a killer," Lis told Ruby. "So much sugar. Suger'll kill you."

"Everything'll kill you if you have too much," Ruby replied.

"True enough, but do you know how much sugar is in just one of these?" Lis held up a bottle of cola.

"I can read, good as you." Ruby took the delivery invoice and headed back to her little office. "I just sell them. I don't give judgment when I do."

"I never saw you drink one."

"And you never will. Not to my taste." Ruby paused in the doorway.

"Earl Grey all the way?"

Ruby nodded. "That, or water. Got some good spring water here, no need for bottled. Others, they can have what they like."

Lis reflected for a minute. "You never let us drink it. Soda, that is. When Owen and I were living here."

"Don't remember." Ruby went into her office and closed the door. Lis laughed out loud. She'd bet a bundle that Ruby damn well remembered.

Lis had just finished loading six-packs of soda onto the shelves when her phone rang.

"Lis, this is Carly Summit. From the art center?"

"Of course. How are you?" After an exchange of pleasantries, Carly asked, "Are you free in the morning?"

"I'm free all day," Lis told her.

"Could you stop over, maybe around ten?"

"Perfect."

"I'll bring the coffee. Dress casually. I'll be in work clothes. Don't show me up by dressing like a city woman."

Lis laughed. "It's strictly shorts and tees here on the island in summer."

"Then we'll match. Do you know where the gallery is? Do you need directions?"

"You're on the Enright property, right?"

"Yes. In the carriage house. It's where Hudson Street dead-ends."

"Got it."

"Perfect. I'll leave the front door unlocked. Just walk in and yell."

"Will do." Lis disconnected the call. She liked Carly already.

The next morning, Lis found she liked her even more after meeting her in person. Carly was petite and blond and full of energy and enthusiasm, especially for the gallery, which was still relatively new to St. Dennis.

"We haven't even been open for a year," Carly told Lis, "but we've attracted some big-name collectors and have made some nice money for some of our local artists."

Lis glanced around the main room, where paintings of various degrees of talent hung from the walls and the partitions.

"These works were all done by local artists," Carly explained. "Some, as you can see, are really quite good. Others are . . . well, some of them are pretty terrible."

"The cats with the wild yellow eyes on black velvet . . ." Lis stood in front of one such work.

"Ah, yeah. I usually don't have that hanging in here. I tried to use the space for the better works and hang the more amateurish pieces in the mansion. But that one just came in, and the woman saw the empty space there on the wall and assumed I'd left it for her." Carly smiled. "She's a sweet old woman who loves her pets and I wanted to indulge her for a little while. She's proud of her efforts and I do want to encourage that. However scary the results might be."

"That's very kind of you."

Carly shrugged. "The gallery belongs to the people of St. Dennis. Who am I . . . ?"

"Seriously? Who are you?" Lis laughed. "Only one of the most successful gallery owners in New York."

"I made my reputation there, it's true, and my place in the city does very well. I have good people working for me, so I'm lucky there." Carly paused. "Any way I can talk you into letting me exhibit a few of your works at my gallery, or is your arrangement with Casper exclusive?"

"It isn't exclusive, but honestly, I feel obligated to him. He showed my works when no one else would return my phone calls. If not for him, I doubt that high-profile sale—the one that got me all the attention—would have been made."

"Summit International could have done as well."

"Summit International didn't return my phone calls."

"Ouch. Really?" Carly frowned. "I'll have to look into that. But I do admire your sense of loyalty to Casper. He's a pretty good guy and honest as the day is long. I can't fault you for wanting to stay with him. But I did hear he might be retiring in another year or so . . ."

"In which case you'll be my first call," Lis assured her. "Assuming you're still interested."

"I'll be interested. I love the paintings you sent us." Carly led the way into a back room where Lis's watercolors were stacked against the wall. "I love the way you play with light, particularly in this one." She pointed to the first in the stack.

"Thank you." Lis knelt down and considered the painting. It was one of her favorites. "I sat in Battery Park for hours, looking at the river, watching the way the sun played off the water. It took me forever to get it right."

"Well, you definitely hit it out of the park—pun intended. I'm going to display this one so that it's the first thing people see when they come in the main door."

"Nice. I like that." Lis stood.

"How 'bout I give you a tour, and then we'll sit down and have that coffee I promised you."

"Sounds good."

Lis followed Carly through the gallery, then out into the summer heat to the mansion that had once belonged to local attorney Curtis Enright, who'd recently donated the house and grounds to the town for use as a cultural and arts center. The entire walk-through lasted forty minutes, and by the time they returned to Carly's office, Lis was ready for a cold drink rather than a hot one.

"We can do that, too." Carly opened a small refrigerator and took out bottled water. "This okay?"

"Perfect."

Carly handed one to Lis, opened one for herself, and gestured for Lis to sit on a small loveseat that stood along one wall. "So I understand you grew up in St. Dennis," Carly said as she sat on a wicker chair behind her desk.

"Actually, I grew up on Cannonball Island."

"Well, same thing, right?"

"Night and day, depending on who you ask." Lis gave the short version of how some of the residents of St. Dennis ended up on the island.

"Wow," Carly said after Lis had finished her recitation. "I hadn't heard any of that."

"I doubt it's something the town people think

about, if they even know about it. To some of the islanders, it's still a sore subject."

"You?" Carly asked.

"My dad rarely missed an opportunity to rail about it." Lis forced a smile. "Ancient history. Let's talk about something fun. I heard you're married to Ford Sinclair. I went to school with him."

"Yes, I am, and yes, I heard. My mother-in-law mentioned it last night at dinner. She's apparently good friends with your grandmother."

"My great-grandmother," Lis corrected.

"Right. She owns the store out on Cannonball Island, right?" When Lis nodded, Carly continued. "I remember Ford's cousin mentioning something about doing some work for her." Carly's brows knitted together in thought. "And something about getting paid with a boat that one of their relatives had built . . ."

"My great-uncle Eb's boat." Lis sighed. Did everyone know the story?

Carly nodded. "Something that needs a ton of work but Alec wanted it anyway. Oh, wait. You must have gone to school with Alec, too. He and Ford are the same age."

"I did, yes." For reasons she couldn't explain, Lis felt a sudden rise of color from her neck to her hairline.

"Oh, I see." Carly laughed. "It's like that, is it?"

"What? No! It's not like anything," Lis protested.

"Sorry, but that red on your cheeks misled me. Sorry to have assumed." Carly cleared her throat. "Anyway, I'm finding that everyone in St. Dennis seems to have a connection to someone else. Even people who didn't grow up here."

"So you're not from here?" Lis was happy to change the subject.

"I grew up in Connecticut. I love it here, though. Actually, I love that sense of connection—I hope it didn't seem as if I were implying otherwise. I like the tightness of the community. The way people stand together and work together and cheer for each other. That's why I wanted to have certain times of the year when we only exhibited local artists." Carly smiled. "Even the scary-cats-on-black-velvet lady deserves to be acknowledged. Her children and grandchildren and her friends and neighbors come and see her work hanging here, and while they might roll their eyes at the subject matter—not to mention the questionable level of talent—they are supportive of her efforts, so I am, too." Carly stood and lifted a painting from behind her desk and held it up. "And then there is this . . ."

"That is flat-out gorgeous." Lis rose and leaned across the desk to get a better look at the landscape that was done in muted blues and greens and browns. She tried to get closer to read the signature. "Who . . . ?"

"Carolina Ellis. A friend of mine is a descendant, and inherited a house here in town. The place was loaded with Carolina's works. My heart stopped in my chest when I realized what she had there." Carly was beaming. "It was a moment that comes once in a lifetime. If at all." She held out her arms. "I still get chills when I talk about it."

"I remember reading about that. It was the talk of the art world for months."

"I moved to St. Dennis to be able to display the works. I have a few in my New York gallery. Their sales go directly to keeping the gallery here going. I like to think that Carolina would have approved of what we're doing with her work. There's one in particular I think you'd like to see."

Back in the gallery, Carly turned on the lights and led Lis around the partition that divided the room.

"My absolute favorite." She pointed to a painting that depicted a couple who appeared to be picnicking on a beach. "It's the most romantic painting I've ever seen."

"Oh, it is. It's wonderful." Lis studied the work carefully. "Who are the subjects, do you know?"

"We're pretty sure the woman is Carolina, because we've seen her photographs, but we don't know who the man is. Ellie—my friend who inherited it—is pretty sure it was a secret lover."

"Was Carolina married?"

"She was, but this was done several years after her husband died, and the man in the painting looks younger than Carolina's husband would have been."

"Maybe she did it from memory."

Carly shook her head. "She alluded to the work in one of her diary entries. No, we're pretty sure it was a clandestine meeting." She stepped back to admire it. "*Stolen Moments*."

"What?"

"*Stolen Moments*. That's the name of the painting. We even found the place where it was painted. Sunset Beach."

"I know that place. It's on the mainland, the next cove over before the island."

"I've been there. Ford took me. It's certainly the right place for a romantic secret rendezvous." Carly made a face. "It's sad we'll never know who her lover was, though."

"You said Carolina had a diary. Maybe she named him."

"She left tons of journals, and I've read them all. Assuming we found every one she wrote in, he's never been named. Everyone thinks it has to be someone local if he knew where Sunset Beach was. It isn't easy to get to."

"Fun to think that he could be someone's great-uncle or great-grandfather." Lis peered closer. "I love a good mystery."

She turned to Carly. "Is it for sale?"

"No. Ellie would never part with it, and if she had any inkling to, I'd be first in line to buy it. Sorry."

"Just thought I'd ask. It does draw you into their story, doesn't it?"

"My favorite kind of painting. I love a good story, whether it's on paper or canvas or whatever."

They discussed Carly's plans for the reception that would follow the opening of the exhibit of Lis's paintings, Carly telling Lis, "We invited a slew of collectors and critics from the major East Coast cities, so don't be surprised if you get offers for your work. You should probably have prices in mind for any of those you might want to part with." Their business concluded, Carly walked Lis to the door. "And there will be a lot of St. Dennis people here as well. You'll probably see some folks you haven't seen in years."

"And whose names I won't remember."

"I'd offer to have Ford stick close so he can whisper names in your ear, but he's going to be taking photos for the *St. Dennis Gazette*. He's working for the paper—writing features and such. He's pretty much taken it over from Grace after that bad fall she had last year. But Grace being Grace, she still looks over his shoulder, because she just can't resist knowing everything that goes on."

"Old habits die hard, they say."

Carly opened the door and stood next to it while Lis walked out. "I'm so glad you stopped by. The exhibit is going to be wonderful. I'll take good care of your works, I promise."

"I have no doubt you will. Thanks for taking me around. I'll see you soon."

The heat outside hit Lis like a sledgehammer. She had almost forgotten that the weather here in summer could change on a dime. The early morning had been pleasant enough. The afternoon would turn out to be not so much.

Lis got into her car and turned on the ignition. Then she opened the windows and turned on the air conditioner, letting it blow hot for a moment before driving off, the windows once again closed. She'd started back toward Charles Street on Old St. Mary's Church Road, pausing for a moment to admire the old Enright mansion from the street. All brick,

Georgian in style, and set back on the vast property at just the right place, the house was a legend in St. Dennis. Until this morning, she'd never been inside. It was, she realized, everything she'd thought it would be, high-ceilinged and handsome, and filled with beautiful furniture. It was all she could do not to *oooh* and *ahhh*.

On a whim, she made a U-turn at Elgin Road, and at the place where Hudson Street dead-ended, she made a right turn. Halfway up the block on the left stood a two-story house, colonial in style, with a wide front porch and several chimneys sticking out from the roof. The house appeared to have been recently painted, and the porch was lined with a row of rocking chairs painted black. Baskets of colorful flowers hung on the porch, and huge pots overflowing with red blooms stood on either side of the front door. A marker on the front lawn read CASSIDY HOUSE ~ CIRCA 1790.

This was the house where her . . . Lis couldn't even remember how far back the relationship went, how many *greats* came before *grandfather* whose name had been Oliver Cassidy, though his name and the fact that he was a well-to-do merchant was all she knew about him. She suspected her father had known little more. It was a pretty house, certainly not a mansion, but a substantial place, one that in its day must have been impressive and had been occupied by one of the more prominent citizens of St. Dennis. And it was the only tangible evidence that her father had to prove the injustices that had been done to his family.

"We were robbed," he'd tell her and Owen,

who'd be huddled in the backseat of their old sedan not quite understanding what he was talking about. "We'd be living there now, if not for those bastards."

"That's Cory West's house," a confused Owen had once made the mistake of saying. "Why would we be living in Cory West's house?"

Their father's explosion of anger taught them both to never question him again on the subject, no matter how many times he forced them to make the trip and made them listen to the tale. After that, they'd made the ride in silence and tried not to listen to their father's ramblings.

Lis pulled to the curb and parked the car.

"It's just a *house*," she said finally. "It's just a house . . ."

The sad truth was that her father had let this house—and what it stood for in his mind—control his life, to the point of destroying it.

"Dad, it's always been just a house."

She put the car in drive and headed back to the island.

Chapter Six

"Mind where you step," Ruby called to Lis from the front porch of the store. "Floor might be falling in on itself. No one's set foot in there since I don't know when."

"I'll be careful, Gigi. Don't worry." Lis got into her car and rolled down the window only long enough to wave as she drove away. She'd intended to walk to the point, but the early heat combined with the invasion of hungry green-headed flies convinced her that this was not going to be a day to enjoy the great outdoors.

The drive took all of a minute. Lis pulled onto the grass in front of the old cottage and turned off the car, sat for a few minutes savoring the view. Through the windshield, she could see the bay beyond the point, the water glistening in the sun. As a child, she and Owen, and later she and her girlfriends, sat at the end of the pier to watch the sun set. Sometimes storms would blow up from the south, and they'd watch the thunder clouds swirl up the bay and wait until the rain began to pelt the surface of the water before they'd run for cover. They'd played in the ruins of the old building that sat out near the road. It had been their fort, their playhouse, their pirate ship. The point had been one of her favorite places as a child, and she was coming to appreciate it even more as an adult. Peace and solitude were guaranteed. Alone with the pines standing sentinel, she could hear herself think. Even with the windows rolled up, she could hear the *shushing* of the tree branches as they brushed against each other in the breeze. It was, in fact, music to her ears. She'd been living in and around the city for so long that she'd forgotten there was another way to live.

She got out of the car and walked to the front door and stood on the small front porch, slapping the backs of her legs and her arms while she tried to jiggle the lock open. Grateful when it finally turned, she pushed the door open and closed it immediately, hoping to lock out the nasty flying insects that had set upon her like vampires. She stood inside the door and looked around to get her bearings.

The first thing Lis noticed was the smell of rotting wood. The second was the sound of very tiny feet scurrying away and out of sight.

"Oh please. Not mice," she pleaded aloud. But of course there would be. The house had been vacant forever and surely there would be plenty of places for the tiny rodents to enter.

Okay, so there are mice. To be expected, considering the age of the house and the fact that no one had been living there to chase the little buggers out. Put *exterminator* at the top of the list.

Lis walked cautiously into the center of the room, which went from front to back, and in its day had served as both living room and dining room. Beneath her feet, the floor seemed to sag, and that couldn't be good.

A large fireplace stood along the right-side wall. The space was bisected by stairs that led to the second floor, which she'd explore later. To the left of the dining area would be the kitchen. She took a deep breath and ventured toward it. More little scritching noises caused her shoulders to momentarily hunch together, but she moved on to the kitchen. There were no appliances and the cabinets were ancient. The floor was the same wood as the rest of the house but seemed a little more solid than that in the front room. The only light came through the window over the old porcelain sink and there were cobwebs everywhere—in the corners and the windows and hanging from the ceiling. The remains of dead bees, wasps, and flies were on every windowsill, and the counters were covered with mouse droppings.

"Ugh." She made a face. "Disgusting!"

Returning to the front of the house, Lis followed the hall that led to the bedrooms and a small bathroom, mentally noting where the boards felt soft and sagged. The bathroom was a total disaster, the old tub chipped and the floor beneath it indented by a full four inches. The ceiling was coming down in two places and the water stains around the window went clear down to the floor. The sink was small and half hanging off the wall, the screws holding it upright having rusted. She backed out of the room and checked the front bedroom.

Here the windows were covered with a thick layer of dirt and more vines crept through the sills. The ceiling, however, showed no water stains and the floor seemed solid beneath her feet, so that was a plus. But when she opened the closet she came face-to-face with the skeleton of what looked to be a hideous beast, and she'd startled herself by screaming right before she slammed the door. She had no idea what sort of animal might have been locked in there, and at that moment, she wasn't sure she wanted to know. Lis couldn't make it out of that room fast enough.

Her heart still pounding, she headed for the steps to the second floor, then hesitated, uncertain she was ready to make that climb, not knowing what she might find. Blocking out the image of the beast in the bedroom closet, up she went.

The second floor was one large room with windows on all four sides. Cobwebs were everywhere. Four metal beds, the mattresses long gone, marched along the front wall, and several old dressers stood back-to-back in the middle of the room. She cautiously brushed aside the cobwebs so she could look out the back window, but even after she cleaned away the detritus, she found vines had grown up across the bay side of the house and completely obliterated the view. Dead stems, brown and brittle leaves still attached in places, snaked through one side of the window and trailed along the perimeter of the room.

But despite all that, she was drawn to the space.

Here her grandmother Sarah and her sisters had slept, laughed and cried, and probably played and teased each other and told each other tales and shared their secrets. For a moment Lis felt if she closed her eyes, she would see them, hear them. The sensation washed through her and brought a smile to her face. Sarah, of whom Lis had no memories, came alive to her. Aware of the fact that her family's roots were deep in this place, Lis felt determined to save it if she could.

She began to look at the space with a critical eye.

The windows were small, but could be replaced with larger ones, which would broaden the view of the bay. Skylights could be added to bring in more light. Watermarks stained the ceiling in several places, though there were no holes in the roof as far as she could see, and she could feel air seeping in from various places around the room.

Still, if done correctly, the second floor would be a perfect studio. She could paint here.

Lis went back downstairs, mentally adding *landscaper* to her list of people to call. Those vines would have to be cut down along with the jungle surrounding the back of the house where they'd originated.

Taken all together, the project would be enormous. Nothing could remain untouched. Lis's heart sank. There was no way she'd be able to do this alone. Either she'd have to hire someone—that would be Alec, if Ruby had any say in it, and of course she did, since the house belonged to her—or Lis would have to give up on the idea of bringing the old place back to life.

She made a second tour of the first floor, trying to look at each room from a practical viewpoint. The kitchen could be redone. It would need a stove and a refrigerator, but the cabinets, despite their age, were in good condition and her optimistic self thought they might look fine with a coat of paint. She could do that. The floor was the biggest problem. It would need to be shored up somehow, and she suspected that whole sections would need to be replaced. She had no idea what that might entail, but she was pretty sure it would be a pricy project.

Almost all the window frames were damaged by insects or water, and some were rotted. Windows, like the floors and the plumbing and the electrical wiring, would require a professional. The brick fireplace looked fine, but there was no telling what was inside it. A chimney sweep was a must, and judging by the loose bricks that lay broken in the firebox, a mason would probably be a good idea as well. The bathroom would need to be entirely replaced, and the smaller of the two bedrooms would make an adequate office. She supposed she could use the larger one as a bedroom, but the thought of not spending the night under Ruby's roof was disconcerting. What if Ruby needed her in the middle of the night?

She brushed the thought aside. Ruby had been doing quite well without her for a very long time. Why would she need her now?

The back door was stuck shut and Lis was afraid that forcing it would break the jamb, so she let it go.

She went back out the front to inspect the foundation more closely, but she was met by a cloud of flies, all of which seemed to attack her at once.

"Damn." She ran to the car and hopped in. Several flies managed to follow her and she chased them around the front of the car with a magazine she found under the passenger seat. She was able to dispatch three of them, but several others managed to outwit her, and they bedeviled her all the way back to the store. She got out of the car and ran inside.

"Look like you seen a ghost, Lisbeth Jane," Ruby observed from the counter, where she was helping a customer pack up her purchases.

"If I spent enough time out there today, I would be a ghost before too long." Lis slapped a fly that settled on her calf. "Ha! Got him."

"Those flies be bad today." Ruby's customer nodded. "'Bout ate me alive when I went to hang the clothes out on the line this morning. Chased me right back in."

Lis recognized the voice as belonging to one of Ruby's neighbors.

"So who hung up all those damp clothes, Mrs. Banks?" Lis asked.

"Nobody. I left that basket right there by the back door. Get to it when the wind shifts and blows the flies back where they came from." The woman turned around. "Heard you be back to show off them paintings of yours over to the mansion, Lisbeth."

"You heard right." Lis put her arms around the tiny white-haired woman and gave her a hug. "How are you, Mrs. Banks? How are D.J. and Mac?"

"Good, good. Married nice girls, got nice families, both of 'em." Ada Banks looked Lis up and down. "Got skinny since you been gone. Ruby, the girl needs some meat on those bones."

"She be fine, Ada." Ruby finished packing the bag. "Eats like a horse, this one."

"Thanks a lot, Gigi." Lis grinned good-naturedly. "Speaking of which, I think it's almost time for lunch."

"Soup's in the fridge, top shelf. You could go on back and heat it up, you have a mind," Ruby told her.

"I have a mind," Lis said as she went into Ruby's new living quarters.

She found the soup right where Ruby said it would be, and she set it on the counter while she looked for a pot to heat it in. She loved Ruby's new pull-out shelves and decided that she'd put them in the kitchen in the cottage when the time came. She had just selected a pot and poured the contents of the soup container into it when she heard someone come into the kitchen.

"For the record, you look pretty good for someone who eats like a horse. My cousin Cynthia really does eat like a horse, and she'd make three of you, easy."

Lis looked over her shoulder, knowing who she'd find.

"Alec, what are you doing here?" she asked.

"Ruby asked me to stop over and do some touch-up painting in her bathroom." He leaned back against the doorjamb, a paintbrush in his right hand. "When Ruby calls, I'm there."

"That's nice of you." She tried to busy herself, first by turning on the burner and adjusting it, then looking in the drawer for a spoon with which to stir it.

"Yes, it is."

She knew without looking that behind her he was wearing that goofy, self-assured smile she remembered from high school. The same smile he'd worn right before she turned him down for the prom.

"So I hear you're thinking about doing some work at the cottage down on the point."

"I am." Ruby strikes again, Lis thought.

"You took a look at it this morning?" he asked, though obviously he knew that she had.

Lis nodded.

"So what's it look like inside?"

"What you'd expect a place to look like after it's been sitting for, I don't know, twenty, thirty years? I don't know how long. Ruby would remember, though."

"Yeah, for one hundred years, she's amazing. She doesn't forget a damned thing."

"Finding that out, are you?"

"Found that out a long time ago." He came into the room and leaned on the island and ran a hand over the wooden top. "Smooth as a baby's butt."

"Gigi said that used to be the old floor." Lis nodded toward the island.

"Looks good now, doesn't it?" He openly admired his work. "It came back so fine." He looked up at her. "What's the floor in the old place?"

"I'm not sure I understand what you mean."

"What kind of wood is it? I'm sure it's wood, local most likely, judging by the time the place was built. So it's probably white pine, but it could be oak. Lots of red oak around."

Lis shrugged. "I don't know what it is. It's dirty, I can tell you that much."

"You'd be dirty, too, if you lay out on the point for all those years."

"Har." She smiled in spite of her efforts not to. "It sags, too, like it's going to break up under your feet and you're going to crash right on through."

"That's not good. Could be termites or water damage. Either way—not good."

"I figured."

"The brick exterior didn't look too bad, though, last I noticed."

"Not bad," she agreed. "But there were bricks in the fireplace. It looked like they might have fallen from inside. So I'm thinking I should call a mason in. At the very least, the brick will need to be repointed."

"Ca-ching, ca-ching."

"I figured that out, too."

"So you think you're really going for it?"

"I don't know. Honestly, Alec, there's so much that's wrong with it right now." She leaned upon the opposite side of the island from where he stood.

"But apparently so much that's right as well."

"There is a lot that is right, yes." She rested her elbow on the island, her chin in her hand, pleased that he *got* it. "The amount of work is overwhelming. But still, there is something about that place . . ." she said wistfully.

"Some places get to you like that. Some places speak to you and some places never say a word."

"This is a place that speaks. Loud and clear," she told him. "Gigi and Great-Grampa Harold lived there, had their kids there. It's part of her." She nodded her head in the direction of the store out front. "My grandmother was born in that house, grew up there. My mom played there when she was little. It's a part of my family. And it's so peaceful there, quiet and serene and wild and untouched. I'd forgotten how much I loved the point. I'm so happy that it's still so natural and unspoiled there, that Gigi's held on to it all these years. I never want it to change. I never want anything on the island to change."

"Nothing stays the same forever, Lis."

"That sounds like something Gigi would say."

"I knew I heard it somewhere." He took a long drink from the water bottle he'd set on the counter and drained it. "Sounds like you're hooked."

"What?"

"The cottage out on the point. Sounds like you're hooked on it."

"Totally hooked," she agreed.

"Well, I guess you should see exactly what needs to be done, see if it's salvageable."

"The first thing that has to be done is to get all the cobwebs out. Oh, and the wild animal in the closet. That has to go, and someone else is going to have to remove it." She looked at Alec meaningfully.

"What's this about wild animals in a closet?" Ruby came into the room, shuffling in her favorite white sneakers.

"There's some kind of dead animal in the front

bedroom closet," Lis told her. "A skeleton of something. It scared the bejesus out of me."

"Probably a possum." Ruby didn't even blink at the news. "Could be a raccoon, though. Got plenty of both in these parts."

"It looked ferocious. It had a long pointy head and beady little eye sockets," Lis told her. "Whatever it was, I bet it was mean when it was still alive."

"Probably got itself trapped between the ceiling and the upstairs floor, fell through the ceiling, poor thing." Ruby went to the stove and stirred the soup, then tasted it. "Alec, there be plenty of soup here. Corn and crab chowder. One of your favorites."

"It is. Nice of you to remember."

"Lisbeth, you bring down three bowls and get some spoons and set the table right there by the window." Ruby instructed. "Alec, you get some glasses and pour the iced tea."

"Thanks, Miz Ruby. You having hot or cold tea today?" he asked.

Ruby paused to think it over. "Hot, I guess. Only had me one cup so far today."

Without asking where things were located, Alec reached behind and over Lis for the glasses from one cabinet and a cup and saucer from another.

"You get pink roses today, Miz Ruby," he said, holding up the delicate china cup.

"My favorite one." Ruby smiled at him.

He winked at her while he filled the teakettle with water, then placed it on the stove and turned on the burner. It was apparent to Lis that this was a scene that had played out before. Alec was obviously comfortable in Ruby's kitchen and seemed to know more about where things were stored than Lis did. They made a strange pair, Lis thought, the elderly woman and the handsome young man.

Wait, Lis caught herself in near panic. Did she just call Alec handsome? And if she had, had she said it out loud?

Apparently not, since Ruby hadn't commented on it and Alec wasn't gloating, as she suspected he might.

Lis ladled soup into the bowls and placed them on the table overlooking the side yard. From there, they could see the bay. She'd enjoyed having dinner there the night before, and breakfast again this morning, though Ruby hadn't joined her for that. Ruby had her early routine in the store with her customers, and nothing interfered with that. The store was Ruby's entire social life, Lis realized—except for the time she spent at the inn with Grace Sinclair. That relationship puzzled Lis—Ruby had a good twenty-five years on Grace, but she'd intimated they had a lot in common. Lis couldn't see what that might be, other than the fact that they were both widows and both longtime residents of the area, but it didn't matter. Ruby enjoyed the woman's company and it did get her out of the store and off the island on a fairly regular basis—something Lis couldn't recall her doing in the past—and that was all that really mattered.

Alec held a chair out for Ruby and waited till she was seated before serving her a cup of hot water on a saucer that also held a tea bag. Lis had watched his movements carefully and it became apparent that he was assisting her without giving the appearance of doing so.

"You been raised right," Ruby told him. She dunked the tea bag into the cup. "You always bring your manners."

"You're my number-one gal, Miz Ruby." He seated himself next to the window. "If you were a few years younger . . ."

"That be more than a few, boy." Ruby chuckled. "Be more like sixty-some, to be sure. But I thank you all the same."

Lis ate in silence, observing the interaction between the two, and it became more and more clear to her that the friendship Ruby and Alec had developed was genuine. She felt almost embarrassed at having suspected him of trying to scam the woman to get his hands on the boat. If she were to be fair, she'd have to admit that the skipjack had been in terrible condition. How much could it have been worth, really, with its rotten hull, and who knows what else might have needed repair?

"Lisbeth Jane, where you be?" Ruby waved a hand in front of her face.

"What? Oh, sorry. I was thinking about the cottage, and how great it will be when it's all fixed up."

"I was saying maybe Alec should go on out there, see what that is in the closet, give it a toss."

"I'm not going to be tossing it, so yes, that would be appreciated, Alec." Lis's eyes met his from across the table, and she felt the color rise to her cheeks again. She got up from the table before he noticed.

"I think I need a little more ice for my tea." She turned her back in an attempt to hide the flush.

"Alec, you be needing more ice?" Ruby asked.

"No, thank you. I'm good." Was there a touch of amusement in his voice?

"I'll need about twenty more minutes to finish the painting," he was saying, "but if you're free after that, we can run up to the point and dispose of the body."

"That would be great, thanks."

By the time the kitchen was cleaned up from lunch, the dishes washed and put away, Alec had finished his painting.

"You ready?" He walked casually into the kitchen.

Lis nodded. "Let me get the key."

She grabbed her bag from the chair in the TV room and told Ruby they were on their way. Once outside, they found that the wind had shifted, as Mrs. Banks had predicted it would, and the flies were nowhere to be seen.

"Funny how that works," Lis said as they walked along the road toward the point. "A while ago, the flies were as thick as I've ever seen them. Now they're gone."

"Just making way for the mosquitoes," Alec said.

"That's a mean thought. I remember when I was a kid and we'd be playing outside and all of a sudden, it was like a cloud of flies would descend on us and we'd be running for cover. Owen used to tell April Smith that if the flies bit you more than ten times in one day, you'd turn into a fly overnight while you slept."

"April never was very bright."

"Owen had a big crush on her. At fifteen he wasn't all that concerned with how smart a girl was."

"None of us were."

They cut through the dunes and along the paths that led to the smattering of small houses that was as close to being a village as there was on the island.

"Those are Ruby's hollyhocks," Lis told him, pointing to the tall stalks covered with pale pink flowers that grew in the front yard of the house they were passing. "And there, too." She walked across the road. "Ruby wasn't kidding. Oh, and her black-eyed Susans."

"What are you talking about?"

Lis pointed to the clumps of orangey-yellow flowers that grew up and over a fence. "Ruby said she and her friends used to trade flower seeds, that her hollyhocks and her Susans were growing all over the island. And there they are."

"Those yellow things? They've been growing around my house for as long as I remember."

"Maybe Ruby or the woman who gave them to her passed some on to . . . to whoever lived there before."

"That was my uncle Cliff. I'm sure he knew Ruby and her husband. We know for a fact that he knew Eb Carter."

They reached the cottage and Lis fitted the key into the lock on the front door and found it already opened.

"I must have forgotten to lock up when I left earlier," she said. "Guess I was more concerned with dodging flies than I was with securing the cottage.

Not that anyone out here would try to get in. Everyone knows it's Ruby's place."

She tucked the key back into her pocket and pushed the door open.

"Watch the floor. It's squishy in places."

She watched Alec test the floor. When he found a section that was soft, he took chalk from his pocket and marked the area.

"Looks like you came prepared," she noted.

"I had it in my pocket from another job I checked out this morning."

"So this is sort of what we call a great room these days." Lis pointed and said, "Living room out here, dining area in the back."

Alec knelt down and with his hand cleaned the surface dirt from the floor. "Looks like heart pine. All random width," he told her. "This would be beautiful cleaned up. Once we cut out and replaced the rotten sections, that is. Not sure how extensive it is. It could be a real problem, Lis."

"What would you have to do to fix it?"

"Depends on whether the beams and the foundation are rotted. We'll have to see what's going on underneath the floor." He stood and looked around. "This is a really nice space."

"It's very cool, with the fireplace over there," she noted as she went into the kitchen. "In here, I thought the cabinets could be cleaned and painted. The wood is in surprisingly good condition and it's solid." She opened one, then another cabinet door. "But the counters are shot."

"Yeah, they're going to have to be replaced."

"If you were going to do the work, would you do wood, like you did in Ruby's? Is there some of her old flooring left?"

Alec nodded. "There's probably enough left."

"And of course I'd need appliances."

"First you need electricity." He turned an old faucet. "And plumbing."

"That should be a relatively easy fix once everything else falls into place, right?"

"Depends on the condition of the pipes. My guess is that they're probably all rusted, and it won't be easy to repair the water damage." He pointed to the kitchen ceiling. "There's been a leak there. And here, under the window. I bet most of the windows had leaks."

"They're all bad—at least they looked bad to me. But they're all fixable, right?"

"Hard to say. More likely than not, they'll have to be replaced."

"Looks like the only thing I'll be able to keep will be the cabinets."

Alec nodded. "I think you'll be able to salvage those."

"It would be nice to keep something original."

"What's on the second floor?"

"One big room." Lis led the way up the stairs. When they reached the top, she pointed to the windows. "They're all stuck shut, I think."

"That's from the wood swelling up from the water that got in." He glanced overhead at the wide ceiling beams. "Those need to be checked out, but I'd need a tall ladder. I can come back and do that, and I'll look at the roof at the same time, if you want." He nodded in the direction of the vines that crept through the back window. "And you'll need to do something about those."

"I thought maybe a landscaper . . ."

"If you have money to hire one, that's fine, but you can pull these out or cut them off at the base outside."

"That sounds like the easiest part of the project."

"Oh, it will be a project, all right, but it will be worth it in the long run." He looked out one of the side windows. "You planning on living here at some point?"

"Right now, I just want to paint here. I like staying with Ruby for the time being."

"Sounds like you're thinking about sticking around for a while."

"For a while." She wandered through the rest of the second floor, peeked into the cubbyholes that had been built into each of the eaves. They were all empty except one. "Hey, look. There's something in there."

"What?"

"I don't know."

He stood behind her, peering over her shoulder. "What are you looking at?"

"See back there? In the corner?"

Alec stepped around her, looked closer, then crawled into the cubby. "It's a box," he told her. He handed it to Lis as he emerged.

The box was made of wood and had a scene painted on the lid. The colors had faded over the years but she could see one of the figures was a woman in a very fancy dress in the style of the pre–Civil War era. She opened the lid and stared at its contents.

"What is it?" Alec asked. "What's inside?"

"It looks like . . . jacks and a ball." She picked up the small silver play pieces.

"I played with those when I was a kid," Alec told her. "Cliff had a set."

"I wonder who these belonged to." Lis folded her fingers over the pieces and felt the knobs dig into her palm.

Alec leaned over her shoulder and pointed to the bottom of the box. "There's a piece of paper, there in the bottom."

Lis looked deeper into the box, then stuck her hand inside for the paper. It was yellowed and brittle, and she unfolded it carefully and started reading. "This was Sarah's. My grandmother. See, she was playing with someone named Ceely and they were keeping score." She smiled. "Looks like Ceely was kicking her butt."

"Sarah wasn't much of a jacks player, but I guess she liked the game well enough to hold on to it."

"Wait till I show Gigi." Lis was still smiling when she returned everything to the box and closed the lid.

She turned to Alec, the box in her hands, and was caught totally off guard when he leaned down and kissed her tentatively on the mouth. Her instincts took over, and she kissed him back without hesitation. She hadn't been expecting it, but somehow it seemed the most natural thing in the world.

His lips barely brushed hers at first, but she reached her arms around his neck to pull him closer.

His lips were warm and soft, and she pulled him even closer. She wasn't prepared for the heat that rose between them or the jolt she felt straight to her toes. That wasn't her usual reaction to a first kiss, and it had taken her by surprise. The simple fact was that it had taken her breath away, and as much as she wanted more, she was the first to pull away.

"Been wanting to do that since fifth grade," he said.

"Fifth grade?" An eyebrow rose. "*Fifth grade*?"

"Yup. I noticed you the minute you walked into that classroom. I did everything but stand on my head to get you to notice me, but you never did."

"I did. I noticed."

"You had an odd way of showing it. I talked practically nonstop during class to John Beyer to get Mrs. Warner to move my desk away from his. But she only moved me two rows over. So I had to talk to Kate Drummond to get the teacher to move me again."

"You sat behind me. I remember that."

"That was my third move and I was afraid it was going to be to the principal's office, that maybe I'd overplayed my hand. But it turned out to be the last move, because I got what I wanted. It took me awhile—and I might add, several nights of extra homework—but it got me where I wanted to be." He whispered in her ear. "Pretty slick, right?"

"You thought that up all by yourself?"

"I did," he said solemnly. "But of course, that put me next to Cathy Shelburn, who thought I'd done all that to sit next to her, and she rigged the bottle at the next party, so I had to kiss her." He paused. "I pretended it was you."

"You played spin the bottle in fifth grade?"

"Well, yeah. Didn't you?"

"We must have all been socially delayed. I don't remember playing kissing games until seventh grade, and the games were short-lived because we all knew each other too well. It wasn't fun for anyone."

"Let me guess: You only went to parties on the island."

She nodded.

"I imagine you had a lot of time to make up for when you hit college. I'm sorry I wasn't there."

"Me, too."

She disengaged her arms from around his neck. Her right hand still held the wooden box.

"I guess we should finish up here. Gigi's going to be wondering what's taking us so long." She took a step back.

"Okay." He exhaled a long breath. "So. Let's take a look at that foundation."

Still rattled from the unexpected kiss, Lis nodded. "It's outside."

Alec nodded and mumbled, "Good place for it."

They went back down the steps, and once outside, Alec proceeded to walk around the house, stooping to poke here or to move a pile of leaves away there. When he'd gone all the way around the house, he said, "You might have some moisture problems and the brick needs to be repointed. The salt from the bay has weathered the wood, so a lot of that needs to be replaced. Once I've had a chance to look at the roof,

I can tell you what else we need to do. I'm sure it all needs to be replaced, but how much damage has been done to the plywood under the shingles, I have no way of knowing. I suspect termites."

"That sounds really bad."

"It is bad. Termites are no joke. Luckily the exterior is brick, so if they chewed up the windows and areas around the roof, the outside walls are still good."

"Do you think you'll have some time to take a look at the roof?"

"I'm tied up tomorrow morning, but I can stop by later in the afternoon. Once I have a better idea of what it's going to take to bring this place back—assuming the damage under the roof isn't too extensive and that termites haven't eaten away the floor beams—then you and Ruby are going to have to decide what you want to do, how much you want to invest. If it can be saved, that is."

Alec brushed the dirt from his hands onto his shorts.

"All right. We'll wait until you're finished." Lis folded her arms across her chest. She'd wanted to say, *Doesn't matter, we're going to restore even if that means totally rebuilding*, but she kept that to herself.

"Want to lock up and we'll head back to the store?" he asked.

"No. I want you to go inside and go into that front bedroom and remove that . . . that thing."

"I forgot about that." He went inside, then came back out a minute later. "I need something to put it on. I don't know that I want to drag it out with my bare hands. And we need a shovel. I'm going to have to bury it somewhere."

"I'll run back to the store and see if Ruby has a shovel and I'll get a plastic bag to put that thing in."

"Ruby's shovels are in the shed near the side of the house."

"It's a miracle that old thing is still standing." She started toward the road. "Even more of a miracle that you haven't rebuilt it."

His lips curved in a slow smile. "It's on the list."

Lis broke into a jog and ran back to the store, replaying the walk through the cottage. She knew exactly how it would look when she—they—were finished with it. There was no doubt in her mind that Alec would be working with her. Which was fine, she thought. Better than fine.

She decided she wasn't going to read too much into that kiss. Not right now, anyway, when she was going to go back to the cottage where he waited. She'd think about it later.

"Of course you will, Scarlett," she murmured as she jogged the last fifty feet to Ruby's.

She reached the general store and poked her head inside to tell Ruby what they were doing, then went out to the shed and opened the door. The exterior may be shabby, but inside, everything was neat as a pin. That would be Ruby, she thought. She's always been a stickler for putting everything in its place. She found the shovel and tossed it into the backseat of her car, then went inside for a plastic trash bag for the remains of the critter. She drove back to the cottage and was surprised to find an unfamiliar car parked off road on the grass. She pulled up next to the white Cadillac and got out of her car with the trash bag in one hand and grabbed the shovel from the backseat with the other.

"Alec?" she called, but there was no answer.

The front door was open, and she walked in. "Alec?"

Silence.

Lis walked back outside and looked around, then saw Alec and another man—the owner of the white Caddy, maybe?—out on the pier. They were too far away for her to hear them, but she could see that Alec was standing with his hands on his hips, and the other man was gesturing with both hands, first toward the bay, then toward Lis. What in the world could that be about? she wondered.

She stood the shovel up next to the front door and placed the bag on the ground next to it, debating whether to walk out to the pier to see what was going on. After all, it was her property. Not hers, exactly, but her family's. She heard the man's voice, loud and angry, and could tell by Alec's stance that he was trying to calm him down.

Lis decided it was time to join the party.

She was no more than halfway to the pier when the man turned and headed toward her. As he approached, she smiled and started to say hello, but he went right past her in a huff. Clearly annoyed, Alec followed, his hands in his pockets.

"Who was that guy?" Lis asked.

"Just a client," he replied.

"What's his problem?"

"He doesn't take disappointment well." Alec stopped when he reached her. "So did you find a shovel?"

"How could I not? That shed is more neatly organized than my apartment. It has Gigi's fingerprints all over it."

"Uh-uh," he told her. "Mine."

"You did that? Lined up all those tools in alphabetical order, stacked the pots by color . . . ?"

"Wouldn't you?"

"No." Lis shook her head. "I can't believe there are two of you. What are the chances you'd find each other?"

The white Cadillac reversed off the grass, barely missing Lis's car, the engine revving as it pulled away.

"He should slow down," Lis said. "There aren't a whole lot of little ones on the island, but there are a lot of old folks."

"I'll remind him next time I speak with him." Alec watched the car disappear down the road, then clapped his hands. "So. The shovel. The plastic bag."

"Right by the door."

He set off for the cottage, bent down for the bag, then disappeared through the front door. Moments later he returned, the bag in hand.

"It's definitely an opossum," he told her.

"Good to know. Could you just bury it now?"

He found a spot a hundred feet from the cottage and began to dig. The earth was soft and sandy, and within minutes he had a hole deep enough for the bag. He placed it at the bottom of the hole and filled the shovel with soil.

"Want to say any words over the deceased?"

She walked closer and peered into the hole.

"I'm sorry you got stuck in the closet and couldn't get out. I could say that's what you get for breaking and entering, but I realize you were unable to foresee the consequences of your actions. So I'll just say if there's a rainbow bridge for wild animals, I hope you crossed in peace and have joined your family and friends on the other side." She looked up at Alec. "How was that?"

"Impressive." He nodded. "Really impressive."

He filled the hole and handed her the shovel.

"Now you have something to cross off your list of things to do to make this place habitable."

"And I'm grateful. Thanks, Alec."

"My pleasure. Any time you find critters in the old place, you know who to call."

"There are more," she told him.

"More?" He frowned. "More what?"

"Mice. I heard them when I was inside earlier."

"That's a given. We can get rid of them."

"I don't like traps."

"We can get someone in to clean the place out."

"How?"

"You really want to know?"

"I guess not."

They reached the house. "I'll lock up and then give you a ride back to the store." Lis fished in the pocket of her shorts for the key.

"Thanks anyway, but I think I want to walk around a bit."

"Walk around the island?"

Alec nodded.

"Oh. Okay. Well, thanks for coming out here and disposing of the body and for doing a walk-through with me."

"You're welcome. I'll be in touch after I've gone over the roof." He opened the back door of the car and put in the shovel. "Make sure you put it back where you found it."

Lis rolled her eyes.

"Maybe you should take the key in case you need to get back inside." She handed it to him.

"Good idea. I'll lock up and I'll drop it off at the store after I finish tomorrow."

"Okay." Lis nodded. "Well, thanks again. See you."

"I'll be in touch."

She got into the car and turned it on, put it in reverse, and backed out onto the street. Alec was still standing on the grass, his hand raised in a wave as she pulled away.

"That was too damned odd," she said aloud.

Something strange had happened, but she had no idea what. It was as if the arrival of the man in the white car had provoked a change in Alec, but she couldn't put her finger on exactly what it was.

"And things had been going so well, too," she muttered as she parked behind the store. One minute he was kissing her and it felt all cozy, the next minute he was distracted.

She found Ruby inside, sitting at the table in the front of the store, reading her book. She looked up when Lis entered.

"Alec do you right?" she asked without looking up.

"Yes. He's going to go back tomorrow with a ladder to look at the roof. I let him keep the key."

Ruby nodded. "He's a good boy, Alec is. Glad to see you getting along."

Lis's eyes narrowed. "What's that supposed to mean?"

"Nice to be in touch with old friends again."

"We were never really friends," Lis told her.

Ruby looked up. "Whose fault would that be?"

"Mine."

"Some learn from their mistakes. Some don't make the same one twice." Ruby went back to her book.

Lis wanted to remind her that she hadn't been allowed to make friends, hadn't been allowed to think beyond the island, but what was the point. She went upstairs and took a shower, the kiss still on her mind. He said he'd been wanting to do that since fifth grade. Should she have told him about all the nights she'd dreamed of him? Of all the times she'd watched him in the hallway, taken the long route to class so she could pass his locker, tried to get a table near his in the cafeteria or the library, just so she could watch him, hear his voice, listen to his laughter?

Probably not, since she'd barely admitted it to herself, then or now.

She'd just finished drying her hair when she heard a car door slam. She looked out the window and saw Alec's Jeep heading toward the bridge. She watched, expecting him to drive over it, but instead, he made a left and headed back onto the island. The dark car disappeared momentarily, then she saw it pull up in front of the old Mullan place and park. Alec got out and walked through the overgrown lot and around the side of the house.

Odd, she thought. No one's lived there in years.

Moments later, a black pickup drove over the bridge and made its way around the curve and reappeared to park next to the Jeep. She watched as someone got out and presumably joined Alec around the side of the house.

It could well be that the family has decided to sell the property and has asked Alec to give them an estimate to make it presentable.

And that would make sense, but why hadn't Alec mentioned it when they were back at the point? It would have been perfectly natural for him to have said something about renovating other places on the island, but he hadn't.

Her thoughts went back to the man in the white Cadillac.

Something about him didn't feel quite right. She knew it wasn't any of her business, but all the same, she couldn't help wondering who he was and what he was doing on the point.

Diary~

    Ruby tells me the visit with her great-granddaughter is going well, which I was sure it would, but then again . . . well, you know how families can be.

    Speaking of which, our little family is about to grow again! Our Lucy and Clay have announced that a little one is on the way and will be born just in time for Christmas! Now, I cannot lie and say I did not know, but "knowing" and being told are two different things. When you know before others do, well, you can't share, and where's the fun in that? Okay, so I did tell Ruby, but her lips are always sealed. If you want to share a secret that you know will never be passed on, Ruby Carter is your girl. One hundred percent guaranteed.

    And speaking of girls, well, that's what Lucy will be giving birth to, though she doesn't know that yet. I even know the name they'll choose, but I won't even commit that to writing. That would be bad luck.

    But back to new babies—Ellie and Cameron O'Connor's baby boy was born a week ago. Cameron Junior, I'm told.

They're a lovely family and I know that somewhere on the other side, Ellie's great-aunt Lilly is rejoicing along with Ellie's mother, Lynley, who left us all too soon.

So that's my news for today—only happy news this time around, I'm so pleased to say. Though Ruby tells me a storm is brewing over her island, a storm guaranteed to cause some waves, if you'll forgive the pun. I'm just hoping—praying—it doesn't spread to St. Dennis. Though I know my nephew Alec is right at the center of it, and that his heart is at risk. Oh, if only I could move that along just a little. I suppose I should just let things play out, but one gets so impatient sometimes. It's so tempting to just give a little bitty push, if you know what I mean . . .

Grace

Chapter Seven

His hand still raised in a wave, Alec took a few steps toward the road as he watched Lis drive away. When her car had disappeared, he went back to the cottage and locked up. He was still annoyed that Deiter had popped up unexpectedly the way he had. The last thing he wanted to do was explain to Lis that someone else wanted to buy the point, knock down the cottage she'd just set her heart on, and build a bunch of houses there. The look on her face as they'd walked through together had told him everything he needed to know about the future of Ruby's old home. He'd been hard-pressed not to tell her what he really thought the prospects were for the old place. He'd wait until he could determine how extensive the termite damage was, and whether the support beams had been compromised. He'd really hate to burst that happy bubble of hers, especially if renovating the cottage meant that Lis would be around for more than a week or two. She had stayed tucked away in the back of his mind like unfinished business; perhaps it was time to explore what might have been.

More than time. He hadn't planned on kissing her today, but he was damned glad he had. He hadn't been kidding when he told her he'd wanted to kiss her since fifth grade. He could have added that he'd wanted to kiss her every year after that as well, but he was pretty sure she got the drift. Kissing Lis had been everything he'd thought it would be, and he knew it wouldn't be long before he kissed her again.

Now was a good time to warn himself that the situation on the island was going to be touchy enough without tossing his own heart into the mix, and that was exactly what he was doing. It had been hard to keep his eyes off her—harder still not to touch her, even if only casually while they walked through the little house. Lis was still the golden girl as far as he was concerned. Over all the years, she'd been the only one who'd gotten into his head and stayed there. The last thing he expected was for her to come back to Cannonball Island and talk about staying. What were the chances that would happen now, of all times, when he was involved in what some might see as the exploitation of the island and its few resources?

From the start he'd tried his best to make the right decisions where the potential development of the island was concerned. He loved the wildness of it, the archaic cabins and the deserted chapels built by dueling ministers, but his fear was that someone who didn't appreciate its idiosyncrasies would ignore the history and the natural beauty and destroy everything that made Cannonball Island unique.

He'd debated with himself before he turned to the one person whose opinion and instincts he trusted above all others.

Of everyone he knew, Ruby Carter was the wisest, the most grounded in reality. He'd sought her counsel even before he'd accepted the job, and he'd laid out everything he knew about Deiter and his company. The developer had made it very clear at their initial meeting that he wanted to buy up as much property on the island as he could. Since the point was the single largest parcel on the island, Alec knew that it would draw Deiter's attention immediately. Before he had any conversations of any substance with Deiter, he wanted first to work through his own doubts about whether this project would be good for the island, and second, to learn whether Ruby had any interest in selling that particular bit of ground. If not, he'd have to find a way to steer Deiter away from it and point him elsewhere.

He'd sat with Ruby on her new back porch on a Sunday night and laid it all out. She'd listened without interruption until he finished.

"You say this man—this Brian Deiter—he be wanting to build new houses here on the island," she'd said. "How many houses he got in mind?"

"We didn't talk about any specific number, but I made some calls, spoke to some people who have dealt with him in the past. They say he likes big projects that will make him a lot of money, that he'll want to build the maximum he can." He'd rocked slowly in one of the two rockers he'd brought outside at Ruby's request. He found the gentle motion calmed him, and he thought Ruby knew what she was doing when she told him they'd sit out here and go over whatever it was that was on his mind. "But they also said he was reasonable if you present a logical case to him."

"You be a logical boy, Alec." Ruby rocked even more slowly than Alec. "He been here? On the island?"

"He has. He said he drove around and noticed there was lots of empty space out here."

"Different reasons for that," she replied. "Some folks left their places and moved away. Just locked the doors and left. Their reasons be their own. Others got tired of bailing out after the storms. Had some come through here, battered the island something fierce. Some folks had enough of putting their roofs back on and trying to dry out. Others places, don't even know who owns them legal these days; folks died and left no kin."

"There are a lot of places on the island where you can't build because the area's protected, or it just isn't suitable," he reminded her. "The wetlands, the salt marsh."

"Don't seem to me there be too much else to build on." She rocked for a moment before adding, "'Cept maybe the point."

"You still own that, Miz Ruby?"

"You know I do. If you're asking me if I'd sell it, I don't know. Never gave it thought." Her gaze was out over the dune, toward the point, though it was too far away to be seen from the opposite end of the island. "That place been in my family since the big move, when the folks in St. Dennis drove us out. Never thought about selling it. Thought to keep it in the family. Only ones who ever come back are Owen and Lis, once in a while Chrissie. Owen would do right by it; he's island through and through, though he don't know it yet. Lis, well, I be waiting for that girl's heart to catch up with her head, and enough said about that. Chrissie—no, no. Wouldn't leave it to Chrissie. She'd sell it to the first person who flashed green in front of her face, and that's the God's truth."

Alec had remained silent. He let Ruby talk out the possibilities.

"What good would come to the island, all these houses be built?" she asked.

"Well, Deiter would have to pay the owners for the land. Then he'd be hiring some local people to work."

Ruby nodded. She understood the financial benefit.

"The general store would be selling a lot more coffee early in the morning and cold bottled water all day long," he added.

"I already figured that," she told him.

Alec smiled. Of course she would have picked up on that immediately. Nothing got past Ruby.

"Tell me what harm you see."

"If the building isn't done right, if too many homes are built, it could be a disaster. From an ecological standpoint—it could kill the salt marsh and everything living there. As far as the environment is concerned, just the amount of human waste to dispose of would quadruple, at the least. If it wasn't done properly so that it seeped into the bay . . ."

Ruby nodded. She understood completely.

"And if the houses weren't right for the island, if consideration isn't given to the places that are here, how new would fit in with the old, the entire look of this place will change."

She nodded again. "What's in your head, Alec?"

"My head tells me that sooner or later, there will be development on the island. It's happening all up and down the bay. If Deiter gets his way, it will be sooner."

"Who'd be in charge of all this building?"

"The developer—Deiter—would be."

"I been feeling a change coming for some time now. You wondering if you should work with this man?"

"That's what it's coming down to, yes."

"Someone with no feel for the island could do harm," Ruby said thoughtfully. "Could be two hundred years of island living be gone."

"That's what I'm worried about."

"Seems to me you'd take good care. Respect what's here. What's been. Maybe know best what should come next. Keep the marshes safe. Keep a keen eye on what's going on." They both rocked in silence for several minutes.

Finally, Ruby said, "What would happen to the old places? The chapels? The first houses?"

"I'll see if I can get them protected. They should be on the National Register of Historic Places, given their history."

"You would do right by us. Guide this man and his people right, maybe it be for the best." Ruby closed her eyes. "Change be coming . . . time to get out of the way. Might as well try to make the best of it, do it right. Once all be gone, there be no bringing it back."

"That's what I was thinking," he said.

Without opening her eyes, she replied, "I know."

Alec had played that conversation over and over in his head, and in the end, he'd decided it would be best all the way around if he was involved with the project. Ruby had promised that if things got to the point where the development was a go, she'd be willing to take Alec's part if anyone on the island had misgivings. If Alec could steer Brian Deiter in the right direction, and if Ruby Carter had his back, the project could be beneficial for everyone involved, especially for the people of Cannonball Island.

It was clear that Ruby hadn't mentioned anything to Lis about the changes that might be coming. It was anyone's guess how she was going to react to the news, especially after telling Alec that she'd fallen in love with the cottage all over again, and how much she loved the unspoiled beauty, how she wished it would never change. If she reacted the way he thought she might, he was going to have to be able to make her understand that in the long run, he was the lesser of all evils when it came to the island's future, that development to some degree was inevitable. Whether she'd see it that way remained to be seen.

Brian showing up at the point had escalated things a bit. He'd told Alec all he could think about was the view from the point: He had to have it. He was going to build his own house there. Alec knew that with

Lis's heart set on renovating the cottage, there was no way Ruby would sell even an acre of the point. He'd need to line up some other properties that he could hope to interest Brian in.

Tommy Mullan had told him just last week that he and his sisters were interested in selling off some ground owned by their parents on the island. Both their father and mother were in a nursing home and could use the money, he had said. As soon as Lis drove off, Alec called Tom and asked if he could meet him at one of their properties. Tom, who was living close by in Ballard, dropped what he was doing and drove over.

"What have you got in mind, Alec?" Tom asked.

"I know of someone who might be looking to buy something on the island," Alec said cautiously. The last thing he wanted to do was set the gossip machine going before he needed to. "He asked me to look around, see if there was anything suitable to build on that might be for sale."

Tom pointed to the house, which was boarded up all the way around. "You came to the right place, pardner. What's he paying?"

"I don't know. The conversations haven't gotten that far, but I imagine it would be fair."

"What do you suppose is fair market for these old places?" Tom rubbed his chin. "You got any idea?"

"There's a lot to take into consideration. These older places, the original homes—they can't be replaced once they're gone. There's a lot of history here."

"But does history have a price tag? And does

anybody really care if the houses on Cannonball Island are knocked down?"

"I think there are ways to make them care."

"These old places, they're small and have been beaten down by the weather over the years. Hell, my grandparents' place over near the village is damn near falling down."

"You selling that, too?"

"If we can."

"Who owns the lots next door?" Alec asked.

Tom pointed to the right. "My dad's sister owns the one there, and his brother owned the one that runs behind them both. Over to the other side, my grandfather owned that one, too."

"So you could conceivably sell them all?"

Tom nodded. "I guess the only value—assuming there is some—is in the land. The roof fell in on my aunt's place—I guess you can see that yourself—and she never bothered to fix it. Her husband died about five years ago, and she just packed up and moved on. The house my uncle lived in is still in somewhat decent shape—he lived there up until Christmas, when he fell and broke his hip, went to live with his son in Baltimore. They're all really small, though."

"I can see that."

"It was like growing up in a shoe box; this place was too small for the five of us." Tom was gazing at the house. "You ever been in one of these places?"

"No."

"Come on in, then, and take a look."

Alec followed Tom around to the back of the house, past the tiny white markers that seemed to grow out of the side yard, each marking the final resting place of one of the Mullans who'd come before. Alec wasn't sure what to do about them, but he'd worry about it later. Tom unlocked the door and held it aside for Alec to enter. He found himself in a kitchen smaller than the one in Ruby's cottage. A walk-through confirmed that every room was smaller than he'd expected. The tour lasted less than ten minutes.

"Well, you were right. It is pretty small," Alec said when they'd gone back outside. "And the amount of work it would need . . ."

"Yeah, it's a tear-down, far as I can see. You find out what this guy is offering and I'll talk to my sisters. I have power of attorney for our folks—the girls don't live local anymore. Kate is in Chicago and Amanda is in Charleston. Between you and me, we don't expect a lot for it."

"Do yourself a favor and don't tell that to anyone else. And it might be a good idea to keep this under your hat for now, at least until we see if this guy decides to make an offer."

"Gotcha." Tom nodded. "I won't say a word to anyone until this guy comes back with a number. *If* he comes back with a number."

"Right. You don't want to be telling people you're selling it and then have this guy decide that the other side of River Road looks better to him."

"Yeah. I'd look like a damned fool." Tom put his hand out to shake Alec's hand. "You have my number. I'll be waiting to hear, either way."

Tom opened the driver's door of his truck, but

before he got in, he turned to Alec. "This place has been pretty wild all my life. Hard to imagine it with new houses on it. Shame, in a way, to see it change, see something different here. But I guess that's progress, right? Wouldn't surprise me at all if someone decided to do a lot of building out here. That's what's happening over near where I live. Someone bought up all that strip along the river and started building these huge places there. Heard they're going for a million and up. Nice-looking places, but when you look across the river, you can't tell where you are anymore."

Without waiting for Alec to comment, Tom got into his truck and drove off.

Alec walked around the property again, this time trying to gauge the size of the lot. Judging by the placement of trees around the perimeter, he had a pretty good idea. He'd call Tom later to confirm.

His instincts told him that the existing houses would be too small to sell the developer on for rehabs, even if they could be saved, which was doubtful, but the properties were well located, and he'd noticed several things in his quick walk-through with Tom. Inside, there was a lot of good wood—beautiful wood—that could be reclaimed and used again. The interior doors were in good condition, and the brick in the fireplace was prime, even after all these years. All he needed was to convince Deiter that this was the way to go, the architect to see things as he did, and a Realtor to pull it all together.

If the architect were to design new houses that reflected the old, filled with wood and brick reclaimed from the original houses that stood on these lots, and with the right marketing plan . . .

It wasn't a new concept, but he'd bet it would be new to Deiter.

Energized by the possibilities, he hopped into his Jeep and headed for home. He had some phone calls to make.

Chapter Eight

A fat blue glass vase spilling over with flowers sat in the center of the round table near the window in Ruby's store.

"So pretty," Lis said as she sat with her coffee after the morning rush of watermen had ended. "What are these orange things?"

"Zinnias." Ruby joined her, a cup of Earl Grey in hand. "They exploded out there near the front corner. Picked as many as I could, but there's still a mess of them out there. I thought you might like some for upstairs."

"I'd love some, thank you. They're so colorful." Lis touched the blooms with a fingertip. "I like the big ones. They're so bold."

"Some flowers be bold, some be quiet. Just like people."

"That's you and me, right there," Lis said. "You're the bold one."

"Live as long as I have, no point in hiding behind yourself. You have something to say, you say it.

Something you want to do, you do it. Life catches up with you, whichever way you decide to live." Ruby took a sip of tea, then put the cup down. "Like now. You got something to say."

"I'm still working it out, Gigi." Lis's fingers tapped on the side of her mug. "How I want to live. Where I want to be. I used to be so sure of myself, what I wanted, and now . . ."

Ruby nodded as if she understood. "Now you're not."

"I like my life, I do. I like where I live, and I like being close to the city. I like the bustle, that sense of urgency, the energy there. I like the work I did there."

"But . . ." Ruby raised an expectant eyebrow.

"But when I'm here, the slower pace feels, I don't know, more natural to me, maybe. I like talking to the oystermen when they come in every morning. I like the connection I feel here. I tried to work on a sketch last night, something I'd started a few weeks ago, but as much as I tried, I found I had no feel for it."

"Maybe you be wanting to paint something different. Change might be due."

"I do have something else in my head right now, something different from what I've been doing, and I'm excited about it and I can't wait to work on it." Lis sighed. "I just hate to put something aside once I started it. It goes against everything I've been taught."

"Unfinished business weighs on the soul and preys on the mind. My Harold used to say that." Ruby blotted up a spilled spot of tea with a napkin. "What picture's in your head?"

Lis hesitated, wondering if she should tell Ruby

about the portrait she was itching to start: Ruby at the table, just as she was now, her face thoughtful and her eyes shining and wise and loving. No, she should hold on to that for now. What if she's unable to bring that face to life, to show the beauty of the woman as it should be shown? Best to let that be for now.

Instead, Lis said, "There was a view from the point—you know, where it looks over toward the cove where Sunset Beach is hidden? I keep seeing that in my mind, the curve of the land, the pines that shelter the beach from view, making it such a mysterious place." She paused. "Carly mentioned the beach the other day. She has a painting in the gallery that was done by Carolina Ellis a long time ago. Carly thinks it's Sunset Beach."

Ruby nodded knowingly. "A good woman, Carolina was. A mite confused at times, but she came into her own, by and by."

"You knew her?"

"Of course. She be a friend of my aunt Helena. Now, I only know what I heard, and I only knew her when she was an older lady."

"Why do you say she was confused?"

"Carolina was always a headstrong young thing, the way I heard tell. Always drawing, painting. Like someone else I know." Ruby smiled. "She knew her mind. Some say she be a bit wild, that she had a secret beau. Didn't know her then, but that's what they say. Then she up and married that James Ellis, and it seemed he had a lot to say 'bout what she did and that sort of thing. Didn't like her painting."

"Why didn't he like her to paint?"

"People say he thought painting was unseemly for a woman to do. People who knew better say it was because it took her mind off him."

"Wow. Talk about selfish, self-centered . . ."

"Like all the Ellis boys, truth be told."

"Who was her secret beau?"

"Well, now, it wouldn't be much of a secret if you knew, would it?" Ruby teased, and got that look on her face, the one that said, *Maybe I know and maybe I don't, but either way, I'll not be speaking of it now.* "That's a story for another time."

"Gigi, I want to hear your stories. All of them. We're going to start tonight, unless you have something better to do."

"What stories you want to hear?"

"I think I want to start at the beginning. I know what my father's side of the family thought about the old times, but I don't remember hearing about it from you."

"Time long past, doesn't mean a whole lot now. I don't recall that my family ever held bad feelings the way Jack did. They called it 'the move,' but they didn't dwell on it."

"No one ever talked about what they had to leave behind in St. Dennis?"

"Not that I heard. Didn't really matter, you think about it. Can't change what was."

"So you've said." Lis mulled it over. "When I went to meet Carly the other day, I drove up Hudson Street. I stopped in front of the Cassidy House, the one my father said belonged to his family. I didn't feel anything at all, looking at that place, except that it's a pretty house and that the people who live there are taking very good care of it." She sipped her coffee and found it cold. "Did your family have a place like that? A house you left behind that was given to someone else to live in?"

"Don't know. Maybe." Ruby shrugged. "Guess no one cared, once they be here."

"That's a much saner way to look at it." A question came to her suddenly. "Gigi, who built the house on the point?"

"There be two houses there."

"Well, both of them, I guess. Do you know?"

"The one that's falling down, well, my grand-daddy lived there as a boy, that be right around the Civil War. Could have been his daddy built it. No way to know now. And the other place, where me and Harold lived? That be my grandfather, for sure. Built it when he and my grandmother married. Lived there until they took over the store from his mother."

"The store's been in our family since it was built, right?"

"That be true. Once they got over here, they looked around to see what needed to be done. Thought a store would be useful, since no one would be going back to St. Dennis to buy what they needed. That little bit in the back there, where my sitting room is, that be the first to be built. Built more on as they could."

"How did they get supplies in? Where did they get the items they sold?"

"Come by boat," Ruby said. "Old Sam—he was the

one who built it up—had a brother over to Cambridge. Loaded up his boat and brought over what was needed. Became a merchant himself, by and by."

"So they really weren't destitute."

Ruby laughed. "Only those who wanted to be. Fair to say that some like to be the victim."

"Like my father."

"He not be the only one, but yes, he enjoyed all that talk somehow. Others saw what was here to see and did the best with it."

"How did your family come to own the point?"

"Never heard tell of that. It just was our place, much as this place is. Does it matter?"

"Not really. I'm just curious about who decided to build out there. That's the best part of the island to me. I would think everyone who came here would have wanted it. So it makes me wonder how your family got their hands on it."

Ruby patted Lis's hands. "Your heart be set on that old place, Lisbeth?"

"I'm afraid so. There's just something about it . . . it's mysterious and romantic, but there's a practical aspect to consider, too, because it would make a great place for me to work."

"Until then—assuming the old place can be put back together—where will you work? Seems to me that it won't be fixed up anytime soon."

"I have to think about an alternative. Alec said he has to look at the roof and some of the beams, the supports, before he can give me any estimates of time or how much it might cost. He thinks the house has termites. Frankly, he wasn't very encouraging. And you're right: Even if it can be repaired, it's not going to be a quick fix."

"Lord knows what other critters been in there all these years. You give thought to what to do if the old place can't be fixed?"

Lis shook her head.

"Maybe you should. Disappointment's always easier to take when you have something else in mind. Sometimes it doesn't pay to hang your hat on just one thing."

"Well, I certainly learned that where Ted was concerned." Lis tried to laugh, but the sound that came out was anything but funny.

"You missing him, Lisbeth?"

Lis shook her head. "You'd think I would, wouldn't you? Since we were together for almost two years? But I don't miss him. I think the fact that it doesn't bother me bothers me, if you know what I mean. It seems like I should care more than I do that he's out of my life. Like I invested a big part of my life and it's just gone, and I don't feel much of anything. Except maybe relief, if you want to know the truth."

"Time will come when you see it for what it was," Ruby said. "Maybe not meant to be part of your life after all."

When Lis didn't reply, Ruby said, "You learn anything from him? From that time?"

"I found out what I don't want." Lis leaned back in her chair. "I don't want someone who hangs over my shoulder all the time. I don't want someone who is dependent on me for everything, from doing his laundry to telling him how smart he is. I don't want someone who looks at my paintings and tells me there should be a little more *green* there and a little less black *there*. I don't want someone who doesn't respect what I do. And I don't want someone who slowly closes me off from everything except himself." She thought about what she'd just said. "Sounds like Carolina wasn't the only one who got involved with the wrong man." She shook her head. "I don't understand why I let that happen. It sure as hell won't happen again."

"Well, then. Learned a lot, I'd say."

Lis sighed. "I guess I did. I hadn't really been able to put my finger on it like that before. It took me awhile to admit that he wasn't right for me." She corrected herself. "We weren't right for each other."

"Long as you know better now, should be easier to see who's right and who's wrong. Could be something right be on its way."

"Maybe. But I'm not really looking for anyone right now."

"Always find what you're not looking for when you're not looking for it."

The door opened and a woman came in holding the hand of a young child.

"Well, now. Look who came to see her old friend Ruby." Ruby pushed herself from the chair with both hands. She turned back to Lis and said, "Go on and take that vase up to your room while I have a visit with my little friend Charlotte. Then you go on over to the beach and take a dip in the bay before it gets too hot to sit out there on the sand. Get a little color, do you good. Don't want to look pasty at that big party Carly be throwing for you."

Lis had been meaning to hit the beach. She knew she needed some color, but seriously, *pasty*?

She carried the vase of flowers up the stairs. As she climbed, she could hear Ruby's voice.

"Now, Hedy, what you and this little peach be after this morning?"

The voices faded as Lis walked down the hall. She placed the flowers on her bedside table, then changed into the one bathing suit she'd brought with her. As she put it on, she realized it had been over a year since she'd worn it. She'd had invitations to friends' pools and beach houses, but Ted hated sand and found most of her friends boring and always said he was allergic to the sun.

"That should have been my first clue," she muttered. "What was I thinking . . . ?"

Hindsight was always twenty-twenty.

She grabbed her sunglasses from her bag and a towel from the linen closet in the hall and slipped her arms into a button-down shirt to wear over her suit until she reached the beach. She went downstairs and took a bottle of water from the cooler.

She was halfway out the door when Ruby stopped her. "Sunscreen," Ruby called to her.

"You have sunscreen?"

"Never go out into the sun without it. Some think I don't look a day over ninety-five. That be the reason." Ruby pointed to her living quarters. "In the cabinet in my bathroom."

"Thanks, Gigi."

Lis retrieved the lotion and passed back through the store.

"For the record, I'd have said ninety. Maybe, on a good day, eighty-eight."

"I think that be more like it." Ruby nodded, a twinkle in her eyes.

Lis headed over the dune, stopping midway to take off her sandals. She paused at the edge of the road, where one car was speeding in her direction. She stepped back onto the sand as it passed in a flash, way too fast for the island.

That same white Cadillac again. At least she thought it was the same one. What were the chances there'd be two different but identical cars this week on Cannonball Island?

She frowned as it rounded the curve near one of the old chapels, wondering if he was headed toward the point again, though she couldn't imagine what business the driver might have there. Alec had said the man was a client of his, and she'd assumed that meant for a boat or some sort of renovation, neither of which explained his presence on the island again today. She'd ask Alec about him when she saw him.

Lis crossed the road, recalling that she had noted once before that there were no speed signs posted, and wondered if drivers took that to mean there were no limits. She'd have to look into that, though she wasn't sure who was responsible for law enforcement on the island, since they had no police department of their own. In the meantime, she had sand and sun and the Chesapeake at her fingertips—and at her toes. She walked onto the hard-packed sand of the beach and tossed her water bottle and towel onto the ground and took off her shirt before slathering on the sunscreen. She picked her way around the dark helmetlike shell of a horseshoe crab as she headed for the water.

The bay was calmest on this side of the island, the waves barely registering as blips as the water rolled onto the beach and brushed against her feet. She knew that a mere three feet from the shore, the sea grass grew thick enough to hide crabs and small fish. She'd walked there as a child once, and never did again. Lis could still feel the slippery fronds of the seaweed as it undulated around her legs, and the sharp pinch of the crab that had grabbed one of her toes when she disturbed it. From that moment on, if it was swimming she was after, Lis headed to the point. For walking along the shore, or for sunbathing, this narrow stretch of beach would do just fine.

She tried to recall the last time she'd brought a towel down and soaked up some sun, but she couldn't say for certain if it had been last summer or the one before. It was a shame, either way. It was quiet here and peaceful, with no crowds to fight for a place to sit. She placed the towel out flat on the sand and folded the shirt for a pillow, then lay down on her back and closed her eyes. She could relax here, clear her mind and let her thoughts drift as the tension lifted from her shoulders and her back. She imagined herself on a raft, floating aimlessly on the bay, no destination, no worries, no deep thoughts to mar the peace of the moment.

For a while, the sun was delightfully warm, but

before too long, she began to feel like she'd been basted and put into an oven. She got up and walked to the water's edge to wet her arms and legs to cool off. Ruby had intimated that she was pale and could use some color in her cheeks, but Lis figured she probably had that covered by now. She'd had enough for that first day out in the sun, sunscreen or no.

Lis gathered her things and started toward the road, but had to stop for another car. She was just thinking how at one time seeing more than one car in the same morning would be notable when the car slowed to pull up next to her, then stopped.

"Hey." Alec leaned over the seat.

"Hey yourself." She walked to the passenger door as the window slid down.

"How's the water?"

"Here?" She pointed back toward the bay. "I don't go in past my ankles along here. Too much seaweed. Reaches out and wraps itself around your legs." She pretended to shiver. "Creepy."

"You could always take a dive off the pier up at the point."

"Not today. Hey, I'm pretty sure I saw your client go by awhile ago. He was headed in that direction."

Alec shrugged. "Who knows? By the way, I looked at the cottage roof this morning. There's no way to salvage it. The entire thing is rotted. I can't believe it hasn't blown off."

"I figured as much. What about the beams? You were worried about them, too."

"I called a termite guy but he can't come out until

the weekend." Alec paused. "Speaking of which, you have a big day coming up next Saturday."

"I do. My debut in St. Dennis as an artist." She tried to make light of it.

"Hey, it's a big deal." He put the car in park. "People take their art real serious around here. Everyone I know is going."

"Seriously?"

"Sure. You're famous. Celebrities buy your paintings and talk about them in TV interviews. Everyone who ever said hello to you back in high school is claiming BFF status now. Last I heard, two TV stations from Baltimore are covering the opening."

"Oh my God." Lis put a hand over her face. "I didn't realize this was going to be such a big production. Carly didn't mention anything to me about media coverage."

"Hey, St. Dennis is a happening place. It's a tourist destination these days. Carly is expecting a packed house. I heard Beck is bringing in a couple of part-time officers from Ballard to help control the traffic and make sure no one parks in front of anyone's driveway."

"Beck? Do you mean Gabriel Beck?" Lis rested her arms on the open window.

Alec nodded. "He's chief of police now."

"Is this the same Gabriel Beck who used to spend most of his time in the principal's office back in the day?"

"The same. Hard to believe, right? He's married and has a sweet baby girl and another one on the way. His wife, Mia, is a former FBI agent, works for the state police now."

"It is hard to believe. My mother always blamed him for leading my brother into trouble." She realized Alec's gaze appeared to have drifted to her cleavage. Pulling the shirt closed and buttoning it, she said, "It's not nice to stare."

"Sorry." He looked like he was about to make a wisecrack but decided better of it. "Wait. How do you know what I'm looking at? I'm wearing superdark glasses." He took them off and held them up to make a point.

"A girl always knows, Alec."

"Sorry, but it's sort of hard not to notice . . . never mind." He slipped the glasses back on. "So I was wondering if you'd like to have dinner with me after the whole thing at the gallery is over."

"I'm going to have Ruby with me."

"She's welcome to join us," he said without hesitation. "I don't mind having your great-grandmother come along on our first date."

Lis laughed. "Well, in that case, sure."

"Great. Do you have any preferences?"

"I don't even know what restaurants are in town, other than Lola's and Captain Walt's and the inn. They've all been around forever."

"I'll choose, then. Unless Ruby wants to."

"She'll be fine, whatever you decide."

"Great. Well, I'll see you before then, I'm sure."

She stepped back from the side of the car and waved as he drove on. It didn't occur to her to wonder what he was doing on the island—again—until she got back to the store.

"Alec wants to take us to dinner after the gallery exhibit," she told Ruby.

"Well, that be nice of him." Ruby was busying herself refilling the sugar jar at the coffee station.

"Ummm." Lis disposed of her empty water bottle. "Is he always on the island so much? I don't remember that he was around so much the other times I've been here."

"Guess he has business 'sides me. Heard he was helping Abby's boy fix their garage door."

"I guess." That would explain it, of course, but still, something felt off to Lis.

"I'm thinking about lunch right now." Ruby finished filling the sugar jar and opened a new box of tea bags. "You have anything in mind?"

"I'll go see what we have." Lis started to the back of the store. "Gigi, how do you get groceries?"

"From the grocery store in town. How else?"

"How do you get there?"

"I don't get there. I make a list, and when I go over to visit with Gracie at the inn, she gives my list to someone to go to the store for me. Andrew down to the market sends me a bill every month and I pay it."

"That's a nice arrangement."

"It is. Been doing it that way for a long time now." Ruby looked across the counter at Lis. "Funny you're just asking now."

"It didn't occur to me until now."

"That's just another way of saying what I said."

Ouch. Another reminder that Lis has been MIA for too long.

"I think I'll just go into the back and fix lunch now."

"Be a good time to do just that," Ruby murmured.

RUBY CLOSED UP the store around eight and turned off the lights.

"Can we sit and talk now?" Lis asked. "I'd like to record you talking about the island and how your family came here."

"You know all that already," Ruby reminded her.

"I don't have it on record in your voice." Lis set her phone to record and placed it on the table between them.

"All right, then." Ruby rested her head against the back of her favorite chair in her sitting room. "Where you want me to start?"

"Start where you know."

"Well, that would be the War of 1812. Everyone taking sides. Mind, now, America be new then. Some stood with them, some with the British. My folks be English, through and through. Thought that England going to win that war and we be under the crown again. Thought they be cutting their losses by standing with the British." She smiled wryly. "We know how that worked out. People in town didn't take kindly to those folks who were helping their enemies, so they run them out of town. Right across the river where it's shallow there, right around where the bridge is now. Took what they could carry, clothes on their backs. Ended up here. You know the rest."

"How'd they survive? There were no houses here, right?"

"Built their own. Some had kin in Baltimore or Virginia who brought in wood, supplies, things they needed here on the island. It all worked out." Ruby closed her eyes. "Things always work out . . ."

"Oh, I forgot to tell you. Wait right here." Lis got up and ran up the steps to her room, grabbed the wooden box, and was back downstairs in a flash.

"I found this in one of those cubbyholes upstairs in the cottage." Lis placed the box on the table in front of Ruby.

"Well, well." Ruby's smile lit her face. "I wondered what happened to that."

She picked it up and studied the lid, one finger tracing the painted figures.

"Where did it come from? Was it yours?"

"Came from my great-aunt Louisa. Said her mama brought it with her when she came from Fauldhouse. That be a little place outside Edinburgh."

"That's in Scotland."

Ruby nodded. "That be right."

"I thought you said we were English."

"We were. Louisa's daddy was from Kingsbury— that be right around London."

"So Louisa's mother brought this with her. Did she give it to you?"

"On my fifteenth birthday. It had a little silk handkerchief inside. Don't know whatever happened to that. Be long gone now, I guess."

"Open it. Look at what's inside."

Ruby lifted the lid, then smiled. "Jacks and a ball. My girls loved to play."

"There's a piece of paper in there. Take a look."

Ruby lifted the paper from the bottom of the box and unfolded it. After she read silently, her smile broadened.

"Sarah and that Barden girl used to play together for hours. Looks like Ceely got the best of her that day." She closed the lid and held the box in both hands. After a moment, she handed it to Lis. "This be yours now."

"Oh no, Gigi. It belonged to you."

"Once upon a time, that be so. I be fine without it all these years." She reached for Lis's hand. "Something to keep your wishes in. That's what Aunt Louisa told me when she gave it to me."

"I will treasure it then, and thank you."

"You be most welcome."

"Gigi, I was thinking that I hardly know anything about your children. You had two sons, right?"

Ruby nodded. "Harold Junior and Simon. Both went to war over to France. Only Simon came back. Left the island in 1945 to go to school up north. Died in a train crash outside of Boston."

"And your daughters? You had three others besides my grandmother."

"Four daughters not counting the one I lost when she was a wee one. Right smart and pretty, all four of them. Lisbeth—you were named for her, like she be named for my grandmother—she married a boy from Virginia, moved down that way. Mary Cathrine, she married a local boy, but after the war they moved to Baltimore. Ann taught here on the island till she got the polio. Died when she wasn't but twenty-two. All gone now. I birthed eight babies. Buried two before they were grown, six lived to grow up. Not one of them left now."

They sat in silence for a while. Finally, Ruby said, "It's a sad day when a mother buries her child."

Lis watched a tear form in the corner of each of Ruby's eyes, but neither fell.

"What about your sisters and brothers? I don't know anything about them."

"Stories for another day, Lisbeth Jane. I be tired now. Think I'll head to my room."

"Can I get you anything, Ruby? Another cup of tea . . ."

"Thank you, but I be done for the night. You turn off these lights before you go up, hear?"

"I will." Lis watched Ruby cross the floor toward the door to her living quarters, her feet moving slowly, her back uncharacteristically hunched.

"Gigi, I'm sorry," Lis called to her.

"What you sorry for?" Ruby called back but did not turn around.

"For making you think about your children."

"I think about them every day, child. Whether I talk about them or not. Always be with me, Lisbeth."

Ruby continued to her sitting room, then closed the door quietly behind her. At the table, Lis picked up the wooden box, turned off all the lights in the store, and went up to bed.

LIS ROSE EARLY the next morning, and before she went downstairs to the store, she walked to the

other end of the hall and opened the last door. Once
Ruby and Harold's bedroom, it was now totally
empty, the furniture all having been moved downstairs to Ruby's new living quarters. Lis opened the
drapes on one side of the room and pulled up the
shades, leaned on the wide windowsill, and gazed
at the view. From here she could see the dunes and
the bay, and in the distance, the green of the point.
There were windows on two sides and plenty of
light. She could work well here if need be, if Ruby
okayed it, and there was no reason she wouldn't
that Lis could think of. There was still another bedroom up here for Owen, should he return anytime
soon.

Last night she'd tossed and turned in her sleep,
and she recognized it as the restlessness she always
felt when she'd gone too long without working. It
had been almost a week since she'd held a brush in
her hands, or felt the satisfaction of having mixed
the exact shade she was looking for. She'd only
planned on staying on the island until the reception.
She'd come early to spend some time with Ruby, but
deep inside, she knew that she'd needed a change of
scenery. She'd been at loose ends since Ted moved
out, not because she missed him, but because she
felt out of place. After five years in the same apartment, two of those years with him, it felt stifling
and she felt closed in, as if she no longer belonged
there. Even the work she'd tried to do there didn't,
well, didn't work. She wasn't satisfied with anything
she'd done over the past three months, and hadn't
finished anything new. For the first time since she

decided to be a working artist, she felt self-doubt creeping in.

Everything felt different since she arrived on the island, and she wasn't sure what that meant in the long run. Things seemed fresher, her ideas more vibrant. Had she gotten into such a rut that any change would seem epic? She thought about the works she'd left unfinished back in her apartment. Not one of them raised enthusiasm or that sense of joy she had when she was into her work and knew it was good.

The view out the window where she stood raised her pulse rate, just as the view from the pier on the point had made her heart beat faster and her plans to paint a portrait of Ruby excited her. The thought of working in the cottage—that made her soul sing.

"*Know where you belong,*" Ruby always said.

Well, maybe just for a while, maybe for right now, she belonged here. There was so much for her to do that felt meaningful. Ruby's stories. The cottage. The joy that swept over her when she stood on the point and looked out at the bay. And Ruby wasn't getting any younger.

And then there was Alec.

"*Unfinished business weighs on the soul and preys on the mind,*" Ruby had said.

Alec definitely felt like unfinished business.

Maybe it was time to return to New Jersey, gather her supplies, and bring them back to the island. She itched to work and she hated to waste time, especially when scenes were forming in her head and impatient to take form, when Ruby's beautiful face was waiting to be memorialized.

In her mind, she was already packing up what she'd bring back, which palettes and papers and brushes. Her sketchbook. Antsy to get started, she headed for the stairs to share her plans with Ruby.

Chapter Nine

Lis gathered the mail that had spilled from her mailbox and piled on the floor in the vestibule outside her apartment and made a mental note to have her mail forwarded to Ruby's store for a while, how long she still wasn't sure. She turned the key in her door and went inside. It was so quiet and felt so empty that she was tempted to tiptoe. The air was still and stuffy, and the first thing she did was turn on the air-conditioning.

She checked her plants on the windowsill and found them in need of a good drink. Clara across the hall had offered to keep an eye on them, but apparently her idea of plant sitting and Lis's were not quite the same. Lis put down everything she carried—her bag, an overnight, the mail—and went into the kitchen. She filled a glass with water and poured generous amounts into the dry pots.

Her studio was in the small back room and it was there she went next. The door was closed, and inside everything was just as she'd left it. She should have felt better about being there, surrounded by all she valued most. Instead, she felt more like a visitor, one who looked upon the room and all it held with a curious eye. How could things change so quickly in a week? How had she left here so recently, only to return feeling like a stranger looking into the details of someone else's life?

If the truth were to be told, the feeling of not belonging, of not feeling at home, began when she first started to realize that she and Ted were a huge mistake. It had grown from that moment until they parted, and had only intensified since. She'd been almost relieved to have received the invitation to exhibit her works in St. Dennis. She'd been wanting to escape, but hadn't been willing to admit it to herself until she had a reason to leave that had nothing to do with Ted.

The paintings stacked against the wall were all works in progress that she'd been unable to finish. The inspiration had been there once, but then . . . wasn't. She knelt down and pushed her hair behind her ears and went through them one by one. Nothing spoke to her. Nothing said, "Finish me. Finish me now!" Scenes from a park in winter, from a bridge, from a busy street corner in the city—all stood waiting for the brushstrokes that would complete their story, but looking at them now, Lis couldn't recall what those stories were. She debated if she should take them with her back to the island, but decided against it. Their straight lines and grays and blacks and muted greens would look out of place there, where the colors were the clearest blue of a cloudless

June sky and the deeper blue of the bay, the golds of the sand and the crayon box of colors that reflected the flowers that grew everywhere on Cannonball Island. With some reservation, she left them where they were.

She packed up what she thought she'd need and stacked her supplies near the front door, then went into her bedroom. Shorts and T-shirts were placed in piles on the bed, followed by several long tees to sleep in. She opened the closet and stared at the contents. She'd taken a sundress with her to the island for the reception, but had since decided she needed something special, dressier, something pretty and feminine. But the selection was meager, and almost all black except for a little brown number that she'd bought on sale two years ago and never wore because Ted said it made her skin look sallow, and she'd had to admit he'd been right about that. She pulled out one short black sleeveless sheath and held it up. Maybe. Shoes? Something strappy and high. She'd had a pair she bought last summer. After searching through one box after another, she remembered she'd loaned them to her friend Pam for a wedding she was going to. Lis found her phone in the bottom of her bag and pulled up Pam's number, then hit the call icon.

"Hello?" A voice that sounded oddly like Ted's picked up the call.

"This is Lis Parker. I was calling Pam?" she said uncertainly.

"Oh. Lis. How are you?" It *was* Ted. An awkward, uneasy Ted who most certainly wished he hadn't answered.

Ted and Pam? Pam and Ted? Seriously?

When had that happened?

"I . . . I'm good, Ted. You?" For a moment, Lis's mind went numb.

"Good. Listen, Pam's in the shower. Can I have her call you back?" Smoothly said, as if Lis were any other friend of Pam's who might have called.

"Ummm . . . no, that's okay. I'll catch up with her another time."

"Okay, well, nice talking to you."

The shock had worn off slowly, but once it did, Lis couldn't just fade away.

"Wait. Ted. You and Pam . . . ?"

"Ah . . . yeah."

"I don't know what to say. Seriously? You're with Pam now?" Lis fought to keep the anger she felt from seeping into her voice lest he think it mattered to her.

"Ah . . . yeah. We're . . . ah, we're together."

Did it matter to her?

"I thought you said she was fat and that her voice gave you a headache." She couldn't stop herself.

Ted laughed uneasily.

"And you know, she always said you sweated too much and bored her to death. Sounds like you guys have found a way to get past all that."

He cleared his throat. "Lis . . ."

"Well, it was nice chatting. Be sure to tell Pammie I called."

Lis disconnected the call feeling just a tiny bit guilty for having been so petty, but really. Ted and Pam?

I never, never would have guessed the two of them would hook up, that I could be replaced so quickly in his life, and by someone who professed to be my friend. And do I care, really? Aside from my feelings being singed, do I really care? Is what I'm feeling anger or relief?

A little of both, maybe. But then again, it isn't as if I haven't already turned my gaze elsewhere.

Yeah, but Alec and Ted weren't besties.

Apparently, neither were Pam and I.

She wrote off the shoes—if Pam had been wearing them with Ted, Lis would set fire to them before she would ever put them on her feet again. Pam was welcome to her shoes and her ex.

But still. Ted and Pam? Her old yoga buddy Pam who couldn't keep a job to save her butt and who lived in a sparsely furnished apartment in Hoboken the size of a fishbowl? How was Ted coping with that? He'd thought Lis's two-bedroom flat was too small.

Not my problem, Lis told herself as she closed the closet door. *Not anymore.* She expected to feel worse than she did at that moment. After all, she and Ted had been together—had started planning a wedding . . .

No, they hadn't, she reminded herself. They should have been planning a wedding, but she was too busy to look for a dress or think about venues or flowers or any of the other things brides were supposed to be happily responsible for. The few times Ted had suggested they start thinking about where the ceremony should be, or when, she'd had an excuse to put him off.

Pam, on the other hand, looked at every first date

as a potential lifetime commitment, would tell anyone who'd listen that her goal was to find a husband before she turned thirty-five. If Lis remembered correctly, Pam's birthday was in October. She just might make it.

Lis sat on the edge of the bed and tried to look at the situation objectively. Did she miss Ted? No. Did she want him back? Good Lord, no. Would she miss Pam's friendship? She mulled that over for a moment or two. Not really.

"All righty, then." Lis slapped her hands on her thighs, then stood and stretched. Onward.

She'd take the black dress and a pair of plain black heels, but she wasn't sold on either. There was that cute little boutique in St. Dennis, though. Maybe she'd find something there. If she couldn't find something different, her not-so-fashionable black dress and generic black heels would have to do. She packed them into a large canvas bag. She stuffed underwear and a pair of yoga pants in next to the dress, then carried the bag into the living room.

She and Ted had picked out the furniture—the sofa, two chairs, and several tables—when he first moved in with her. Or more accurately, they'd gone to pick out furniture together, but once they hit the store, it was Ted all the way. He'd shot down her choice of a small cozy sectional that she could see piled high with pretty pillows and went in search of black leather. She wouldn't have given the black leather sofa with its modern straight lines a second glance, but Ted was into watching TV and movies. In the end, she'd agreed because she knew she'd never sit on it to watch television. When she had downtime, Lis preferred a good book to the shows Ted enjoyed, and she had a cushy chair in a corner of the bedroom for reading. Until then, she'd only had a desk and an antique round oak table and four chairs next to the bay window. Because she spent most of her time in her studio, she hadn't felt the need to furnish the front room before Ted moved in. Once he had, her things had been pushed aside to make room for his, the table and chairs being relegated to a corner. One of the first things Lis did after Ted moved out was to move her table and chairs back to the bay window.

She should probably email Ted and tell him to pick up the sofa and move it to Pam's apartment. Not that it would fit. She toyed with the idea of calling a moving company and having it delivered to Pam's apartment. Let her figure out what to do with the annoying thing. Both of them.

On the other hand, did she really want to pay to have Ted's things moved for him? Not really.

If Lis were to do the room over on her own, she'd do it in deep blues with touches of gray and gold. Maybe she'd do just that. Maybe now, on her own again, she'd spend less time in the studio and give herself more of a life. She'd spent so much time trying to convince Ted and everyone else she knew—including herself—that she was a serious artist that she rarely gave herself downtime. Now that she had nothing to prove, that she finally had acknowledged that she was not only good, but *damned* good, maybe she could give herself a break.

Then again, maybe the biggest break she could give herself would be to move to another apartment.

Of course, she could stay for as long as she liked with Ruby. The island had always given her a boost. Why had she stayed away so long? It would be easy to blame it on Ted, but that wouldn't be fair. She could have gone on her own to Cannonball Island. She wasn't sure why she never did.

There was nothing in the refrigerator that didn't have a layer of white fuzz growing on it. She tossed everything, considered calling for her favorite takeout, then grabbed her bag and left the apartment. Two blocks down, Curcio's served the best Italian in North Jersey. Just thinking about Lena's gnocchi made Lis's mouth water.

Cool air rushed out as she opened the door to the storefront restaurant. She took off her sunglasses and eased them to the top of her head. There were twenty tables, seven of which were occupied. She waited at the hostess station to be seated.

"Hey, girl. Where've you been?" Marianne Curcio, the owner's daughter, greeted her with a smile.

"Visiting family in Maryland," Lis replied.

"Looks like you got a little color in your cheeks, on your arms. Looks good. Relatives must live near the ocean?" Marianne picked up a menu from the desk.

"Chesapeake Bay." Lis grinned. "Better than the ocean."

"Nothin's better than the ocean." Marianne gestured for Lis to follow her to a table on the side of the room.

Out of habit, Lis glanced at the table in the front window. *Their* table, where she—she and Ted—had spent so many nights with a bottle of really good red and a plate of whatever Lena's specialty was that day.

"No, you're not sitting there." Marianne dropped the menu on the table she'd selected for Lis. "Not anymore."

"Oh, you heard . . . ?" Lis pulled out a chair and sat.

Marianne nodded. "Yeah, I heard. Straight from the horse's mouth." Marianne leaned over the other chair at Lis's table. "You know that ass had the nerve to come in here with that skank—"

"It's okay, Mare. I know. My ex-friend and former yoga companion Pam."

Marianne rolled her eyes. "Had the nerve to sit at that table with her. Seriously? After it was your spot for what, two years? Believe me, they got the worst service anyone ever had in this establishment. My mother didn't even want to cook for them."

"Mare, it's okay. I don't care." As soon as the words were out of her mouth, she knew they were true. Happily, gloriously true. "It isn't worth you losing customers over."

"Sorry, some things are sacred. *The table* is sacred. You don't bring the new girl to the table you shared with your ex. It's a violation."

Lis laughed, though she knew Marianne was serious.

"So what can I get you?"

"What are the specials?"

Marianne went over the menu and Lis settled on mushroom gnocchi in brown butter sauce and a salad. Along with the salad, Marianne's mother brought Lis a glass of wine.

"My daughter says you're fine," Lena said as she placed the glass in front of Lis.

"I am, thank you."

"I can see in your eyes that it's true." Lena rubbed Lis's shoulders for a moment. "Good for you. You'll find someone better."

Lis could have added, *I already have.*

She devoured the gnocchi and passed on dessert, but Lena insisted on packing up a generous piece of tiramisu for Lis to take with her.

"So you're back and you'll be around the neighborhood, right? We missed you this past week," Marianne told her.

"Thank you. I appreciate that. But I'm not sure of my long-term plans. I want to spend some time with my great-grandmother in Maryland. She's one hundred years old, and she—"

"One hundred! God bless her. Of course you should spend some time with her while you can. Who knows how much longer?"

"Oh, she's not going anywhere anytime soon. She is the toughest, strongest person I know. I just want to spend some time there, where I grew up."

"Well, don't be a stranger, right?" Marianne gave Lis a hug, handed her the bag with the tiramisu, and walked her to the door, where she greeted a family coming in and patted Lis on the back as a good night.

Lis walked back to the apartment, swinging the bag and wondering how long before she'd break down and eat that mountain of Lena's tiramisu, which in this neighborhood was as legendary as her pasta.

Darkness had begun to settle in and she flicked on the lamp on the desk near the front door. When she first moved to the apartment, she'd placed the desk on the wall near the kitchen where she'd see it every time she came into the apartment. It was mission-style tiger oak, and the first real piece of furniture Lis had ever bought for herself. She'd found it in a tiny garage three towns away when she first moved from the city and she was looking for a shop that sold art supplies. The desk had been piled high with other objects that were being sold that day, and it was a miracle she'd even seen it. She'd wanted it so badly that she hadn't even tried to negotiate the price. She just handed over the cash and asked the seller to help her load it into her car.

Ted had moved it because it "crowded" his TV stand.

The TV and its stand having left with Ted, Lis moved the desk back to the space it had originally occupied.

"You look so much better there," she told the lamp as she plugged it in and placed it back on its corner of the desk.

She sat at the oak table in the chair closest to the front window and listened to the sounds of the street from below. From somewhere across town she heard the shriek of a siren. While not in the city, the apartment was located in a town with a population ten times that of St. Dennis and the island combined. Over the last several nights at Ruby's, she'd grown used to the quiet. Here it seemed she heard every car that passed and every voice that called from one side of the street to the other. She'd picked the apartment for its size, the number of windows and the amount of light they let in, and its proximity to New York. It was still spacious and bright, but it no longer suited. She felt the remnants of the relationship that had soured, and she couldn't not hear the words that had been spoken here. It was, she thought, much like that accident on the highway you couldn't unsee.

But she was lucky. She could go to the island and put the bad feelings behind her. She could stay until she figured out where she belonged. Once Ruby's cottage was ready, she could divide her time between there and here as the spirit moved her.

Here, she decided, wouldn't be this apartment. There were too many bad memories, too many bad decisions made here, and the negative vibes had choked out her creativity. She couldn't work here: She'd tried since Ted left, but nothing seemed to work. It was time for her to make changes in her life. She'd send Ted an email and tell him to remove whatever he wanted from the apartment by the end of the month or she'd have it sold. She'd take with her to the island only those things that were important to her, put in storage the things she couldn't bring. First thing in the morning, she'd call the landlord and give notice that she'd be moving out. She'd find a place to store her chair from the bedroom, her oak table and chairs from the living room, and her desk. Ted was welcome to everything else—he'd selected most of it, anyway. She sent Ted the email, then called Ruby to tell her she'd be here for another day or two to tie up some loose ends.

The realization that she'd taken control of her life again energized her, and for the first time in a long time, Lis felt free.

ALEC SAT IN the front seat of the Jeep, the driver's door open, and waited for Brian Deiter and Cass Logan, his architect, to arrive. He'd asked them to meet him at the Mullan place with the hopes of selling Brian on the idea of smaller houses placed around the island rather than one big concentration of homes that screamed new development. He was hoping that once the architect saw the island and had a chance to see what was available for reuse, Cass would be intrigued enough by the challenge to agree with him. They'd never met, but he'd spoken with her on the phone, and she hadn't sounded sold on the idea, but he thought perhaps if she saw the island, saw with her own eyes what he'd tried to describe, she'd see the potential in his idea.

They were fifteen minutes late, and Alec was beginning to wonder if perhaps Brian had decided to skip the meeting and just go ahead with his plans when the white Cadillac pulled up behind the Jeep.

"Sorry we're late," Brian told him. "There was an accident on Route 50." Without taking a breath, he pointed to the leggy blond woman who accompanied him. "Cass, meet Alec Jansen. Alec, Cass Logan. Now, where are these houses you think I should buy? This it?"

The architect was young and beautiful, not at all

what Alec had expected. After polite greetings, they followed along behind Brian as he walked to the deserted house.

"This is one of the houses, yes. The house next door, and the one behind are also available, and I think you'll see—" Alec was cut off by the impatient developer.

"Key?" Brian held out his hand.

"I have it." Alec passed him and unlocked the front door. Tommy Mullan had been more than happy to loan him the key when Alec told him he wanted to show the property to the potential buyer.

"Small," Brian observed. "Way too small. Who'd want to live in a place this small? This is what you think I should buy and try to make something out of? Maybe I called the wrong guy."

"The idea wasn't to renovate it, Brian," Alec explained patiently. "The idea was to buy the lot— which is a good size—don't let the size of the house fool you—and take down the house—"

"Now you're talking." Brian nodded and went to the nearest window. "Yeah, I can see the bay from here. A nice big, two-, maybe three-story place . . ."

"Ah, no," Alec told him. "No one will sell you so much as an inch of ground here if they thought for one minute you were going to build something like that. For one thing, it would block the view of the bay for everyone who lives on the back of the island. For another, it wouldn't fit in architecturally." He glanced at Cass, hoping for her agreement, but she said nothing. "For another, houses that big would create ecological nightmares. We already discussed that, Brian. I thought you understood you'd be limited in what you can do here."

"I don't like restrictions." Brian turned from the window. "I don't like being told what I can and cannot build."

"It's up to you how you want this to proceed. You can try to get variances and you can try to deal with the EPA and the state agencies. It will cost you a bundle and you won't win," Alec reminded him. Damn, but he hated dealing with hardheaded clients who wanted what they wanted and didn't want to hear the truth. If Brian thought that anything had changed since the last time they had this conversation, he was wrong.

"You think anyone would buy this place? Even fixed up?" Brian stood with his hands on his hips.

"No, but I think if Cass were to design something that maintained the architectural integrity of the historic structures, and utilized some of the original features of the old places within the new, I think you'd have people falling over themselves to buy one."

Brian glanced at Cass and said, "Well?"

She knelt and licked a finger to wet it, then rubbed away dirt on the floor. "Nice hardwood. It does have some scrapes and scars, but that adds character." She inspected the wainscot along one kitchen wall but said nothing.

In the living room, Cass took a long look at the fireplace. "The brick is in great shape." She turned to Alec. "Local?"

"Made in St. Dennis at the old brickworks," he told her.

She went from room to room, noting the placement of archways and windows.

"The doors are in remarkably good condition," she pointed out.

When she completed her second tour of the house, she said, "I see what Alec is saying, and I think his idea has merit. I'd like to take some time to study the exteriors of this and the one next door. Then, if I could have a tour of the island . . ."

"Absolutely." Alec led them outside and locked the door behind them.

"You think this is a good idea, Cass? You really do?" Brian was on her heels with every step.

"I think it could be brilliant, if it's done right." She kept walking. "I haven't heard of anyone else doing something like what Alec is proposing."

She walked ahead of him and looked at the house from different angles, stopping several times to take photos with her phone. When she was finished, she said, "I'd like that tour of the island now."

"I'll drive." Alec pointed to the Jeep.

Brian still looked annoyed, but he got into the car without comment.

With Alec at the wheel, the tour took forty minutes. Careful to point out all the original structures, he wanted to make sure that the architect saw exactly what he wanted her to see. When they passed Ruby's, Cass asked, "Is that really a general store like the sign says? Like, a real old-fashioned general store?"

Alec nodded. "It's been there for well over a hundred years. The woman who owns it is that old herself. Which means the store has been there since the 1800s, because she told me once that her parents used to run it, and their parents before them."

"Amazing," Cass said.

"You mean to tell me that an old lady owns that prime piece of real estate?" Brian leaned out the window to take a better look.

Alec laughed. "Brian, that 'old lady' is one of the sharpest people I've ever known." He wanted to add that Ruby Carter could chew up the likes of Brian Deiter and spit him out, but Brian was, after all, a client.

"That could be a great selling point," Cass told Brian. "Here you have this unspoiled island, complete with an old-time general store. The ambience alone will pay off in the long run."

"You really believe that?" Brian asked her again.

"I really do. Let me work on some ideas."

Alec had returned to the Mullan property and parked the car. Cass got out first and took a few more photos with her phone.

"Having seen the rest of the island, I agree with Alec that we shouldn't block the view. I think a one-story design would be best," she told Brian, who didn't look happy.

"You didn't see the point," Brian told her.

"The point is not for sale," Alec hastened to tell him.

"You know that for a fact? You asked the owner?"

Alec nodded.

"You have no idea what kind of money I could offer," Brian persisted.

"It's not for sale, Brian."

"Everything's for sale at the right price, buddy." Brian got into the Cadillac and slammed the door. He rolled down the window. "Cassie, let's go."

"One minute, Dad," she called back. She took one more shot, then walked past Alec on her way to the white car, an amused smile on her face. "Didn't see that coming, did you?"

Alec laughed and shook his head. "I did not."

"You're lucky you got me today and not one of his lackeys," she told him. "I think what you have in mind to do here is wonderful. I love the concept. I want to be part of it. It's fresh and exciting and my father would be a fool to ignore your vision, and make no mistake, my father didn't get rich by being a fool. But anyone else who might have come out here today would have agreed with him, that bigger is better, because that's what he wanted to hear. They'd have convinced him that it would be a good idea to throw around as much money as possible and take on the state to get around whatever regulations stood in his way."

"So you think he's coming around?" Alec asked.

"He already has. He doesn't especially like it, but he's on board." She punched his arm playfully before walking away. "Like I said, today you got lucky."

Alec stood next to the Jeep and watched the Cadillac drive off, stopping briefly in front of the grassy section that marked the beginning of the point. Moments later, the white car sped off. He got behind the wheel and headed for the store, where he'd have a chat with Ruby.

He hadn't been completely honest with Brian. Ruby hadn't come right out and said she wasn't interested in selling the point, but he was 100 percent certain that as long as Lis had eyes for that cottage, no force on earth could talk Ruby into selling it. But his conscience would nag him until he told her just how much those prime twenty-two acres could bring, and how badly Deiter wanted them. Sometimes, even when you knew the answer, you had to go ahead and ask the question.

Chapter Ten

With the most-pressing of her apartment-related to-dos crossed off her list, Lis packed her car and headed south. Traffic was miserable and due to an accident, she sat on the New Jersey turnpike at Exit 8 for almost fifty minutes before the traffic began to move. Once she was over the Delaware Memorial Bridge, cars moved at a steady clip and she made it to St. Dennis by late afternoon. But here, too, tourists snagged Charles Street, cars and pedestrians both, and after crawling along for several minutes, she found herself stopped in front of Bling, the upscale boutique in the center of town.

She'd been wanting to check it out, and she decided now was as good a time as any. She put on her turn signal and made a right onto Kelly's Point Road and into the municipal parking lot.

Even Bling was crowded, with customers going through the racks of clothing and accessories. Behind the counter, a pretty dark-haired woman was ringing up a sale. In search of the dress section, Lis shimmied past two women who were blocking the aisle as they went through the bags on display. The chatter in the store wasn't loud, but it was lively and enthusiastic.

Lis found the dresses near the back of the store. She thumbed through the hangers in her size range, and while she found several things she liked, nothing gave her that zing she was looking for.

"Looking for anything in particular?" a woman's voice from behind asked.

"I was hoping to find something pretty, something special. Something that . . ." Lis wasn't sure what she wanted.

"Something that could knock the socks off a special guy, maybe?"

Lis turned around and met the eyes of the pretty dark-haired woman she'd seen at the front counter when she came in.

"Well, now that you mention it . . . yes. Something like that." Lis nodded.

"This is pretty. And this shade of green matches your eyes perfectly." The saleswoman reached past Lis to pull out a hanger holding a chiffon dress. When Lis didn't reply, the woman said, "Too dressy?"

"I think maybe. It's beautiful, but I think I want something more . . ."

"More sexy? More of a statement?"

"Yes. More of a statement."

"Something came in this morning that I think might be what you have in mind." She disappeared into the back and returned holding a dress bag, which she hooked onto the rack and unzipped.

"Does this make the statement that you want?"

She held up a dress of water-colored silk. It was sleeveless with a V neck and was light as a feather.

Lis nodded. "That could be it, yes. May I try it on?"

"Of course. The dressing rooms are on the right just inside the back room." The woman handed Lis the dress. "I'm Vanessa, by the way."

"Thanks, Vanessa." Lis stepped into the dressing room and changed. The dress floated like a cloud over her shoulders and her hips, and once zipped in the back, it fit like a dream. Lis didn't look at the price tag. She didn't care what it cost. The dress was hers.

"How are you doing in there?" Vanessa asked.

"It's perfect." Lis stepped out of the dressing room.

"Wow, it is that. Turn," Vanessa said, and made a twirling gesture with her index finger. "The fit couldn't be better. It's nicely fitted where it should be without being too tight. It's lovely on you. It's elegant, classy . . ."

"Done." Lis laughed. "I'll take it."

"Excellent." Vanessa beamed. "Easiest sale I made all day."

Lis removed the dress carefully—somewhat reluctantly because she loved the way it looked on her—and took it to the front counter, where Vanessa was waiting on another customer. Lis fell in line and took the opportunity to look at the jewelry under the glass.

"This was great on you, Brooke," Vanessa was saying to the customer who'd just handed over her credit card. "Is this for the rehearsal dinner?"

"No, I'm covered there. This is for the reception at

the art gallery tomorrow night," the woman replied. "You're going, right?"

"Of course. Everyone's going," Vanessa said.

"Even Jesse," the customer told her. "He said the artist is the great-granddaughter of one of his clients, so he wanted to go."

"I heard the artist is from around here," Vanessa continued. "Did you know her?"

"I knew her brother, Owen. Adorable—and really a nice guy back then, if a bit of a player, but I haven't seen him in years. I heard her work was really good, so I'm looking forward to it."

Vanessa completed the transaction and returned the credit card, then handed over the bag holding the purchases. "So I guess we'll see you tomorrow, Brooke."

Brooke? Lis frowned. Brooke Madison? The town mean girl? Lis had been too many years behind her in school to have known her, but her meanness was the stuff of legends, though she hadn't sounded so mean just then. Lis smiled to herself. She'd never heard her brother described as adorable before. A player, yes. Adorable, no.

"Did you need anything else?" Vanessa turned her attention to Lis.

"No, I think I'm— Oh! Shoes!" Lis cringed at the thought of wearing the gorgeous new dress with her old black heels. "Where can I buy shoes?"

"If you're looking for shoes to wear with this pretty little number, try right over there." Vanessa pointed to the left side of the shop. "I don't have a huge selection, but I do have some gorgeous high strappy sandals to wear with something like this." She reached for the dress. "I'll hold this here for you if you want to look."

"I do." Lis made a beeline for the shoe section. It took her all of a minute to zero in on the exact pair. She took the display shoe back to the counter and asked Vanessa hopefully, "Size seven and a half?"

Vanessa nodded. "I'm pretty sure." She went into the back room and came back with two boxes in hand. "I have them in black and in a soft gray."

Lis tried on the gray. "Perfect."

"I love them. High enough to say it without screaming it, if you know what I mean," Vanessa said.

"My thoughts exactly."

While Vanessa wrapped Lis's dress and shoes, she chatted. "So what's the occasion?"

"Big night tomorrow night," was all Lis said.

"Lucky guy." Vanessa smiled.

"Maybe." Lis paid in cash and gathered up her bags. "Thanks. I'm glad I stopped in."

"Me, too. Come by again if you're in town."

"I'll do that. I'll be around for a while."

Lis all but whistled on her way back to her car. She had, in fact, wanted to knock the socks off Alec Jansen. She just hadn't been aware of it until she put on that silk dress and zipped it up.

She was still in a happy frame of mind when she reached the island, but she frowned when she pulled around to the side of the store to park her car. An unfamiliar SUV, the color of dried mud, occupied the space she'd been using and had come to think of as hers. Gathering the bag she'd packed in the apartment and the one containing her new purchases, Lis went in through the back door.

"Gigi?" she called out.

When there was no answer, she dropped what she was carrying and went into the store. She found Ruby deep in conversation with a man whose back was to Lis.

"Gigi, I'm back," Lis told her.

"'Bout time." Lis's brother, Owen, turned and stood at the same time. "How long did it take you to just pack up a few things?"

"Not as long as it took you to get your ass back to the island." Lis threw her arms around his neck and hugged him. "Where the hell have you been?"

She stood back and took a good, long look. Owen was deeply tanned, his dark hair showing some natural highlighting from the sun he'd obviously spent a lot of time in.

"Been around. Alaska. Australia. Costa Rica. New Orleans." Owen gave her one last squeeze, then let her go.

"Doing what?"

"Having adventures." He pulled out a chair for Lis and she sat.

"Did you know he was coming today?" Lis asked Ruby.

"Not till he walked in that door, big and bold. Near gave me a heart attack. For a minute, I thought he be my brother John, come back from the dead." Ruby's hand fluttered over her heart. "Spittin' image, I swear."

"Was this your brother John the pirate?" Lis asked.

"No pirates on my side," Ruby all but harrumphed. "Now, on my Harold's side, there was tell of some shady sailors."

"That's you, Owen. The shady sailor," Lis teased.

"Speaking of sailors, where's Uncle Eb's boat?" Owen asked.

"Down to Ellison's boatyard, where it belongs," Ruby told him.

Owen raised a questioning brow. "What's it doing down there?"

"Gigi traded the boat to Alec Jansen in return for work he did for her," Lis explained.

"What kind of work was worth a skipjack?" Owen's eyes, green like his sister's, narrowed with suspicion.

"The lot of you," Ruby exclaimed. "Peas in a pod. One more suspicious than the other. You, Owen, get on up and I'll show you what kind of work be worth a skipjack." She pointed to Lis. "You can wait out here, take care of anyone who stops by."

Lis watched in amusement as Ruby herded her big, strapping brother into the living quarters.

She wandered around the store, stopping to straighten a shelf here and there. She took her bag and her new dress and shoes upstairs to hang in her closet, then came back down and hopped up onto the wooden counter to wait for Owen and Ruby to make their way back. She had no doubt that her brother would be as impressed as she'd been with the work Alec had done to turn unused space into comfortable and modern rooms for Ruby, and she was just as certain that Owen would be as embarrassed that it had taken a stranger to recognize Ruby's needs and to ensure her health and safety.

She could hardly believe her brother was there. The proverbial rolling stone, Owen came and went as he pleased, and had since he was eighteen.

"So what do you think?" she asked him when his tour was completed and he and Ruby returned to the store.

"I think it's lucky for all of us that Gigi has people looking out for her. I owe Jansen a whole lot of thanks for this." He leaned against the counter and added, "He's welcome to the skipjack and anything else he sets his sights on."

"He did a beautiful job, that's for sure. Gigi, did you tell Owen about the cottage?"

"What about the cottage?"

Lis proceeded to fill him in on her plans, and Alec's part in helping her determine how viable those plans might be.

"Sounds like Alec has more in his sights than Eb's boat," Owen noted.

"He's interested in the island and concerned about preserving what's here."

"Yeah, well, we'll see what he's really interested in." Owen turned to Ruby. "Say, if Captain Walt's is still open and serving the best rockfish on the bay, what do you say I take you both out for dinner to welcome me home?"

"Dinner suits me fine, but I've got a taste for Emily Hart's crab cakes," Ruby told him.

"Mrs. Hart is still doing her thing?" Owen looked surprised.

"She is indeed," Ruby assured him.

"Does she even have a restaurant license?" Lis asked.

"No one be needing a license to cook in their own kitchen and serve at their own table."

"I'm pretty sure you do if you're charging for the food," Lis told her.

"Yeah, the board of health might disagree," Owen chimed in.

"Emily Hart been serving up for folks every Tuesday and Friday nights for more years than either of you been alive. Never heard tell of anyone ever having a problem with what came out of her kitchen."

"Which is probably a good thing for Mrs. Hart," Owen said. "If she doesn't have a license, chances are she didn't bother with liability insurance, either."

"You hush and go change into something respectable. Those ripped-up shorts be fine for the beach, but not for being seen in public."

"Yes, ma'am." A chastised Owen headed for the second floor, winking at his sister as he passed.

"And you, Lisbeth, you go on and get everything out of your car. You be driving. These old legs of mine don't reach high enough to climb into that big old thing your brother's got parked out there." Ruby placed her large black purse on the counter.

Not for the first time, Lis wondered how that small woman could carry a purse that looked to weigh almost as much as she did. God only knew what she was carrying around with her.

"Brush your hair before we go, Lisbeth. You be looking like you drove all the way from New Jersey with your head out the window . . ."

EMILY HART'S WHITE clapboard house was a mile down the road from the general store. Built in 1883 by the grandfather of Emily's late husband, Phillip, it was one of only a few houses on the island that was two stories and the only one with any true Victorian touches. The porch was wide, wrapped from front almost to the back of the house on one side, and was framed with elaborate gingerbread trim. Several rocking chairs, set out in groups of two and three, were placed on the porch for diners who liked to relax in the soft bay breezes after dining on nights when the mosquitoes weren't biting. Inside, the dining room was large and formal, with a table that could seat ten, more with the leaves added. Diners would be seated with whomever else had shown up that night. Emily, who was seventy-seven years old, took no reservations, had no set menu, served one sitting per night at seven on the dot, only took cash, and offered no alcohol. If all the chairs were taken when you arrived, you were turned away. You ordered what she cooked that day—which was whatever her nephew Pat had brought in from the bay—and if you wanted beer or wine, you brought it with you along with the glasses you'd drink from.

Emily had a set of very fine crystal wineglasses that no one ever drank from. Including Emily.

"Well, look at you, Ruby Carter." Emily's eyes lit when Owen and Lis followed Ruby into the dining room. "You got that boy of yours and your girl with you. Glad you brung 'em to see me." She patted Owen on the back. "Got soft-shells tonight, big guy. Rockfish, too."

"I don't know that I can choose between your soft-shelled crabs and your rockfish, Mrs. Hart." Owen held a chair out for Ruby. "That might be asking too much."

"Well, boy, lucky for you, you don't have to choose." Emily turned to the five others who were already seated at the table. "That there joining you is Ruby Carter. She owns the general store up this side of the drawbridge. That be her great-grandchildren, Owen and Lisbeth. These nice folks here at the table be the Hawkins family, all the way from Ohio."

There was a chorus of *Nice to meet you*'s and *How are you*'s, *So you live here*'s, and *What brings you to Cannonball Island?* before the two families retreated back into the sanctuary of their private conversations.

"This is so pretty. The white-lace tablecloth, the pretty china . . ." Lis said. "It's just the way I remember it."

"The jelly glasses for water," Owen murmured.

"You mind your manners, Owen Parker," Ruby chastised even as her lips fought a smile.

"If I'd known we were going to come here for dinner, I'd have stopped at Miller's for a bottle of wine when I came through town," Lis said.

"I'm more a beer guy myself," Owen told her. "Last time I was home, I had some of that MadMac beer that Clay Madison and his partner are brewing. Good stuff. I think I'll run over to St. Dennis after dinner and pick up a six-pack or two."

"Been a tea drinker all my life," Ruby said. "Never did see a reason to fuzz my brain. Life can confuse your thinking all on its own." She poked Owen with a slightly bent finger. "How long you be sticking around this time?"

When Owen failed to reply, Lis kicked him lightly under the table.

"Owen?" Lis poked him with her foot. "Gigi asked how long—"

"I heard. I'm trying to think how to answer."

"Was the question too hard for you? 'Cause we can rephrase it . . ." Lis rested her arms on the table.

"Actually, it is," Owen said slowly. "To tell you the truth, I wasn't thinking about coming back for a while, but something got into my head about this place and I just felt like I had to come home."

"Was that something my art exhibit?"

"I wanted to come home for that, of course. But it was more than that. It just felt like it was time."

"Time for what?" A prickle had gone up Lis's spine. She hated when Owen talked like that. He'd been doing it since he was a child. "Were you worried about Gigi's fall?"

"That not be it," Ruby said almost unperceptively.

"At first that's what I thought, but it doesn't feel like that. Oh yeah, Gigi told me about her fall, and I'm real grateful that she was found when she was and that she's all right. But this isn't about that. It doesn't feel like that."

Ruby nodded and exchanged a long look with Owen.

"I just felt like I needed to come home," he said. "That something important was waiting for me here. I can't explain it better than that."

"Don't need more explaining," Ruby told him. "Sometimes things just be what they be."

"What would be important enough to make you want to stick around?" Lis asked.

"Don't know yet." Owen shrugged.

"So what have you been doing?" Before he could offer a glib response, Lis added, "And we don't want that nonanswer, 'Having adventures.'"

"Hey, I'm all about adventure."

When Lis made a face, he said, "Okay, for a while I was fishing in Alaska. Then it occurred to me that I really hate the cold. A guy on the boat with me was from Australia. He was going back and talked me into going with him. His family owned a cattle ranch, so I did some ranching for a while. Fixed fences. Looked for lost cattle. Didn't stay there very long, but it was a good experience."

"And Costa Rica?"

"Surfing and diving, mostly. I hooked up with a salvager—guy I knew in college. Ran into him on the beach down there one day. His company was doing a salvage operation on a ship that went down off the coast, and they needed one more guy on the diving team."

"Small world," Lis noted.

"Really. I hadn't seen Jared Chandler in ten years. Then all of a sudden, there he was. So yeah. Small world." Owen fell quiet for a moment. "You know,

I've always liked to dive. Never occurred to me that I could make a living from it. Funny how it all worked out."

"How did it work out?" Lis asked.

"Long story short, Jared offered me a job. His company's salvage operation is going to be working on a ship that sunk out there in the bay about two hundred years ago."

"Going to take another hundred years to bring it up," Ruby said. "Bay be busier than a beehive in July. How you figure to bring up a ship around all the crab traps and oyster beds?"

"Well, I guess that's for Jared to work out."

"Did you take the job?"

"I did, Lis. I don't know what led me back here, but it seems now I have a reason to stay. At least for a while. We'll see what comes next."

"You were always creepy about stuff like that." Lis couldn't help herself. She had to say it. "You and cousin Maryclaire. Always had these creepy feelings that this or that was going to happen. And sooner or later, something always did." She turned to Ruby. "And you, too, Gigi. You always know stuff before it happens. You don't always give it away, but I know you always know."

Ruby smiled.

"You're just jealous because you don't have the eye." Owen seemed to almost gloat.

"I don't want 'the eye.' I don't want to know what's going to happen before it does. I like being surprised."

"I don't always know what's going to happen."

Owen turned to Ruby. "But she's right about you, Gigi. You always know stuff you don't talk about. You never seem to be surprised about anything."

"Surprises be overrated sometimes," was all Ruby said.

"Well, speaking of surprises, how surprised were you when you were asked to exhibit in the new art center?" Owen turned back to his sister.

"Very surprised. For one thing, I didn't know about the gallery—didn't know there was one."

"Just goes to show how far and wide your fame as an artist has spread."

"The woman who runs it owns a very well-known and prestigious gallery in New York, among other places. She heard about a sale I made up there, read a few of the articles that followed that sale, realized I was from Cannonball Island, and since she likes to show the work of local artists, invited me to exhibit. She's a very clever lady, this Carly Summit. She'll exhibit local artists regardless of taste or talent. I've seen some of the stuff some of the locals have done, and I have to tell you, some of it is pretty bad. I think it's so kind of her."

"Kind of her to inflict terrible art on St. Dennis?"

Lis laughed. "Look, most people who are terrible artists don't know how bad they are. She gives everyone the opportunity to see their work exhibited, makes them feel like a real artist, if only for a little while."

"I get it. So will your paintings be hanging be-tween Elvis on black velvet and the paint-by-numbers red-covered-bridge scene?"

"Please. It's cats with scary eyes on black velvet,

and I'm not sure, but I think maybe Carly draws the line at paint by numbers."

"I guess the line's got to be drawn somewhere."

"Hazel Stevens been painting those cats for years." Ruby shook her head. "Cats been gone longer than your daddy. Think she'd find something else to paint."

Emily appeared in the doorway, two of her nieces behind her carrying trays.

"Dinner be served now. Hope you brought your appetites." Emily came into the room, then stepped aside so the two girls could place bowls of creamy mashed potatoes, string beans, and new carrots on the table. "You all know it's family style here, so Mr. Hawkins, you go on and start up here at this end of the table, serve yourself, then pass the bowls around the table clockwise. You get to the bottom of the bowl, you let me know and we'll fill it up again."

The girls left the room, then returned with platters piled high with soft-shelled crabs and fat wedges of lemon. A second platter of rockfish cut into fillets came next.

"Plenty more in the back," Emily told them, "so you all go on and enjoy your dinner."

She disappeared back into the kitchen, and for a few moments, the only sound in the room was that of spoons clinking on the sides of the well-used bowls.

By the time dinner was over and dessert had been served—blueberry pie with homemade vanilla ice cream—Lis found herself wishing she'd worn a tank dress or anything without a waist.

"I haven't eaten like that since . . ." She paused to reflect. "Maybe never. I may need a forklift to get me out of this chair."

"I know what you mean," Owen agreed. "I think I just ate about five times my normal caloric intake."

"That might have something to do with all that butter on the soft-shells," Lis reminded him.

"Look who's talking, Miss Please Pass the Potatoes."

"I only did that once, and only because I never get mashed potatoes."

"Seems to me calories not be the point," Ruby said as she struggled to stand. Before she could blink, Lis was on one side, Owen on the other, to help her out of her seat. "Seems to me some people have eyes bigger than their stomachs."

"Sad but true, Gigi," Owen said. "I'm the first to admit it."

Emily came out from the kitchen to applause from her diners and accepted their praise with pride.

"Been doing this longer than most of you all been alive," she told them. "Nice to see I'm still appreciated. Now, you all go on out and set a spell on the porch, if you have a mind to." She turned to Ruby. "You be staying a time?"

"Not tonight, Emily. I think I'd best be getting these two on home. We be back before long, though," Ruby assured her.

"Don't be a stranger, then." Emily walked them to the door. "And you, Lisbeth—I'll be by to see your paintings. Wouldn't be missing it."

"We'll be looking for you, Mrs. Hart." Lis held the

door till everyone filed out, then along with Owen, helped Ruby down the steps and to the car.

"I'm glad you suggested that tonight, Gigi," Lis said as she started her car after they'd strapped themselves in with their seat belts.

"Nothing like what comes out of Emily's kitchen." Ruby nodded.

"I am looking forward to trying Captain Walt's while I'm home, though. I've heard a lot about it."

"Wait. You've never eaten at Captain Walt's?" Owen eyed her with disbelief. "And you're how old?"

"I just never think about going to town, Owen. And most of the time when I'm home, I hang out with Gigi here on the island."

Owen muttered something under his breath, but when Lis asked him what he said, he just shook his head.

It was still light out when they arrived back at the store, but only barely. The sun was setting across the bay and the fireflies were already dancing across the dune when Owen and Lis helped Ruby up the front steps.

"Wouldn't need help out here if that railing was a little more stable," Ruby complained.

"I'm surprised Jansen didn't fix that, too," Owen noted.

"Alec be spending his time inside and out back," Ruby told him as she unlocked the door. "Seems to me someone else could toss a hammer just as good."

"You're right. And first thing in the morning I will do just that." Owen went back out to the handrail and wiggled it back and forth. "Looks like a few nails at the base and another few at the top should do it."

"Hammer's in the shed, nails are, too." Ruby looked over her shoulder and told them, "I'll be reading a bit before I turn in. Owen, I 'spect you'll be wanting pancakes in the morning."

"I expect I will." One foot on the first step, the other on the ground, Owen grinned. "Want me to make them this time?"

"I'm sure I do not." Ruby closed the door.

"How do you rate pancakes?" Lis asked. "I never get pancakes."

"You would if you were as pretty as me." Owen came up the stairs and sat on the top step. He patted the space next to him.

Lis sat and looked out across the dune.

"It's so peaceful here. I hope the island never changes," she said.

"Everything changes," he said.

"Not Cannonball Island. I bet it's looked pretty much the same for the past eighty, maybe a hundred years."

"Maybe it's time."

"Time for what? A Dairy Queen and a 7-Eleven?"

"Nothing that drastic, but maybe some new blood."

"Owen, there's not even a lot of old blood around anymore."

"My point exactly. You wouldn't want to see the island die out, right?"

"Of course not." Lis frowned and picked at a fingernail she'd split when she was unloading her car.

"So you need some new blood. New energy. Change can be good."

"I like things just the way they are around here." She dug in her bag for a nail file.

"This from someone who wants to renovate that old shack down on the point?"

"It's not a shack, and that's different. That's part of our family history, and if Alec thinks it can be salvaged, then yes, that's what I want to do. But there are probably termites and water damage and I'm not sure what else. I'd love for it to work, though, Owen. The place is magic."

"Well, then, let's hope Jansen's a magician. Maybe I'll pay him a call tomorrow, see what he's thinking."

"You don't have to check up on it for me. He'll let me know when he knows."

Owen stood. "I want to stop over at the boatyard anyway, pay my respects to Uncle Eb and the *Annie G.* Plus I owe him my thanks for looking after Gigi. Whether he ended up walking off with the boat for his troubles or not, it was good of him. Jansen always was a good guy. Sounds like he still is."

"He and Gigi are really tight," Lis told him.

"That speaks well of him, then. She isn't fooled easily."

"She isn't fooled at all."

Owen went out to his car and opened the back, took out a duffel bag, and closed the hatch.

"Your old room is still up there," Lis told him as he walked back to the porch. "You'll probably have to put sheets on the bed, though. Look in the hall closet. Towels are there, too."

Owen grinned broadly. "How many thirty-eight-year-old men can say their great-grandmother keeps a room ready for them?"

"My guess is that most grown men wouldn't admit to it."

"Hey, I don't have a problem with it. Doesn't threaten my masculinity. Most guys don't have Gigi." He stood on the ground and looked up at the store. "What do you think is going to happen to it when she's gone, Lis?"

"The store?" She shook her head. "I don't know."

"And the rest of it? Poppa's old place, the point?"

"I'm hoping to stake a claim to at least a little piece of the point. Gigi seemed pleased that I wanted it."

"It should stay intact, stay in the family. There's a lot of acreage there, but it should stay intact. Keep it together, Lis."

"If I have any say in it, sure. But it's Gigi's to decide what to do with. As far as Poppa's place is concerned, I haven't even been over there. I forgot about it, to tell you the truth. I'd be surprised if it was still standing. Last time I was over that way, the old chapel next door was falling down and that little graveyard was overgrown. I said something to Gigi about it and she made a few calls and got some people out there to clean it up. She was threatening to go herself, but we—me and Hedy and Essie—were able to talk her out of it."

"I'll take a look tomorrow. You coming in?"

"In a minute. You go on up. I'll see you in the morning."

"See you in the morning." He opened the screen door and took a step inside.

"Owen?" She heard him pause in the doorway. "I'm glad you're here. When I'm here, I mean."

"Yeah, kiddo. Me, too." He closed the door softly behind him.

Lis sat on the porch step for a few more minutes, her head back, and watched the sky for shooting stars. She was in the mood to make wishes—there were a number of wishes on her list tonight—but stare as she might, there was no movement in the dark sky. Finally she went in, locked up the store, and went to bed.

ALEC HAD JUST finished sanding the repaired hull in preparation for paint when he looked out the window and saw a tall man with dark hair and dark glasses approaching the warehouse. He put down the sander and went to the door and looked out through the glass. The man stood with his back to Alec's shop, his hands on his hips, and stared out at the bay. The visitor turned around just as Alec stepped outside.

"Hey, Alec," the man called.

"Owen Parker, that you?"

"It is." Owen offered a hand in greeting and Alec gave it a shake. Owen's grip was just a little bit tighter than Alec would have expected for someone he hadn't seen in a long time.

"How've you been?" Alec asked, waiting for the bones in his hand to recover. "Where've you been?"

"Here and there."

"You planning on being around for a while?"

"A while." Owen tilted his head in the direction of the warehouse. "Is that where you're hiding her?"

"Her?" Alec frowned.

"*Annie*."

Alec smiled. "Ah, the lovely *Annie G.* Yes, she's safe and sound inside. Want to see her?"

Owen nodded. "Came to pay my respects."

"Right this way." Alec opened the door and gestured for Owen to go in. He followed and closed the door behind them.

"Just as pretty as ever. Showing her age, but still pretty." Owen walked around the boat, a smile on his face. He patted the hull, took a long look at the hole in her side, and asked, "Dry rot?"

"Yeah. I'm replacing it, piece by piece." Alec pointed to the stack of new wood. "I just finished sanding one that I'll be replacing on her soon."

"Shame she sat out there for so long. I bet there's plenty of work before she's ready to get back on the bay. Assuming that's your plan."

"That's the plan." Before Owen could ask, Alec told him, "Not going to use her for fishing or oystering or crabbing. I'll just be taking her out for show, a couple of races in the summer. Otherwise, she'll be treated like a valuable racehorse put out to pasture."

"A worthy future." Owen slapped the side of the boat lightly. "Are you making a new mainsail yourself?"

"No. Too tricky. I'm going to have one made when the time comes."

"Well, I'd have liked to have kept her in the family, to be honest, but all things considered, she's better off in your hands. There's no one who can do for her what you can."

"Thanks, Owen. I'm glad to hear you say that."

"That was a sweet deal you made with Ruby."

Alec let out a sigh. "If you're going to imply that somehow I took advantage of an old lady, let me assure you, your sister already covered that base."

"I think in terms of cold cash, Ruby got the best of the bargain. She told me about all you did for her." Owen paused before adding, "I appreciate it. And I'm embarrassed that it didn't occur to me to come home to watch out for her."

"I don't think she wanted that. She always talks about how good she thinks it is that you're seeing the world now while you're young, before you settle down."

"Settle down?" Owen snorted. "I hope she's not counting on that anytime soon."

"You should take that up with her."

"So I hear you're going to help my sister fix up Ruby's old cottage down on the point."

"I did look at it, but I'm not so sure that it can be salvaged. There's a lot of water and termite damage. I know Lis has her heart set on it, but I don't know that it's going to happen." Alec added, "I hate to disappoint her. You should have seen her face when she was walking through it. It's obvious that place means a lot to her."

"If there's anything I can do to help out, just let me know. My sister's had a rough year. I'd like to see her happy."

"I'll do that. I think she's glad to be back on the island, and she has that big showing of her work tonight."

"Yeah, it's a big night for her, all right. I'm looking forward to it myself."

Owen walked around the boat one more time. "I have to admit the landscape on the island isn't quite the same without *Annie* standing guard in Ruby's backyard, but I guess it's time she moved on. And that new living space for Ruby—well, we should have done something about that a long time ago."

"No harm, no foul, as they say."

Owen moved toward the door and Alec fell in step with him.

"So are you planning on building any more boats here, or are you keeping busy enough with your home-remodeling business?"

"Keeping busy all the way around." They'd reached the door, and Alec pushed it open. "Though eventually I would like to start where my uncle Cliff left off. Build a skip from scratch. Maybe a few other bay boats. We'll see."

They stepped out into the sun. "So I guess I'll see you tonight at the gallery," Alec said.

"Wouldn't miss it. My little sister, showing off her paintings to the hometown crowd." Owen shook his head. "Who'd have figured that?"

"She'll draw a crowd, all right." Alec slipped on his sunglasses. "So, you planning on being around for a while?"

"Not sure how long, but yeah, for a time. I met up with a guy I knew from school who's going to be doing a salvage operation in the bay. I'll be working with him."

"I heard someone was going to try to pull up

some old boat from the War of 1812. That your friend?"

Owen nodded.

"Great. Good luck with that," Alec told him. "Guess I'll see you tonight."

"See you there." Owen walked off down the sidewalk.

What, Alec wondered, was the point of that? Just to let me know that he's back and he's looking out for Ruby? Or is it Lis he's watching over?

Alec turned and went back into his shop. He had a few more hours before he had to quit and go back home to clean up for Lis's showing. He'd sensed that she might be a little nervous about tonight, and he wanted to be there for her. Besides, this was a date that had been seventeen years in the making, and he wanted to savor every minute they had.

Chapter Eleven

"What do you think?" Lis came down the steps and into the store, where Ruby and Owen waited. "Do I look okay?"

"Other than the fact that the dress is a little low in the front and a little short on the bottom, I guess you look okay," Owen told her.

"You hush, you." Ruby frowned at him. "She looks just right."

"Thank you, Gigi." Lis planted a cheek on the older woman's cheek.

"Just right" was one of Ruby's highest compliments and was exactly what Lis needed to hear. Knowing that she and her work would be on display for all the world to see that night was enough to make the butterflies in her stomach go wild, but it was her date after the showing with Alec that was making her nervous. What if it didn't go well? Once she got past her initial suspicion and realized he was really helping Ruby and not taking advantage of her, they'd gotten along just fine. Better than fine, considering that kiss in the cottage the other day. But say the word "date," and things have a way of changing, sometimes for the better, sometimes not.

"You be driving, Lis," Ruby reminded her. "I can't—"

"We know. Climb into that beast I drive. I promise that my next car will be more Gigi friendly." Owen took her arm and helped her down the steps while Lis locked the store and put the CLOSED sign face out on the window.

The drive took fewer than ten minutes, and by the time Lis, Ruby, and Owen were walking toward the door to the carriage house turned art gallery, Lis's heart was in her throat. What if everyone thought her work was ugly, or boring, or worst of all, silly? She tried reminding herself that other paintings of hers were at that very moment hanging in a respectable, well-known New York City art gallery, but having anonymous strangers looking at your work with a critical eye was entirely different from having people you know judge your talent. And that was exactly how Lis felt walking into the crowded gallery: that everyone was there to judge her.

She did remind herself that Carly had contacted her, had *invited* her to show her work here, so that should count for something. Then again, Carly had crazy-eyed cats painted on black velvet hanging in the very room where Lis's paintings would be displayed.

It seemed to Lis that everyone she'd ever met in St. Dennis—and many she hadn't—came through the receiving line. The biggest shock was the number of people from her class in school who came to see her, many whose names she couldn't even recall because she'd never really known them. Hadn't been allowed to know them. Everyone was so friendly, so complimentary of her work, that by the end of the night, she'd promised herself that for as long as she was living on the island, she'd make more of an effort to involve herself in whatever way she could in whatever was happening in the town. Maybe she'd even make a friend or two.

"You're Vanessa, from the dress shop," Lis said when she recognized the woman from Bling.

"And you're the pretty lady who bought my favorite dress." Vanessa smiled and leaned a little closer. "And you do wear it well. It looks stunning on you. How do the shoes feel?"

"Terrific. Thank you. I was in a bit of a rush yesterday, but I'll be back in to see what else you have," Lis told her.

"Good. And since you're our newest resident artist, you qualify for my friends-and-family discount."

"Even better. I'll see you soon."

Vanessa passed through the line to make way for the next person.

"The ice cream shop," Lis said when she recalled where she'd seen the tall blond woman.

"Steffie MacGregor. I love your work. It's so moody. It's such a nice contrast to some of the other works here." Steffie stepped aside and eased another woman forward. "Mom, this is Lis. She likes strawberry mousse with a chocolate thunder chaser."

"I'm Shirley Wyler, and I apologize for the fact

that my daughter tends to identify people by their choice of ice cream flavors." Shirley Wyler was a very stylish, well-preserved sixtyish woman, with the same tawny blond hair as her daughter. "I've been so excited to meet you. Your work is so . . ." She appeared momentarily lost for words, then added, "So full of energy."

"Thank you. It's hard to paint New York without reflecting the pulse of the city," Lis replied.

"Mom's an artist, too," Steffie told Lis.

"Oh no. No, I'm . . ." Shirley protested. "Not like—"

"Don't listen to her," Steffie said. "Ask Carly to show you some of her work. She paints as Shirley Hinson, her maiden name."

"Oh, you . . ." Shirley was beet red. "Really, Miss Parker . . ."

"It's Lis, and I'd love to see your work. You have something displayed here tonight?"

"Oh, just a watercolor or two," Shirley said. "But really, you don't have to . . ."

"I'd be delighted. Maybe when I'm finished here, you can show me," Lis told her.

"I haven't had any formal training, and I—"

"Some of my favorite paintings were done by artists with no formal training. I'm sure if Carly has been displaying your work, it's better than you're giving yourself credit for." Lis checked the size of the line. "There are only about twenty-five more people to greet, so I should be finished here soon. I'd really love to see what you've done."

"All right. I'll catch up with you in about twenty

minutes or so." Shirley took her daughter's arm and disappeared into the crowd.

"Having fun?" A voice whispered in Lis's ear. "Or are you ready to run screaming back to the island?"

Lis laughed and tried to pretend she hadn't felt the softness of Alec's breath on her neck or the shiver that ran through her when he touched her bare arm.

"Actually, I'm having more fun than I thought I'd have. But you wouldn't believe how many people from our class are here."

"I believe. I've been talking to them since I got here. Everyone's so tickled that our class produced such a great artist."

"I couldn't remember most of their names," she told him. "It's embarrassing."

"Well, put that thought aside for a while and enjoy yourself while you're here." Alec stepped around her and embraced the small, white-haired woman next in line. "Hello, Aunt Grace. You look great. I love the way you coordinated your dress with your cane."

Grace pretended to swipe at him with the cane even as she laughed. "Out of my way, young man. I'm here to see the artist."

She leaned over and kissed Alec on the cheek before moving on to Lis. "What a wonderful crowd tonight. I think everyone in town is here. There's nothing we love more than a local success story." She took Lis's hand. "You've done lovely work. You're every bit as talented as Ruby said. Now, where is my friend? Someone said she was here."

"She's probably holding court in the next room.

Carly found a comfortable chair for her, so I doubt she's moved from the spot where I left her."

Behind Grace, her entire family was lined up: daughter Lucy and her husband, Clay; her oldest son, Dan, and his fiancée, Jamie; and Ford, her youngest, Carly's husband. Alec stood and chatted with his cousins, and before long, the line had dwindled down to a few old friends of Lis's mother, and Emily Hart and one of her nieces, who'd served them dinner the night before. Lis accepted their compliments and promised to pass on their best wishes to Kathleen next time she spoke with her.

"Have you had anything to drink yet?" Alec asked her when the receiving line had broken up.

"No, but I'd kill for some water. My throat is so dry from talking so much. I swear, I talked more tonight than I have in the past three months," she told him.

"Must have been a lonely three months," he replied.

"Now that I think about it, I could use a champagne chaser with that water." Lis forced a smile.

She hadn't realized just how lonely she'd been until she returned to her apartment on Thursday. The contrast between her life there and what her life was beginning to look like here was like night and day. Here she had family, and maybe even the makings of a friend or two.

And then there was Alec, and who knew where that might lead?

"Coming right up." Alec headed toward the makeshift bar that Carly had set up for the occasion.

No sooner had he left than Shirley Wyler walked over. "Listen, I'm sure there are a lot of people who'd like to talk to you. I saw a reporter from the *Baltimore Sun* here, so I know your time is in demand. You can take a look at my paintings another time. It's really all right. I won't be offended."

"Don't be silly. There's no time like the present." Lis took Shirley's elbow. "Which way?"

"On the other side of the main partition," Shirley told her.

Alec appeared with a glass of water in one hand and a champagne glass in the other. Lis grabbed the water and took a long drink.

"I'll be back in five minutes. Hold on to the wine," she told him.

"I'll get you another one," he said as he raised the glass to his lips. "I'll be around."

"This is yours?" Lis asked after Shirley stopped in front of a large painting of a garden in early morning.

Shirley nodded.

"It's beautiful. You really have a way with color and design. You're very talented," Lis told her sincerely.

"Thank you. You don't have to say that to be nice, but thank you anyway." Shirley looked as if she could cry.

"I'm being honest. It's lovely. You can almost feel that tiny bit of breeze that is setting the flowers swaying just the slightest bit. Are you exhibiting anywhere other than here?"

Behind Shirley and halfway across the room, Lis saw Alec engaged in conversation with a pretty blonde in a slinky black dress. She was wearing a lot of gold and mile-high heels.

"Not yet. I've had offers from other galleries, but I don't know what to do, or who to trust. I don't even know how to price my paintings. I don't know any other artists, so I haven't had anyone to ask."

"Well, you do now. We can have coffee some morning. Ask me anything you want to know." The blonde leaned closer to Alec and was whispering conspiratorially in his ear. He was smiling as if whatever she was saying was exactly what he wanted to hear. Who, Lis wondered, was she? Competition? Lis's heart dropped. Why should she be surprised if someone else was as interested in him as she was? Alec was pretty much what every woman was looking for.

"That would be great, thank you. I'd love to."

"Great. I'll be in touch."

Alec's smile had faded, and he was nodding slowly as the woman spoke.

"So you're staying in St. Dennis?" Shirley asked.

"On the island, yes. I'm not sure yet how long, but I'll be around." Lis watched as Owen joined the party of two.

"Let me give you my number." Shirley took a card from her bag, wrote on the back, and handed it to Lis. "Just whenever you have an hour to spare . . ."

"Thanks. I'll be sure to call you." Lis moved in Alec's direction, but he'd already walked away from the blonde, who at that moment seemed to have captured all of Owen's attention.

Alec swiped a glass of champagne from a passing tray.

"You're a huge hit tonight, you know." He handed the glass to Lis. "Everyone loves your work."

"Pinch me." She took a sip. "This is beyond anything I expected. How did Carly get everyone to show up?"

"She just put a little item in the *St. Dennis Gazette*: who, what, when, and where. It's not such a big town that people forget you when you leave." He pushed a stray strand of hair behind her ear. "People remember you and Owen. And of course, everyone knows Ruby. From what I understand, she wasn't shy about telling people about it."

"I'm sure the item in the paper let people know about the exhibit, but I wouldn't put it past Ruby to bug people until they agreed to show up."

"Does it matter who got them in here? You're a hit. Everyone now knows how very talented you are. You should feel great."

"I feel better than I did when I arrived tonight, that's for sure," Lis admitted.

"Then things are looking up."

"Alec, who's that woman talking to Owen?" she asked casually.

"Cass Logan."

When he offered no further explanation, she said, "Is she from St. Dennis?"

"No. She's just visiting." He looked at his watch. "Only about another twenty minutes or so before people start to leave. I made reservations for nine at Captain Walt's."

"Oh great. I was just saying last night that I wanted to go there while I'm home. Owen suggested we go last night but Gigi wanted to go to Emily Hart's."

"I just saw her a few minutes ago. I can't believe she's still running her little operation over there on the island. She must be under the radar to have been operating all these years without someone from the board of health showing up."

"If they did, she'd feed them and they'd go away so happy they'd forget why they were there in the first place."

"Captain Walt's might not be quite as good, but they're good. And they have live music on Saturday nights, so I thought you might like that," he said.

"I do."

"They used to have music on Friday nights only—jazz groups, mostly. Then Walt realized that he was losing a lot of Saturday business to a new place out on the highway that had a live band, so he started bringing in local musicians. Some of them have been pretty good." He lowered his voice and leaned a little closer. "Some of them have been dreadful."

Lis laughed. "You know what Forrest Gump always said."

"You never know what you're going to get," Alec said solemnly.

"Wise words from a wise man."

"Your glass is empty. Another?"

"No, thanks. I'm good." Lis watched as several people made their way to the door. "Looks like the exodus has begun."

"Good. That means we can leave anytime we want."

"I should check on Ruby, and remind Owen that he's going to have to drive her home."

It took several minutes for Lis to make her way from one room to the other, since many of the attendees stopped as they were leaving to tell her they admired her work and the reporter from the Baltimore paper caught up with her at the door for a quick interview. She had intended on tapping Owen on the back, but she noted he was already on his way toward Ruby, and the blonde was nowhere to be seen. By the time she reached the side room, Ruby was already on her feet and saying her good-byes to her audience. Lis smiled. Even at her age, Ruby was still the center of attention.

She caught Owen's eye.

"I can take it from here," he told her.

"I know. Thanks for being here."

"Even though I barely saw you all night," he reminded her.

"Doesn't matter. I knew you were here. You know that I love you both." She handed him her car keys.

"I do. Have a good time. Do I have to tell you to behave?"

She poked him in the side. "Don't play the big brother card now. We're both too old, and it's a little late."

"I'll never be too old, and it will never be too late."

She rolled her eyes. "I'll see you at home."

"Nice crowd came out to see you, Lisbeth." Ruby approached on Ford Sinclair's arm. "Lots of folks told me how pretty your pictures are. I said to them, I hope you're not surprised."

"Thanks, Gigi." Lis kissed her cheek. "I'll see you when I get home."

Lis joined Alec near the door, where he was talking to Carly.

"Congratulations. That was some homecoming. St. Dennis welcomed you back with open arms." Carly was beaming.

"It was great," Lis said. "I can't thank you enough for arranging this."

"My pleasure. Let's make it a point to get together sometime while you're still in town."

"Will do." Lis looked up at Alec. "Ready?"

"When you are."

"Bye, Carly, and thanks again."

Alec held the door for her, and Lis walked outside into the evening air. The day had been hot but not humid, and a cool front was expected to move through that night. It was almost but not quite dark, the streetlights just coming on to light the way.

"So what was the best part of the night?" he said.

"I'll have to think about that. Some of it was surreal. People I didn't think I knew acted like they knew me."

"I think people—especially people from our class—felt they did know you back then." He seemed to choose his words carefully. "Not as well as they might have liked, but everyone remembered you."

His fingers grazed her elbow when they got to the car, and he opened the passenger door for her.

"There are people I wish I'd known better," she

admitted, "but I was really discouraged from making friends in town."

"I don't think anyone was aware of that." He slid behind the wheel and started the car.

"Well, it wasn't something that I walked around talking about. 'My dad is prejudiced and thinks everyone from St. Dennis is a crook.' Talk about how to win friends."

"How'd Owen deal with that?"

"Owen couldn't have cared less what our father thought. He always did his own thing. Besides, by the time he was fourteen, he was bigger and stronger. I don't remember Dad ever messing with him."

"Have you and your brother always been close?"

"Yes and no. He was a few years older and he was out of high school by the time I got there. Then he went off to college and after he graduated, he joined the navy. These past few years, it's been hard for us to keep in touch. He's been traveling a lot since he and Cindy got divorced. This will be the most time we've spent together in a long time."

"He came to see me yesterday at the boatyard." Alec stopped at the Stop sign, waited while a few cars passed, then made a left onto Charles Street.

"He mentioned he might do that."

"Yeah, he said he just wanted to see the *Annie G.* I thought he was going to give me a hard time about it—like someone else who shall remain nameless did—but he didn't."

"Both Owen and that someone else who remains nameless are both grateful that you've been so good to Gigi." Lis smiled and looked out the window. "I believe that she who remains nameless already told you that."

"She did. I just didn't expect to hear it from her brother."

Alec turned right at the light and drove slowly down Kelly's Point Road, past the municipal parking lot to the smaller lot at the end reserved for Captain Walt's customers. The lot was full, and he had to backtrack and park farther up the road.

"Looks like a packed house tonight." He and Lis got out of the Jeep and walked along the side of the road to the boardwalk that ran along the bay at the marina.

The door at Captain Walt's opened and a crowd spilled out, and for a moment, the music from the band followed them. Then the door closed, and it was quiet again, the water lapping against the sides of the boats that were docked at the pier the predominant sound. Alec and Lis followed two other couples into the restaurant and were greeted by the smiling hostess.

"Alec, I have you down for nine o'clock. You're a little late," she told them.

"Sorry, Rexanne. We were at the gallery opening."

"Lucky for you, so was everyone else." The woman raised a finger to beckon a waiter. "We're really busy right now, so I'm just going to have Craig show you to your table."

"I requested a table near the windows looking out onto the bay," Alec told the young man who led them through the restaurant toward the back wall. "I hope one's still available."

"How's this?" The waiter stopped at a cozy table for two with a great view.

"Perfect. Just the table I had in mind."

The waiter held out Lis's chair while Alec seated himself, then handed them both menus. "We also have a shrimp special and tuna that came in this morning."

"Yum." Lis had relaxed as soon as she was seated. There was something about the ambience of this restaurant that made her feel like she was home.

They talked about the menu, and after they'd both ordered the tuna, Alec ordered wine for Lis and a beer for himself.

"I don't know if you like beer," he told her, "but St. Dennis has a local brewery now, and the beer is not like anything I ever had anywhere else."

"I do like it occasionally."

"MadMac Brews. Clay Madison—who is married to my cousin Lucy—and Wade MacGregor started it about two or three years ago. Clay grows the hops organically at his farm, and they set up their brewery right there in an old barn on his property. It's quite the operation."

The waiter appeared with their drinks.

"MacGregor." Lis thought for a moment. "Steffie who owns the ice cream place, her last name is MacGregor."

"Wade is her husband. He's also Dallas MacGregor's brother."

Her mouth hung open for just a moment. "Dallas MacGregor, the movie star?"

Alec nodded. "She lives here, too. Married her

old sweetheart, who just happens to be Steffie's brother."

"She lives in St. Dennis?"

"Girl, where have you been?" he teased. "She not only lives here, she bought some old warehouses on River Road and turned them into a studio. She has her own production company and they're right here. They're just starting work on their third film."

"Wow. I had no idea."

"Don't you read *People* magazine?"

She shook her head no.

"Watch *Entertainment Tonight*?"

Another no.

"How do you keep up with the beautiful people? Don't you care how real celebrities live?"

"Apparently not." Lis laughed.

"Me, either. The only reason I know about Dallas is because she lives here and our paths cross now and then."

"She's one of the few Hollywood types I'd recognize, but only because her looks are so distinctive. I watched one of those award shows on TV about six months ago, and I swear, I didn't know who anyone was."

"That's because you don't read culturally informative publications."

"More likely because I grew up in a house where, culturally speaking, it was still the 1800s."

"Ancient history," he told her. "Time to move on."

"For the most part, I have, but then something happens, some little thing like seeing Jody McGovern at the gallery. We were always in the same English class, and I thought she was so smart and so funny, and I bet she was fun to be with. She was the one person I really wanted to be friends with back then. Tonight I had about three minutes to talk to her before I had to move the line, and I wish it had been more."

"You can see Jody anytime you want. She's still around. She's the assistant librarian."

"Maybe I'll stop in and say hi one day. But it doesn't make up for all the times I wished . . ." It was hard to put into words what she wished. "I missed a lot back then. When I got to college, it was hard for me to make friends because I never really had to. The kids I'd hung around with in school, I'd always known them. So I didn't have to *get* to know them, if you follow me. I didn't know how to make friends. I've always been awkward with new people."

"If you felt awkward tonight, you hid it really well."

"Really?"

Alec nodded. "You looked relaxed and charming and gracious."

"Charming and gracious," she mused. "I don't think I've ever been described in those terms before."

"Maybe not to your face. You just don't see yourself the way others do."

"That's nice of you. I appreciate it. I think I will stop at the library one day next week and see if Jody is there. Maybe it's not too late to be friends."

"It's never too late, Lis." He looked directly into her eyes. "It will never be too late."

Something told her he wasn't talking just about friendship.

The waiter brought their dinners and Lis tucked away the conversation for later.

"Thanks for asking for a table near the bay. I never get tired of looking at the Chesapeake. I didn't realize how much I missed it until last week. I love watching the lights on the boats at night when everything else is so dark. It's like watching fairies dancing on the water."

The fish was perfectly cooked and she said so, adding, "Fish never tastes as good to me as it does here. Crabs—hands down, the best come out of the bay. Rockfish—no comparison. Maybe that's why I eat so much of it when I'm here."

"My uncle Cliff used to take me crabbing. He had an old green rowboat that we'd take out, mostly in the river. I loved those times with him. He was such a good man." Alec finished his meal and placed the knife and fork on his plate. "He took me in when my folks died, and treated me like a son from that day on. Everything he did, he did for me. He taught me to fish and crab and where to find oysters when it seemed like they'd all been taken by the professionals. He never missed a parent-teacher meeting or a lacrosse game or a basketball game. There was always a cake on my birthday and a party with my cousins at the inn. Christmases were the best. He always made the holidays worth the wait." He cleared his throat. "It's been sixteen years, and I miss him every day."

"He sounds like a great guy." Lis thought back to the conversation she and Ruby had had just a few days ago. "We don't stop loving people just because they're gone."

"I had great parents. We were a really happy family. I'll never understand why things had to be the way they were."

"If Ruby were here, she'd say something like, *'Can't change what was.'* She tells me things like that all the time."

Alec smiled. "I've heard that one, too. That, and, *'It's all in his hands, and he keeps his plans to himself, no reason to let me know ahead 'a time.'*"

"*'Times be changing. Keep up.'*" She grinned.

"How 'bout, *'You go on about your business, now, and let me go on about mine.'*"

"And to whatever it was that she wants you to do, it's, *'Do you good.'*"

"She's the best. I don't mind saying that one of my best friends is a one-hundred-year-old woman."

"Funny. Owen said something sort of like that last night. That he didn't mind living with his great-grandmother because she's . . . well, because she's Ruby."

"Loved and respected by all who know her." Alec realized that Lis, too, had finished eating. "Dessert?"

"Not another bite for me. But thanks."

Alec signaled to the waiter for the check. Ten minutes later, they were walking along the boards, hand in hand, looking out at the bay.

"It's such a pretty night," Lis said.

"Too pretty a night, and too early to take you home. Unless you're worn out from being 'on' tonight."

"No, I'm good."

One Scoop or Two was already dark, and the parking lot was mostly empty.

"I hadn't realized that St. Dennis had become such a tourist destination," she told him as they walked to the car.

"It's been growing steadily over the past ten years or so. There are some Friday nights you can't park in town and it takes half an hour to go from Sinclair's Inn out to the highway. It's been a boon to the shopkeepers, though." He opened the passenger-side door and held it while she got in. "And I've lost track of the number of places that are now B and Bs. There's at least one on every street." He walked around the car and got into the driver's seat.

"I guess if I were looking for a vacation place, I'd consider St. Dennis."

Alec turned the key in the ignition. "My cousin Dan has had a lot to do with the way the town has grown in popularity. I don't think most people are aware of the contribution he's made by all the changes he's done to the inn. There's a kids' park there now, tennis courts, a restaurant with a phenomenal chef. The entire building has been updated and the grounds are beautiful. There are weddings there almost every weekend, thanks to Lucy, who was an event planner in California before she came home a few years ago."

"Lucy was so pretty, with all that long strawberry-blond hair straight down her back. She's still pretty." Lis fingered her own dark curls. "I always envied her hair. Mine never went straight like that."

Alec drove over the drawbridge, and Lis assumed he was taking her home. Instead, he pulled the car onto the grass at the point and parked in front of the cottage.

"Have you figured out yet what's what here?" she asked, wondering if he had bad news and had brought her here to break it.

"I'm still waiting to hear from the termite inspector. He was supposed to be here this morning, but something came up and he had to put it off. He thought maybe he'd get to it by Monday or Tuesday."

"For a second, I was afraid you brought me here to give me bad news."

"Well, it might not be good in the end. I already told you there was water damage, but I don't know how extensive. Let's wait and see what the termite report tells us. The place may need some major rehab, but we don't have enough information right now. You'll have a decision to make soon enough. In the meantime . . . I see moonlight."

"Then let's not waste it." Lis kicked off her shoes. "Let's walk out onto the pier."

"Remember there are a lot of loose and missing boards. We won't be able to see them in the dark, and—"

Lis was already out of the car and heading toward the water. She heard Alec's car door slam and his footfalls behind her.

"So let's make a plan ahead of time in case one of us falls through the pier," he said as he caught up with her.

"Whoever doesn't fall through pulls out the one who did."

"Good plan." He took hold of her left hand. "Heck of a plan."

Lis laughed. "We'll just go slowly and be careful where we put our feet."

"Very careful." He glanced at her bare feet. "You know you're inviting a mass of splinters."

"I'll take my chances."

They reached the pier, and Lis stepped onto it, with Alec following behind, still holding her hand.

"I wish we had a flashlight," she said.

"Hold up. There's an app for that." He let go of her hand and pulled out his phone. A moment later, a beam of light illuminated the pier.

"That's very cool." She kept her eyes down and successfully avoided the missing boards all the way to the pier's end.

"I can show you how to get it on your phone, if you like," he told her.

"That would be great. Thanks."

They stood at the end of the pier looking out on the dark water. What had been a hot, sunny day marked by clear blue skies had turned into a cloudy night where the moon played *now you see me, now you don't* and the stars were mostly hidden. Still, it was beautiful there on the edge of the bay.

"Well, there had been moonlight." He sounded disappointed as clouds moved across the face of the moon, and poof! The light was gone.

"And there will be again. Look"—she pointed overhead—"the clouds are moving."

Alec stood behind her and slid his arms around her waist. Lis melted back into him as if it were the most natural thing in the world, as if they'd stood like this before a thousand times. She was mentally urging him to kiss her when he turned her around and did exactly that. This time, there was nothing tentative about the kiss. It was hot and urgent and full of promise and passion.

This is what it's like when you kiss someone who matters, a voice inside her head told her, and she wondered where the thought came from. *This is how it feels when it's right.*

And then he was whispering in her ear, "Next time I'm bringing a bottle of wine. We'll sit on the end of the pier, and after we finish drinking it, we'll take turns spinning it."

"Sounds like a plan." Lis nodded.

With Alec's arm over her shoulder, they walked back to the car. The radio was playing softly as they drove back to Ruby's. Alec pulled up behind Lis's car and turned off the headlights. He was just about to reach across the console for her when he noticed the back porch light was on and someone was sitting in one of the rocking chairs.

"Looks like your brother waited up for you." Alec nodded in the direction of the porch.

"Oh, for crying out loud." Lis got out of the car and went straight for the porch. "Owen Elliott Parker, what do you think you're doing?"

"Just sitting here, enjoying the night." Owen raised a hand and waved to Alec. "Hey, Alec. I meant to tell you earlier—real nice job you did on this porch. This is real quality work here."

"Thanks, Owen."

"You're welcome. Can I offer you a beer? I picked up a six-pack of MadMac Brews's Honey Ginger on my way home. It's really good."

"You're not going to go inside, are you?" Lis asked.

"Nope."

"You're being a jerk."

"Probably. But it's amusing me, so I'm okay with it."

Lis rolled her eyes. "Alec, thanks for a great night. I really enjoyed dinner."

"We'll do it again soon," Alec told her, obviously more amused than she was.

Lis stood on the top step and leaned over to kiss Alec lightly on the lips. "I hope so."

She smacked her brother on the head as she went into the house.

"Sure I can't get you a beer?" she heard Owen ask Alec.

She didn't wait to hear Alec's reply. She went straight up to her room and closed the door. What was it with Owen, anyway? She was thirty-five, not fifteen—not that he'd ever pulled a stunt like that when she was younger.

She tossed her bag onto the bed. It had been a long day, one filled with emotion on several levels, and she had to admit that as annoyed as she was with Owen, exhaustion trumped even that. From the porch below, she heard voices, and she opened the window and tried to hear what was being said. If she knew Owen, he was trying to pump Alec for information about the blonde. She smiled in spite of herself. All in all, it had been a great night, one she would never forget.

She changed out of her dress and hung it in the closet next to the black backup number she'd brought with her from her apartment. It was hard not to compare the two. It was like looking at her old life alongside her new one, like before-and-after pictures. She pulled her nightshirt over her head, turned off the light, and got into bed.

Outside, the conversation went on in murmurs and occasional laughter. She turned over and fell asleep listening to the sound of Alec's voice.

Chapter Twelve

So what did you think of my sister's artwork?" Owen raised the bottle to his lips after Lis had disappeared into the house.

"She's obviously very talented," Alec replied.

"That was too easy, Jansen. Too politic. Of course she has talent. She's always had talent. Her *talent* is not what I'm asking you." Owen tapped the side of the bottle with his fingers. "What I'm asking is, what you thought of the paintings. As in, did you *like* them?"

"Well . . ." Alec cleared his throat and lowered his voice as if he thought Lis were standing behind him. "The subject matter is . . . well, sort of foreign to me."

"You mean city streets. Skyscrapers. Three lanes of traffic jammed with cars. Crowds gathered on street corners waiting for the lights to change."

"Well, I did like that last one, the one with all those people on the corner, standing in the rain. And I liked the ones in Central Park."

"So what you're saying is you can't relate to most of the others."

Alec sighed. "More or less."

"Yeah. Me, either." Owen took a long drink, finished the bottle, and set it on the porch next to his chair. "I know she's made her name painting that other stuff, but I feel she could do better, you know?"

"I guess." Alec had no idea where this was going.

"I mean, I don't understand how a girl who was raised among all this"—his arms spread to include the entire island—"would want to paint eighty-or-more-story buildings. Makes no sense to me. All that glass and steel . . . I don't get it."

"I'm sure she could paint whatever she wanted," Alec said cautiously, still not sure why he and Owen were having this conversation.

"It's like she was trying to ignore the fact that she grew up on an unspoiled island." Owen turned to face Alec. "You see what I'm saying, right? That what she paints is the exact opposite of where she came from?"

"Well, I agree that the two places are very different. Country versus city, you could say. But if you're asking me if I think she's deliberately trying to separate herself from her Eastern Shore roots—I don't know that I'd go that deep, Owen."

"I don't think it's all that deep. It looks to me that she's almost running away from her past. Like she's trying to forget." Owen took two more beers from the cooler, opened one and passed it to Alec before opening the second one for himself. "Are you part of that?"

"Part of what?"

"Of what she's trying to forget. What she wants

to put behind her. Did you do something to her, back then, that would make her want to leave, to forget—"

"Owen, if anyone should have been wanting to put the past behind where Lis is concerned, it should be me. I'm the one who was humiliated when she turned down my invitation to the prom. I'm the one who everyone snickered at behind their hands when she shut me down in front of everyone."

"What are you talking about?"

Alec told him.

"Why would you ask someone to the prom in front of an audience?" Owen asked in disbelief. "Even I—who was never turned down for a date, I should add right about here—even I wouldn't be dumb enough to do that for the simple reason that the girl might be that one in a million who might say no."

"Yeah, well, your advice is about seventeen years too late. So to answer your question, no, I'm pretty sure that I'm not what Lis was running from, if in fact she was running from anything or trying to forget something from her past." He tilted the bottle back and took a drink. "You know, you could probably ask your sister why she chooses one subject over another. There could be a very simple answer that has nothing to do with Cannonball Island."

Owen rocked for a moment, the bottle dangling from his left hand.

"So how do you feel about her now?" he asked.

Alec sighed. "About the same way I felt about her back then."

"Which was?"

"You're going to make me say it, aren't you?"

"Yep."

"I fell for your sister in fifth grade and my feelings have never really changed. Back then, I thought she was that one-in-a-million girl. I still do. That answer your question?"

"Pretty much, yeah." Owen gazed out across the dune toward the bay, then looked back at Alec. "You know if you hurt her, I might have to hurt you. Just sayin'."

"I would never do anything to hurt her," Alec said softly. "I think I've been waiting for her to come back. I didn't even realize it myself, but I think all this time, I've been waiting for Lis."

"Good. I'm glad we understand each other."

Alec started to get up, feeling he'd been dismissed.

"By the way, what do you know about Cass Logan?" Owen asked, his voice casual but his expression intense.

Alec hesitated before answering.

"I know she's not from around here. That she's staying at a B and B in town for a while."

"Yeah, yeah. Eastern Shore. Vacation. Blah blah blah. Why's she really here?"

"What makes you think . . . ?"

"Hello? Naval intelligence?" Owen sighed. "We both know she's not here for R and R."

"What makes you think I'd know otherwise?"

"I saw you talking to her, heads close together," Owen replied. "And since we've already established that you've got it bad for my sister, I'm going to assume you're not dating Cass, because you'd never stand there and have a cozy tête-à-tête with another girl while my sister was standing ten feet away. Especially not with me in the room."

Alec debated how much to tell Owen. Some parts of the deal with Deiter were still up in the air, and the last thing he wanted was to start rumors.

"Cass is an architect," he told Owen.

"I know that much."

"Her father is Brian Deiter. He's a builder who's responsible for a number of housing developments up and down the Eastern Shore."

"And he has his eye on St. Dennis?" Owen frowned.

"What makes you think that?"

"Why else would she be here?"

Alec shrugged.

"Don't play with me, Jansen," Owen said quietly.

"That's all I'm at liberty to say," Alec told him. "Sorry."

Owen glared at him for a long, hard moment.

Alec finally broke the silence. "I guess I should be going. I have some oyster beds to check on in the morning. Thanks for the beer."

"Anytime."

Alec got up and went to his car.

"Hey, Jansen," Owen called to him just as Alec opened the driver's-side door. When Alec turned around, Owen said, "Good luck with my sister."

"Thanks." Alec started the Jeep and drove off.

He waited while two large SUVs tried to pass each other on the bridge, and thought about Owen's obvious interest in Cass Logan.

Alec weighed what he knew about Owen against the little he knew about Cass. He couldn't even venture a guess what the outcome might be, but he knew it would be interesting to watch. The bridge cleared of its minijam, and Alec stepped on the gas and headed to St. Dennis, amused by the thought of the big guy possibly—finally—striking out.

Alec drove home through the quiet streets of St. Dennis to the house he'd inherited from his uncle Cliff. For his money, it had been an exceptional evening. He wished he could relive that moment when Lis first walked into the gallery in that dress that made him catch his breath. It was silky, of soft, misty colors and gentle curves, and he'd found it smooth and cool when he finally got close enough to touch it. She'd worn her hair down in a sort of ponytail that had been worked into a knot at the left side of her neck and spilled over her shoulder. It was simple and exotic and sexy all at the same time. And as a bonus, he'd been able to look at her all he wanted without having to explain to anyone why he couldn't keep his eyes off her, because it was her show, so everyone else was looking at her, too. She was the guest of honor, and for Alec—as much as he admired her art—she *was* the show.

And then Cass Logan popped up.

"Hey, Cass." He'd come up behind her.

"Hey, yourself," she'd replied.

"So what are you doing here?"

"I'm an art lover. I saw the notice in the paper that there'd be a showing tonight, so I thought I'd drop by, see what all the fuss is about. You know, there's really not much for a newly divorced woman to do by herself on a Saturday night on the Eastern Shore. Besides, I like to know the area I'm going to be working in."

"That sounds like decisions have been made."

"Let's just say I've already started on my part of the project."

"So when am I going to get to see what you've designed?"

"It will be awhile before I have anything to show you. Maybe you won't like what I've done. Maybe my dad won't like it. Maybe he'll decide the cost per unit versus the sales price isn't cost-effective. Maybe your people will decide not to sell, or maybe not enough of them to make enough to offset the cost of the project." Cass took a drink from the glass she was holding. "Lots can happen between here and there. Plenty can go wrong. That's why we take it one step at a time."

"Okay. I get it. I'll be patient."

"I hope you'll also keep it all close to the vest. If word gets out about the project, who knows—another builder could get wind of it and decide it sounds like a good idea to them, too. They offer more money to the sellers, and boom! Deiter's out, someone else is in. It happened to my dad not too long ago, so he's understandably gun-shy about people talking. Loose lips and all that."

"Tell me how it's a bad idea for someone else to pay the islanders more money for their property."

"I'm surprised a man as astute as you needs to ask." She leaned closer to him and lowered her voice.

"Let's start with the fact that you'd have no guarantee that another builder would be willing to work with you to make sure the houses all fit in architecturally. I can make that guarantee. I can promise that nothing will be built that doesn't look like it could have been here two hundred years ago. I can also guarantee that no corners will be cut during construction. You can ask anyone who's ever worked with my father. Yes, he can be tough, he can be annoying as hell, he's stubborn and wants what he wants, but you can count on him to deliver exactly what he says he will."

Alec listened without comment.

"And someone else might be willing to play fast and loose where the environment is concerned."

"There are regulations—"

"That can be overlooked if the price is right. We both know that."

"Sad, but true."

"We both know that sometimes the impact on the environment doesn't manifest itself for years. How many times have you seen the EPA go after a builder only to find out he's gone out of business and maybe he's operating under a different corporate name. We both know who's on the hook, right? The homeowners, or the insurance company for the builder, depending on how his policy was written." She shook her head. "I promise that Deiter Homes is the best company for the job. We'll do it your way, from design to construction, and we'll go by the book when it comes to the regulations. Clean, quick, and honest."

"So in other words, trust you."

"Yes. Trust me. You will love my designs. They're going to be fabulous." She leaned a little closer, a smug smile on her lips. "So fabulous that I already decided that one of them will be mine."

"I can't wait to see them."

"You'll be the first. But I'd like your word that you won't discuss the project until we're ready to start talking to potential sellers." Cass had paused. "You haven't already talked it around, have you?"

"I did discuss the possibility of some development with one person, but it won't go beyond her."

"How can you be sure?"

"Because I know her." Ruby was Ruby, and not into idle talk or anything she might construe as gossip. "And I did mention the possibility of a sale with Tom Mullan, who owns the properties we looked at this week. I did ask him not to talk about it, though, and he agreed."

"I guess you had to confide in him in order to get the key to the house."

Alec had been just about to respond when he realized Owen had joined them.

"Alec," Owen had said, his eyes on Cass, "aren't you going to introduce me?"

And of course, he had, and then he'd taken advantage of Owen's presence to back away and rejoin Lis.

But for tonight, he'd already given enough thought to Cass and the project and where it was going. He'd rather think about Lis, and how great the evening had been for her. She'd been right when she said that most of the town had come to see her work. His aunt Grace had been diligent in beating the bushes on behalf of her friend Ruby, who'd been telling Grace for weeks how proud she was of Lis and how she hoped a lot of people would show up. Grace had taken that as her personal mandate to ensure that the town turned out in droves, and she'd done a damned good job of it, judging by the number of people he'd seen filing in and out of the gallery.

Lis had commented on the fact that many of their classmates had come, and while he assured her that everyone was happy that she'd returned home a successful artist, he hadn't told her about the part where he'd called a lot of them himself, or that the vast majority of them had remembered her as a snob.

"Lis Parker? Yeah, I remember her. She never had two words to say to anyone."

Or: "Oh, Lis Parker, right. I heard she was living in New York or something. She any friendlier these days than she was back in school?"

Or the one that stung the most: "Lis Parker? You mean the one who turned you down for the prom in front of half the student body and made you look like a dork? That Lis Parker?"

Yeah, he'd sighed. That Lis Parker.

They just didn't know what she had been dealing with at home, didn't know what a crazy man her father had been, how he had blamed St. Dennis for everything that was wrong in his life. Alec hadn't known it back then, but over the years, he'd heard enough to piece it together. Hearing it from Lis only confirmed the rumors.

But the friends he'd called had all come tonight, and as Lis had come away with a different outlook on them, so they, too, had seen her in a different light.

"I didn't remember her as so friendly and nice. I guess you were right, Alec. Or maybe I had her mixed up with someone else. It has been a long time . . ." more than one person had said.

"Hey, people change, right?" he'd replied.

He felt sorry for her in a way. He'd had such a great time in high school, had good friends and had enjoyed his life back then immensely. He was always able to look back and smile. Lis seemed to have no such joyful memories. It was a shame, he thought as he pulled into his driveway. Kids should have fun times to look back on. Life is serious enough as you get older.

Of course, the best part of the evening came after the exhibit, when he and Lis finally got to be alone. And, he was happy to recall, the kiss they'd shared tonight had been everything he'd hoped it would be, filled with the promise of other kisses to come. No need to rush the journey, he'd told himself. He wanted to savor every mile of the ride.

He pulled into his driveway and parked near the small garage that housed his bike, a kayak, a canoe, and his tools. The Jeep was too large to fit even without the kayak, so he'd gotten into the habit of leaving it in the driveway. He got out and locked the car behind him and walked around to the front, where he picked up some litter from the lawn and tossed it into the trash can on the side of the house.

Once inside, Alec turned on the light in the front hall, which his cousin Dan had jokingly told him wasn't large enough to be considered a foyer. The house was relatively small but it had suited Alec and his uncle Cliff just fine. Cliff had never married, so it was always just the two of them until Cliff died.

Then the house fell to Alec, who'd been grateful to inherit it. He loved the place, small though it may have been. To the devastated, frightened orphan boy he'd been, the warmth he'd been offered here had gone a long way in helping him past the tragedy that had befallen his family. He'd known Cliff well before the accident, had spent plenty of time in St. Dennis, so it wasn't as if he'd been sent to live with a stranger in a strange place. He already loved the older man, had always been welcome in this house, and as he'd told Lis, from the moment Cliff was named his guardian, he'd treated Alec like his own son.

This small house was home to him, and it had never occurred to Alec to live anywhere else. After college, he came back to St. Dennis, and to this house. Even during those few years he spent in Havre de Grace working as an environmental consultant, he returned to this house every weekend. He'd passed up job offers in other places that he considered geographically undesirable because they weren't a quick and easy drive to St. Dennis; had lost a woman he'd thought he loved when it came down to a choice between moving to Portland with her and living on the other side of the country, or losing her and staying where he was. He wasn't sure if his choice said more about the way he felt about this house, this town, or the way he felt—or didn't feel—about the woman. Either way, he'd never second-guessed his decision.

As Ruby was fond of saying, "You need to know where you belong." There was no doubt in Alec's mind that he belonged right here, in this house, in this town.

He was hoping that sooner or later, Lis would come to the conclusion that she belonged here, too.

"HERE, LET ME give you a hand with that."

Owen had come outside when he saw Lis struggling to get something out of the trunk of her car.

"Like you gave me a hand last night?"

"Did I interrupt something?" He took the easel from her hands and carried it toward the house. "Where did you want this?"

"In the front bedroom, and you know damned well you did."

"Lisbeth Jane, you watch your tongue. It's the Sabbath." Ruby had come out onto the porch and stood with her hands on her hips.

"Sorry, Gigi. But he—"

"Hush. Don't be telling tales." Ruby turned and went back into the store, and Lis laughed out loud in spite of having been chastised.

"What else?" Owen appeared by her side at the back of the car.

"You could grab that box of paints, and my other suitcase."

He reached past her, picked up the box and the suitcase and was gone again. She finished emptying the trunk and took the last box inside.

"Are you going to have breakfast with Gigi and me?" Owen asked as he passed Lis on the steps.

"I had coffee earlier. I just want to get my stuff set up."

"You're going to use Gigi and Pop's old bedroom as a studio?" he asked.

Lis nodded. "It has the best views and the best light, and Gigi said she had no use for it now, so I was welcome to it."

"I thought the old cottage was going to be your studio."

"Even if it can be restored, it's going to take a long time before I can set up shop there. I can't sit around doing nothing while I wait." She went up a few steps past him, still talking. "I have a painting in my head for Gigi that I want to get started on right away. This is just temporary."

"What if the cottage can't be saved?"

"Then I'll think of something else."

"Sounds like you're making plans to stick around for a while more. Wouldn't have anything to do with old Alec, now, would it?"

Ignoring the question, she said, "What was all that about last night, anyway?"

"Just taking some time to renew an old friendship, that's all."

"Owen, even you said you hardly knew him back in the day. You can't renew a friendship you never had." She smirked. "You just wanted information on the blonde."

"Maybe. No harm there."

"So what did you find out?" Lis shifted the box in her arms. "About the blonde."

"Curious, are you?"

"Don't make me hurt you, Owen."

"Right. As if you could. All I know about her is that her name is Cass—"

"I know that much."

"—and she's an architect."

"I knew that, too. Tell me something I don't know."

"She likes art—that's why she was there last night. She's renting a place over on Dune Drive, and she went to Penn undergrad and Columbia for graduate school."

"That's it? You talked to her all that time and that's all you found out?"

"She's divorced."

"So I guess the rest of the time you talked about yourself."

"Pretty much. Now that you mention it, yeah."

"Self-centered much?"

"Hey, I didn't offer to talk about myself. She just kept asking me about me. Not saying that I might occasionally bring up my accomplishments, but last night, I didn't have to. She asked."

"Interesting."

"What is?"

"That she found you so fascinating." Lis turned to start back up the steps.

"Lighten up, Lis. It may come as a surprise to you—you being my sister I can overlook it—but there are some ladies who find me hot."

"I personally don't know any, but we'll let it go. So did you get her number?"

"No," he admitted.

"I would have put real money on that. She declined?"

"I didn't get a chance to ask her. I meant to. But when it was time to go, I went to check on Gigi. When I came back, Cass was gone."

"So I guess she didn't find you all that fascinating after all. Better luck next time."

"Say it like you mean it." Owen went downstairs and disappeared into Ruby's sitting room.

Lis reached the landing and headed for the room in the front of the house. The door was open and she left the box she'd been carrying on the floor near the side window. With light coming in from two sides, the room was perfect for her to work in. Owen had set up her easel, and earlier she'd carried up a small table from the storeroom to hold her paints. She opened her case and set it on the table. She'd once told her mother that all she really needed to be happy was a place to set up her easel and some great light. Now that she had both here on the island, she could work, and few things made her happier than working. She sat on the edge of a stool she'd brought up from the store and gazed out the window.

The sky was clear and blue and the water dark and as smooth as the deepest blue silk. The rocks that formed the jetty were the color of granite, and the sand along the shore was pale gold. The dunes were paler still, and the grasses that grew along their mounds were shades of green and gray and brown. In the distance the pines grew in a haphazard pattern and overhead gulls swarmed and dove. In her mind, Lis was already mixing the colors she would need.

She sat in front of the window, a sketchbook resting on her knees, while she quickly drew the rudiments of what she saw beyond the window. She wanted it to be right, to be as near perfect as possible. This was the scene that had greeted Ruby and her Harold every morning for so many years, and Lis felt a compulsion to preserve the view. She'd learned long ago that sometimes you had to go with your gut, and since she'd arrived here, she had the urge to paint the iconic island scenes, especially those that might mean something to Ruby. She told herself that the feeling had been born of wanting to record the island's stories in Ruby's words, so wouldn't it follow that she should record the way the island had looked for so long? There had been some changes over the years, but the island she'd known and grown up on basically remained the same. Maybe Ruby had spooked her with her "change is coming" talk. Whatever, Lis's hands itched to feel her brushes and she needed to work.

When the sketch had been completed, she lined up her brushes, her tubes of paints, and her palette. She repositioned the easel so that the surface was horizontal. Soon she was lost in perfecting the blue of the sky and the nuances of the sea below. Sun sparkled off the bits of mica in the granite, and she worked to get that right. When she stopped for her first break, she found she'd been working for almost three hours. She looked around for water but realized she hadn't brought any upstairs. She rested her brush on its holder and went down into the store and found a cold pitcher of iced tea on the island in the kitchen. She poured herself a glass and leaned against the counter to take a long, cool drink. There was a shuffling noise at the doorway and she looked over to see Ruby leaning on the jamb.

"This is great iced tea," Lis said. "Thanks for making it."

"That be your brother's making," Ruby told her. "He likes to poke in the kitchen. Made chicken salad for lunch, too. That boy spent half the morning in here."

"Are you talking about Owen?"

"You got a brother I don't know about?"

"I had no idea he liked to cook." Lis frowned. "Why didn't I know that?"

"Maybe you two spend more than half a minute talking twice a year, you might learn something 'bout each other." Ruby turned to go back into the store.

"Gigi, can we talk again tonight?" Lis drained the glass and rinsed it out at the sink.

"We talk every night, best I recall."

"I mean, about the island. About what you remember from what your mother and father told you, about the old days."

Ruby nodded. "I be around."

"Do you mind talking about it? Does it bother you?"

"Bother me more if things that should be remembered be forgot in time." Ruby turned toward the store and called, "Essie, you go on and make yourself some tea. I be just a minute."

Essie called back but Lis couldn't hear what she said. Ruby was still in the doorway looking at Lis.

"Is something wrong, Gigi?" Lis asked.

"Things be right, by and by. Can't change what's meant to be, Lisbeth Jane. Time be coming when you be needing to think with your head *and* your heart. Mind you take care."

"Take care with what?" she asked, but Ruby had already walked away.

It was so like Ruby to be cryptic sometimes. There were times when she would appear to be giving a warning of sorts, and then something would happen and Lis would wonder if that was what Ruby had meant. There was no denying that what people on the island said was true, that Ruby had "the eye," and if that meant the ability to sometimes see things that other people didn't see, Lis could attest to that. It was just a little spooky in a way. It used to scare her just a little when she was younger, especially when she'd hear Ruby talking to Lis's mother.

"*I see nothing good coming of this, Kathleen,*" she'd hear Ruby say, and Lis's mother would back off whatever she'd had in mind to do. Lis supposed that maybe her mom had experienced enough of Ruby's "seeings" that she found it more prudent not to tempt fate.

Whatever, it was disconcerting sometimes, especially when Ruby would get that expression on her face and sort of look past you, and she'd say things without explanation, like just now: *Mind you take care.* As if disaster was about to strike at any minute.

Lis refused to dwell on the fact that sometimes it appeared that Owen had inherited the ability.

She shook it off and went back upstairs to work.

The sketch of Ruby she'd started a few days earlier
was on the table. She picked it up and studied it, then
put it aside. She'd work on that more when she and
Ruby sat down to chat later. That painting would
be for herself. The watercolor painting of the island
would be for Ruby, and she wanted to finish that first.

Her phone was buzzing to alert her to an incom-
ing text message, and she picked it up.

Congrats again on a great exhibit. Celebrate tomorrow? Parade starts at nine.

Lis frowned. Parade? What parade?

She looked at the date on her phone: July 3.
Tomorrow would be the fourth.

St. Dennis always had a huge parade to commem-
orate the Fourth of July, but as a child she'd never
been permitted to attend and she'd never been back
on that particular holiday.

Love to. Meet you there.

A minute later, Alec replied.

We'll never find each other. Will walk over to Ruby's
around 8:30.

If all she'd heard about the parade in the past held
true, he was probably right.

It's a date. See you then.

She smiled, picked up her brush, and turned her
focus to the view out the window and the colors that
were swirling around in her head.

Chapter Thirteen

The local high school band marched along Charles Street behind the ancient baby-blue convertible carrying this year's Miss Eastern Shore that led the parade.

"That's some car," Lis observed.

"A 1957 Olds Super 88," Alec told her. "She's a beauty. You don't see fins like that these days."

"Well, I think it's safe to say they don't make 'em like that anymore."

"No, but when you see one that's been restored the way that one has, you have to admit, that's a beautiful machine."

"It is." Lis pointed at the band coming along next. "Oh, look! Bagpipes!"

"Don't have to look to know bagpipes are on the way."

"I love the sound of the pipes. My dad used to play them," Lis said.

"He did?"

"All the men in my family played bagpipes."

"Somehow I don't see Owen playing the bagpipe."

"Well, except for Owen. But he did play the violin."

"Didn't see that coming, either."

"He wasn't very good at it." Lis laughed. "Don't tell him that I said so. He thought he was quite the virtuoso."

A seemingly endless sea of kids of all ages on bikes festooned with red, white, and blue crepe paper streamers followed the pipe band. Behind the bikes came the strollers similarly decked out in crepe paper streamers, their little occupants dressed in patriotic finery. Next came a string band from Philadelphia, and then a World War II tank.

"Where do you suppose they got the tank?" Lis asked.

Alec shrugged. "No telling. I think my aunt Grace was on the committee this year, so I can ask."

The parade went on for a respectable thirty minutes, with bands from all over and different organizations represented by floats and marchers. By the time the local middle school jazz band went by to end the parade, most of the onlookers were done—well done, because the temperature had risen to ninety-three humid degrees and they were standing in direct sun. Alec ducked into Sips, where he stood in line for fifteen minutes to buy cold drinks behind a lot of other hot, thirsty parade-watchers.

"Sorry it took me so long," he said as he returned with two large bottles of cold water. "The place is jammed."

"No surprise there. Thanks." Lis pulled the elastic

from her hair and redid her ponytail, lifting it higher in an attempt to keep it off her neck. Alec handed her one of the bottles and she took a long drink. "That was one heck of a parade. Thanks for bringing me. I enjoyed the festivities."

"Babe, you haven't even begun to see festivities. That was just the appetizer." He took her hand and led her toward the center of town.

"Where are we going?" She noticed everyone else was headed in the same direction.

"First to the park, where we'll watch the little kids run footraces and toss water balloons at each other and carry raw eggs on spoons while we eat ice cream and try to keep from passing out under this merciless sun and talk to people we haven't seen since last year's parade. The agenda hasn't changed in fifty, sixty years." He looked down at her. "You seriously never did a St. Dennis Fourth before?"

She shook her head.

"Well, after the games and the socializing, we go back to the inn. We have lunch on the terrace and then we go down to the water and sit on the grass and watch the sailboat races. That will take us to around three o'clock, at which time we will probably fall asleep in the shade of one of those big old trees. After that, we have dinner—they do a barbecue for the inn's guests and the family always grabs a plate before the fireworks start." He paused. "What did you used to do on the island to celebrate the Fourth?"

"Nothing like what you all do on this side of the bridge. Mostly it was just watching one of the big-city parades on TV and a barbecue in the afternoon."

She shrugged. "Most years we'd go out on someone's dad's boat to watch the sail races in the afternoon, and at night we'd sit out on the pier and watch the fireworks from St. Dennis and from across the bay."

"Guess you didn't have much of a marching band."

"Very funny. A couple of the kids from the island were in the school band. Everyone's parents weren't as prejudiced as my dad was."

"What about your mom?"

"My mother didn't much care one way or the other. I had the feeling that when she was younger, she tried to buck the system, defy my dad, but I don't think that ended well for her." Thinking about the relationship between her father and her mother made her sad, and she said so. "We didn't have the happiest home life. I think my mom was getting ready to leave my dad when he got sick. She stayed till the end, then she left to go as far from the Eastern Shore as she could get. She has a friend who lives in Mesa, so she went out there to visit and decided to stay."

"That was senior year, right?"

"Right. My dad died in July following our junior year, and as soon as the dust settled, my mom left for Arizona. I didn't want to go because I had one more year left in high school and I couldn't see starting over somewhere else as a senior. So I stayed with Gigi. After graduation, I did visit Mom, but it was just too hot and I missed the bay, and I missed Gigi, so I came back."

"And promptly left for college."

"Art school in Philly," she told him.

"I remember seeing you one day that summer at the library here in town."

"You did? Did we talk?" Lis was pretty sure she'd have remembered.

"No. I was with a bunch of the guys, and since they'd never let me forget that you turned me down for the prom . . ."

"Oh God, you remember that." Lis covered her face with her hands. "I was hoping you'd forgotten."

"A guy doesn't forget rejection like that."

"I am so sorry."

Alec shrugged. "It was my own fault for being so cocky. It never occurred to me that you'd say no. In my own foolish head, I thought you'd be dying to go with me."

"I was."

"Was what?"

"Dying to go with you. It never occurred to me that you'd ask. Which is why I had nothing to say after I said no. I knew I wouldn't be allowed, but I really wanted to, and it was too hard to explain in front of everyone."

"Is that why it took you so long to respond?" Alec tried to make light of it. "It seemed that in my head, I heard that Final Jeopardy music playing while I waited for you to answer. And of course I expected your answer to be yes."

"I wish I could have said yes."

"Did you go with someone else? To the prom? I remember looking for you but never did see you."

"Jerry Willets asked me."

"Now, that I would have remembered."

"I stayed home."

"Seriously? You didn't go?"

"Seriously. What was the point?" Lis shrugged. "Get all dressed up to go someplace I didn't want to be, with someone I didn't want to go with? It was easier to stay home."

"Did you go senior year?"

She shook her head no.

"So you've never been to a prom?"

"Nope."

"Not even in college? Homecoming dance? Sorority formals?"

Another shake of the head. "I didn't join a sorority."

"So are you as antisocial as you sound?"

"I'm really not." Lis laughed. "I had friends and I had a good time in college, but I was really focused on my art classes. You may not have noticed, but the art department in our high school left a lot to be desired. When I got to Philly and had all these incredible instructors, it was like someone had turned the lights on after I'd been sitting in the dark for a long, long time. I had a ton of raw ability but I'd had very little direction. I got that in Philly."

"Did you date?"

"What kind of a question is that? Of course I did."

"A lot?"

"Enough."

"Did you have a steady guy?"

"Sometimes. How about you?"

"I did it all. Fraternity. Homecoming. Sorority date nights. Played lacrosse."

"And somehow you still managed to graduate?"

"I did."

"Were you lucky or were you that smart?" As soon as she said it, she remembered just how smart he'd been in high school. It was one of the things that had attracted her to him back then.

"A little of both, I guess."

They reached the park and filed through the open gates along with a few hundred others. The distance to the playing fields where kids would compete for prizes and medals wasn't far, but it took twenty minutes or so, because they ran into so many people who complimented Lis on her paintings, or who asked Alec how the boat renovations were coming along.

"Does everyone in town know about that boat?" Lis asked.

"Pretty much. Not much goes unnoticed around here." He put his arm around her waist. "Like right now, Nita Perry is telling Barbara Noonan to check out Alec Jansen and Lis Parker. The game is always on around here."

"What game?"

"Telephone. By this time tomorrow we'll be engaged, and by Thursday we'll be expecting our first child."

They reached the middle of the park, where an announcer stood on a wooden grandstand and made announcements. The footraces for the four- and five-year-olds would begin right after the national anthem and the Pledge of Allegiance. A girl in her late teens who'd been a finalist on one of the televised singing competitions sang and the leader of the local grange hall led the pledge.

"Want to watch the races?" Alec asked her.

"Sure."

They made their way to the makeshift track and cheered for no one in particular, then stayed for the races for the ten- through twelve-year-olds. The temperature continued to soar, and finally Alec told her, "They're giving out ice cream over by the grandstand if you—"

She didn't wait for him to finish. "Yes. Anything cold."

"We don't have to stay till the last race has been run, you know. We can leave whenever you want."

"I kind of want to stay, despite the heat. I haven't been before, so it's new to me. If you're bored, though, we can go."

"I thought maybe you were bored."

"I'm enjoying it. The kids all seem to be having a great time." She glanced around at the crowd. "The adults, too."

After another hour had passed, Alec said, "We can pack it in anytime now. They're not giving out prizes for staying till the end."

Lis nodded, and they walked to the back entry to the park.

"If the marsh wasn't there," he told her when they came to a stand of cattails, "we could walk straight over to the inn instead of going all the way out to the road and down the lane to get there."

"It's a nice walk, now that we're in the shade. I don't mind. But I think I should get back to Gigi's."

"Why? She isn't there."

"She isn't?" Lis frowned. "How do you know?"

"Because she's at the inn. Ford was going to pick her up after the parade, but Owen said he'd bring her. I thought you knew."

Lis shook her head. "When you live with Gigi, it's one surprise after another."

"She'll be at the inn all afternoon, right up to the fireworks. She said she loved fireworks and hadn't seen any up close in a long time, so my aunt invited her to spend the day at the inn."

"I didn't see Owen this morning before we left, so I didn't know what anyone's plans were. I wonder if Owen went to the parade."

"I guess you can ask him. I imagine he'll stay for the barbecue."

They reached the end of the marsh and stepped onto the shoulder of the road. Another twenty steps and they were at the winding lane that led to the inn. Already a crowd had gathered on the lawn and the smoke from several large grills was drifting upward. The tennis courts were filled, people were dragging kayaks and canoes down to the water's edge, and several teenagers sped past them on bikes headed toward the road.

"I had no idea there was so much going on here." Lis looked around as if she were lost. "And I always thought of the inn as an old building with peeling paint."

"That was before Dan decided to make it *the* place to go on the Eastern Shore. There's a beautiful playground for the younger kids and a lot of activities for the older ones. You can take tennis lessons or learn to sail or take out a kayak or one of the canoes. There are activities for every month of the year. Like in November, the chef runs a cooking class weekend where you can learn to make dishes that use the local catch from that morning. December, Laura from the flower shop comes in and does a wreath-making day." Alec smiled. "There is no grass growing under my cousin Dan's feet, that's for sure. And I should add that since Lucy came back from California, the wedding business here has skyrocketed. There are weddings every weekend, sometimes during the week as well."

"That accounts for the full parking lot," Lis observed. "Oh, there's Owen's car. He and Gigi must be here already."

"Then she's probably on the back patio with Aunt Grace. That's one of her favorite places to hang out." Still holding her hand, Alec led Lis around to the back of the building and the covered veranda that stood beneath a long line of magnolia trees.

"Well, there you are." Lis joined Ruby and Grace. "I didn't know you'd be here."

"Slipped my mind, I suppose." Ruby noted Lis's and Alec's joined hands with obvious satisfaction. "Can't pass up my day with Gracie, and since the Fourth fell on Tuesday, I get to enjoy a barbecue and the view at the same time I get to visit. How was the parade?"

"It was fun," Lis told her.

Ruby appeared oddly satisfied at this admission as well. "Long time coming," she said to no one in particular.

Lis couldn't tell if Ruby was referring to the fact

that Lis had finally experienced a St. Dennis parade, or to her changed relationship with Alec, or both.

Just as Alec had promised, there was nonstop activity until late afternoon when, sure enough, he fell asleep on the grass beneath the pines. Lis tried to stay awake, but the heat combined with the barbecued chicken and potato salad she'd eaten made her drowsy as well.

"Must have been the Smith Island cake," she muttered as she stretched out on the grass next to Alec, her head on his shoulder. Within minutes she was sound asleep, and when she awoke, her head was on his chest and his arm was wrapped around her. She felt momentarily disoriented. It seemed so natural to be lying there, so close together. On the other hand, it felt almost too intimate, and she was trying to figure out how best to extricate herself from his embrace when he said, "Are you awake?"

"I am."

"Good. My arm's asleep."

She sat up at the same time he did.

"Sorry," she told him.

"Not your fault, and not a big deal. The blood will return in a few minutes."

Lis smothered a yawn with her hand. "I didn't realize I was that tired."

"When I told you that a nap on the lawn was part of the day, I wasn't kidding. Now, how 'bout we get a couple of beers and check out the sailboat races. They're probably almost over, but at least we'll see who crosses the finish line."

By the end of the day, Lis's head was spinning. She

hadn't done that much socializing, hadn't talked that much, in years. They were just getting ready to watch the fireworks when Lis saw her brother. He was seated on the lawn next to Cass Logan.

"Something wrong?" Alec asked when he saw her staring. His gaze followed hers.

"Not really. I was just wondering how Owen ended up here with Cass Logan."

"Does it matter?"

"Not really."

"Then let's get a seat down front for the fireworks. They'll be starting soon."

They sat close together on the grass, Alec's arm around her. When she startled at the first loud boom, he drew her to him almost instinctively, and when the finale filled the sky with exploding colors and one boom after another, they walked together back up the lawn to the inn.

"We can probably get a ride back to the island with Owen," Lis told Alec. "He's probably going to take Gigi back."

"Would you rather ride or walk? I don't have a preference."

"Then let's walk. It's a beautiful night."

They said their good-byes and walked leisurely toward the road, their hands entwined, their arms swinging between them. The air had cooled with the setting of the sun, and a gentle breeze had picked up. Even though they'd spent the entire day together, Lis wasn't ready to watch Alec drive away. As they strolled across the bridge, fireworks could be heard in the distance.

"Where do you suppose those are coming from?" Alec asked.

"Let's walk out to the point"—Lis tugged him toward the road—"and you'll see. It's my turn to show and tell."

The walk to the point took another fifteen minutes, but once they'd seated themselves at the very end of the pier, it had been worth it. From across the bay, fireworks spewed huge pinwheels of color far into the sky. The show lasted for close to an hour, each display grander and louder than the one before.

"That was a perfect ending to a perfect day." Alec stood and reached a hand to Lis to pull her up. "A perfect night."

"It was. I can't remember when I—"

Whatever Lis couldn't remember was lost when he wrapped his arms around her and covered her mouth with his. The last time he'd kissed her, Lis had thought it was the best kiss ever, but that had been before tonight. Last time, she realized, was only the warmup. This was the real deal, deep and hot and soul stirring, and the only thing that went through her mind was *more*. More of his lips, more of the way his tongue mingled with hers and then teased the corners of her mouth. More of the heat that built up between them. More of Alec.

A last boom from across the bay jolted them both, and Lis pushed back, startled, then they both laughed somewhat nervously.

"I thought for a moment someone was shooting at us," Lis said, only half joking.

"It could happen." Alec stared toward the road, at the far end of the property from where they stood on the pier.

Two figures appeared near the road, moving toward them.

"Who do you think that is?" Lis whispered.

"Probably a couple of kids looking for a spot to make out," he replied.

They watched as the figures drew closer, then stopped. They walked side by side some distant apart, not touching, nor were they hand in hand the way would-be lovers would be, though one was clearly a man and the other a woman. Suddenly the two stopped and stood as if staring at something.

"Alec, they're stopping at the cottage," Lis said. "Do you think they're going to try to break in?"

"I don't know, though anyone from around here wouldn't bother. Everyone knows the place is about to fall down."

"Really?" Her attention shifted from the trespassers at the cottage to Alec. "Really? Is that your final, professional contractor assessment?"

He cleared his throat. "I wasn't going to say anything until I got the written report from the termite inspector, but I ran into him yesterday morning, and he told me from everything he's seen, it's not good. There's a lot more damage than I'd suspected, and frankly, I suspected there was a lot."

"But you can fix it all, right? You'll fix it for me?"

"Lis, sometimes things can't be fixed. The foundation is rotted and now we're finding out that the support beams were riddled by termites. It doesn't look good."

"So what you're saying is . . ."

"It's probably a teardown. I'm sorry. I know it meant a lot to you."

"Damn it. Why can't you build a new foundation and replace the supports?"

"We'd have to take up the floor to do that."

"But you could do that, couldn't you?"

"We're talking about a lot of time and a lot of money, and even at that, I don't know that it would work."

Lis fell silent, and disappointment bled through her, stronger than she'd imagined.

"Look, we can rebuild it to look like the original. We can replicate the floor plan, but we can make it even better. We can make the rooms larger, put in central air, new windows that actually open and close."

"It won't be the same." She tried not to sound petulant, but she'd had her heart set on moving in and setting up a new studio in a new place that had new energy. In her mind's eye, she even saw herself creating great works of art there.

He stroked her hair, from the crown to the center of her back, where it had flowed when she took out the elastic that had held it back all day.

"No, it won't be the same, but we can put in it everything you love about the old place. We'll reuse as much as we can and we can make it look the same from the outside. You can position it anywhere you want on the point, like closer to the bay with windows overlooking the water, bringing in the bay and the sky. You can have skylights upstairs, more than one fireplace—whatever you want."

"I wanted Ruby's place. I wanted the floors she and my great-grandfather walked on and the steps they climbed." She'd felt such a sense of history, of family there.

"You can have those things," he assured her. "We'll take up the floorboards, and the ones that aren't damaged, we'll use in the new place."

"But you can't re-create the whispers and the tears and the laughter, the emotions that are in the walls and in the air there." The things that mattered most and could never be duplicated.

"No," he conceded, "I can't do that."

"Well, thanks anyway." She broke away from him except for her right hand, which sought his. "I guess it wasn't meant to be. And maybe you're right, maybe it's too far gone to fix. I was just hoping . . ."

Alec sighed with resignation. "Look, maybe I can take another look. Maybe there's some way . . . I can talk to Cameron O'Connor, see if he has any ideas."

"I knew you'd do it." Her expression went from sad to smug in the blink of an eye.

"Just understand that it's iffy at best. I will do whatever I can, but no guarantees. And if you decide you want to rebuild it, I promise you it will be everything you want it to be."

"My hero." She wrapped her arms around his neck.

"Don't get ahead of the game here."

"I know you can do it. I know you can make it work." She stood on her tiptoes to kiss him.

Alec sighed. "I'll give it my best."

Hand in hand, they walked the length of the pier to the grass. As she and Alec drew closer to the cottage, the couple they'd noticed earlier backed away. A minute later, they heard the sound of a car engine and something small and sleek drove off.

"I guess they were just poking around," Lis said. "They wouldn't be the first to drive out here just to look at the place."

"Probably," he agreed.

They walked back to Ruby's along the western side of the island, past the abandoned chapels and the old churchyards.

"Do you have a key for the front door, or do you want to walk around the back?" Alec asked her when they arrived at the old store.

"I have keys to both," she told him. "I'll go in here."

Ruby had left on the porch lights both front and back, so the lock was easy to find.

"I'm glad she's locking the door these days," Lis noted while she unlocked it. "For a long time, she never bothered."

"Even Ruby recognizes that it's a different world."

Lis turned the key and added, "She said as much, that change was coming."

"Did she tell you what kind of change?"

Lis shook her head and pushed the door open. "No, but I'm sure she knows. She always seems to know."

"Change isn't necessarily a bad thing," Alec told her. "Sometimes a little change is good."

"True. At least, it's been good for me. The change in scenery has been good for my work."

"Not so many tall buildings to paint around here."

"I think I might be ready for something else." She told him about her second-floor studio and the painting of the island she was working on for Ruby. "I want to paint her as well," she told him. "I've been working on sketches. Her beauty is so hard to capture on paper. Her bone structure is perfect and her features are classic. There's no one else who looks quite like her."

"Does she know you're doing it?"

Lis shook her head. "I don't think she does. I've been sketching her in bits and pieces but I don't think she's caught on that the sketch was the first step to a painting."

"I'm sure she'll love it when it's finished."

"I hope so. But it isn't for her. It's for me. I keep thinking about the time when . . . when . . ." Lis couldn't make the words come.

"When she isn't with us anymore." Alec finished the sentence for her.

"I can't even bring myself to say it. I know she won't live forever—none of us will—but I can't imagine what life would be like without her. It's one of the reasons why I closed up my apartment and brought a lot of my stuff down here. I want to spend as much time as I can on the island."

"What are the other reasons?"

Her arms slid around his neck. "I think you can figure that out for yourself."

"Maybe. But I want to hear you say it."

"I want to spend more time with you, here. I want to see where this leads." She kissed him. "Is that what you had in mind?"

"That just about covers it, yes." He pulled her closer. "I've waited a long, long time for you. I didn't even realize I'd been waiting until I saw you again. We both deserve the chance to see where this goes."

"And in the meantime, we can work together on my house."

"Wait. Does this mean you're only interested in my rehab skills?"

"I'll bet you really rock your tool belt."

"So I've been told."

The lights from a car rounded the bend in their direction, and seconds later Owen drove past the front of the store and around toward the back.

"Kiss me good night, Alec, before Owen shows up and ruins the mood." She stretched to reach his mouth. "Thank you again for an absolutely perfect day. Maybe one of my most favorite days ever."

"Even after me telling you that the cottage might not—"

She put her hand over his mouth and grinned. "I have faith in you. You're going to figure it out."

Chapter Fourteen

"So how was your date last night?" Lis asked Owen over coffee the next morning.

"I didn't have a date last night," he replied.

"Oh. My mistake. I saw you and Cass Logan at the inn yesterday. And since you mentioned she was staying someplace on Dune Drive and the barbecue was for paying guests at the inn plus Sinclair family and friends, I assumed she had come with you. As your date." Lis stood at the counter, pouring half-and-half into her coffee. She didn't have to turn around to know what expression was on her brother's face, but turn around she did, because she couldn't resist. "Since you qualify as one of the aforementioned Sinclair family and friends . . ."

"Not that you are entitled to the information, but she is staying at the inn. She was on the waiting list for a long-term room, and when one became available, she checked out of the place she was staying in and moved her things into the inn." He put his mug of coffee aside and took a container of orange juice from the refrigerator. "And before you ask, no, I don't know how long term it's going to be."

"What's she doing in St. Dennis?"

He seemed to hesitate. "Vacation. Like about five thousand other people who come here in the summer."

"If you drink right out of that carton, I'm telling Gigi," Lis warned.

Owen laughed and poured juice into a glass. He held the carton out to Lis.

"No, thanks," she told him, and he returned the juice to the fridge.

"So you just ran into Cass when you went over to the inn to drop off Gigi and you decided to stay?"

"Pretty much, yeah. It was just a coincidence. Speaking of yesterday at the inn, you and Jansen looked pretty cozy, all snuggled up in the shade under that big tree down near the water."

"You're just jealous because no one was snuggling with you. Though you and Cass looked pretty cozy, off by yourselves chatting away. What do you and an architect have to talk about for so long, anyway?"

"None of your business."

Owen took his coffee, and a slice of toast from Lis's plate, and went out onto the back porch.

Lis finished her breakfast and washed Owen's and her dishes before going into the store, where she chatted with a few of the latecomers that morning.

"Did you sleep in this morning, Mr. Eisner?" she asked the elderly gentleman who leaned on his cane as he waited for a new pot of coffee to brew. Lis looked at the clock over the door. "You're usually in by seven."

"Late night, yes indeed," he told her. "Damned fireworks kept me up past eleven."

"They stopped by ten, if I remember correctly."

"Maybe so, but I still heard 'em in my head. Boom! Boom!" He shook his gray head. "All that noise."

"Well, it's only one night out of the year," she reminded him.

"One night too many, you ask me." He continued to grumble after he poured his coffee and snapped on the lid, and even as he paid Ruby at the cash register.

"Well, now, Fred, you know, you'll be sleeping long enough, by and by," Ruby told him. "Time to enjoy what be in this world. Time enough to sleep in the next."

He harrumphed and shuffled off to the door, his cane in one hand, his coffee in the other.

"Lisbeth Jane, you should know better than to put a bee in his bonnet, 'specially so early in the morning," Ruby chastised her, but there was a hint of a gleam in her eye. "To hear him tell, that man never had a good day in his life."

"That's so sad," Lis said.

Ruby nodded. "That's a fact."

A delivery truck pulled into the drive and several large cartons were brought into the store. While Ruby chatted with the delivery man, Lis took Ruby's box cutter from a drawer near the counter and sliced the tops of the boxes. She shelved the cans of soup and the boxes of tissues and rolls of paper towels, then hauled the empty shipping cartons out onto the porch.

"Thank you, Lisbeth," Ruby said when she came back inside. "You be getting real good at that."

"Ha," Lis chuckled. "Anyone can open a box and put the contents onto a shelf."

"You be fast. Take me all morning to do what you just did in ten minutes."

It was on the tip of Lis's tongue to remind Ruby that she was a hundred years old, and Lis only thirty-five, but the words stuck in her throat. Any reminder of Ruby's age only served to make Lis sad and dread the inevitable even more.

"I'm going to go upstairs to work for a while," Lis told Ruby.

"You finding it a good place to work, that front room?"

"It's a great place to work. The light is perfect and the view can't be beat."

"You be okay there, then, if the cottage don't work out?"

"I could paint here, yes, I could. Would I rather be at the point? Sure. But I'm good here, Gigi. Thanks for asking."

Ruby nodded with apparent satisfaction.

"If you need anything, just call me." Lis turned toward the steps.

"I got Owen here today, for a while, anyway," Ruby told her. "Though there be no telling what that boy . . ." She walked to the window and looked out. "What is that boy up to?"

"Looks like he's searching for something in the shed." Lis stood next to Ruby at the window. On impulse, she put her arm around Ruby's waist. Who knew how many more opportunities she'd have to tell her without words how much the older woman meant to her?

"Now, now, Lisbeth." Ruby patted the arm that encircled her. "Don't be thinking such thoughts. It be what it be. No need to worry now."

Lis didn't bother to ask how Ruby knew what she was thinking. It just seemed that more and more, Ruby knew. It was as much a part of her as her arthritic hands and the narrow folds of wrinkles that lined her face.

"That boy messes up my shed, there be the devil to pay." Ruby opened the door and went outside. "Owen, you put it all back where you found it, every piece, hear?"

Lis smiled. Ruby still ruled. It settled Lis's heart.

Once in her makeshift studio, Lis moved the easel to better catch the light from the side window, and opened her palette. Soon she was lost in her own world, where color and form blended into sky and sea. Sometimes it almost seemed as if she were seeing the island as it was before anyone inhabited it, before any of the cabins had been built and no boats stood on pilings looking out at the bay. She painted what she saw, and what she did not see. She worked until the light began to fade and shadows lengthened across the floor.

"Hey, you still alive here?" Owen stood in the doorway.

"Yep. I'm good," Lis replied without looking up from the paper on which she worked her watercolor magic.

"Wow, that's . . ." Owen paused. "That's really good. Beautiful, even. What made you think to do that, to take out all the cabins and everything?" He inspected the painting closely. "There's no road," he said. "Did you forget to put in the road? And no store. Though I guess if you're painting from the perspective of the store, there wouldn't be . . ."

Lis glanced up at him and smiled. "It's just the way I saw it today. I don't know why." She stood back and seemed to study her work as if she hadn't seen it before.

"Well, wrap it up. Gigi wants to have dinner early, the three of us, and she's ready. Now."

"Gigi cooked?" Lis frowned. She had taken over most of the cooking chores since she arrived.

"I cooked."

"You . . . ?"

Owen nodded. "And I'll thank you to keep your comments to yourself. I just figured Gigi's cooked enough meals for other people over the years. It's her turn to have someone cook for her."

"I agree." Lis began to clean her brushes. "Am I allowed to ask what you made?"

"Gazpacho."

"Seriously? Does Gigi know?"

"It was her idea." Owen turned to go downstairs and over his shoulder added, "And she asked for extra spicy."

"GIGI, WHAT DO you know about the people who built this store?" Lis, Ruby, and Owen sat on the back porch at dusk, Lis's old tape recorder between them on the table.

"That be my great-great grandfather Sam and my great-great-grandmother Edna. They be the ones who made the crossing, May of 1813." Ruby sat in her rocking chair, her arms resting along the chair's arms, and stared into the streaks of color shed by the setting sun as it spread across the water.

"Why'd they side with the British and not the Americans?" Owen asked.

Ruby shrugged. "Best I recall hearing about all that, Sam's brother—I believe he was Edwin—was in the British navy. A captain or such. Sam wasn't about to go against his own flesh and blood."

"But they were Americans by then."

"Plenty of folks on the Eastern Shore thought it best to be loyal to the king." She began to rock slowly. "Not be my place to say they be right or they be wrong. Didn't walk in their shoes. Would I go against my own kin?"

"But it had to be something more than who in St. Dennis sided with who," Lis pointed out.

"I been thinking back to what I heard from the old folks, since you asked before. Seems I heard tell that some boys from St. Dennis were taken and put on a ship and told they be sailing for the king. Their kin wanted their boys back, didn't take kindly to anyone telling them that the king be the king and can do what he please. Said anyone who wouldn't fight to have them boys be brought back home got no business in St. Dennis, and if they wouldn't move out, they'd be moved. That be when folk be sent over the bridge to the island and not be left back."

"Doesn't it bother you?" Lis asked.

"Can't change what was. No point in holding a grudge against people who had no hand in it. Seems silly to me, but like I say, I never walked in any shoes but my own."

"If they couldn't take anything with them, how were they able to build the store?" Owen leaned forward in his chair.

Ruby told him about Sam's brother bringing supplies up from Cambridge.

"They had money, some say. Some say there were things smuggled over by some who lived in the town and didn't like that their neighbors or friends or kin be run out."

"That makes sense," Lis noted. She'd been making notes along with recording their conversation. "Have you given any more thought to how your family ended up owning so much of the land? The point, the store, that lot over on the western side of the island where Poppa built that cabin?"

Ruby shrugged. "If I knew, I've forgotten. Maybe it be written down somewhere, but I don't know."

"What do you know about the three chapels?" Owen asked.

Ruby chuckled. "They be built by three pastors, men of God who couldn't get along with anyone," she said sarcastically. "The first one built the chapel that looks over toward Sunset Beach. Jeremiah Sharpe, he was. Someone in the congregation didn't like him, started his own chapel—that be Reverend Moore. Same thing happened to him. Chapel number three be built on the opposite side of the island. Reverend

Patterson." Ruby shook her head. "Foolish men with foolish thoughts."

"Did you ever attend any of them?" Lis wondered.

"We went to Reverend Smith when I be small. He preached in Reverend Sharpe's old church. Then he died, and Reverend Pace came to the island, stayed a long time. When he died, Reverend Bristow came, but after him, there be no one. The chapel be boarded up, last I saw."

"It still is," Lis told her. "I wonder what the future holds for them. It's sort of weird, three houses of worship standing empty like that."

"Maybe there be some use for them," Ruby told her. "Not my place to say."

Owen asked Ruby what it was like for her growing up on the island, and Ruby replied, "Growing up like anyplace, I suppose." Ruby and Owen fell into a conversation about her childhood, but Lis was so tired she couldn't keep up. She rubbed her eyes, made sure the recorder was still on, and said her good nights. Tomorrow she'd play back whatever was on the recorder, but tonight she wanted nothing more than to close her eyes and sleep.

ON THURSDAY MORNING, Lis was totally engrossed in painting and barely heard the ping of her phone. She finished the section she was working on and checked the text.

Friends getting married this weekend. Be my date?

She replied, Day? Time? Attire?

Friday. 7 p.m. Dress you wore to gallery, he responded.

Lis laughed. There was no way she was going to wear the same dress twice. She sent back a short text, Sure. Thanks. Then set aside her brushes and went into the bathroom to wash the paint off her hands and the smear on the side of her face. She changed from her old ratty shorts, which were almost threadbare from having been worn and washed so many times, and put on a knit tank dress.

"Gigi, if you don't need me for anything, I'm going into town," Lis told her after she'd gone downstairs. She found Ruby at her table, reading the newspaper.

"Owen be here if I need help. Which I won't. You go on." Ruby had glanced up at Lis, then back to whatever article she'd been reading.

"I won't be long." Lis headed toward the door.

"Take your time," Ruby said. "You be sure to get something nice. But nothing that be showing your business all over St. Dennis."

Lis paused in the doorway, then shook her head. There was no point in asking Ruby how she knew where she was going.

Okay, could be that she figured if I changed into something nicer than shorts, that I was going into town. And if I'm going into town, I might be stopping at Bling. And if I'm going to Bling, I might be looking for a dress. If I'm looking for a dress, it shouldn't be too revealing lest I scandalize the entire town.

Yes, Lis nodded to herself as she started her car. *That had to be it.*

That Ruby was able to cut to the chase so quickly

was still a mystery, but at least Lis had come up with what sounded like a logical explanation.

She parked on Cherry Street and walked around the corner to Bling. Vanessa waved from the counter as she rang up a customer and had several more in line. Lis went straight to the rack where the dresses were separated by color, not size, and began to search through them. She found several contenders and caught Vanessa's eye to let her know she was headed for the dressing room. Three try-ons later, Lis returned two dresses to the rack and went to the counter.

"Found something?" Vanessa's eyes lit when she saw the dress in Lis's hands. "Oh, I love that one. I wish I'd seen it on you. I bet it looked fabulous."

"Thanks. I wasn't sure about the style." Lis held up the dress with the V-neck and halter straps that tied around her neck.

"The fabric's so pretty," Vanessa went on. "And I love the colors. The shoes you bought last week will be perfect. Any particular occasion?"

"Something came up for the weekend." Lis hadn't wanted to say she was going to a wedding but had no idea who was getting married. Vanessa would have asked whose and she'd have had to admit she didn't know. Or maybe she did and didn't realize their wedding was the one Alec had invited her to. Chances were that if the wedding was in St. Dennis, Vanessa would be there, too.

Lis drove back to the island, singing along with the radio. George Michael's "Father Figure." She belted out the chorus as she pulled into the driveway.

"Whoa, kiddo." Owen came down the steps. "If you're going to sing like that—and that loud—roll up your windows."

Lis laughed. "Some oldies just beg to be sung along to. That's one of them."

"Where'd you go?"

"I went to Bling." She rolled up the windows and got out of the car, then reached into the backseat for the dress bag.

"New dress?"

She nodded and went past him on the steps.

"Didn't you buy a new dress last week?"

"Yes, I did." She went into the store and straight up the steps.

Lis couldn't remember the last time she'd shopped for dressy clothes two weeks in a row; wasn't sure she ever had. She hadn't had that many places to go to before. Gallery openings, yes, but all in New York, where black is practically mandatory. Weddings? Once, in a restaurant, and it had been very casual. Even the bride had worn pants. And that had been the extent of her social life, other than going out for lunch or dinner or drinks with friends or with Ted, sometimes with her friends and Ted. At one of those get-togethers, Ted must have decided that Pam's voice didn't bother him so much after all, and Pam must have found that maybe he wasn't as much of a bore as she'd first thought.

Lis shook her head as if to clear it. What had she seen in him that she couldn't see now?

Love certainly can be blind.

She hung the new dress over the door in her

bedroom and admired the colors. If the dress she'd worn to the showing at the gallery had been sky and sea, this one was sunset. Pinks and lavenders and golds. Once again the contrast between the colors of the new dress and the singular black of the old one was apparent. It was the difference between the way her life felt now and the way it felt when she looked back on her life before she returned to the island.

Funny, how things go. She sat on the stool in front of the front window and looked out on a beautiful day. She'd come back to the island to kill two birds with one stone—since she had to return for the showing of her work, it made sense to come early and spend some time with Ruby. Now, after just a few weeks here, she couldn't remember why she'd stayed away so long, and was seriously considering moving back permanently. She thought about keeping a condo in Hoboken, just someplace to hang her hat when she had business in New York, but even that lacked appeal. She felt more and more that this was where she belonged, and the prospect of leaving and living somewhere else, even for a short time, seemed less desirable. Yes, of course, her relationship with Ruby was part of that, but her brother was now back and planning to stay, at least for a while, and despite their occasional squabbles, she loved Owen and knew he loved her, too. Life had taken them in different directions for years, but now they were both here, where they'd grown up, and finally had the chance to reconnect as adults. Their mother was so wrapped up in her own life—her new marriage and her stepchildren and their children—that she had little time for

Lis or Owen and had no intention of ever setting foot on Cannonball Island again. In a way, Lis couldn't blame her. Kathleen may have had a great childhood, but her marriage to Jack had sapped away every bit of love she'd had for this place. But for Lis—and possibly for Owen—the island was offering new beginnings and new challenges and new opportunities. She felt invigorated here, and creative in ways she hadn't felt in a long time.

Invigorated, creative, and free.

And then there was Alec, and the second chance they might have to discover what could have been. Whatever they were destined to find once the dust settled, for better or worse, Lis was all in.

Diary~

    I have always had a romantic soul—oh, it may have taken my Daniel awhile to find it, but it was there, all along. I love weddings and I love watching those I care about fall in love, and it seems that right now I can enjoy both, and I could not be happier.

    I woke up with my sister Carole on my mind. I can see her face as clearly as if I'd just seen her yesterday, and not—oh, dear, could it really be almost thirty years since she's been gone? Almost thirty years since that too-tired truck driver crashed into the car that carried her and her husband—a wonderful man, her Allen was—and took them from us. Almost thirty years since we had to tell their darling son, our Alec, that his parents had left this life and traveled on to the next. I can still see his face, so filled with confusion. How could his mother be somewhere she could not reach him? How could his father have been taken from him, just like that?

    That boy cried for so long and so hard that I know Carole

was crying through her son's eyes. And oh, how Cliff had wept—Carole had been the youngest in the family and Cliff had treated her like a little princess. That his princess was gone had broken his heart as surely as it had broken her boy's. There was no question that Cliff would take Alec in and raise him, and he did a fine job of it. By the time Cliff passed on—another unexpected blow, well, to everyone except me (I wish I could say that I don't see certain events unfolding, but I do, all too often, but that's a tale for another day). Anyway, as I was saying before I so rudely interrupted myself—by the time Cliff passed, Alec was grown and already in college, and he left the boy quite well off. Not only had Cliff invested money from the insurance settlement Alec received from the accident, but he'd saved enough money to cover all of Alec's college expenses. But more than financial security, Cliff had given Alec a home where he was loved and where he was told that he was loved. He gave the boy a future by passing on his carpentry skills and his love of the classic bay boats. But most of all, he taught him to love the bay and how best to protect it. Alec has grown into a fine young man because of the love he'd always had—Carole's and Allen's and Cliff's—and we are all proud of him.

All of this to say that I see that which he's been long-ing for so close to him now, and I want to tell him it will be all right, it's going to be fine. But he has to be true to himself and do what he knows is right for him. He cannot—he must not—deter from his path.

It's so hard to see these things and not share. I can see, but I cannot do anything that might change the outcome. And my, but it's hard to hold my tongue sometimes. Like now.

Grace

Chapter Fifteen

This may be the coolest place for a wedding ever," Lis whispered to Alec after they'd been shown to their seats in the open-air cathedral that had been created by cutting down trees in a forest of hardwoods to create a sort of chapel.

"Jason, the groom, is a landscaper. He cut down the trees himself—well, with some help from guys on his crew. Sophie Enright—she's the bride—owns the land straight down to the river, and Jason owns all the property next door, where his business is located. She opened the restaurant last year and they've been living in the apartment on the second floor," Alec told her.

"So they both live where they work? Awesome."

"Especially for her. She opens the restaurant at five, and I've heard her say she's down there by three thirty at the latest. She makes everything from scratch, so she has to get an early start," he explained.

"The restaurant looks adorable." Lis had peeked through the window on her way from the parking lot to the area where the ceremony would be held. "And I love the name. Blossoms. It sounds so cheery."

"There's a story behind the name. There were three ladies in St. Dennis who were friends for a long time. Lily, Violet, and Rose. Rose was Sophie's grandmother. She died about twenty years ago." Alec repeated the story he'd heard from his aunt Grace. "Lily is long gone, too, but Violet is still alive and well. She worked for Sophie's grandfather, Curtis Enright, for years. Now that he's retired and having some health issues, he deeded his family home to the town and he's living in Violet's house."

"The Curtis Enright of the Enright Mansion?" Lis asked.

"Right. He was *the* attorney in town for many years. Represented my uncle Cliff for a number of things, including his estate. Now his grandson Jesse has taken over his practice. Jesse's my lawyer. Ruby's, too, I understand. Sophie's a lawyer as well, but she spends most of her time at the restaurant now, only goes into the law office when Jesse needs help." Alec sat with one arm over the back of Lis's chair and leaned in so as not to be overheard by everyone in their vicinity.

"It was a really cool idea to carve out this area and bring in chairs. It's like a church, only outside and with natural air-conditioning." The shade from the trees was welcome on this hot July day, and there was a bit of a breeze off the river.

"I'm sure that was the idea." Alec glanced around, then said, "There aren't that many chairs set out, so I'm guessing they were trying to keep the wedding small."

From somewhere behind them, violins began to play, and everyone stood as the bridal procession began.

"You're going to have to tell me who everyone is," Lis whispered.

"That's Jesse Enright with their mother, Olivia," Alec said as a young man walked up the center aisle with a handsome older woman on his arm.

"Who's the bridesmaid?" Lis asked as a pretty blonde who moved with incredible grace walked toward the makeshift altar.

"I think one of Sophie's half sisters, Georgia. She's a dancer."

Lis nodded. The woman moved like a dancer.

"That's Zoey, Sophie's other half sister, coming up the aisle," Alec said. "I remember her from a party they had for Curtis when he turned seventy-five.

"And . . . there's the bride. That's Curtis walking her down the aisle."

"Where's her father?" Lis asked. "Why isn't he walking her?"

"Estranged from the entire family, last I heard. He's the black sheep, apparently."

The bride passed by in a cloud of tulle and lace, the dress high in the front and low in the back. Her pace slowed to match that of her elderly grandfather, who was beaming with every step he took. Flowers wound through her dark hair, and she carried a huge bouquet of roses in every imaginable shade of pink and cream.

"Roses," Alec whispered, "for Rose."

"So pretty," Lis murmured. The bride was being handed over to her groom, a tall, handsome man in a dark suit. Between them stood another dark-haired man. "Who's the minister?"

"The bride's half brother, Nick Enright. He got some sort of license to marry off the Internet for the occasion."

"You're kidding. Is that even legal?"

"Shhh," came the demand from behind them.

Lis cringed at having been chastised—though she knew she probably deserved it—and said nothing further throughout the brief ceremony, at the end of which the bride and groom were showered with rose petals and pops of a dozen champagne corks. Waiters immediately filled, then passed flutes of bubbly as the newly married couple went row by row greeting their guests.

"So much nicer than the usual grand exit with a receiving line," Lis noted. Minutes later, Alec introduced her to the happy newlyweds, and she was surprised to learn that neither had grown up in St. Dennis.

"I lived in Ohio with my mom, and Jason is from Florida, so we're both new to the St. Dennis family. Where are you from, Lis?"

"Cannonball Island," Lis replied.

"Isn't that right over there?" Sophie pointed in the general direction of the island.

"It is." Lis nodded. "But it's not St. Dennis."

"Oh. Well, it's nice to meet you. I'm sure we'll see you again." Sophie and Jason moved on to the next row.

"You know, you really do confuse people when you say things like that," Alec told her.

"Things like what?"

"That you're not from here, you're from Cannonball Island. It's confusing, because most people think the island is part of the town."

"You're right. I need to stop doing that. Without an explanation, it makes no sense. And I'm tired of explaining. I'll try to be more conscious of that from now on," she agreed.

"I noticed that Owen doesn't do it," Alec noted.

"No, he doesn't. I don't know that he ever did." She watched the rows ahead of them begin to blend together into the center aisle, and the two of them moved toward the end of their row. "What were you two talking about the other night, anyway?"

"Just guy stuff. Why? Do you think we were talking about you?"

"Actually, I think you were talking about Cass Logan."

After what seemed to Lis to be one beat too long, Alec said, "Why would you think that?"

"It's obvious that he's interested in her, and it looks like no one else around here knows her but you."

"I don't really know her. I met her once before the art exhibit."

"Who introduced you?"

"Her father. He's a client."

"The client who was on the island? The one who drives the big white Caddy?"

"Yes, that one."

"What kind of client is he?" Lis asked.

"What do you mean?"

"I mean, is he a boat client, or someone who wants you to renovate some property for him?"

"He's looking to renovate some properties, yes." It appeared to Lis that Alec was about to elaborate, when a voice called from across the aisle.

"Hey, Alec."

"Hey, Dan." To Lis, Alec said, "Have you ever met my cousin Dan? Ford's older brother?"

"I'm not sure. I don't think so."

"I kept looking for him at the inn the other day, but I guess he was really busy, with so much going on. Come on. You should meet him and Jamie."

Alec took her by the hand and together they joined Dan in the center aisle, where Lis was introduced to Dan and his fiancée, Jamie. Soon Ford and Carly appeared with Grace, and the entire group was off to the tent where the reception would be held.

"Sophie is actually catering her own wedding," Grace told Lis. "She's an amazing chef. You'll be impressed, I'm sure. I know I was when she opened Blossoms."

"Did she bake the cake, too?" Lis noticed the tall white confection on a flower-laden table just inside the tent.

"No, Brooke is the baker. Sophie's sister-in-law. She owns Cupcake, the bakery in town. Her brother, Clay, is married to my daughter, Lucy. He's the Mad in MadMac Brews."

"The local brewery." Lis nodded. "I remember. It's hard keeping everyone straight."

"We are a tightly knit group here in St. Dennis," Grace admitted.

"I think *slightly incestuous* might be more accurate," Carly said. "Everyone is somehow related to everyone else. It's tough at first for us outsiders."

"Why, Lis isn't an outsider," Grace protested. "She's just lived away from home for a while, and now she's back. There's a lot to catch up on, granted, with so many new faces in town, but she's hardly an outsider." Grace patted Lis's arm. "Her people were here long before mine were."

"Sounds like there's a story there. I'd love to hear it. Come sit with us." Carly took her by the hand. "Have you met Jamie, Dan's girl? You know she's J. L. Valentine, right?"

"The writer? *The Honest Relationship*? *The Honest Life*?"

Carly nodded. "Yes, and the mother of the bride's half siblings? Delia Enright."

"Stop." Lis's eyes grew wide. "My favorite mystery writer? Is she here?"

"She is. Would you like to meet her, too? She's a good friend of Grace's," Carly confided. "She always stays at the inn when she's in town."

"Damn. And I left all my Delia Enright books at my apartment. Not that I'd have brought them for her to autograph, of course," Lis hastened to add. *Though it would have been a temptation,* she silently admitted.

"Come on. Let's see if we can find her . . ." Carly led Lis in search of the writer.

Delia was surrounded by her children and talking to Grace. Lis was introduced and found the writer to be charming and warm, and when Lis told her she'd read every one of her books, Delia promised to leave a copy of her upcoming release at the inn for Lis.

"This has been the most incredible day," Lis told Alec when they were seated for dinner. "I met Delia Enright, and J. L. Valentine, and Dallas MacGregor is here, and I think if I play my cards right, I'll meet her, too."

"Too bad you didn't bring a little book to get autographs in," Alec teased.

"I might have been tempted, but my good manners would have trumped the impulse. You just don't expect to find people like that all in a place like this and all at the same time."

"If you mean St. Dennis, you still have a lot to learn. When Dallas is shooting a film at her studio, you wouldn't believe who you'll see walking down the street, or having coffee in Cuppachino, or dinner at Lola's or Walt's, or shopping in the local stores. We may be a small town, but these days, we're mighty."

Dinner was served—rockfish over a bed of wild rice with a stir-fry of local vegetables—and Lis was, as Grace had predicted, impressed. After dinner, a band began to play, and the bride and groom took to the floor, but instead of the expected slow, romantic dance, they wowed their guests with a carefully choreographed tango.

"They've been taking lessons over in Annapolis for months," Carly told the others at the table.

"That was amazing," Lis replied.

"Would you like to dance?" Alec said as the band began to play a slower number. "I'm afraid I don't tango, and I don't really know any steps, but I can probably push you around the floor adequately."

"How could I resist an invitation like that." Lis stood and Alec took her hand.

"I'll try not to embarrass you," he said as they reached the dance floor, a patio that in good weather served as a charming outside café.

"Judging by some of the other moves I'm seeing, you'd have to go to some lengths to embarrass either one of us. Check out the guy in the light gray suit," she giggled.

"That's the bride's brother-in-law. I forget which one."

"He truly does have two left feet. I've never seen anything like it." Lis tried unsuccessfully not to stare. "He's sort of the male equivalent of Elaine from *Seinfeld*."

Alec laughed and turned her in the opposite direction, and the band began to play a slowed-down version of "Every Breath You Take."

"Now, this takes me back," Alec said. "This was big at that prom you turned me down for."

"I always thought it was just a teensy bit creepy," she told him. "Like he is always following her, watching her."

"It's nice to dance to, though. I think it was considered romantic back in 1997."

"There had to be a better song to dance to," she said.

"There were several," he told her. "I'm sorry we missed out on dancing back then."

"So am I."

They danced for a few minutes more, Alec holding her close and she resting against his body.

"I have an idea." He broke the embrace and, taking her by the hand, led her from the dance floor.

"What are you doing?" she asked when he stopped and looked around.

"Locating the bride and groom so that we can say thank you for inviting us, it was a lovely party, good night, and enjoy the honeymoon."

"It isn't over."

"It is for us."

They found Sophie and Jason at the bandstand, where they were making several song requests. Alec said their thanks and good wishes and good nights, then they left quietly.

"Where are we going?" Lis asked when they reached the parking lot.

He handed her a rose he'd snagged from one of the table arrangements on the way out and had been holding behind his back.

"I'm taking you to the prom."

IT WAS QUIET and very dark when Alec parked the Jeep near the cottage at the point.

"What are you up to?" Lis asked.

"We're going to have the prom we missed." He unbuckled his seat belt. "Come on."

Alec got out of the car and Lis followed.

"There's no music," she told him.

"Ah, but there will be." He took his phone from his pocket and spent a moment doing . . . she wasn't sure what he was doing, but his face was intent.

"There we go." He held up the phone. "Pandora. Just programmed with the most romantic tunes from the mid- to late nineties."

He slipped the phone into his jacket pocket, and when music began to play, he drew Lis into his arms.

"May I have this dance?" he whispered.

Lis nodded, not trusting herself to speak. She wrapped her arms around his neck and snuggled in. For a few moments they swayed to "(Everything I Do) I Do It for You."

"Romantic enough for you?" he asked.

"Totally romantic," Lis sighed. She paused and pulled away from him just long enough to kick off her heels before returning to his embrace.

The clouds moved away from the face of the full moon, and just a hint of moonlight spread across the point.

"How did you manage that?" she asked. "The moonlight, I mean."

"Anything is possible tonight, Lis." He held her closer. "Anything at all . . ."

She closed her eyes, and for a moment, she could almost believe she was sixteen and wearing a blue Cinderella ball gown that swirled around her when she moved. The rose in her hand could have been a nosegay (she never did like corsages) and the sandy soil could have been the gymnasium floor. For just a moment, she was at the prom she'd dreamed about so long ago.

And then she realized that this moment with Alec, here amid the unspoiled natural beauty of the place she loved, was so much more wonderful than that night ever could have been, even in her most wonderful fantasies. This moment was real, and the boy she'd dreamed about was now the man who was holding her and kissing her neck and the side of her face.

"Is this the part where the chaperones tell us to separate?"

"This is the part where we dance into the darkest corner of the room, so we can do this." His mouth covered hers and claimed her in a way no sixteen-year-old boy could have done.

Lis pressed herself to him and returned his kiss with every yearning fiber of her body. His hands slid down her back and up to her shoulders, and a shiver the length of her spine followed his touch. It took her less than a minute to realize that kissing him tonight was not enough, might never be enough again.

"Is this where we move to the backseat of your car?"

"I'm not sure how that would work out." He held her against him and she could feel the rapid beating of his heart. "I have a better idea. Grab your shoes and let's go."

He led her back to the car and opened not the back passenger door but the front.

"Where are we going?" she asked when he got into the driver's seat and turned the key in the ignition.

"You'll see."

He backed the Jeep onto the road, then drove to the end of the island and crossed the bridge into St. Dennis.

"Gigi's still awake," Lis noted as they passed the

store. There was a light in the back room, where Ruby liked to sit at night to watch TV or read. Tonight the light was slightly blue, which meant she had the TV on and would probably fall asleep in her favorite chair.

Alec made the second left off Charles Street onto a side street Lis had never noticed.

"Where are we?" She looked around for a street sign.

"We're on Lincoln Road."

"What's on Lincoln Road?"

He pulled into the driveway of a small house with a wraparound Victorian porch and a light shining brightly at the front door.

"Who lives here?"

"I do." Alec turned off the car and turned to face her, as if asking without words if she wanted to go inside and all that might follow.

"Yes," she said simply. "Yes."

"You sure?"

"Totally. Absolutely." She opened her car door and got out, and stood on the sidewalk waiting for him to join her.

"No doubts?" He moved toward her.

"Not a one."

He reached for her hand and they walked up the front steps. Alec unlocked the front door and stepped aside so she could enter first.

"This is darling," she said when he turned on the lamp on the desk that stood just inside the hall.

"It was my uncle Cliff's," he told her. "He left it to me when he died."

She peeked through an archway off to the left. A

fireplace filled one corner, and the room was slightly overfurnished.

"This was mostly Uncle Cliff's stuff in here. I have some things from my parents, but I've never been able to decide what to move out of here to make room for their things."

"It's a pretty room," she said. "That sofa—my dad's sister had one like that. Mohair, right? From the 1950s."

He moved closer and put his hands on her shoulders, and that slight touch brought her back into his arms. His lips all but devoured hers, his tongue filled her mouth, and she found it hard to breathe. The heat that flashed between them overwhelmed her, and when his lips began to trail her neck, she reached behind her and pulled down the zipper on her dress, then slid the silky fabric from her shoulders down to her waist. His hands were as hot to the touch as the skin on her body, and he backed her to the sofa and watched the dress sink to the ground. He tossed off his jacket as she unbuttoned his shirt, her eyes never leaving his. He finished undressing himself just as she did, and when she eased herself back onto the sofa, he asked, "Lis, are you—"

"Shut up, Alec."

And then his mouth and his hands were everywhere. His fingers toyed with her breasts while his lips traced a line from her throat before his mouth replaced his hands. The jolt that passed through her arched her back and caused her to cry out, the sensation was so overpowering. She was lost, and she knew it, and she wanted more, couldn't get enough of him.

She raised her hips, inviting him in, desperate to have him inside her, and as he entered her she wrapped her legs around him, urging him to move with her. Their bodies rocked to the rhythm from the unheard music of the ages until her entire world exploded.

The waves of pleasure seemed to go on forever, but when she was finally able to speak, she cleared her throat and said, "That was one hell of a prom."

Chapter Sixteen

The sun was just about to rise when Alec walked Lis to the front door of Ruby's store. She debated over which door was least likely to rouse Ruby or Owen, and decided she'd rather take her chances with Owen, though if she was really quiet, she'd probably get away with sneaking inside.

"I don't think I've ever done this before," she whispered.

"Come home at dawn after a night of incredible lovemaking?" Alec whispered back.

"Come home at dawn after anything and had to sneak into the house."

"You really did live a sheltered life."

"You have no idea." She slid the key into the lock and pushed the door open slowly. She knew just how far she could open it before the hinges creaked.

"I'll see you later," Alec promised. "Come have lunch with me at the boat shop. I'll bring in something from . . . somewhere good. You can even choose the take-out place."

"I would love to do that, but I can't promise."

"Got plans for the day?"

"Just this painting I've been working on for Gigi. I want to work on it this morning, but once I start, I lose track of time."

The lights went on in Ruby's quarters, and Lis said, "I'd better get inside and upstairs. It's almost time for the watermen to start coming in for their coffee. I need to get changed out of this dress."

"Good idea. Especially since it's on inside out."

She looked down to check, then she laughed. "Great. My dress is inside out and my underwear is in my bag."

"At least you remembered to pick it up off the floor." He leaned in for one last kiss.

"Go. Get out of here." She suppressed a giggle and tiptoed inside, closing the door behind her as quietly as possible. She had managed to avoid the squeaking hinge, and hoped she'd do as well with the creaking stair steps. There were three of them, she knew, and she carefully made her way around them. She crept down the hall to her room and ducked inside.

Not a sound from Owen's room. Good. She was home free and undetected. Not that she felt guilty about where she'd been or what she'd been doing—at thirty-five, she'd left her guilt behind long ago—but she wasn't in the mood for Owen's teasing jabs. She stripped off her dress and hung it in the closet, put on her robe, and headed to the shower.

She wished she could take her time, could savor the night and every touch they'd shared, but if she didn't make it downstairs as usual, Ruby might wonder why, and Lis wasn't prepared to have that conversation.

She was dressed and at the counter when the first of the early birds arrived, and feeling pretty smug, when Owen sidled up next to her and whispered in her ear, "Big night last night, eh?"

"You don't know where I was," she said blithely.

"Yeah, right." He leaned closer. "Two words, sister. Lincoln. Road."

She felt her eyes widen. "How do you know Lincoln Road?"

"I know who lives in the house in the middle of the block on the right side. I suspect you do, too."

Before she could speak, he added, "Look, I don't care. As long as you're happy, I don't care who you're with or what you do. Just be happy, Lis." He uncharacteristically leaned down and kissed the top of her forehead. "Just be happy."

"I am happy," she told him.

"That's all that matters."

"But how did you know where—" She began but Ruby cut her off.

"You, Owen, go into the back room and bring us out some more lids for those to-go cups," Ruby called from the counter.

"Will do." Owen winked at Lis, then went off to obey Ruby's orders.

When the morning activity ceased, and Ruby had settled at the round table near the window with her cup of Earl Grey and her newspaper, Lis went back upstairs and studied the work she'd left partially done on the easel and debated whether to add those landmarks that were missing from her painting. In the end, she decided to leave it as it was, and to complete the painting she'd started. She prepared her paints in the palette and picked up her brush. This was the part she looked forward to, when her vision would blot out everything else and she would be lost in the world she was creating. But she was haunted by the songs Alec had played last night and this morning, the love songs he'd programmed into his phone so that they would play over and over. As she painted, she could hear Whitney's "I Will Always Love You" and the Goo Goo Dolls' "Iris," Steve Winwood's "Higher Love," and a song she wasn't familiar with but that Alec said was one of his favorites: Herb Alpert's "This Guy's in Love with You."

"I never heard this song before," she'd told him.

"It's really old," he'd replied, "like from the sixties."

"How do you know it?"

"My dad used to sing it to my mom."

Thinking about it brought a tear to her eyes. It was obviously something that meant a great deal to him, and he'd shared it with her. She found herself humming the tune while she painted.

By the time she put down her brush and stretched, it was midafternoon. She checked her phone and saw that Alec had sent her a text at one.

What's the decision on lunch?

She hit reply and typed, Sorry. Worked all morning. Lost track of time. Later, maybe?

Lis waited, watching the screen and listening for the familiar ping, but the phone was silent.

He does have a life, she told herself, and things to do besides stand around staring at his phone waiting for a response from me.

She went back to work, but the intensity of the morning was gone. Her stomach reminded her that she'd skipped breakfast and had missed lunch, so she ran downstairs and picked at some tuna salad. She was thinking about how best to replicate a certain blue-green she'd seen in the bay that morning and couldn't quite get right.

"A penny for them." Ruby came into the kitchen carrying her cup and went right to the sink to rinse it.

"Hmmmm?" Lis looked up. "Oh. I was just thinking about a color."

"Color of what?"

"Just a sliver of water out on the bay. It's a blue-green with some gray in it, and I've tried mixing it but can't seem to get it right."

"Put your mind to it, you will." Ruby dried the cup and put it away.

"I thought I had something like it, but I guess it's in the box I left back at the apartment. I'm pretty sure if I added just a little touch of green to it, I'd have it right."

"Maybe you should be thinking about that apartment."

"Thinking about it how?"

"Thinking about how much money you be wasting on rent and such when your heart be here."

When Lis didn't respond, Ruby went on.

"How much longer you going to be thinking about it, Lisbeth? How much longer till you know for sure where you belong?"

Ruby left Lis standing in the kitchen, leaning on the shiny wooden countertop that Alec had so lovingly created.

"HOW MUCH LONGER *till you know for sure where you belong?*"

Ruby's words rang in Lis's ears for the rest of the day. She tried to paint, but she was too distracted, so she cleaned her brushes and put away her paints and turned off the overhead light. Owen was outside washing mud off his car's tires when she ran into him in the yard.

"Where are you off to?" he asked.

"Just a walk. Maybe to the point." She hadn't thought about it, but now it was clear to her where she was headed.

"That place really calls to you, doesn't it?" Owen turned off the hose.

Lis nodded. How to explain, even to her brother, the feeling she got when she was there, when she walked the length of the pier, or roamed around the cottage where Ruby and her Harold had been so happy?

"Well, I hope it works out for you, but it doesn't look good, does it."

"What are you talking about?"

"Jansen told me he didn't think the cottage could be habitable again."

"When did he tell you that?"

"I don't know. When we were talking the other night, I guess." He stared at her for a moment. "How disappointed are you?"

"I would be majorly disappointed, but I haven't given up. I'm pretty sure Alec will figure something out."

"Think maybe he's just telling you what you want to hear?" Owen turned the hose on and sprayed one of the front tires. Lis stood there watching for a few minutes, thinking about what he'd said.

"I think he knows what he's talking about. Have you gone through the house?"

"I don't have to go through it. I can see the rot and the water damage and the places where animals have gnawed at the wood. I'm surprised you even went inside that place. You and Jansen are damned lucky you didn't fall through the floorboards or have the steps give way or that the roof didn't come down on your heads."

"Well, on that happy note, I think I'll take that walk now."

"I just don't want you to be disappointed."

"I don't intend to be. It's in good hands, Owen."

Lis walked over the dune and across the road. She stepped down onto the beach and walked along the water's edge. A wave rolled onto the shore, so she took off her sandals and carried them in one hand. The sun had disappeared behind some fast-moving clouds, and she wondered how much time she had before the rain began. She picked up a piece of driftwood that had bleached in the sun and stepped around the empty shells of several horseshoe crabs.

When she neared the place where the rocks began, she cut off to the left toward the road and walked the rest of the way to the point on the shoulder.

She made it all the way to the end of the pier before the first low rumble of thunder rolled in from somewhere down the bay. Ignoring what she knew about lightning, she sat on the pier, her feet dangling in the water as fat drops of rain landed all around her. She could see the movement of the clouds heading north and figured the rain wouldn't last but maybe another ten minutes at the most. Right then, she didn't care if she got wet.

Owen could be right about Alec. Was he just telling her what she wanted to hear to placate her for a while?

She was pretty sure Alec wouldn't play that game. He knew how much the cottage meant to her. The cottage as an art studio had become a sort of Holy Grail. Why hadn't she thought of it sooner?

Maybe if she'd stayed around instead of moving to New York, if she'd had someone look over the place with an eye toward renovating it years ago, perhaps it could have been salvaged before it had deteriorated so badly. Now, after the cottage had suffered so many years of neglect, Alec's first impression could be correct. She'd smelled the rotted wood the second she opened the door, had smelled it in every room including on the second floor, where, if she were to be honest, the odor had been even more prevalent.

She skimmed her toes over the water and watched it ripple.

The last thing she'd expected when she came here was to find her old dreams come to life, but last night, they had. Last night had been magic, and it had started right here, in the moonlight. She raised her legs from the water and turned her back so that she was facing the cottage and the place where they'd danced the night before. She could see the tire marks from the Jeep on the grass, and she was pretty sure if she tried hard enough, she would see them dancing there. Could memories manifest themselves into visions?

Last night, she wanted to weep for all the time they'd lost. If not for her father's stubbornness and prejudices, she'd have had that prom date long before last night. And if she had, in its aftermath, would she and Alec have fallen in love, stayed together after graduation, gone on to . . . what? Would she have left for art school, where she'd had such amazing instruction? Would she have created the art she was so proud of?

"Change one thing, change all," Ruby had said.

Lis sighed. Ruby was always right about things like that. So maybe things have worked out the way they were supposed to. Who she had loved, or who he had loved, between then and now no longer mattered. What counted, what was true and important, was that they'd found each other. They hadn't needed words to tell each other how they felt. She knew— and Alec knew, too.

Know where you belong. Right always feels right.

Lis blew out a long breath and noticed that the rain had stopped. She stood and picked up her sandals, and started home.

She knew where she belonged—and it felt exactly right.

It was time to move back home for good.

"WHERE YOU GOING with that bag, Lisbeth?" Ruby asked when she called Lis down for dinner.

"Owen, your meat loaf smells amazing." She leaned over the pan that sat atop the stove and inhaled deeply.

"Thanks. I used some of the herbs from Gigi's garden." Owen looked very proud of himself.

"You're becoming a regular master chef," Lis said.

"Someone's got to pick up the slack around here." He took three plates from the cupboard.

"You're going to have to save me a piece."

"Oh? Big dinner date?" He took a closer look at his sister. "Ah, probably not dressed like that."

"These are my traveling clothes, the most comfortable things I own." She held on to the hem of the faded navy T-shirt, which she'd put on over old khaki shorts.

"Traveling?" Ruby asked. "Where you be traveling off to?"

"I'm going to my apartment. I left a lot of things undone there." She took a knife from the drawer and sliced off an edge of the meat loaf. "Oh, yum. I can smell the thyme." She took a bite. "Perfect. You really could get a job making this stuff."

"I have a job, remember? I start next week."

"Making meat loaf has to be easier than diving under the water with an oxygen tank on your back."

Lis sliced off another piece and bit into it. "Really. This is delicious."

"Maybe easier but not as adventurous."

"Ah, that's right. Mr. Adventure. I guess things have been too quiet around here for you this past week or so. Nothing to get your heart pumping." She grinned and lowered her voice. "Except maybe a certain blonde."

"Lisbeth Jane, you put down that knife and stop hacking away and sit down at the table proper and eat your dinner with us."

"I really wanted to get on the road early, Gigi."

"That road still be there in another half hour. Here." Ruby handed her a bowl of green beans. "You put this on the table and come back in here for the salad."

"Guess I'm here for dinner," Lis muttered.

"Better than driving a couple of hours on an empty stomach." Ruby harrumphed. "Taking off when dinner be ready to be put out. What nonsense be that?"

In the end, it had taken more than a half hour to eat, clean up, and get going. Before she left, Lis called Alec, but he didn't pick up, so she left a voicemail telling him she'd be back probably by tomorrow, maybe the day after. She wasn't sure how long it was going to take to set things in order once she got to New Jersey. But she'd made up her mind that Ted had to step up and take whatever of his things remained in the apartment. She'd clean out her closet, pack up her clothes and the remainder of her painting supplies and the books she wanted to keep. She'd donate what she didn't want and she'd store, for now, those pieces of furniture she couldn't take with her. Of course, she'd planned to do all these things during her last trip, but in the end hadn't taken any real steps to accomplish any of it. Now she had resolve. She knew where she belonged, and it wasn't in New Jersey. This time around, she was determined to clear her things out of the apartment. She didn't really own all that much, she reminded herself.

How long could it take?

Chapter Seventeen

"You sure you have everyone lined up?" Brian Deiter stood on the front porch of Ruby's general store. "Everyone's going to come?"

"I spoke with Mrs. Carter about an hour ago. She contacted everyone who has a property that she believes they might want to sell," Alec told him.

"What if she's wrong?" Brian grabbed Alec by the arm.

Alec removed the man's hand.

"Ruby Carter is never wrong. But if no one agrees to sell, well, then you know where you stand as far as this project is concerned."

"Yeah," Brian grumbled. "Nowhere."

Alec shrugged and went inside to look for Ruby. There were seven or eight property owners who Ruby had identified to Alec as possibly wanting to sell. Tom Mullan was one of them. He'd already agreed, but he'd allegedly come to offer moral support to Alec, though Alec knew his motives weren't quite that altruistic. If no one else sold, the chances that Deiter would build anything on the island were practically nonexistent. It was too costly to do all the testing necessary and apply for all the required permits to build two relatively small houses.

Cass came into the store carrying the display she had made earlier that morning. It showed the island as she projected it would look when the new homes had been completed. She wanted to assure the potential sellers that the homes on the drawing board were as island friendly as she could make them, with simple architectural features that would blend into the existing buildings, and with landscaping that would utilize only native trees. And the builders would respect the wildlife on the dunes.

"Where would you like these?" Cass asked Alec.

"Maybe stand them up over on the counter." He took a quick glance at the poster in her hand. "That looks fabulous, Cass. You captured . . . really, it's just what it should be."

"I listened, buddy." She took the posters and the display to the counter and began to set them up. "I wasn't sure I could get this all done on such short notice, but it worked out okay."

When Ruby came into the room, Cass stopped what she was doing and watched in fascination as the elderly woman approached her.

"You must be Mrs. Carter," Cass said in a tone that was almost reverent. "I'm Cass Logan, the architect."

"I know who you be." Ruby appeared to study Cass for a moment. "You be welcome here, Cass Logan."

"Thank you, Mrs. Carter."

"Alec said you be doing some pictures of the houses your daddy wants to build."

"They're right here." Cass scrambled to put the posters in order. "Here's what we're looking at for the Mullan property."

Ruby studied the poster, then moved on to the next, nodding slowly. "And this one—this be the whole island?"

"Yes. With the houses we'd like to build on the lots Alec thought might be available."

"There be nothing built on the point," Ruby noted with satisfaction.

"Alec said you had no interest in selling the point."

"Alec be right."

"You should know that my father hasn't given up on getting you to sell it to him."

"He be wasting his time."

"I know. He wanted me to sketch in a couple of houses out here toward the pier . . ."

"No point wasting time on something that never going to happen."

"That's exactly what I thought." Cass smiled. "But I did have to humor him with a mock-up of how the point would look with houses on it. He *is* my father. . . ."

"Get along just fine, you and me, Cass Logan." Ruby patted the woman's arm.

Alec had eavesdropped on the conversation and was relieved that his overall assessment of Cass as being someone he could trust was holding true. Brian

Deiter might be disappointed at the end of the night, but Cass had won over Ruby, and that was more important than feeding the developer's ego.

Alec wished he'd been able to get in touch with Lis, but when he called yesterday, and then again today, she hadn't picked up the call. The night before last she'd phoned him from her car to let him know she was going to her apartment to pick up some things she needed, but he hadn't heard from her since. The request from Deiter to bring everyone together had been made the afternoon following what Alec had begun to think of as prom night. Yesterday Alec sat with Ruby and they'd gone over the names of people she knew had been thinking about selling, those who had moved away and had property to sell, and those who might be interested if the price was right. He'd spent yesterday and today tracking down the people on the list, and by five that evening had made personal contact with every single person. They weren't all able to attend, but some had sent family members and others had said straight out that they'd be happy to sell for the right number. To make sure that the amounts offered were fair to everyone—especially the property owners—Alec had invited Hamilton—Ham—Forbes, a local Realtor, to be part of the conversation that evening. Forbes for Homes had been in business in St. Dennis for over sixty years with good reason. Everyone knew Ham's father, and they knew him and his reputation for being fair and honest.

The past two days had kept Alec crazy busy, and he figured that was a good thing, with Lis out of town. He was having a really hard time focusing on anything but her. He'd never really believed a time would come when she would be in his arms, even though she'd been in the back of his mind for as long as he could remember. Lis was everything he'd ever wanted in his life, and he spent the past few days pinching himself every time he thought about the night they spent together.

He tried everything he could think of to find a way to make the cottage come alive for Lis—had even asked his friend Cam O'Connor to take a look at the place and see if maybe he saw something Alec hadn't seen. While Cam's assessment pretty much echoed Alec's, he had agreed that it might be possible to salvage the place by removing the floorboards on the first floor section by section, and replacing the foundation piece by piece. Both men agreed it was a gamble, but for Alec, it was a gamble worth taking.

But just in case the old cottage couldn't be saved, Alec had turned to Cass and asked her if she'd be interested in designing a house that replicated the cottage with maybe a few concessions for modern living, like air-conditioning and central heat. Cass had been intrigued and hadn't wasted a moment. The drawing she showed Alec was perfect in every way. He had to admit that Cass really had a feel for the island. He hated knowing that Lis would be disappointed if Ruby's cottage couldn't be made whole, but he hoped that Cass's plans might take out some of the sting.

People began to drift into the store, hesitantly at first. Alec greeted them, as did Ruby, and one by one, they gravitated to the counter to look over Cass's plans. Soon there was a comfortable buzz of chatter in the room, and Alec began to relax.

Until Owen came in and looked around. He went straight to Ruby, who talked to him for a moment, after which Owen began to rub his chin, then nod his head. Then he made his way through the small crowd to the counter, and walked up behind Cass. He touched her shoulder, and she turned around with a smile on her lips.

Oh boy, Alec thought.

Owen Parker had always had a love-'em-and-leave-'em reputation. When it came to girls, he'd made it clear that he didn't like to work hard at it, and back in the day, he'd never had to. Girls had always flocked to him like lemmings to a high cliff. He was a natural-born player.

Alec smiled. Yup. Owen Parker just might have met his match.

He glanced at his watch. He'd told everyone Ruby thought should be included to come to the store by seven thirty. He knew there would be questions, and if they weren't asked, he'd bring up certain points himself. He wanted to make sure that everyone understood what was going to happen if they decided to sell, all the pros and all the cons. Once this door was opened, it could not be closed, and he wanted everyone to understand, as Ruby had, that change can be good if things are done the right way. He never forgot who had hired him, but at the same time, he knew that in the end the best interests of the island and those of his client would be the same. Cut corners led to costly problems—it was better to do the right thing from the start. He'd been pounding this into Brian Deiter's head for the last few weeks, and it had been a godsend that the architect was the boss's daughter and she agreed with Alec's philosophy.

The last of the islanders wandered in and went straight to the displays on the counter, which everyone crowded around. It was time to get their show on the road.

Alec cleared his throat and said, "Folks, we'd like to get started, so please take a seat, and we can begin. I know you all have questions, so now is the time to ask them . . ."

LIS STOPPED AT the red light on Charles Street and craned her neck to get a better look at a bathing suit in Bling's window. The light turned and the car behind her blew its horn, so she stepped on the gas. She could pop into Bling tomorrow, she thought as she drove toward the island. Or the day after. She'd found the green paint she'd been looking for, and the tube, along with the rest of all her supplies, were piled amid her clothes in the backseat. She'd sort it all out when she got back to Ruby's. She'd been looking for her phone for the past two days, and she suspected it might be somewhere in that pile of dresses, sweaters, shoes, pants, and art supplies.

Everything had gone surprising well. Ted had been cooperative, renting a truck, and having bribed a few friends with promises of pizzas and beer, had moved all his belongings from the apartment. He'd even offered to move Lis's table and chairs and a few other pieces to the storage unit she'd rented. At first she declined: The sooner he was gone, the better. But when he'd repeated his offer, noting there was still room in the truck, she'd thanked him and supervised the carrying of her furniture to the truck. What the hell, she'd thought as she drove to the storage facility. It was the least he could do for her. Besides, her only other option was to hire a truck and movers of her own, which would require her to stay a few more days in the near-empty apartment. She'd already checked with several reputable movers, and the earliest she could get a crew, even a small one, would have been the beginning of the following week. It wasn't the cost that had changed her mind. She just didn't want to spend that much more time away from the island—from Alec and Ruby and Owen—and the new life she was building there.

And Ted had been cordial, making the most of the awkward situation. Thankfully, Pam had not tagged along. Lis wasn't sure she could have been as pleasant to her former friend—the friend she'd cried to when she and Ted first broke up, the friend who'd patted her hand and told her it was all for the best and she deserved someone better than Ted. All in all, Lis had been grateful for Ted's help. Clearing out the apartment meant she could load up her car, give her key to the landlord, collect her security deposit, and say good-bye to the past.

"*Close one door, open another,*" Ruby would say. Lis smiled as she did, literally, close the door behind her and headed home.

Home to Cannonball Island and her cottage on the point. Home to Ruby. Home to Alec and her future.

SHE DROVE OVER the bridge, and as she approached the store, she noted that cars were parked along the road where normally there were none. When she pulled into the driveway and saw not only Alec's car but the white Cadillac as well, she felt a sense of panic. Why were there so many cars there? Had something happened to Ruby? Had Alec or Owen tried to call on her phone, which she'd been unable to locate?

She hopped out of her car and all but ran up the steps and pushed open the front door, then stopped short and stared in confusion at the gathering inside.

"What's going on?" she asked.

"Lis." Alec put down whatever he'd had in his hand and went to her. "I've been trying to call you, but—"

"What is going on here?" she said a little louder. "Where's Ruby? Is she all right?"

"I'm right here, where I always be, and I be fine," Ruby said from her chair at the round table. "Why wouldn't I be?"

"Why are all these people here?" Lis turned to Alec. "What the hell, Alec?"

"There's a meeting here, with a developer who wants . . . that is, he's thinking about buying a few lots here on the island and . . ."

Deep frown lines creased her forehead, and she

pushed past him and went directly to the counter. Her eyes scanned the displays.

"Gigi, did you know about this? Before tonight?" Lis asked.

Ruby nodded. "Known from the start."

"You didn't think to mention it?"

"At the time, it were just talk. And not my place to tell."

"Whose place was it to tell? Yours?" She glared at Alec.

Lis picked up one of the posters showing where the new houses would be located around the island. "This looks like more than just talk."

"Could be, but none of them places have your name on them," Ruby told her.

"Miss . . ." Brian Deiter reached out to her with a meaty hand, which she ignored. "I'm Brian Deiter. Deiter Construction. I think if you'll listen to what we have to say, whatever fears you might have will be put to rest."

In his hand he held a poster, and Lis turned her head to get a better look. She took it from him and placed it flat on the counter.

"This is the point." She looked up at Ruby.

"Nothing wrong with your eyes."

"You're thinking about selling the point to a developer?" She turned on Alec. "Is this why you told me the cottage had to be torn down? So that you and your developer friend could build on it?"

"Lis, I would never do something like that. You should know that. And Ruby has made it clear to Brian that the point is not for sale," Alec tried to

explain, but she pulled away and picked up the litera-
ture that Brian had brought along with him.

THE DUNES AT CANNONBALL, the one-page flyer
read. The principals were listed as Brian Deiter,
Builder/Developer; Cassidy J. Logan, M.Arch.; and
Alec M. Jansen, PhD, Environmental Consultant.

Lis stared at it, then held it up.

"PhD? You have a doctorate?" She waved the
paper. "Environmental consultant? I thought you were
a carpenter. A boatbuilder."

"I am, but—"

"You didn't think to tell me you have a doctorate?"

"Lis, it's kind of hard to fit that into a conversation. What was I supposed to say, 'By the way, you
should call me *Dr.* Jansen'? It just never came up, and
frankly, it's really not all that important."

"It's important, *Dr. Jansen*, that you are who you
say you are." He reached for her, and she pushed him
away. "I don't think I really know who you are. I'm
not sure I want to know."

She walked from the room, and even Ruby's
"Lisbeth Jane!" failed to slow her down. She got into
her car and drove to the point, unlocked the door to
the cottage, and stepped inside, ignoring the sagging
floors.

"No one is going to sell you," she said aloud.

She went into the large room and sat on the floor
near the fireplace, mindless of the dirt.

"No one is going to sell you," she repeated. "Ruby
promised you to me."

Had Ruby lied?

Lis shook her head. If Ruby had, it might well have been the first time in her life. The woman was honest to a fault, and everyone who knew her knew that about her. Ruby would never lie to her or make a promise she did not intend to keep.

So what the hell was going on back there at the store? Why would anyone want to change anything on Cannonball Island? As far as Lis was concerned, it was perfect just as it was. The fact that it hadn't been developed was what made it different, made it special.

"Changes be coming . . . time to get out of the way," Ruby had said. God knows Ruby had seen enough changes on the island, and in her life, in her hundred years. Judging from Ruby's stance back at the store, she was just fine with whatever changes were about to occur. How could she be okay with all that construction? How could she have given her blessing to such a project?

And why was Lis the last to know?

Lis thought about the view out the front window at Ruby's, and how she could see so clearly the way the island looked before anything had been built there. It was almost as if somehow it was her job to record what had been, as if she'd been given a window of another sort, one that opened onto a view of an island that was no more before it was lost forever.

She heard the front door squeal open and heard footsteps cross the floor.

Alec came into the room and sat down a foot away from her.

"Lis, nothing is the way you think it is," he said calmly. "Nothing."

"Are you working with that developer to build on the island?"

"Yes. I am. I'm his consultant."

"*Environmental* consultant."

He nodded

"Then things are exactly the way I think they are."

"You're wrong. And if you would listen to me for just five minutes, I'd like to tell you how things *really* are."

"All right, *Dr. Jansen*, I'm listening." She looked at her watch. "Your five minutes start now."

"Brian Deiter contacted me about building a bunch of houses on the island. A lot of houses. And yes, he wanted to build on the point, but Ruby would have none of it. I've told him more than once that it isn't for sale."

"Then why did he have that poster that showed houses built out here? A whole *bunch* of houses out here."

"That was his last-ditch ploy to appeal to Ruby. He had it in his head that if he showed her what it could look like, told her how much he was willing to pay her, she might cave." Before she could ask, Alec said, "And no, of course she did not. She knows what it means to you and she couldn't care less about the money. All that time and energy and money he'd spent trying to change her mind—it was all a waste."

"But the rest of the island . . . does she know what he wants to do with the rest of the island?"

"Of course she knows. Actually, she was the first

person who knew he was interested. When he first contacted me about working for him on this project, I came out and talked to Ruby before I accepted the job offer. She was the only person I consulted with. I needed to know how she would feel about the changes that would come to the island. Hers was the only opinion that mattered to me."

"When was that?"

"Awhile before you came home."

"I can't believe she'd go along with it. What did you say to make her think this was a good idea?"

"Do you really think that anything I or anyone else might say could make Ruby go along with something she didn't think was a good idea?"

"You're telling me she thinks this is a good idea?"

"She's a realist, Lis. She reads the writing on the wall more clearly than anyone I ever knew. You know how she is."

"How is changing the island in any way a good idea?"

"Lis, there is development going on up and down the Chesapeake. Some of the developers are good and are trying to do the right thing, build in a way that has the least impact on the environment. Others couldn't care less about where the herons and the osprey nest or whether there's sludge or waste in the bay. You need to understand that there are other consultants who aren't above overlooking certain regulations for a price. If I'd turned Deiter down, he'd have hired someone else."

"So what you're saying is that you're the lesser of the available evils."

"If you want to look at it that way, fine, yes, I am. But the truth is that it's only a matter of time before someone builds on the island. I know this and Ruby knows it, too." He shook his head. "Lis, it's inevitable. Ruby recognized right away that sooner or later, it's going to happen, and it would be better for the island that I be involved to make sure that nothing is done that shouldn't be done. I didn't talk her into it. It was really the other way around. Ruby knows she can trust me to do the right thing, to make sure Deiter does the right thing."

"But why does it have to happen at all? Why can't this island, this one place, stay as it is?"

"Most of the island will remain as it is. There won't be a concentration of homes like Deiter originally wanted, only a few dotted here and there around the island. So it isn't going to look like a housing development plopped down onto the island, I promise. Cass has spent considerable time studying the existing buildings and she's come up with plans for the new places that are spot-on. Beautiful little cottages that look as if they could have been here from the first. She's even agreed to reuse whatever wood and brick she can salvage from the original structures in her designs, so each will be a little different from the others but they'll retain the history. She's done a remarkable job." He ventured a little closer to her. "Look at them, please. I'd asked her to be respectful of the architecture that is here, and she has been."

"And this place?"

"I promised I'd do my best to fix it and I will. I had Cam O'Connor come out to look it over. To tell you the truth, he thinks I'm crazy to try, but I told him we were going to give it our best shot because it means so much to you and because I'd do anything to make you happy. I waited so long for you, Lis. You are . . . you are everything to me. There aren't words for me to tell you what the other night meant to me. I waited more than half my life for you. Do you really think I would do anything—anything—that would make you unhappy? Knowing that maybe we could have a future here, don't you think I would move heaven and earth to make it happen for you? For us?"

She slid over to him, winced when a splinter pierced her shorts. She touched the side of his face, then leaned over to kiss his mouth. "I'm sorry I second-guessed you. It was just . . . walking in on that meeting, with all those people there and seeing the posters and the displays and that man . . ."

"I understand. I wouldn't have wanted you to find out that way."

"Then why didn't you tell me? Why am I the only person on the island who didn't know all this was going on?"

"At first, I didn't tell you because I'd agreed to keep it confidential until we could determine if enough of the property owners would be interested in selling to make it worth his while. Brian had an experience recently where another builder came in and outbid him on a project, bought it right out from under him. Didn't even give him the option of bidding back. And like the man or not, I believed the island's best interests would be served if Brian was the man who did the building, so I didn't discuss it with anyone. You have to understand, he's my client, and in this, my first obligation is to him."

"Except Ruby."

"That was before I even agreed to take the job. You weren't back then, and I had no reason to believe you might be." Alec smiled. "Ruby is so sharp. She got it right away."

"Got what?"

"That a change was going to come, like it or not, so it would be best if we found a way to like it. Brian is offering to pay fair market price, and that's good for the people who are interested in selling. He also promised that he'd give first consideration for hiring to residents who have construction skills. It's going to be a bit of a windfall for some of the families here."

"How can you be so sure he'll be fair when it comes to buying the properties?"

"I asked Ham Forbes to come out this morning and look over the properties in question, and to give us fair evaluations. Deiter has promised to honor that."

"So just like that, all those people are willing to sell off their families' land? I don't get it."

"Not all of them are selling. But some of them don't have a choice. Some of the older people have no relatives to leave their property to, and some of the younger residents don't want to stay on the island because their futures are limited here, but they can't afford to leave."

"You mean because they can't afford to start over someplace else."

"That's exactly what I mean. And then you

have Tommy Mullan and his sisters. They are selling property that has been in their family since the island was populated. And before you say, 'How can they do that?' you need to know that Tommy's parents are both in a nursing home. Frankly, the family needs the cash. The money they get from the sale will ensure that Mr. and Mrs. Mullan can stay in the nursing home they're in and get the care they need."

Lis nodded. She got it.

"The two houses that Brian will build on the Mullan land will reflect the original house that Tom grew up in. I don't know of another developer who'd have made that promise. There won't be any modern boxes, and nothing over one story, so the views of the bay won't be blocked. And there will be no deep dredging to allow for big boats to dock in the cove." He held his hands out in front of him. "It was the only good solution to the problem, Lis. I did the best I could do. It was going to happen, was only a matter of time. Ruby saw that right away."

"I just wish I'd known. I wish I could have been part of that conversation, that you'd trusted me enough."

"It wasn't a matter of not trusting you. I gave my word to my client. I signed a contract." Alec reached into his back pocket but there was nothing there. "Wait. I must have left it in the car."

"Left what?"

"A surprise. Be right back." He was on his feet, out the door, and back in a flash.

In his hand he carried a rolled-up piece of paper.

He spread it flat on the floor. Lis leaned over his shoulder and studied the picture.

"It's the cottage," she said.

"It's the new and improved cottage," he corrected. "This is obviously the exterior. And this"—he unrolled a second sheet that was under the first—"is the interior."

"It's just the same . . ." she said.

"It's the same but different. Better. It has all the modern comforts and conveniences but retains all the charm and the history. Here's the second floor." He pointed to a sketch in the top right-hand corner. "See? It has all those windows that you love across the side, but it has skylights and everything is energy efficient. There won't be massive gaps between the windows and the walls, so no cold wind, no water, will be blowing into your studio when you're trying to paint."

"That would be nice," she admitted.

"I've told Cass that I wanted her to incorporate as much of the original woodwork and floors from the old into the new, just like she's doing in all the others she's designing."

"So I'll still have the floors Gigi and Harold and Gramma Sarah walked on."

"If enough can be salvaged, we'll use the old, and we'll try to match what we can't use to complete the floor. If not, we'll do counters, like I did for Ruby." He rested his chin on the top of her head. "Cass drew up these plans for new construction if we had to go that way, but this is how I see the place after we've finished the renovations. There's no reason why we can't use her plans and adjust them to restore the original building."

She nodded. "All right. When does the work begin?"

"As soon as you say the word."

"You've got it. Let's do it. Tomorrow."

"Tomorrow might be tight. We need permits, we need to see when Cam's schedule is free, we need to order supplies and equipment, and the foundation has to be shored up and—"

"Okay, okay. Do all that." She sat snuggled next to him for a long moment, then asked, "Is there any way to make the front bedroom bigger?"

"Not if we stick to the original foundation. If we build an addition, it can be as big as you want, I suppose. Cass can adjust the floor plans. Why?"

"Because I'm thinking maybe I'll want to live here when it's finished. Maybe I'll want a big bed in there."

"Big enough for two?"

"Oh, easily big enough for two. Big enough for two and maybe a big dog."

"I'll talk to Cass first thing in the morning, before you have a chance to change your mind."

"No way I'll change my mind. You?" she asked tentatively.

"Are you kidding? After all the time we've lost? You're stuck with me now."

They sat quietly, caught up in their own thoughts of the future.

"Were you going out with her?" Lis asked.

"Going out with who?" He frowned.

"Cass."

"Me and Cass? No. I think you might have me confused with someone who wishes he were dating her."

"You mean Owen."

"I fear he's smitten."

"Owen is never smitten, and she's not his type. Or maybe he's not her type."

"Don't make assumptions about her, Lis. She's really very nice. Get to know her." He smiled. "Owen doesn't know what he's getting into if he's set his sights on her."

"Might do him good to have to work for it for once. But that's his problem." Lis wiggled out of Alec's arms and stood. "We need to go back to the store. I feel an ear-whipping coming from Ruby." She waited for him to get up. "I have never in my life walked out on her when she called my name, and I know I am going to hear about it. '*Lisbeth Jane, you be taught better than that. You listen when I talk to you, hear?*'"

"Lis, are we okay?" Alec stood at the door with it half opened. "Before we go, I have to know."

"We are okay. More than okay. We're going to be okay for a very long time, Dr. Jansen." She put one hand on each side of his face and kissed him. "We are as much okay as we were on prom night."

"That was pretty darned okay."

"Well, okay, then." Lis went outside and walked toward her car. "I'll meet you back at the store. I'll be the one in the back room getting the lecture on respecting one's elders . . .'cause you're never too old for Ruby to 'put some manners on you.'"

Lis got in behind the wheel, started the car, and

slipped the gear into reverse, then paused. Alec walked to his Jeep, then raised a hand to wave to her, and in that moment she was overcome with gratitude. For the love she knew they would share in that cottage on the point and the years they would spend there. Even for the tongue-lashing she knew she was going to get, because it meant Ruby was still there with them, alive and feisty as ever. For whatever it was that had brought her back to this place that she loved with the people she loved. The family she had and the family she and Alec would make.

Know where you belong.

"I know, Gigi," she whispered as she drove off. "I know . . ."

Epilogue

September

"Gigi, you about ready for me to drive you over to the inn?" Lis stuck her head into the back room, where earlier Ruby had been watching the morning news.

"I been ready. Been waiting on you." Ruby eased herself out of her chair with some difficulty.

Lis had to stop herself from rushing over to help. She knew it would have earned her a swat on the hands and a verbal rebuke. So she waited patiently while the elderly woman gathered her purse and the book she had borrowed from her friend Grace and was returning.

"Owen, you be sure to tell Tommy to take back that extra case of orange soda he left here last week." Ruby stopped in the doorway and called to Owen, who was sitting in her chair at her table. "Don't know why he be bringing that here. Never did sell much of it."

"Sure thing, Gigi." Owen looked up from the newspaper he was reading.

Ruby stared, squinting at him from across the room.

"If you don't look like your great-granddaddy sitting there." Ruby shook her head. "Hm-hm. Just like my Harold."

"I do?" Owen put the paper down.

"You do. And I'm going to tell you 'xactly what I used to tell him."

"What's that?"

"Don't be getting too comfortable in my seat."

Lis laughed out loud and followed Ruby out the door.

"We can take our time," Lis said as she opened the passenger-side door. "We're a little early."

"A little early be better than a little late." Ruby got into the car with minimal assistance, but she did need a little help with the seat belt.

Once Lis had Ruby safely strapped in, she started the car and drove slowly onto the narrow two-lane road that wrapped itself around Cannonball Island. They crossed into St. Dennis, the tires bumping along on the grate of the drawbridge.

"How old do you suppose that bridge is?" Lis asked after they'd crossed.

"Well, now, let me put my mind to that." Ruby looked out the window. "I watched it be built, back in the day. Guess I be around nine or ten. So maybe 1925 or so. Before that, you couldn't go straight around the island. If you were in a boat in the river over beyond the store, you would have to turn around, go all around the point, then all along the far side of the island. Guess at some point, someone got tired of it and said the bridge should open up."

"Who built it?"

"The state of Maryland built it. They had a couple of engineers come around, studied the area. Built a bunch of those small drawbridges around the shore, I heard."

They reached the turnoff for the Inn at Sinclair's Point and Lis made a left to follow the long, winding drive. Once they'd reached the back of the building, Lis found a spot close to the back door and parked, then helped Ruby from the car and across the parking lot without appearing to be helping.

"Hold my hand, Gigi." Lis took Ruby's hand in hers.

"You think I need help walking?"

"I like to hold your hand, like I did when I was little and needed help crossing the road or walking on the jetty."

"You think I don't see what you're saying there?" Ruby held Lis's hand despite her protest, even giving it a squeeze.

"I know you better than to think that there's anything that you don't see." They reached the back steps and Lis waited for Ruby to climb them with her.

Alec was so right to move her downstairs when he did, Lis thought. *Sooner or later, she would have killed herself, falling down those steps in the store. At the very least, she could have broken an arm or a leg.*

They reached the landing and a bellhop rushed to open the door for them. After they stepped inside,

Ruby pointed to the grand staircase in the lobby. "Those be the steps Grace fell down last year. Broke her arm and her leg."

Lis smiled to herself, no longer questioning how it seemed that Ruby could pluck words or phrases or thoughts from her mind.

"There you are, my friend." Grace greeted Ruby with a broad smile and open arms. "I'm so glad you're here. I wanted your advice about something . . . oh, and Lis, dear. Happy to see you, too, of course. Can you stay and join us for lunch? The chef is making crab cakes with a little extra spice, just the way you like them, Ruby."

"I'd love to join you, but Alec asked me to meet him at the cottage after I dropped Gigi off. He said he has a surprise for me."

"Well, who doesn't love surprises?" Grace's eyes sparkled. "You never know what that nephew of mine has up his sleeve."

"Knowing Alec, he probably got in a shipment of windows." Lis laughed. Alec had been happily showing off the materials for the cottage's renovation as they were received.

"Is he ready to put in windows already?" Grace shook her head. "My, it seems like only yesterday he was telling Dan that he wasn't sure any of that place could be saved." She leaned closer to Lis. "Of course, I knew he could do it. It means the world to him to be able to do this for you, you know."

Lis nodded. She knew.

"And I can't wait to see it once it's finished, can you, Ruby?" Grace took the arm of her old friend.

"I know just how it be looking," Ruby said simply. "Boy be doing it right." She and Grace exchanged a long look that spoke volumes, but Lis couldn't understand a word.

Lis sighed. It was always like this when Ruby and Grace got together. The two women just seemed to *know* things.

"Well, I should get going, see what Alec wants to show me."

"I'm sure it will be a happy something, whatever it is." Grace smiled.

"Alec always makes me happy, Grace." To Ruby, Lis said, "I'll be back around two or so. Call me if there's a change."

Lis hummed all the way back to the island. It was still hot, still summer on the Chesapeake. While the mornings might have just a touch of crispness and the evenings might come just a little sooner, summer hadn't quite said good-bye to the Eastern Shore. Some of the maples and the oaks on Charles Street had begun to drop a leaf here or there, but fall was still a good month or so away. Maybe later she and Alec could take out a couple of kayaks or his old rowboat and head to the sound to do a little crabbing. They'd caught a couple of jumbos last week, and Grace talking about crab cakes made her think about catching a few more.

Up ahead on the left, a flashy little sports car was pulling into the old Mullan place behind a line of trucks. Lis waved as Cass got out of her car juggling her briefcase, a three-ring binder, and a cup of coffee. She returned the greeting with a smile and nod of her head.

"Looks good," Lis called, pointing to the frame of the house that was going up, the first of the new homes to be built on Cannonball Island in many years.

She'd heard from Owen—who said he just happened to be walking past the Mullan place the other day when Cass just happened to be there—that they might use that first house as a spec house. Cass, he went on to tell her, was thinking about building one of those new places for herself, but she hadn't decided on a location yet.

"Maybe she'll want to buy Poppa's old place, next to the old chapel."

"A, that place is mine, and B, that place is mine."

"Yeah, I guess it would be a hard sell, being that it sits right next to a graveyard where the most reviled man ever to set foot on the island is buried."

Owen had snorted. "I think Cass could handle Reverend Jeremiah Sharpe, on either side of the grave."

Yeah, but can you handle Cass? Lis wisely chose not to respond.

Lis was still smiling when she pulled onto the grassy area in front of the cottage and parked next to Alec's Jeep.

"Alec?" The front door stood open and she stepped inside. The walls were down to the studs and there were gaping holes where the new windows would be, but the floor beneath her feet no longer sagged.

She went into the kitchen, where the cabinets and the counters had been removed and the floor torn up. Here, too, as in the great room, the windows were missing. With Cass's help, the redesigned kitchen included a bumped-out back wall that enlarged the space and made room for an island and a greenhouse window, and French doors opening to the back where a patio would eventually be built. The space would be bright and cheery, and Lis couldn't wait to cook on the new stove she'd ordered the week before.

Every inch of the cottage was going to be glorious, made more so because she would be sharing it with Alec.

She heard noise upstairs and took to the steps.

"Alec?"

"Up here, babe."

"So it looks like we'll have windows soon." She reached the top of the steps and looked around. Alec was standing in front of the cabinet where they'd found her grandmother's ball and jacks. "What are you doing?"

"I found something I must have missed when we looked in here before." He turned around with a small box in his hand.

"Oh, what is it?" She peered over his shoulder. "Something that belonged to my grandmother?"

"No." He turned to her and opened the box. "Something that belonged to my mom."

"To your . . ." Lis looked down at the open box, at the sparkly ring that sat upon the dark blue velvet interior, and her mouth dropped open.

"It's the engagement ring my dad bought for my mother." He took the ring from the box and dropped to one knee. "I know she would be so happy to pass it on to you. Will you marry me, Lis?"

"I . . . well, I . . . I . . ." She couldn't seem to get a word out that made any sense.

"Was that a yes *I*, or a no *I*?"

"It's a yes. Of course it's a yes." Her hand trembled as he slid the diamond onto her finger. "Yes, of course . . ."

Alec stood and wrapped his arms around her. "Kiss me to seal the deal," he said, and she did.

Lis held her hand out in front of her, staring at the pretty stone.

"It's beautiful, Alec. I love it. And I love it even more knowing that your mother wore it first. But how . . . where . . . ?"

"My aunt kept it in the safe-deposit box in the inn. I always knew it was there, along with some other jewelry of Mom's that Aunt Grace saved for me. It was just waiting for me to find the right girl." He held her close and rested his chin on the top of her head. "It was waiting for you to come back. To come home."

"I am home. *We* are home. *This* is home." She smiled and looked into his eyes. "Ruby knew. She knew all along that I'd be back."

"A wise woman, that Ruby Carter."

"Oh." Lis pulled away slightly. "*She knew*. About the ring. She and Grace both knew."

"Of course they knew. I had to ask Aunt Grace for the ring," he reminded her. "Do you care? That they knew before you did?"

"Grace and Gigi?" Lis laughed. "Knowing the two of them, they knew long before *you* knew."

Diary~

I always look forward to my mornings with my friend Ruby—she is just a font of knowledge. Besides the obvious— if she doesn't know about it, it never happened on Cannonball Island. Naturally, since my nephew and her Lisbeth have finally found each other—and didn't we wait long enough for that to happen!—we got to talking about family: Ruby about her Kathleen, and me about my brother Cliff. He was such a good man—imagine him, a lifelong bachelor, taking in a young boy the way he did. Daniel and I were set to bring Alec to the inn to raise him along with our three, but Cliff said no, Alec was meant to be with him. And so it was, and it was best for both of them. Next to Alec, I don't think anyone mourned Carole the way Cliff did, but that's not what's on my mind tonight.

Thinking about Cliff got us thinking about Eb Carter—I guess because Eb used to spend so much time hanging around the boatyard, passing the time of day with Cliff, having a beer or two, and chewing the fat, as my brother liked to say. Of course, everyone knew about Eb's lost love, Annie Gregory—the love of his life, the woman he'd named his skipjack for—and how she disappeared one night and was never heard from again.

Anyway, the conversation this morning went something like this:

Me: You think they'll ever find out what happened to Annie?

Ruby (without so much as the blink of an eye): I know what happened to her.

Me: You do?

Ruby: Course I do. Annie took off with one of the Mason boys, I forget which one. Andrew, maybe. Or Peter. One of them.

Me (aghast): Huh! Eb always swore that Annie just disappeared out of that house in the middle of the night, like she'd been spirited away.

Ruby: Annie never wanted to marry Eb in the first place.

Me: Here he always said he didn't know what happened.

Ruby: Well, I don't think he did.

Me: You didn't tell him? Wasn't he your Harold's brother?

Ruby: Sure enough he was, but what good would telling that tale have done? Man's heart be broken, don't need to know why. Long as he don't know, he can put the blame on someone else.

Me: But he might have moved on, found someone else to love.

Ruby: Not Eb. He never had eyes for anyone but Annie. Sometimes it's best to just let things find their own way.

Which is Ruby's way of saying that things will always turn out the way they're supposed to without any interference from anyone else. In other words, best to mind your own business—something that's deeply ingrained in Ruby's philosophy of life.

"Nobody's business but theirs," she likes to say.

Which is probably why it's taken Alec and Lis so long to find each other. There have been times when I've been tempted—so tempted—to move fate along just a little tiny bit. Now, I'm not talking about a grand spell here. I just thought maybe a pinch of this or a little of that (nothing I haven't done successfully before, mind you, and always with the best intentions). But no, Ruby said. "They be together, by and by. Don't be meddlin', Gracie. They'll find their way."

Well, when Ruby says don't meddle, I don't meddle. I didn't, and she was right, of course. They're finding their way.

So was I surprised when that nephew of mine asked me if he could open the safe-deposit box? Hah! Of course I gave him the key, and of course I knew what he was after. He held up the ring Allen had bought for Carole so long ago and asked me if I thought it would be all right if he gave it to Lis. Well, I told him that I knew his mother was standing right there, smiling, and I don't mind saying that we both shed a tear or two.

And for the record, my sweet sister was there, and she was smiling to see her boy finding his happiness, just as she had found hers. Love is a celebration of life, and I know that wherever she is, Carole is still celebrating with Allen and Cliff.

Now, the big news everyone's been talking about is that there's going to be development on the island. Of course, we've been discussing it, Ruby and I have, since we saw the winds of change picking up about a year ago. It won't change the character of the island, but it will bring new people in, and that can be a good thing.

Ruby's Owen is back and he'll be staying longer than he thinks he will—Ruby says he has a "comeuppance" on the way, which is long overdue, if you ask me. That boy was a wild one when he was young. No reason to believe he's changed, but Ruby says all will be well in its time. He'll be around to take over the store when Ruby . . . well, when she's moved on.

Now, she can't see how much more time she has, but lately, I've had glimpses. I wish I didn't know, wish I hadn't seen what's coming—it makes my heart so very sad. Even though it isn't imminent, I cannot imagine not having her counsel and her friendship. Ruby always says that she'll always be there if I need her, on this side or on the other, but it won't be the same.

That's life, I suppose—and since Ruby isn't leaving us anytime soon, well, as she would say, I won't be worrying about what I can't change, what's past or what will be.

Grace

P.S. Of course, Lis and Alec will move into the cottage when it's finished, but that doesn't mean my brother Cliff's house will be empty for long. Ruby says Owen will be staying there for a time—not all of that time alone. I, for one, can't wait to see how that will play out. As Ruby would say, there be mischief afoot . . .